OF LIGHT AND DARKNESS

Of Light and Darkness

Book I

Rai Jaeger

Of Light and Darkness

Published by Rai Jaeger
https://www.raijaeger.com

To contact the author please email raijaeger.fh@gmail.com

ISBN: 979-8-9943768-0-5
ISBN (ebook): 979-8-9943768-2-9
Library of Congress Control Number: TXu 2-505-909

Cover art and design by Cliff Cramp
Editing by Emily Macadam
Interior design and typeset by Katherine Lloyd, The DESK

PROLOGUE

The night should have been the pinnacle of peace and tranquility, a display of undisturbed harmony and unmatched beauty. But the stars gleaming in their blanket of darkness could hardly be seen on this evening. The commonfolk wondered if the very night shuddered at the sight which awaited its return, defying its natural occurrence for its own sanity. It would be forever remembered as a night of despair and despondency, a point from which Skana herself could not recover—the beginning of a display of tyranny that would ravage the continent with unbridled carnage and unrestrained hate, carried out by those who sought vindication for perceived wrongs. The prior years had been long and woeful, and now the worst had finally come to pass.

The Valeriaans and their allies conquered their adversaries, proving themselves victors as they inflicted grief on the world they felt was rightfully theirs and had been denied to them for far too long. They acted well on their threats of retribution and were keen on taking complete advantage of the spoils war now afforded them. But it was not gold or treasure they sought. It was fire. It was cleansing. It was the unmitigated devastation of a world they wanted to punish as they had once been punished—the first undertaking in a great saga of wrath.

The epicenter of what transpired was a city which prided itself on being the heart of knowledge, boasting the largest library in all of Skana. This library held every book and transcript that had ever been written, its many levels forming a pillar that reached to the sky. The privileged visitors who patronized this monolith of material proclaimed rather dramatically, but in all seriousness, that it would take more than a lifetime to peruse every book on every shelf, and even an attempt did not guarantee the success of such a feat. And those who did indeed try were left unsettled and discontented in the afterlife. Heímdäll was the great city's name, home of the proud and recalcitrant Noldarín clan whose ancestry could be traced back to the once wild and ruthless Viklands. These arbiters of knowledge descended from barbarians, as this city's inhabitants boasted, unknowingly made themselves the ultimate target of what was soon to befall the land, catching the wandering eye of the Valeriaans' wrath.

The fateful night fell. Heímdäll, riddled with the corpses of its erstwhile denizens and foreigners, had already been laid to ruin by the war, rendered a mere shadow of its former beauty and splendor once known throughout the whole of Skana. All that remained was that towering library, left predominantly untouched in the midst of the devastation around it. But the appearance of its salvation was purposeful, and very much short-lived as would soon become clear, for the Valeriaans were meticulous in exacting their enduring retribution. The tower had borne witness to, and served as a prominent symbol of, what the Skana folk had accomplished from clansmen to civilization, and its downfall was much more than the mere destruction of an imposing structure. Even its reputation and the ideas it represented were no match for the flames of the torches carried by its soon-to-be antagonists. Yet despite its impending doom, an unescapable fate, there was something furtive at work—a force of which no Valeriaan had been even tenuously aware, a force witnessed by only that which dwelt within the walls of the library.

When the Valeriaans made their way up the grand steps, flames their weapon, they were still none the wiser. As their hands grasped the handles of the elegant wooden doors fitted into stone walls, there was a sudden flash of light which swept through the inner recesses of the library—a swell of white that traveled as one might imagine a visible echo, an iridescent shine that put even the sun's rays to shame. From floor to pinnacle, it traveled amongst the levels of shelves and books until at last it dispersed as an ocean wave parting against a stony shoreline, a ghostly apparition vanishing as suddenly as it appeared. When the doors swung open, all traces of this phenomenal happening had already departed, leaving no evidence of its presence. The Valeriaans carried on with their mission to deeply wound the folk of Skana for generations to come.

The soldiers moved swiftly about the obelisk, reaching all corners so the fire would neglect no single book, leave no segment unscathed. There was no sating the hunger of the flames once they had but licked the spines of the books, and they feasted on those cherished pages with a terrifying ravenousness, melting away the elegant covers, and engulfing the adjoining occupants upon the shelves. What had taken ages to produce took only moments to destroy. The works created as a result of many lifetimes of commitment perished without any protest. The Valeriaans stood and observed long enough to ensure the fire would continue to spread, that it would soon consume the entirety of the building around them. When at last the second floor caught fire, the flames lapping eagerly at the precious material, they retreated to the city. The Valeriaans' weapon of choice might have been fire, but even they themselves were not immune to its fatal embrace.

They withdrew upon their steeds of white beyond the city limits and to the hills surrounding Heímdäll's borders. There they were awarded the most magnificent of sights, the beauty of their doing a spectacle for them to observe with a voracious eagerness. The destruction claimed almost the full duration of the evening, but for the Valeriaans the interval passed all too quickly.

The library, which towered high above Heímdäll, which once bestowed upon the land of Skana an elegant and conversant gaze, soon found itself completely engulfed in the flames that would bring about its demise. At last, the tower would join the rest of her city and her folk.

The olden tale goes that the spire could be seen for miles, making even the mountains envy its standing. Travelers lost in the Icelands needed only to look for the library and it always set their path aright. That night was no different. The library could still be seen as the fire rose high and burned brightly with all it claimed in its gluttonous jowls. As the wooden interior succumbed to devastation, the stone exterior began to collapse slowly and certainly. Stone by stone, the tower revealed the flames devouring its innards, spouting smoke to the clouds above. A blanket of darkness completely and utterly consumed a sky where the stars and the moon herself were on the cusp of arriving.

Those who were privileged enough to have escaped their own demise during the war, were the unfortunate witnesses of the aftermath. What they observed was the unrelenting obliteration of their homeland, the fall of all they knew, the rhythms of their lives shattered beyond repair. What the Valeriaans saw, however, was not despair, but a much-awaited reckoning. The hues of the ravenous inferno were only the commencement of something much bigger, something much more devastating to come.

As the dark smoke stretched across the already tarnished sky, a never-ending sea of black, a comparable glow appeared in the distance. There was but one at the beginning to the east, the arising of flames consuming yet another dwelling called home by Skana folk. Then there came another to the west. And at last, the north. The horizon was lit by a uniting orange glow which made the whole of the world look as though it had been cast to the purging flames. To spectators the fires appeared to be isolated incidents, though this was hardly the truth of the matter. They could only watch their respective lands perishing before their very eyes. But in truth, the entirety of Skana was set alight. The major cities, villages, towns—every place folk once called home—the centerpieces of olden kingdoms and past empires, would be but the graveyards of a history meant to be scorned or lost altogether.

Entire livelihoods were upturned as the zenith of the darkest of times began to announce itself.

Spreading ash and suffocating smoke, the flames could be felt no matter the distance they were observed from. The once lush, green land and the rich browns of the surrounding mountains emerged at dawn in a coat of grey. The fresh waters were tainted, the sky set to the farcical appearance of night. No one could recall if the day had indeed retired completely by the time the smoke engulfed the sky above, nor could they recall if the night had indeed taken up its domain in the subsequent hours. All that was remembered was the bite of flames, the choking ash in the air about them, and the stains of tears on blackened faces as the entirety of Skana wept helplessly. It was all they could do—weep for what was lost and what would never return. The spoils of war had been given to those who should never have prevailed.

When at last the spire of the library collapsed upon itself, all of Skana lit up once more as though life were breathed yet again in the ravenous flames consuming her. Wood cracked and the library's foundation fell upon the city below with such force that it could be felt throughout the land. The Valeriaans spoke of how marvelous the sight truly was, observing the structure within its final moments. With delight they recounted the thunderous crack of stones and debris, told of the fire suddenly growing with an intensity achieved by the sheer power of the structure's collapse. A wave of flame and cinders dispersed throughout what was left of Heímdäll, and neither soldier nor horse flinched as they felt it brush against their skin and pierce their ears, blinding them momentarily. It was all part of the spectacle.

Skana burned, so fiercely that olden tales speak of how neither moon nor the sun appeared on their respective horizons for many a day. They refused to lay eyes upon the bloodshed awaiting their unblinking gazes. Hardly anyone could blame the deities, the representatives of all that was good and natural, of peace and serenity. The skies remained a sickly black and the clouds a dirtied brown. Ash continued to fall akin to rain on the living folk, the scorched bodies of those they once called family and friends, and the dwellings they had called home.

Skana herself was weeping beside her folk. She could hardly avert her gaze from the butchery that transpired, for she had seen all as she has always seen all. She was witness to man's greatest moments as she was to his pitfalls, both folks' capacity for sacrifice and the folly in their character. She had seen many a war, many an empire fall at the hand of another poised to take its place, but this—this was a devastation of catastrophic proportions never previously achieved. Skana was distraught as she felt the pain and despair of the folk just coming to know the true meaning of the word, as she also felt every bit of anger consuming the Valeriaans, the sentiments and passions that drove them to enact such a sin without hesitation, without remorse. It was in those coming days that she too finally wept—tears which extinguished the remaining flames cast about the land looking for more to feed upon in such barrenness. It was her tears which brought an end to it all at last. And though the land burned no more, what her tears could not heal was the unseen toll upon her folk and the repercussions it would have for an already uncertain future. There was no remedy, even given all her great might, that could ever heal such a wound.

The folk called the tragedy *Mordúnn*—the Black Dawn—to memorialize the sorrow of Skana. To remember the time they wept in solidarity with one another. It was the end of a world they once knew, and the beginning of one that would not let them forget the victors' capacity for ire.

That was over two hundred years ago, and the Valeriaans are as much in power now as they were then. Their despotic reign is the bane of all prosperity and contentment of the commonfolk, who live in fear of the Empire all too quick to punish and all too obliged to be unforgiving. The commonfolk live in a world with a past torn away from them and a future long faded from sight, a world in which most knowledge and skills are forbidden to them, the promise of prosperity left only to those who laid claim to the spoils of war. But that does not stop them from longing. It is all they have left. While the many can only hope there will come an end to the Valeriaans, others have taken to their courage and raised a blade in a stoic defiance.

It was on the day proceeding the fall of Heímdäll, as the commonfolk gazed upon the ruins they once called home with both heaviness in their hearts and an indignation thought to be possessed only by the Valeriaans, that a glimmer of hope appeared. It was a call, a beckoning to action—to take up arms ever so defiantly in opposition of the newly formed Empire. They called themselves the Oathbound, for they did make an oath to resist the Valeriaan reign just as they had in olden times. As they always would, no matter what the future held.

But oaths were a disregarded concept left behind in the ages in which men gave their lives to the most sacred of promises, to uphold the word they so valiantly pledged. The Valeriaans sneered at this concept, at a notion they confidently deemed archaic and foolish.

What was used as an expression to deride the folk of a region thought to be of an uncivilized and barbaric nature, now was proclaimed loudly upon the tongues who adopted what would become a title, a legacy. For Heímdäll.

For the folk who were denigrated because of the circumstances they were born into. For the folk who had taken up arms against the Valeriaans in olden times. For the homeland which birthed the defiance. A rebellion was formed of unlikely heroes, the hearts amongst the commonfolk that responded to the call.

The two adversaries have stood at odds with one another for over two hundred years, and the Oathbound remain the last hope of the commonfolk of Skana. Though they may not outwardly display support due in part to the grave consequences, it has not stopped the commoners from furtively yearning in the shadows, behind closed doors, in the company of trusted parties, for the victory that had been lost to them all those years ago.

CHAPTER 1

It began again as did every morning from the dawn of time—the darkness extended a gracious hand, and from the depths of night pulled forth the coming morning. The vibrant colors, a soft gradient, pushed back the blanket of stars that once ruled the sky. The sun had not yet peeked, nor did it need to, for the mountains to become almost monstrous silhouettes overlooking a vast landscape of forests and plains that were still asleep, quiet and serene in their present dormancy. Only when the snow-riddled peaks began to glisten of gold, and the rays of the morning star began to extend their own hands across this vast landscape, did it begin to wake.

Creatures of the night took to slumber, relinquishing their nocturnal domain for the time being, and the land became alive in a completely new way. The morning dew, akin to a blanket of crystal, glistened on the brush with an almost iridescent glow, splashing a touch of bright color in contrast to the gentle browns and greens of the forest. The forest faeries, who fluttered about in gleaming magenta, began to flit away in the coming light. The birds ruffled awake with a fluff of their plumage, twittering about up high within the trees, unseen as they sang and danced and filled the forest with a harmonic melody. The stags stretched their elegant legs and sharpened their equally elegant horns before they began to roam.

Where the moonlight once pierced through the trees to the depths of the forest floor below, now did the sunlight, and in these early morning hours when the land had only just stretched to life once again, came the eager footsteps of a young boy walking about the trail he had traversed with his father many times before. Beginning in the garden of their home, it was a trail he knew well and found comfort in traveling alone. As of recently did he take this walk in his own company, bucket and fishing pole in hand, to try for the morning catch down by the river not too far from his village, Trivaden.

He was the important age of twelve and thus was in the midst of seeking as much independence as he could be granted, to become the young man he thought himself already—one no longer in need of the determined support or guidance of his parents. He thought himself a quick learner and possessed a level head upon his shoulders, the teachings throughout his childhood having done well to shape his temperament and inform the decisions he made. It was just fishing, after all—his favorite hobby, nearly second nature at that point. And he would always stay to the path his father marked for him, even when traversing a forest with which he was well acquainted, whose atmosphere was peaceful and undisturbed by any predators that elsewhere posed terrifying threats.

His name was Arturias Sigurdsson, but he preferred the nickname Artur; he felt it suited him better. A thicket of raven-black hair framed his face, his peachy skin often flushed with youthful excitement. His bangs bounced over his forehead, lending him boyish charm, as he marched down the beaten path worn by the constant trips to and fro. Dark eyebrows lifted above large, grey eyes which were full of delight and the vivacity youth afforded. They were a tad greener today, with glints of brown in the iris, as they often were on days he went fishing, and when the days grew warmer, his mood particularly high. Both parents commented flippantly, but with slight suspicion, that it was due to the hobby being associated with his father, who himself possessed deep green eyes. It was when the moon returned and the sky darkened that the boy's eyes would revert to deep grey. His mother, who possessed eyes of fathomless blue, the abyss of an ocean, wished she saw a bit of herself in Artur's gaze. Yet never in his twelve years of life had they ever shifted to such a hue, not even the slightest.

"Just akin to his father," the neighbors would often remark on the stark resemblance to the man they knew as Thelric Sigurdsson. Yet it was his mother, Ygrayne, whose raven-colored hair lay thickly around her, that Artur inherited his own from.

On many a night he would hear the two of them disputing one another's claims as to who he most resembled. But in truth, they loved seeing the other in him and were quick to capitulate.

Artur was generally a jovial young lad. Full of vitality and in possession of a pleasant, but shy, disposition. Free-spirited until he needed to listen to his parents, grudgingly deferring to their authority.

None of that mattered in the current moment, however. He was about to partake in one of his favorite hobbies, his love of fishing instilled in him by his father as he too had a passion for it in all its peace and simplicity.

"Stay to the path your father marked out for you!" his mother always called out to him from the kitchen window before he could even reach the tree line behind their home.

"I know, Mama!" Artur huffed, doing well to avert his face to hide the blush of embarrassment in his cheeks and the rolling of his eyes. Artur often mistook Ygrayne's motherly instincts and well-meaning concerns for nagging, given his unwavering opinion that he already knew how to tend to himself. It was, again, just fishing.

"Better watch that mouth," Ygrayne would mutter under her breath in response to Artur's cheekiness.

When the serene music of the river could be heard, did Artur quicken his pace with eagerness, and when at last it came into view through the trees, could he feel the coolness of mist about his face, the smell of the fresh rushing water filling his nostrils. The sun was a warm embrace about his arms and legs when he removed his boots and rolled up his trousers and sleeves to his knees and elbows. The sands tickled the bottoms of his feet as the chilly water lapped at his toes. With his bucket beside him and a satchel of food to keep his stomach occupied, Artur cast his line into the water, a small splash carried away by the current, and he lay back on the riverbank to wait patiently.

"We wait, so we can eat," Thelric would say when Artur would fuss about with boredom. When he was first learning how to fish, he could hardly stand the silence and lack of commotion. Patience was first and foremost what his father taught him—a very long and arduous lesson for a young child to study, indeed.

"That doesn't make any sense!" Artur often retorted in frustration before he was hushed by Thelric, who would always respond in a quiet whisper, "The fish will hear you."

Artur loathed it so when his father told him that, for he would be left thinking, *How do fish even hear anything?*

Even in the present, Artur still wasn't certain if his father's proclamation was true. But he had eventually resigned himself to silence after much, much discipline. The boredom didn't set in as promptly as it once had, and he had come to adore the peace the forest afforded and the gossipy whispers the river was all too keen to share.

The surroundings were so familiar but he never tired of taking his place amongst them—the gathering of boulders and rocks that had long ago settled across the river to form steps that connected the opposing banks, the river itself that weaved through the land until it was eventually swallowed by a line of trees, disappearing into the vastness that was the world around him. He was awed by the mountains, forever in the distance, looming so high they could touch the sky above and part the clouds as they passed by unassumingly. Their peaks were illuminated by the vibrant colors of the Nerúnors at night.

The running water couldn't conceal the splendor that lay beneath, even as it glistened with the touch of the sun. The riverbed needed not be as grand as the mountains to boast the bountiful beauty of colors and shapes. But such magnificence was not without its perils, as Artur had often been sternly reminded.

"You are not to cross the river. Go no farther than the riverbank if you are by yourself," was a common admonition in his household, brought upon by a singular unfortunate event when Artur was younger. A moment in which his boundless curiosity had compelled him to traverse the waters one leap at a time.

Back turned as he stood in the midst of the river to fish farther down from their usual spot, Thelric was unaware of his son's innocent mischief. That was, until those paternal instincts were called forth, often awakened whenever the youngling was in proximity to danger. Indescribable and mysterious, the roused sense prompted Thelric to turn in time to see Artur bounding across the river upon those boulders, his balance at the time not yet honed. The stumbling of his feet against those wet and moss-covered surfaces made Thelric's heart descend into his abdomen.

At the time, only Thelric knew the waters in that particular area were deep and quickened—a child could be swept up and cast away by the cruel and indifferent force of nature in an instant. Thelric lost his favored fishing pole that day, but such a loss paled in comparison to the devasting possibility of losing his son.

He caught Artur just as the boy's foot slipped from the edge of one of the boulders and into the waters below. It was the barest disturbance in the vastness of the river, but it was more than enough for a panicked father. Thelric grabbed Artur about the arm and pulled him to safety. Looking back, Thelric felt he had yanked Artur back too harshly, but in his distress, he could at least forgive himself.

"That's too dangerous for you!" Thelric brought Artur back to the riverbank, where he scolded him further.

"Never cross the river! You know this is the boundary!" And as Thelric pointed with a stern finger at the stones, the harshness in his voice prompted the onset of tears that streamed down Artur's face, the terrified boy to whom it had never occurred that he was doing anything wrong.

The admonition remained with Artur for the rest of his life. The hesitancy in crossing into the unknown wasn't brought on by an inward fear of his own inabilities, but the desire to refrain from provoking the worried anger he had witnessed on that day—an anger he had never seen from his father before, or since. An anger which hurriedly faded away as a father brought his son into his arms to embrace what he almost lost, and to hide the tears stinging his own eyes.

Those years were behind him now. He was older, stronger, and not as fearful of inciting the wrath of his parents. Certainly now they would understand he was more than capable of performing such a feat; at least, that was what Artur hoped. The river he'd once thought of as perilous now seemed but a stream to him, unassuming and gentle. He could even stand in its center without slipping or falling, and that had to mean something.

Artur stood just before the first boulder, whose white glistening surface had been sculpted by ages of rushing water, and his gaze followed the trail of stones to the riverbank his feet had never had the chance to grace, to feel the sands, or walk the makeshift path leading into the forest beyond. There was hesitancy at first. The long-ago ordeal replayed in his head as a warning of how he had previously tempted his own fate, and the consequences awaiting him should he do so again. Artur longed to put one foot atop that nearest boulder, but found himself hesitating once more. His father's words intruded upon his mind as those of nagging parents have a habit of doing. As improbable as it was, Artur felt his father would burst through the forest at the very moment he dared to take that first step. Parents were always spoiling the fun in such a way—suddenly appearing just in time to witness moments of defiance. It would mean no more fishing on his own—he knew that for certain—until he could be trusted again. That was the most frightening outcome, even more so than the prospect of death. But no child his age had truly contemplated such a prospect, nor even considered it a possibility when so much life still lay ahead of them.

The cruelest of outcomes was certainly not drowning, nor being swept away to unfamiliar shores. No. Never fishing again was the trepidation currently gripping his conscious, making him go pale with fear. No matter how strong the urge to defy his parents' orders was in his ever-growing desire for individual autonomy, he couldn't bring himself to tempt it. Not right now.

It seemed akin to an eternity that he spent waging this internal battle, but eventually he found himself retreating to the safety of the riverbank as he had been told to time and again.

Artur grimaced at his failure with a begrudging huff. He sat by his fishing pole, a pout contorting his features, for the remainder of his time at the river.

"One day," he whispered to himself, as if it were a mountain to be conquered, or the barrier to his growth as an individual.

Artur could brood on the issue no longer when his stomach gave out a growl despite having been fed a sufficient breakfast, procured with finesse by his mother, before he left the cottage. Artur pushed aside his intrusive thoughts and focused instead on grabbing a small bite to eat from the satchel that lay beside him: a few slices of bread and some jam cultivated from the fruits of the region. He ate his snack angrily. The flush of his cheeks only intensified as the disappointment in himself deepened, reminded as he was that he had failed to defy the laws of his parents each time his gaze fell upon the trail of stones. But amidst the quiet and serenity of his surroundings, there came a blatant disturbance.

It started out as but a sound against the natural melody of the nature around him. It was no wind, nor water, nor the activity of the forest residents. From the distance, there came the faint sound of horses neighing, the familiar rumble of the heavy carriages they towed with leather and iron. It was peculiar enough for the river to not drown out such sounds, as few noises from the main road connecting their village to the major city of the region, Falkhearth, were loud enough to be heard in Trivaden. Trivaden was small and insignificant, as were many of the villages in the region, often left unnoticed and forgotten. Even the occasional travelers making their way through the village only did so to return to the main road, having lost their way.

Something was different, however, and Artur could feel it so. He wasn't certain how, or why he felt the way he did, but there came an unfamiliar air sweeping through with the gentle breeze, unnerving and uncomfortable. Unable to find any reason for his misgivings, he ignored them as most often do. He pushed aside the shifting of the winds around him to tend to his fishing pole, as it gave hints that the line had finally snagged a fish.

Little did Artur realize that there was indeed something coming, carried by folk not native to the lands he called home, passing through unheeded by the folk so often left undisturbed in the course of events happening around them.

CHAPTER 2

The heat of the day gave way to the cooler air of the afternoon. Artur followed the familiar path home with enough fish in his bucket for supper, and an eagerness to spend the remainder of the day with friends before then.

The place he called home was a modest cottage, with the main quarters consisting of the eating and kitchen area, which also served as his parents' bedroom. The loft overseeing the main quarters was the place that served as Artur's own room with a single window above his bed, offering the privacy a growing boy needed. The outdoor area was a modest garden surrounded by a wooden fence, where they grew their vegetables, not just for their household, but for the rest of their neighbors as well; onions, cabbage, garlic, and turnips were their main crops. Each resident played a part in contributing something for the benefit of their small village, whether that was food, herbs, livestock, or various other goods. Meat was a special commodity, venison the most common due to the bountiful population of deer in the forest that surrounded them. The natural resources and abundances the terrain provided them gave them the opportunity to sell such goods in Falkhearth, which was their main means of income. Select caravans would travel the few hours to Falkhearth and stay for the remainder of the week, selling their goods and purchasing other resources the village needed that could only be obtained from the city. Falkhearth was the heart of vast and rich trade within the region, situated between the Folklands and the Viklands, and it provided a variety of goods that would otherwise not be found in the region itself.

When the dirt path transitioned into the stones that made their way to the garden, did Artur see his mother appear in the window as if she had never left since the morning, going about her baking as she so greatly enjoyed doing when times were unhurried. He could smell it, well before he drew close. The scent of fruits picked directly from another neighbor's garden filled the air as if wafted by the wind itself to tease him. The smell of sugar and bread was so delicious that it made him salivate.

It was only then Artur regretted giving his mother a bit of arrogance that morning, thinking perhaps she had indeed caught sight of his eyeroll and sensed the defiance in his tone before he sped down the path; it seemed mothers had an intuition for catching such insolence. If she was still angry with him, asking for a taste would be futile.

But Artur determined that he would not be deterred from the satisfaction of his hunger. He would simply pretend as if nothing had occurred—certainly that would work.

"I'm back, Mama!" Artur called loudly, and his mother's blue eyes shifted from the kitchen counter to him.

"Hello, my boy!" her face lit up, and she brushed back a strand of hair which had fallen about her face with the back of her flour-covered hand.

"How was fishing?" she asked as Artur stepped inside through the back door and placed the bucket at her feet.

"Got a lot of them today," Artur proudly proclaimed, thinking of how his father would be proud of him. He attempted to hide his obvious delight out of embarrassment. "What are you making now?" He peered over the counter to find that he was indeed correct. It was a pie—a delicious-looking pie—and Ygrayne had already begun to make another.

"Your father taught you well," she commented, as she always did, to encourage the hobby. Rolling the dough on the counter before her, she peered into the bucket to see his catches of the day with an impressed arch of her brow.

"Good to have for supper tonight. In the meantime, I am making these raspberry pies. One for us and one you can take across the way to Eogan."

"Can I play with my friends until supper, after I deliver the pie?" Artur asked, his eyes yet to leave the delicacy sitting innocuously on the counter.

"Ah!" Ygrayne gasped as the memory came back to her. "They came by earlier asking for you. Said they will be playing about the hills again if you wish to join."

It was their favorite spot, after all—where the forest opened up into a small valley and a hill overlooking the main road. It helped that Trivaden was always in sight, any of the parents able to observe the children if needed.

Artur hadn't yet responded to Ygrayne, mesmerized as he was by the presence of the pie. Reaching for the bowl containing the concoction of berries that would make its delicious filling, Ygrayne quickly noticed just how filthy his hands were. Blasphemous and indecent! Ygrayne slapped his hand away and said, with her finger pointed at him, "I hardly think so!"

"But Mama!"

"You're not having any pie until after supper!"

There was no arguing with her. Ygrayne was more stubborn than Artur, and he knew it. The rejection nearly had him prancing in place as he had done as a toddler, whiny and petulant. He simmered in his disappointment, unaware of the pout forming about his face to Ygrayne's amusement.

"Deliver the pie to Eogan and go play. I'll send for you when supper is ready." Ygrayne tried to mask the smile that was daring to cross her face at the sight of her son's puckered one.

His endeavor was lost, and so did he resign himself to such defeat. He grabbed the pie meant for Eogan and said hurriedly, "I'm heading out!"

Artur was in the midst of bursting out the back door as he spoke, until Ygrayne frowned and retorted, "Aren't you forgetting something?"

He knew exactly what she meant, and he blushed out of embarrassment once more.

"But Mama…"

"Shush! You get your arse over here!" She bent at her waist and presented a cheek to him. "Or you're not going."

Artur rolled his eyes and, with an exasperated sigh, gave his mother a quick peck on the cheek as she so wanted.

"I'm too old for this," he commented when at last he pulled away, wiping his mouth as if it had been tainted by her very touch.

"I don't care how old you are," Ygrayne said back to him. "You're always going to be my little boy whether you like it or not. Now, get!" she waved a floured hand to dismiss him, and Artur was all too happy to oblige.

He was thankful none of his friends were nearby to witness such torment or he would never hear the end of it.

"And watch that eyeroll," Ygrayne called to him through the window. He waved at her in acknowledgement and sprinted out of sight. She narrowed her eyes and shook her head as she returned to the task before her. Ygrayne hardly tolerated the eyeroll she knew her son had given her earlier that morning and the second was treading in dangerous territory, but she couldn't help but titter to herself. "That part is definitely his father."

As they were found nearly every day, Artur's friends were out in the fields atop the one hill they had claimed as their playground, lying about in the brush overlooking an endless landscape that made their little village seem even more insignificant in the scheme of the grandeur that was Skana. They hardly knew that, however. The mountains off in the blue haze of the horizon seemed just as small as they looked, and the boys had no cause to realize their true magnificence, or that the fields they thought were just an endless abyss of green gave way to snowy plains and great waters beyond their shores. To them, their grass was the greenest, their hill was the largest, their river was the fastest, their forest was the thickest, and their village truly meant a great deal in their life.

"Kian! Ronan!" Artur called to the two brothers with a wave of his hand.

"Get your arse up here, Artur! You have to see this!" Ronan called out to him with neither boy turning to acknowledge him. It was only when Artur flopped beside them that Ronan looked to Artur with a very dissatisfied look and scolded him, "'Bout time you showed up. Where were you?"

Ronan was the eldest, and lankiest, of the three of them at the even more difficult age of thirteen, but this gave him the title of leader in their little group. And it was this reverence which gave him the boldness to speak with such unquestioned authority.

"I was fishing!" Artur felt the answer was obvious. "Have the two of you been lying here all day?" He had half-expected them to be playing hide-and-seek in the tall grass or frolicking through the stream that ran through the field behind them.

"Yeth!" Kian, the youngest at eight, replied in a hushed tone, as if to avoid discovery. "We're on lookout." He was currently looking through a spyglass that their parents had lent to them. Artur paused a moment. Kian's voice was odd, different, with a predominant lisp changing the sound of his speech. Artur perched atop his forearms and peered at Kian over Ronan's back.

"Why do you sound funny when you talk?"

"I don't th-ound funny."

"Yes, you do," Artur retorted.

"No!"

"Yes!" Ronan intervened. "It's because he lost his two front teeth this morning."

"What?" Artur was taken aback.

"I only loth-t my two front teeth becauthe you kicked me in the fathe." Kian glared at his older brother.

Ronan put down the spyglass and looked at Kian with raised brows. "Your two front teeth have been loose for the past week, and you asked me to help you get them out. So, I did. What did you expect?"

"Not for you to kick me in the fathe."

Artur couldn't help but chuckle a bit at the two brothers bickering—bickering which turned into a light scuffle that put Kian back in his place with a hard shove of his head into the grass.

"Be quiet, we're still on the lookout."

"Lookout for what?" Artur inquired, nudging close enough to Ronan that their shoulders were touching.

"Look!" Ronan pointed out to the main road, and Artur followed the gesture motioning to a caravan that was winding along the road, not too far away from where they perched.

It was exactly what he had heard earlier, and what a sight it was to behold. The largest and most terrifying "caravan" he had ever seen. What would usually be a wagon or two with folk accompanying on foot, that day was an endless line of horses prancing down the main road. They moved with such synchronicity that they gave an air of rehearsed perfection upon the thousands. The silver plates of armor glistened with a golden hue in the sunlight, reflecting the world around them, adorning the steeds with a haunting beauty and a terrifying air. Their hooves battered the ground, the vibrations felt as far as the top of the hill, filling the air with a roar akin to thunder on a storming night.

The riders, who were clad in equally grandiose sets of silver armor, sat still as stone in their saddles, poised and controlled in the way they handled their steeds. The faces peeking through the raised visors of their helmets were cold, seemingly permanent scowls about them. Supply wagons accompanied them, harboring contents that could only be speculated upon—terrifying in what they suggested. Then there came large, elaborate wooden carriages whose windows were draped with white silk, pulled only by regal white horses with shimmering coats and elegantly flowing manes. The beauty and grandeur these carriages boasted was dwarfed in significance by the looming presence of the heavily armored horsemen riding alongside them. They were intimidating by appearance alone, their precision and numbers a clear indication of their deadly abilities.

At intervals between the hundreds passing through, there came flowing banners displaying the emblem of the Empire in all force and ferocity. A combination of purples and silvers, intricate designs formed a background behind a rearing horse with a singular horn about its head—a creature which symbolized power, royalty, and majesty.

Merely witnessing such a spectacle made the boys shudder with equal measures of unease and curiosity. Artur himself was stunned into silence, at a complete loss for words. He had never seen anything of such enormity, the sight making him feel as small as his village. He felt daft in the way he gawked and widened his gaze. But his friends had responded the same way upon first sight. Now Ronan and Kian were bemused by Artur's awe, unwilling to admit that their own confident demeanors had faltered.

"What are they?" Artur finally found the courage to muster a whisper, looking to Ronan, as he often did to seek words of "wisdom" from the oldest of the three.

"It's a Valeriaan caravan," Ronan answered quietly. "We think they might be heading to Falkhearth."

Artur had never heard of a "Valeriaan caravan" before, let alone anything "Valeriaan." Yet he felt that he should have based upon Ronan's assertion.

He couldn't let the boys know of his ignorance, and in an attempt to prove he was indeed conversant on the matter, he responded, "Oh, is that so?" His voice was a bit more nervous than he intended.

"They've been marching through all day. Where else would they go?" Ronan narrowed his eyes, lowering himself back to the ground akin to a mountain lion preparing to pounce.

"I wonder why. I haven't heard of anything happening in Falkhearth," Artur stated. But he knew very little about Falkhearth overall. Any information he'd gleaned came from his father, and even then, it was usually just the details of successful trades.

"Let me see." The statement was more of an announcement than a request for the spyglass that Artur nonchalantly took from Kian's hands, even as he protested with a whine. The youngest boy tried in vain to retrieve the spyglass, but Artur held it from his reach with ease and pushed Kian's hand away to discourage further efforts. Kian continued to verbalize his protest but quickly realized that his efforts would be useless. He begrudgingly let Artur be, folding his arms beneath his chin with a "Hmph!" He hated being the youngest sometimes, the smallest and weakest of the three of them, in both the physical and hierarchical sense.

"They look to be awfully important folk," Artur said, now that the sheer magnitude of the situation was intensified before his very eyes. As he began to comprehend that the matter was more serious than he understood, there came that sinking feeling in his stomach again, turning and twisting with nauseating unease. It was the same feeling he had dismissed so nonchalantly at the river.

"You think..." Artur almost squawked, his voice breaking. He took a moment to swallow and tried once more. "Do you think something's gonna happen?"

He turned to Ronan to seek some guidance in the unfamiliar terrain, and Ronan in turn looked at him with a blank expression, his brown eyes meeting Artur's grey ones. There had to be an answer, an explanation. But Ronan was just as ignorant, and though he dared not admit, as frightened, as Artur felt.

The unspoken tier they had constructed amongst themselves suffered a crack in its foundation.

Just when Artur couldn't take the unsettling silence anymore, his lips already parting to speak, Ronan's own lips perked up into a small grin and he said, "Nah, mate. I think everythin's going to be fine."

Ronan was lying—his voice sounded so unusual, lacking the confidence that his tone habitually carried, that Artur could sense it so. He had known his friend long enough to recognize how his demeanor visibly changed, the air about him shifted. As Artur continued to stare into Ronan's eyes, the wavering expression about his face only undermined the words spoken. But who was Artur to question it when he had no answers himself? After all, Ronan should know best of the three of them.

With that, Artur nodded. Neither boy had much they could contribute to the conversation, and the silence settled around them once more—tense, unnerving silence.

CHAPTER 3

The hours passed by in a blur, the boys still waiting for a caravan that had disappeared long ago. But the lull in all the excitement turned out to be permanent for the remainder of the afternoon. When the land no longer trembled, and the silence of evening finally crept in, did they retreat toward the all-too-familiar fields.

The Valeriaan soldiers were now but a memory left at the hillside, never once crossing their minds as they ran through the grass and played about in the stream, looking for any unusual rocks or semi-aquatic animals they could grasp. They loved bringing snakes and lizards home, to the dismay of their parents.

The last time Ronan brought home a harmless river snake to his mother, she nearly fainted from the very sight, believing that non-venomous creature to be in fact dangerous. Ronan's father tossed it back into the river without even the slightest sympathy for it. There had been many such incidents, no matter the scolding and the protests, for the boys found endless amusement in their parents' displeasure.

They were having so much fun moseying about that they eventually lost track of the time. The smell of the households making supper was absent, the breeze not at all in their favor, and as such they had no reminder to return home. Ordinarily, it would be one of the adults who retrieved them with a simple shout as they were not inclined to trek into the fields.

However, it was an unexpected visitor who came to retrieve them in their familial guardians' stead. While welcomed nonetheless, the clump of fur that burst through the tall grass following sounds of rigorous shuffling and the pattering of paws making its way in their direction surprised them all. Artur, who was on top of a boulder at the time, gazing down at the gentle waters below, was the first to see the additional company.

"Vána!" Artur had an immediate smile on his face, and he slid down the side of the boulder to meet the dire wolf who was nearly as tall as him.

The excited beast wagged her tail intensely as she tried to bound atop Artur in her affectionate attempt to give him as many kisses as she possibly could, completely unaware of her weight and her size. She still thought herself to be a pup.

Artur struggled to keep her at bay, until his strained protest brought a state of calm to her, a sudden ease. But it didn't stop her from beaming at

Artur with those bright gold eyes of hers, and a joyous whine further gave voice to her happiness in his presence. Artur scratched behind her ears and about her thick grey ruff, and Vána panted as her long, floppy tongue jutted out from her jowls. Her front paws pranced excitedly in place, her tail wagging so vigorously that the grass behind her danced in the breeze it created.

Though Vána was adored by the entirety of the village, her favorite person in all of Trivaden was indeed Artur, and he in turn adored her. She was a beauty. Her thick, light grey pelt had an even lighter underbelly with hints of light brown on her legs, the top of her head, and inside her ears. Her white face phased into a widow's peak of light grey and brown, and the fur running along her spine was a darker shade of coal.

Vána was brought to Trivaden by Urda, the neighbor who lived across from the Sigurdsson household, upon her return from a routine trip into the forest in search of herbs for her tonics and flowers for her garden.

Urda revealed that she had found the week-old pup amidst the carnage of her dead siblings; the rest of the family had met its demise in the form of a fierce beast thought to be a mountain lion. Though neither beast was believed to be living in the area, a mountain lion was the only potential predator that could have bested a dire wolf suffused with motherly instincts. Vána only survived as she was too deep within the den for the predator to reach her—according to Urda's observations. Despite the strangeness of her account, it was something everyone decided to believe. No one dared to seek out the scene, either because they believed it too dangerous or simply because they were already enamored by the dire wolf in their midst.

Tales spoke of how the dire wolf species had disappeared during the seventh age. In those olden times, they were both wild and domesticated—personal companions, royal household pets, and even weapons of war.

There were even whispers that there once existed dire wolves that grew so large they could be ridden akin to horses. But such anecdotes could neither be confirmed nor denied, given that such knowledge of any kind had been lost in the war. What happened to them or where they went, no one knew. Sightings across Skana amounted only to the number of fingers upon a single hand. The folk of a village as unassuming as Trivaden would never have dreamed they would ever be graced with such a rare and spectacular presence.

The week-old pup grew into a steadfast beast of over a hundred and sixty pounds of fur and muscle, standing at over four feet—her head near the same height as Artur's. Though her stature was intimidating, her sweet and loyal temperament never left her, and she was unconditionally treasured amongst the villagers.

Even still, her happy and calm demeanor was not to be taken for granted. Dire wolves were deadly no matter their dispositions. A single bite could end a person with an alarming promptness should they be so unfortunate as to find themselves caught in their unyielding jowls.

There still existed a tale within Trivaden, frequently referenced in conversations, of when Vána returned from a hunting trip with Garric, one of the more seasoned and older residents of their small village. Locked in her jaws was a stag, its head bent unnaturally at its bloodied neck. Vána dragged its body, muddied and bruised from the journey back home, as though it weighed nothing.

"She growled every time I tried to grab it," Garric commented to his neighbors. "Finally, I just let her bring it back on her own." And a wise decision it was, as he wanted to avoid ending up akin to the stag.

Vána took her trophy to his porch and sat with it for hours until she grew bored and decided to entertain herself elsewhere.

Despite the unsubstantiated tales of such capacity for carnage, dire wolves were undoubtedly the most loving of creatures and equally loyal, and it was their easy adjustment to domesticated life which granted them the title of man's most valued companion. Vána could be found lying on a chosen porch for the day and frequenting a soft warm bed, which every household always had prepared for her. When she wasn't lying about, or out on a hunt, she would often be found playing with the children. Both parent and child trusted her entirely. Vána knew exactly what to do and how to care for them. Somehow, she possessed an understanding unakin to any creature they had encountered before, retaining an awareness beyond description. She listened well and understood the words spoken to her. When one stared into her golden gaze, they always described the experience as akin to peering into the eyes of a person. Vána was baffling. Enchanting. But her most amiable and trusted temperament balanced her unsettling cognizance.

Artur was only five when she was brought to Trivaden, and it was their household that Urda came to first with her new charge.

Ygrayne and Urda were already good friends, given that Urda had helped deliver Artur and had done well to mentor the new mother.

Artur remembered the day Vána arrived as if it had just occurred but the previous evening. All he saw was a clump of fur whining in fear and innocence, a rather pathetic sight in comparison to the majestic beast she was now.

It took but a glance, an empathetic connection made within the very moment, and Artur held up his arms and proclaimed unabashedly, "Mine."

Artur had hardly the faintest idea of what ownership was when he made his proclamation, nor did he truly comprehend what he was declaring. All he knew in his naïve mind was that he couldn't help but feel as though she truly did belong to him.

"She's a dire wolf pup," Urda told him in that moment, rather than question him or chuckle as his parents did in response.

"Pup?" Artur mimicked. It was the first time he had heard the term before.

"A puppy." Urda knelt before him. "See?"

Ygrayne watched nervously over her baby boy all the while, nearly voicing the protest what she kept sealed behind pursed lips. Had Thelric not been there to calm her, she would have most certainly fretted. He was more enthusiastic about the dire wolf, and the prospect of his son forming such a prompt connection. He felt that their meeting was predetermined by Fate, calling forth what had previously been dormant, awakening with a howl. Thelric could see the same sentiment in his son's eyes, as he felt within himself.

Artur had no hesitation in reaching out and gently placing his hand atop the dire wolf's head, feeling the softness of her dirtied fur.

"Puppy."

"That's it, laddie. Be nice an' gentle to the wee thing." Urda smiled, trusting Artur completely despite his lack of understanding and young age.

Both smiled to one another before their gazes returned to the now-relaxed beast nestled between Urda's bosoms.

"I'm gaun'ae name her Vána," Urda stated, already accepting the furry little being as one of their own.

"Vána." Artur repeated her name aloud and it was then Vána turned her head in his direction. Her eyes were still closed, but she could sense him—body and soul alike. She sniffed at his hand to take in his scent and licked at his palms to see how he tasted, and concluded based on such little information, that Artur was her person.

Vána was drawn to him with the same unknown connection Artur himself felt. What exactly passed between them, could not be described. But they felt it whenever they were near, whenever they were far, despite all the ways it sounded inane. When he talked, she listened. When he called, she came to him. When he was sad, she was there for him to hold. In delight and happiness would they share.

Ygrayne was hesitant to have a wild beast in her household and around her baby at the outset, but once Vána began to show her calm and loving temperament, accompanied by vigorous training with Urda, it was soon as if Vána had been born of the same womb as her own son. The Sigurdsson cottage quickly became the dire wolf's favored household.

That feeling, that connection, was not lost upon them as Artur hugged her about the neck, and her foreleg went to his back, the usual greeting they gave one another. Ronan looked up from where he was crouching in the creek, a stick in his hand, prodding at the rocks and tiny polliwogs below.

"Ah! Vána came to visit us!" he said aloud.

Kian paid no mind to any of the commotion. He was too busy trying to catch the same polliwog he had been working to capture for the past hour.

"Did you come to play with us?" Artur asked. It was akin to talking to a peer, she understood words so well, and Vána responded in kind as though man's communication came as naturally to her as her own instincts.

Vána turned her head and pointed her snout at Trivaden with a bark. Artur followed her directional gesture and gazed over at their village. He realized it was time to return for supper, having now noticed the smoking chimneys and discerned the smell of food drifting to their location.

"Aye," Artur turned to Ronan and Kian. "I have to get home. Supper is going to be ready soon."

"Are we actually going to see you tomorrow, or are you going to be fishing again?" The snarky comment made Artur bristle, but he let it be.

"I won't fish tomorrow..."

"Aye!" Ronan couldn't help but chuckle at Artur's reaction. Sometimes he found great pleasure in getting a rise out of the other two. "We'll see you tomorrow then."

"Th-ee ya tomorrow, Artur!" Kian shouted to him, his hands dripping of water, cupped together to ensnare the polliwog he had succeeded in capturing at last.

"You going to come with me, Vána?" He didn't need to ask, but he loved seeing her prance with excitement and respond with a confirming bark.

She never left his side as they made their way through Trivaden. He waved to the various neighbors he passed, a common expression of mutual cordiality and familiarity. His cottage was at the far end of the village, the last one passed when leaving Trivaden, and it was near torture now that all he could focus on was his hungry belly. Even Vána shared his sentiment, eagerly anticipating the treat she knew awaited her, an expectation. All families were more than happy to welcome her in their supper festivities.

But it wasn't just food that was on Artur's mind. Now that his attention wasn't diverted elsewhere, he thought back on the so-called "Valeriaan caravan" he had witnessed. Not even his imagination could have constructed a similar scene, his complete ignorance an obstacle to his understanding. Neither of his parents had ever mentioned such folk—such terrifying-looking folk. He was eager—determined—to find out what exactly was happening around their insignificant village. What was transpiring in the larger world around him, beyond the borders he had yet to pass. Artur had only ever known life in Trivaden. To him, Trivaden was the world. But that cocoon of sanctity had been prodded, and uncomfortable truths were threatening to spill into his reality. Soon he would learn just how wrong he was about everything.

CHAPTER 4

"I'm home!" Artur announced and proudly added, "And I brought Vána." Of course, his mother knew so as she was the one who sent the dire wolf to fetch her son.

"You made it just in time. Very good." She smiled.

Ygrayne set the last plate on the table and ruffled the fur between Vána's ears as the dire wolf came to sit beside the table as if she too were invited to a seat.

"Had you not, I would've eaten without you, and you would have been without supper for the evening." It was an obvious jest, but there was a threat hidden in her words.

How delicious it looked—the seared fish sat at the center of the table, surrounded by a loaf of bread complemented by a set of cheeses, and assorted vegetables from their garden.

Vána received her own portion of fresh fish which Ygrayne was certain to save specifically for the dire wolf. Even when Ygrayne placed it before her, Vána didn't consume her supper right away. She was to wait for Artur and Ygrayne to take their designated seats at the table and serve themselves before she would think of helping herself.

"Is Papa going to be home?" Artur asked, washing his hands as he had been taught to do always before supper.

Ygrayne let out an exasperated sigh, and to the front window did she turn her head in a fruitless attempt to set her gaze upon her absent husband. Thelric had been gone from Trivaden for several days, as it was his turn to trade in Falkhearth. His skill and finesse as a hunter did well to bring in what little money they could and secure the essentials they needed. The major cities such as Falkhearth relied heavily on flowing commerce and abundant trade. It was both a haven for wealth and a breeding ground for poverty, whereas in villages such as Trivaden, the residents had learned to take advantage of nature's generosity and rely on one another to survive. Although they lived modest lives, absent of riches and wealth, they could produce their own food, engage in their own hunts, and stay removed from a life that engendered hunger, sickness, and destitution. Only the royal family and nobles thrived in Falkhearth, as in any city. The war had left them with deep pockets and empty hearts. The spoils of a victory they had so happily claimed came at the detriment of the rest of Skana, and it was an established order they maintained by wielding callousness and cruelty. The grandeur of the city could not hide the decay within its walls.

Ygrayne was thankful that her husband, and most of the men in the village, were willing to tolerate such disheartening sights. She couldn't possibly do so anymore. In her youth, all she had wanted was the energy and excitement she had believed to reside within a city. It was why she traveled to Falkhearth in the first place. Not long after meeting Thelric did she realize how much she missed the quiet and simple life only a village could provide. And back to a village she returned, never intending to step foot within the borders of a place akin to Falkhearth again. But that was the downside to her new life—how much she missed her husband. Even now, did she miss him terribly. It worried Ygrayne, knowing he had yet to traverse the main road. His failure to return could hardly be considered cause for concern yet. But even as she knew it was foolish to hope that a spared glance might somehow summon Thelric, she was left disappointed.

Ygrayne waited a bit longer with her forearms propped at the window frame, her head turning this way and that, only ever seeing that same empty road. The sun was nearing the horizon, the night returning to them.

As much as she wanted to wait, as much as she believed the caravan would turn up before nightfall, Ygrayne didn't want to delay supper much longer. She still had a son to feed, and a rather hungry dire wolf waiting patiently for permission, never minding her own hunger.

"Let us eat." She resigned herself with another longing sigh, and she joined Artur at the table.

The two ate in satisfied silence, basking in the delicacies before them that filled their bellies at last. Vána too began to help herself to her serving of fish, slowly and meticulously enjoying each bite she lapped up into her drooling jowls.

It was apparent by their lack of conversation their minds were indeed heavy with deep thought—Ygrayne worried about her husband and father of her child, and Artur contemplated the spectacle of the Valeriaans. Neither wanted to divulge their musings; Ygrayne was reluctant to show her uneasiness as she needed to be the strength in the household in Thelric's absence, and Artur was uncertain of how to bring up such a subject he himself knew nothing about. Waiting some time more, he realized perhaps there wasn't an opportune moment. It fell to him to choose when to broach the topic.

He paused mid-bite, his mouth full of bread and cheese, while the events replayed in his thoughts, and it was then Vána noticed his sudden change in demeanor. Her eyes glancing at him with obvious concern contorting her brow, she tilted her head to the side as she began deciphering the sudden alteration in mood. When Artur hadn't moved for some time, she nudged his arm with her snout and rested her head within his lap. Artur didn't notice her nearness until Ygrayne took the gesture as Vána begging for food and quickly scolded the dire wolf.

"Vána, no begging! You haven't even finished your first helping." She pointed to the half-eaten fish strewn across the floor.

Only then did Artur feel the weight of Vána's head in his lap, and peering down could he see she was still looking to him with concern about her expression. He knew promptly what Vána's motives were and appreciated the kind gesture becoming of her temperament.

"I'm all right," he whispered to her, patting the top of her head.

"Don't let her do that, Artur," Ygrayne gently reminded her son, still believing her previous notion.

"Sorry, Mama." Artur needed only to nudge the dire wolf's head for her to understand what was expected of her, and as commanded Vána perched beside her meal and began nibbling at it once more.

Artur returned to his withdrawn state, merely peeking up at Ygrayne through his lashes until she caught his gaze. Only then did he divert it to the food before him. He was still too nervous to speak.

But Ygrayne was now astutely aware something was indeed amiss with her son. She could tell just by looking at him, observing his mannerisms. Knew that his mind was elsewhere.

"What's bothering you, my boy?" she asked after swallowing her food. "You're not usually this quiet."

She rested her chin atop her folded hands and gazed at Artur softly.

Artur took another bite and tried to answer the question without thinking of how garbled his response would be with a mouth full of food.

"I 'aw a 'arav—"

Ygrayne held up her hand to halt him and said, rather annoyed, "Chew first then answer. I can't understand, nor do I wish to see your mouth full of food."

Artur almost rolled his eyes at the request he thought was unnecessary, but he could feel the sting of past slaps on his cheek from previous attempts—never mind the awaiting glare he could see foreshadowed about her expression. It all served as a grim reminder of the consequences of such a small, yet snarky, gesture.

So, he finished chewing—thoroughly—and finally said, "Me and my friends saw a... Valeriaan caravan today."

Artur didn't have a chance to continue before Ygrayne's blue eyes narrowed into sharpened points beneath furrowed brows. The smile about her mouth faded, the gentle chewing behind closed lips ceased, jaw unnervingly clenched.

Her face stilled to stone. It was a discomforting sight, one Artur hardly knew despite being well-acquainted with his mother's many expressions. Pushing past his nervousness, Artur finished in a meek voice, "There were many of them. Ronan said they were heading for Falkhearth."

He paused, and Ygrayne took this moment of reprieve to lick her teeth and swallow any remaining food.

"Is that so?" she finally said rather carefully, calmly.

Ygrayne had hoped Artur would never have cause to mention such happenings. That he wouldn't be privy in his youth to the Valeriaans' existence, let alone the atrocities they had committed. She'd hoped Trivaden was remote enough that they would be safe from the Empire's ire. The soldiers had never frequented the village in her time of residence. Any business, as well as all tariffs they owed to the Valeriaans, were conducted and collected in Falkhearth, as was the expectation of all neighboring villages in the region. It made Trivaden the perfect place to live, to grow a family, to raise children; their little village meant nothing to the Empire. And in Artur's twelve years of life, she had been at ease knowing of their unattested place in everything.

Her justification was thus: the truth was more terrifying than being ignorant of the Valeriaans' very existence, of the Empire's gruesome history, and she wanted to spare him the misery that came with such knowledge.

Thelric was always quick to disagree with her on such a choice. He felt the more their son knew, the more prepared he would be for anything. But Ygrayne always contended that such an event would never happen in Trivaden, and so it was better not to address it. Ygrayne didn't want Artur to worry himself over conflicts that didn't involve any of them.

"Yes, Mama." Artur responded with the same caution, sensing the mounting tension in the air. "But Ronan didn't really tell me much about it. Do you know who they are?"

She looked to him and their eyes met in an uncomfortable stare. Her gaze was so intense that Artur felt he would crumble, completely at her mercy.

There were very, very few times Artur had ever feared his mother. He was absolutely terrified in that moment. He had never seen her in such a state, in such unspoken, but palpable, distress.

"Mama?" Artur called to her as his voice caught, slumping back against his chair in preparation for an unpredictable response.

Ygrayne blinked, bringing herself back into a state of awareness in which the fear and anguish dwindled and she was at last seeing her son withering before her—scared of her—and she realized the intensity of her demeanor, felt ashamed that she had put him in such a state.

It would have been the ideal moment, the time to tell him the truth, all of it. He was not a toddler anymore. He was old enough to comprehend what Ygrayne wanted to keep hidden so zealously. Yet as the words poked and prodded at her lips did she so stubbornly keep silent, refusing to let the breath that held the words escape.

I can't... she thought to herself. *I just can't...*

She knew her own fear and denial were her only obstacles, no fault of her son's. Still, she just...couldn't.

"I don't know, my boy." She swallowed hard, her otherwise confident voice shaking. "I really don't know who these Valeriaans are."

She breathed, regained her composure behind the façade of a soft smile about her face.

"I wouldn't worry yourself. Whatever is going on doesn't concern us. Best we forget about it." She took a quick bite of food, hoping that reconvening their supper would end the conversation. But Artur knew the action was no more than a charade. His mother always behaved so when trying to dismiss a concern of his—he hated it.

Artur loathed being lied to, loathed being dismissed so easily. Certainly, she wouldn't think him still too naïve to question her, especially in the face of such blatant deception.

Whether it was a product of a bruise to his own ego, or genuine curiosity now fueled by a small burst of animosity, Artur furrowed his brows and stated rather bravely, "You're lying to me."

The words came out with a bit more disdain than intended, but they were out regardless, and he wasn't keen to withdraw them. Even as he watched, his mother's posture stiffened and her expression hardened, eyes wide with shock and anger at such bold insolence.

"Why can't you tell me the truth, Mama?"

Mother akin to son, both their brows furrowed in the same manner, the intensity returned to their gazes. Neither were willing to concede to the other.

In a moment such as this, Ygrayne would ordinarily wield the sting of a scolding to put an end to it all, conclude the stalemate they now found themselves in. But she could see it—the stubbornness in her son, as she knew it in herself—and if he was growing more akin to her in such regard, there would be no resignation in the face of opposition, only more defiance. Though it was a struggle to do so, Ygrayne took a deep breath and against her habitual temperament, her instinctual urge to become passionate in her combativeness, she softened her gaze and said with the utmost sincerity in her voice, "My love, I don't have an answer for you. Truly, I don't." It almost felt akin to admitting defeat, but feelings aside, it was for the better. "But I will say this: keep your wits about you and stay vigilant. The times ahead are always uncertain."

Ygrayne hoped the path she chose would prompt Artur to cease further questions…at least for now. And her words weren't completely untrue. Ygrayne truly didn't know why the Valeriaans were present, nor what their intentions might be. The last thing she wanted was her own ignorance to add to unneeded disquiet.

Ygrayne reached across the table and held out a hand to Artur as a sort of truce, a way to come to an understanding for the time being.

Artur hesitated a moment, knowing full well she was still somehow deceiving him. It was so unsatisfactory, so disheartening, to know his own mother didn't think him mature enough to handle whatever it was she was still hiding from him.

There was no more pressing her for the truth. His only conclusion, though inadequate, was to take her hand—and he did so.

There was no doubt a feeling of uncertainty weighing heavily on both their shoulders. Yet Artur could see in Ygrayne's eyes, and hear in her voice, the sincerity of a mother trying to do her best for her son. It still stung, the feeling of being talked down to—treated as a child. Even if he didn't understand what was going on, or what his mother might be alluding to, hiding, Artur at least hoped she would be honest with him, to trust him in the future as he had chosen to trust her with his disclosure.

When all but the firelight had been swept into the night's embrace, the village lay quiet and soundless. A deep blue blanketed the land as it did the stars above, brought to life by the stars filling the dark canvas.

Artur could see the wondrous beauty from his window as he lay in his bed that evening, his loft separated from the main quarters by a ladder.

Artur thought he would soon be lost in dreams, but he found his mind instead as lively as the forest surrounding his family's cottage. The night was a welcome domain for those that disavowed the day, the air filled with the chirping of the crickets, the anonymous sounds of various animals, the faelora fluttering about akin to glowing lanterns.

But it was neither nocturnal activity nor instinct which kept him up that night. His thoughts were about him, replaying over and over the sights he had witnessed that day—the soldiers in gleaming, silver armor, and the thundering hooves of their steeds. Despite how sinister he'd felt their very presence to be, he still foolishly hoped that he might see them again.

Artur sat up from his bed, propping himself on the window ledge to take in the fresh night air, his restlessness still about him. His gaze leapt from one familiar star to the next, amongst the series of astral formations he likened to various objects which existed in his world, until Artur happened upon the star deemed the most significant in the Njörden sky, the Normír.

Artur would have thought it to be inconsequential and insignificant amongst the numerous diamonds within the blanket of darkness had it not been for his father, who made a comment one night when they were out in the fields. "'Tis the brightest, and the only constant star in our sky. It never moves, nor ever dims."

He pointed to it, Artur following the gesture with his gaze.

"It has been described as the 'Star that has forever shone, and may it shine forever more.'"

"Is t'at a good t'ing?" Artur asked, a little over three years old at the time.

"Very," Thelric said. "Folk have used it for travel for ages and continue to do so. If you ever get lost, you need only follow the Normír. A guide forever rising in the north. Folk have even wished upon it, swearing by its magic."

Artur couldn't tell if his father was being cheeky or serious with the last comment. All he could comprehend was that the star seemed truly enchanting without need for lore nor legend. Artur went so far as to wish upon it from time to time, and that's what he did that night.

Even if the idea of it being *magic* seemed too childish, he cast to it yet another request—to see those Valeriaan again no matter the reason for their presence, so that he might discover who and what they were.

Artur's eyes lit with the reflection of the Nerúnors bursting across the sky, swaying, turning, coiling about akin to a river in but a blink, shifting blue and green hues leaping from peak to peak, gazing at themselves in the mirrors of various waterfronts. Artur couldn't help but think to himself that their presence was a kind of acknowledgement from unseen and unexplainable forces. The very thought gave him chills all over his body. Yet despite their energetic appearance, the sight of them brought a sense of calm to Artur's mind, enamored as he was by the beauty before him. And he stared until his eyes began to grow heavy. A yawn parted his lips, his body stretching as if to prepare him for the night sleep which up until that point had evaded him.

Artur resigned himself to his bed, and with his window open beside him, he fell asleep in the glow of the lights undulating across the sky.

Ygrayne herself lay awake in her bed with eyes fixated on the dying fire as it danced amongst the stones and wood of the hearth across the living quarters. She thought watching the flames would eventually lull her to sleep. Yet it appeared to have no effect, her mind as active as the flickers themselves. How could she sleep when her mind raced with dark, upsetting thoughts, and imagined events which may or may not come to pass?

She had enjoyed a peaceful day until supper, when her son brought to her attention what she had been trying to keep from him for his own protection, never considering what his growing curiosity would have in store for her as a mother. He was an inquisitive and adventurous boy. Questions would come naturally to him as they would any young lad with a keen awareness not possessed in infancy. Playful jests and casual dismissals would hardly be adequate answers anymore.

The days she feared from years ago were now upon her, and as much as she had tried to prepare for them, she still found herself as ill-equipped as ever.

How could a mother tell her son about the hard truths and cruelties of the world around him? The wars which had brought the entirety of Skana to her knees in complete and utter submission? The violence committed against folk just trying to survive in circumstances inflicted on them by those who wanted nothing more than to eliminate them from existence?

Ygrayne had at least hoped she would have her husband at her side when the time came to tell Artur those truths, for she had never been brave enough to do so. Or at least, to bring her some peace of mind when such thoughts haunted her. But Thelric wasn't there, and Ygrayne didn't know when he would return home.

The realization of the conditions about her brought a tear running down her cheek. The sheer bleakness of the situation filled her with sorrow.

Ygrayne prided herself on being the one who held the family together. She cared for her son, maintained the home while her husband was away so they could afford a decent life. Yet now she found herself vulnerable and weakened by the unknowns surrounding her, by the challenges brought on by the growing youth in their home. She didn't know what was to happen.

The presence of those soldiers had been foretold. It was Thelric who had relayed such information to her, telling her how word had spread weeks earlier from various travelers visiting Falkhearth of the approach of a massive Valeriaan army.

"It's not exactly known where they are headed," Thelric had mentioned. "But they are undoubtedly heading south. And whatever their destination, they will still happen upon Falkhearth."

Ygrayne was quick to dismiss the notion out of her own uneasiness and fear, until their neighbor across the road, Urda, mentioned it similarly during a tea session.

"Have ye heard?" Urda chimed, her teacup clacking against the plate in her hand. "Valeriaan soldiers are headin' south." She said it so nonchalantly and without a hint of concern, it was almost more troubling than the news itself.

"Soldiers are always traveling down the main road, Urda. Nothing new there." Ygrayne dismissed the notion once more.

"No' such as this," Urda retorted. "This is an army. No' the usual patrol we often seen on the main road. Somethin' big is gaun'ae happen sooner than we think, Ygrayne. Something big an' terrible."

Ygrayne was not one to shudder at anything, but this remark made her tremble. And though she still very much desired to believe it a falsehood, idle gossip mistaken for truth, she now couldn't help but inquire further.

"What could possibly encourage the presence of such an army?" she asked.

"The Oathbound, o' course," Urda said in a hushed whisper, leaning closer to the small, rounded table as if they were surrounded by a crowd of ears. "I've heard rumors thon they have a strong presence in Falkhearth."

Ygrayne nearly spit out her tea. She took a moment to regain her composure and attempted to gently place her cup down with a quivering hand, to show no hint of weakness in her otherwise confident air.

"There are no Oathbound here in the region. If they're anywhere else in Skana, fine. But they should leave the rest of us be." It was foolish to say and she knew it, but the words slipped from her tongue regardless.

"Ye know the Valeriaan Empire and their ways. We may be in fer some dark times ahead. Juist bear this in mind, an' keep a close eye on things. Protect yer boy."

"Protect your boy." The words rang in her head akin to the sound of a persistent bell. "Protect your boy."

Ygrayne took in a deep breath and closed her eyes to fight back any more tears that might befall her pillows. But if the wetness of her tears was not to stain her face, then the wetness in her nose would threaten to do so instead. She sniffed rapidly, smiling in spite of herself with trembling lips. Ygrayne opened her eyes and wiped at her face, meeting the golden glow of a gaze framed by the stark silhouette of the dire wolf before her, outlined by the fire behind.

Vána let out a concerned whine and tried to nuzzle her head closer to Ygrayne, ever unaware of her size.

Ygrayne had always known Vána to be intellectually competent and rather intuitive, but she couldn't help but feel the dire wolf understood exactly what she was feeling. She wasn't precisely certain how, nor why such a thought came to her, but it was what she absolutely needed—an empathetic companion who felt her pain and knew of her fear. Someone to hold and let her weep without words, to lend a listening ear.

She sat up from her bed and embraced Vána's head against her chest, gently stroking the fur between her ears—a gesture that Vána herself very much appreciated. And Vána too reciprocated the affection. She gave herself into the arms of the woman before her with a huff, bringing her body to stillness. Both drew unspoken comfort from the embrace.

"Oh, Vána," Ygrayne whispered with sad longing. "Will you always watch over my boy as you have for so many years? Will you be there if I can't?"

Ygrayne was more so talking aloud to herself than making a personal request of Vána directly. But Vána raised her head until they were looking directly into each other's eyes.

It was akin to looking at a person, as silly as it seemed to Ygrayne at the time, but there was a certain contentment she felt, as though her request was understood, and received without question. The tears she thought she had fought back began to fall down her face once more and she found herself wrapping her arms about Vána's thick ruff, the warmth of the fur a greater comfort than the fire itself could ever bestow.

CHAPTER 5

When Artur awoke the next morning, his senses were immediately hit with the smell of freshly baked bread, of honey and butter. The prospect of breakfast in the morning, no matter how normal and mundane it was, was enough to make him sit up in bed and cast aside his grogginess.

And so, he crawled out of bed and peeked over the ledge of his loft down to the living quarters. Their morning's breakfast had been set at the table, as neat and tantalizing as always. The very sight suddenly made Artur's eyes not so very tired and his stomach rather demanding.

"Is breakfast almost ready?" Artur called down to his mother as she placed a plate of that delectable bread on the table.

"It's ready now." Ygrayne clapped her hands together to rid them of crumbs and flour. "Come down here and eat." She gestured to him.

He did so quietly, last night's conversation still looming heavily in the atmosphere, a fact they were both acutely aware of. They avoided eye contact, partook in discreet, or not so, efforts to keep their distance. Even Vána, who didn't hold any stake in the matter, could feel how uncomfortable the air was about them. She decided to quietly escape out the back door—a task which came easily to her, gently tugging the handle with a nimble paw.

Neither Ygrayne nor Artur noticed her absence, they were so distracted as they sat at the table preparing their meals. It was quiet, save for the rustling of their bread pieces as they spread their toppings, the sound of utensils clacking. They were never so reticent in the morning. The early hours were always filled with chatter and laughter. The table was an area of communication for the members of the household. It was as obvious as a thorn in one's foot that tensions were high, that ordinary interactions had ceased.

Ygrayne didn't want it to be so. Out of her own guilt and desire to rid the air of the heaviness that loomed over them from the night before, she initiated the conversation.

"What will you be doing today?" she asked calmly.

Artur looked up from his plate just long enough to see her blue eyes staring directly at him, before he averted his gaze back to his food.

"Probably just go play with my friends today. Or go fishing afterwards," Artur answered curtly, but truthfully. Of course, he didn't mention his ulterior motive, how he wanted to sit atop the hill again and watch for the majesty that was the Valeriaan caravan, to see them pass through if even for a moment. Given his mother's reaction, he doubted she would be very pleased to hear it. Silence on that point was best, he decided.

"By playing with friends, do you mean you're going to see if there are more caravans passing through?" Ygrayne raised a brow to him. She wouldn't be fooled, knowing Artur to be an inquisitive boy, in his period of stubbornness and dissent.

Artur was taken aback. Sometimes he truly believed she could read his mind, as she used to claim in his younger years—back when he didn't think to question it, as he was susceptible to words spoken from the folk he looked to for guidance. But he wouldn't be fooled this time, remaining silent.

Ygrayne chewed and nodded her head, for his lack of a response was confirmation enough.

"If you do go out and play with your friends, please stay away from the hill. I don't care if Ronan or Kian are up there. You are not to be. Understand?"

Artur didn't see the value in arguing with her. He wasn't going to receive permission, nor the answers he was seeking. Any questioning or objection would perhaps lead to her determination that he was never allowed to go to the hill.

"Yes, Mama." Artur sank back in his chair, defeated and dejected.

Though Ygrayne struggled with accepting her choice in letting her boy go at all, she put trust in the fact that he was going to do as he was told, that he was at least old enough to understand her motivations, however his urges of defiance might compel him otherwise.

It would be so much easier just to tell him...so why can't you? she thought to herself, wrestling still with the ongoing conflict that was akin to a storm out at sea.

Would it only serve as a detriment, or would it bring a sense of liberation? In truth, Ygrayne was still too afraid to oblige.

Maybe once Thelric is back. It was a valid excuse to keep the matter at hand at bay. Ygrayne wanted to be spared the conversation she had fretted about all through the night. Artur would ask questions. He would eventually have to know, but Ygrayne trusted it was not this day. She strongly hoped that the soldiers' passing was a mere coincidence. After all, she hadn't heard anything more about it, so she felt it best to maintain an attitude of indifference toward the situation.

"W-why don't you go fishing for a couple hours...at least sometime today. You know...t-to bring some of your catch to share with our neighbors." She was mentally berating herself for not keeping her composure, the grip of regret around her throat when she noticed the look on Artur's face. He didn't believe her motives were wholesome in the least.

"What if I don't catch anything?"

"Then we just won't give them anything today. What they don't know doesn't hurt them, right?"

Artur arched his brow just as she did to him.

When the table had been cleared and the two had said their goodbyes, Ygrayne watched from the patio as her young boy took off down the village road as if he couldn't wait to be free of her company. It hurt to know they were parting on such tentative terms. She let out an exhausted sigh, her body shifting against one of the columns of their patio, arms crossing over her chest.

I know you don't understand right now, but maybe one day you will. That I'm just trying to protect you. Was that the excuse she was still giving herself? *Admit it, Ygrayne. You're the one who's afraid. You're the one who's the coward.* She pressed a palm against her forehead, her eyes closing. *This would be so much easier if Thelric were here.* The darkness of her thoughts soon shifted to her husband and his continued absence.

She thought of him, of the various dreadful scenarios that might be keeping the caravan away. Had they run into the Valeriaans on their way home? Was something happening in Falkhearth after all? As she spiraled into the grim possibilities, Ygrayne unthinkingly tied her thick, black hair up into a loose bun. Strands framed the sides of her face. It was particularly warm that winter morning and it was almost second nature for her to do so in such a moment.

The breeze felt good against her ivory skin, a welcome reprieve now that the curtain of her hair was swept away. She wasn't partial to the warmer weather; she preferred the cold provided by a tundra environment, and the rain and snow which often accompanied it. But winter was coming to an end whether she desired it or not. With the snow nearly melted about the terrain, and the spring come to greet them again, the warmer days indeed would be upon them soon.

Ygrayne's partiality for colder days wasn't shared by her neighbor and friend, Urda. Basking in the sunlight akin to a spring flower, she was across the way tending to the flowers sprouting before her windows, humming happily and absentmindedly to herself. It wasn't unusual to find Urda out in her garden all day, making certain it was perfectly tended to, never once seeming to be flushed nor exhausted from the labor and sun. As Ygrayne's household produced vegetables for Trivaden, so Urda had a talent for making poultices and blends of spices and herbs, even medicinal tonics that the villagers hadn't known of until she arrived shortly after Ygrayne and Thelric.

That was thirteen years ago, just a year before Ygrayne was to deliver Artur. Midwives were not strangers to Trivaden. There were several women who were called upon whenever a child was to be birthed, but Urda appeared dissimilar. It helped that the two of them befriended one another rather quickly when Urda first moved into the once-vacant cottage across the way. Leading up to that auspicious day, Urda introduced methods and home remedies to ease the rather difficult pregnancy far beyond the knowledge within Trivaden at the time, and kept Ygrayne company when Thelric had to be away.

The village thought Urda odd. The things she knew and the way she carried herself were not the norm within Trivaden, nor the region. Moreover, the others were wary of her purely based upon her appearance.

Urda was from an island in the west called Dargdha, home of the folk dubbed the Keltaes. They were the subject to harsh superstitions espoused by the rest of the Skana folk—superstitions which often led to discrimination and horrific executions as they were believed to have immersed themselves in dark magic and human sacrifice. They were easily identified by their pale skin—paler than the average Skanian—their distinct freckles, their vibrant red hair, and complementary green eyes. Even if such drastic discriminatory practices had been left in olden ages, the prejudices still lingered passively in the hearts and minds of the commonfolk.

Urda herself was blessed—or cursed—with that thick, fiery red hair. The strands shifted and bent akin to the contorting of the flames of a wildfire. Her pale skin was creamy and smooth, with a flare of red in her cheeks and freckles scattered about them, and the vibrant green in her eyes was akin to the shallow waters of a lagoon.

Her predetermined reputation was made worse by the fact that Urda was young and a natural beauty, often garnering jealousy from the other women of the village. Even Ygrayne found herself fondly jealous of her dear friend. Urda's vibrant hair and eyes provided a stark and enviable contrast to her own dark hair and deep blue eyes.

Despite the opinions of others, Urda wasn't afraid to flaunt the beauty of her figure, taking pride in its elegance and stature. Dresses with a V-shaped, plunging neckline were amongst the common attire, though often a modesty panel allowed for only the vague suggestion of the top of women's breasts, while the shoulders were exposed.

Urda had no shame in showing off her, as she described them, 'glorious bosoms.' Her necklines often dropped lower and allowed a pleasing peek for the wandering eye. The backs of her dresses boasted an elaborate "keyhole" design to reveal the shapely lines of her shoulders.

Ygrayne found Urda's confidence rather impressive and was even tempted to dabble a bit in the style herself, if only to tease her husband.

Many a night, Ygrayne would hear of Urda as the topic of whatever gossip the village was passing around at the time. She always dismissed the other women's comments as bouts of insecurity, but she couldn't help but take note that the Keltaes' appearance perpetuated archaic superstitions, of which she had never heard until Urda's arrival.

"What do they speak of?" Ygrayne once asked Urda over dinner on another one of those nights Thelric was gone. She would rather hear it from the woman herself than from the sharp tongues of the scorned.

"Oh." A smile played upon Urda's red lips. It was clear she had heard it before, and many times over. "Thar is actually truth in the words they speak." Even her accent was distinctly different from the average Skanian. Ygrayne found it rather enchanting.

"It's an old wives' tale though," she continued. "Superstition which endit the lives o' many innocent women back in the olden days."

Urda took a sip of her tea, more than happy to share. "It wis says thon Keltaes women were witches an' did dealings wi' unfavorable gods in order tae remain young an' beautiful. E'en sae much as tae lay wi' the gods themselves—their bodies taintit an' sullied. The red hair wis a symbol o' the blood spilt from sacrifices. The strands stained from thon veins o' the innocent." Urda couldn't help but chortle again at the absurdity of it, before she continued. "It wis also says they wad enchant an' seduce any man thon wad leuk upon thaim. If she were tae be scorned, she wad ask for the gods tae punish aw those thon she found unfavorable. Curse thaim! But, o' course, this wis aw a silly tale most probably spun by jealous wives. Us red heads caen't help but be beautiful."

Urda flicked her locks with her hands and posed as if to confirm the rumors surrounding her. Ygrayne found it all inane. She knew Urda was nothing that their neighbors claimed she was, and bore no resemblance to the women about whom the legends of old spoke.

"What happened to them?" Ygrayne was hesitant to ask, but she had to know now that they were deep into the conversation.

"They were tortured an' killed. Oftentimes by burnin' tae cleanse the evil within thaim. They were raped tae take away their seductive prowess, an' agency ower their own bodies. Tae defile thaim in the eyes o' the gods thon haed fallen for their charm an' wickit ways. It wis rather gruesome." Urda answered without hesitation, not so much as batting an eye.

Ygrayne couldn't help but stare, her mouth agape.

"That's aw in the past now. Na ane believes thon anymore. Or really remembers the fou' extent o' them olden tales." Urda dismissed it with a wave of her hand.

Ygrayne couldn't comprehend at the time how indifferent Urda was about the whole thing—the rumors and history, by which she and women akin to her, were still judged.

But it all made sense the night she gave birth. Ygrayne only allowed Thelric and Urda to be with her while the rest of the villagers waited in silent anticipation.

Thelric was in dismay, given he was to be a father and had no experience in dealing with a woman going into labor. Urda was Ygrayne's steadfast companion, her support through the entire ordeal. No matter how angry Ygrayne was, nor how frustrated she became, Urda was not the least bit intimidated nor distracted from the task at hand. With deft hands and a calm demeanor, backed by an expertise no one was aware she possessed, she guided the very difficult birthing process as efficiently as conceivable, and by the end of the night, Artur was lying peacefully in Ygrayne's arms after a long bout of crying and expletives.

Urda stayed with Ygrayne and Thelric the entire night, for as long as the new parents were up themselves. She was at their beck and call if they so needed assistance, the picture of a diligent midwife. The malicious rumors and gossip did her no justice, nor were they true in any capacity. It was that night Ygrayne truly acknowledged that Urda was her closest friend in Trivaden, and if the rumors should happen to stretch to her own reputation, she didn't care.

Ygrayne knew the truth, Urda knew the truth of herself, and that was all that mattered.

"Aye, ye are sae pretty!" Ygrayne could hear Urda talking to her flowers again after a good watering, her finger gently tracing the petals.

Some of the harmless rumors were valid. Ygrayne would find Urda talking to her plants more than any actual folk around her, but she couldn't blame the woman when being around the villagers so often meant being in the company of envy and bitterness both. Plants were better company for her in comparison. They didn't talk back or argue, listening in a peaceful silence with hardly the capacity for judgment or biases.

"Greetings, Ygrayne!" Urda called out in that sweet tone of hers, with a delicate wave of her hand.

"Hello, Urda!" Ygrayne called, a swift and easy transition from the deepness of her thoughts.

"Ye leuk as though ye have somethin' on yer mind, deary. Wad ye want tae talk aboot it?" Urda saw the worry on her face, observant as she always was.

"I think I shall take you up on that offer." Ygrayne didn't have any hesitation confiding in Urda, knowing well she could handle even the heaviest of burdens.

"Guid, guid. I think I've bothered ma flowers enouch. Now I must come bother ye!" She chortled.

Ygrayne approached as Urda went to water the last of her flowers—beautiful violets with streaks of magenta, the five petals sprouting out and sloping downward akin to a cascading waterfall. Ygrayne hadn't seen these on Urda's windowsill until that moment, which prompted her to ask, "You've been going out again. Haven't you, Urda?"

"Only as o' lately. The nichts grow warmer an' it makes a pleasant stroll—peaceful an' quiet. I find it's the best time tae cultivate." Urda gently caressed one of them as if cradling an infant's hand and added, "An' there's been too much commotion around here lately. I find it's easier tae get around under the cover o' the nicht."

"What do you mean?" Ygrayne perked up a brow instantly.

"I found there's an increased Valeriaan presence within the region, an' they have watchpoints at various parts on the main road. I e'en saw some encampments in the forest nearby. Last thin' I neit is tae be reprimanded for mindin' ma own business." Urda spoke as though such a situation was nothing out of the ordinary, but Ygrayne couldn't help but feel her stomach turn and curl with agony. The occurrence she'd tried so much to dismiss with an abundance of excuses was becoming all the more real, and all the more unavoidable.

"These Ilyndór flowers are rare tae find. Usually they retreat intae a pod durin' the day, an' sprout durin' the nicht. They give aff a gentle glow in the moonlicht, an' they attract faelora. I juist haed tae get some for ma garden."

Ygrayne found herself slightly taken aback, believing a serious matter such as this would cause some alarm even for Urda. But she was more concerned with finding rare flowers than the escalating presence of the adversaries of the commonfolk.

"Wait! Wait, Urda!" Ygrayne shook her head, motioning her hands in a halting gesture. "What do you mean there's watchpoints and camps?"

Urda looked at Ygrayne for a moment. "Whit aboot thaim?"

"What do you mean, 'what about them?' There are increased numbers of Valeriaan soldiers in the region, and you're more concerned about Faelora?" Ygrayne's brows furrowed.

"Worryin' gives ye wrinkles." Urda playfully tapped between Ygrayne's brow with the tip of her finger.

"My son gives me wrinkles enough. That's not the issue!"

Urda tilted her head slightly just as Vána did when she was confused or trying to comprehend something.

There was a pause before Urda replied, "I don' see the problem here."

"Urda!" Ygrayne was exasperated. "Why are there Valeriaan soldiers here? Why hasn't my husband come back from Falkhearth along with the rest of the caravan? What is going on?"

Urda realized that her dismissive manner regarding the mounting situation was not shared by her dear friend who was seething before her very eyes.

"Oh dear." Urda let out a sigh. "'Tis a very serious situation for ye, it seems."

"Of course it is! I don't know how to explain to my son why he saw an army marching right past our village! I don't know where my husband is! And I don't know what is happening around here!"

"Aye-aye!" Urda dropped her pail and quickly reached into her apron pocket, rifling through the contents until she produced a bottle that contained a clear fluid in which various herbs and petals were floating.

"Smell this." Urda removed the cork and held it up to Ygrayne's nose. The sweet scent of flowers and spices hit her, a feeling of euphoria took ahold of her senses, and a calmness poured through her body.

"By the gods. What on earth is that?" Ygrayne asked, taking the bottle from Urda.

"It's a remedy thon calms the mind an' body. I used it on ye whan ye were givin' birth."

"Damn, that smells delightful."

"I make only the finest," Urda proudly proclaimed, her hands about her hips. "Are ye no' sleepin'?"

"I hardly slept a wink last night."

"I'll give ye a Ilyndór scent tae put on yer pillows. Knocks ye oot. Works akin to a charm."

"Oh, really? That would be fan—No! Urda! Don't change the subject."

"I'm no' doin' anythin' o' the sort!" Urda feigned innocence, an evident jest of performative falsehoods. "I simply am concerned for the wellbein' o' ma closest friend."

"If you're really concerned for my well-being, you will tell me if there's anything amiss!"

The silence which crept between them was deafening, and it was apparent Urda did indeed know something was happening. Why she hesitated, Ygrayne could only speculate. But she also couldn't press Urda regarding her reluctance in light of her own hypocrisy.

"I cannot tell ye for certain. But if I haed tae guess, the Valeriaan soldiers are probably keepin' folk from leavin' Falkhearth.Under lock, for lack o' a better description." Urda needed not say more for Ygrayne to understand what she was implying.

"They have all of Falkhearth under lock? But why?"

Urda let out a sigh. She looked over her shoulder and behind Ygrayne to be confident they were the only ones in the immediate area. She wanted no eavesdropping ears or nosy neighbors to happen upon their discussion of such a sensitive topic, knowing it could very well cause a panic.

When she was certain they were indeed alone, Urda stepped closer to Ygrayne and said in a hushed tone, "Remember hou I mentioned o' thare bein' rumors o' an Oathbound stronchold in Falkhearth. If thon is indeit correct, an' the Valeriaans have been able tae confirm the rumors, they'll lay siege tae Falkhearth."

"That's ridiculous! I told you before there are no Oathbound in Falkhearth." Ygrayne's voice was a tad louder than strictly necessary, and Urda quickly shushed her friend.

"Rumor!" Urda's hushed tone was a bit strained but the silence that settled in gave her a moment to regain her composure.

"That's aw I know, Ygrayne. Ye don't have tae believe it, but it wad explain why yer husband an' the caravan haven't returned from Falkhearth. They're no gaun'ae allow anyone oot o' Falkhearth, nor will they let anyone in. That's whit the watchpoints are for."

"Even if there were Oathbound in Falkhearth, no one from our village has anything to do with this petty war."

"The Valeriaans don't know thon, an' that's aw thon matters tae thaim."

"But…Urda…" Ygrayne was at a loss for words. She could only mutter, "There are no Oathbound in Falkhearth…"

Ygrayne was endeavoring to convince herself in some way. Oathbound in the city would mean Thelric might not return for a long while, if at all, and she couldn't accept such an outcome.

"Dae ye really believe thon? If sae, you're a fool. Or are ye tryin' tae convince yourself o' a lie you'd rather believe?"

Urda easily called her bluff. She wasn't going to let Ygrayne make a mockery out of herself. That wasn't the resilient woman she had come to know.

"For whit purpose? Tae protect yer boy? Tae hope yer husband comes home soon? Well, regardless o' whit ye believe, we're aw gaun'ae find oot the truth very soon." Urda's entire demeanor changed—a sobering reminder of the realities which surrounded them. Her solemnity was almost haunting, bringing a chill to Ygrayne's skin.

"Richt now, yer boy needs ye tae be strong in yer husband's absence. If Thelric isn't involved wi' the Oathbound, then ye more than likely have nothin' tae worry about…"

There was the matter of unintended civilian casualties, but Urda felt it best to keep that out of the conversation.

"There's nothin' any o' us can really dae aboot it at present. Until then, we can only wait an' see what's tae happen."

It was easy for Urda to say.

You don't have a son, or a husband. You only have your plants, and I doubt the Valeriaans are quick to punish them. Ygrayne was ashamed to think of it in such a way, yet she couldn't help but feel a little bitter over her powerlessness in the situation, and having it thrown in her face by a well-meaning friend. There was veracity in Urda's words, however. Ygrayne knew she couldn't abandon her duties as a mother in the face of her fears. She had to reinforce her nerves. Bring soundness to her mind.

Urda quietly walked to the wooden gate, which led to the garden and creaked open with only a slight push.

"At least ye have yer son, an' I have ma plants." Urda's demeanor softened once more, and her words brought a smile to her lips.

Ygrayne felt guilty to hear aloud the thoughts with which she almost invalidated Urda's outlook on the whole ordeal.

"Why don't ye come help me tend tae ma garden? I'll let ye tak' some herbs an' spices home if you'd prefer. It'll help keep yer mind aff things for a bit. Ye neit no' worry now, for thare's no' a damn thin' ye can dae aboot it."

With that, Urda walked into the garden, leaving Ygrayne to contemplate the offer. She was right. There wasn't anything to be done except to focus on her son. To make certain he was kept safe until Thelric returned. She hoped a day in Urda's garden would help clear her mind and bring her the peace she was looking for.

The day was disappointingly quiet and rather testing for young boys with little patience, outside of fishing, and boundless thirst for excitement. It didn't help that Artur had been sitting at the base of the hill, not daring to join Ronan and Kian at the very top as he had the day prior, lest he go against his mother's orders. This was an immense and embarrassing strike to his ego, made worse by the taunts and insults of his friends. All he could do was sit there and sulk while he was omitted from the adventure he had been eagerly waiting for.

"Anything?" Artur had to call up to them periodically, to stay informed of any activity. Though he already reckoned there was nothing, for the land did not tremble as it had; there was no sound of thunder, no clanking of armor.

"Nope," Ronan called back to him. "I don't think they're coming at all today or we would have seen them by now!"

There was some comfort in knowing he wasn't missing anything.

"Then maybe we should just do something else?" Artur called once more to Ronan, hoping his friends would sympathize at least slightly and join him to play out in the fields instead.

"You would want that, wouldn't you, Mama's boy?" Both Ronan and Kian couldn't help but laugh between each other, and Artur skulked deeper in his frustration. Should he be found to have defied his mother's request, he might never be able to go on the hill again. He knew neither of his friends would snitch, but they had big mouths and loose tongues, and the truth could accidently spill in conversation regardless.

"Why can't Artur justh come up here for a li'le bit?" Kian looked to Ronan. "We won' tell hith mama."

"'Cause he listens to his mama." Ronan shifted back onto his stomach. "I swear she's paranoid too."

There was slight disdain in his tone. Their parents had told them to stay away from the hill as well, but the pair couldn't care less about it. To them, what they were doing was harmless and nothing dangerous was likely to happen.

Frustrated, Artur stood with an angry huff and made his way back through the field. If he wasn't going to be included, then at least he could do something he loved by himself.

"Where are you going?" Ronan called after him.

"I'm going fishing. You both are hardly any fun right now!" Artur yelled back at them without diverging from his path. So Ronan had to be the one to leave his spot and chase after Artur, cutting in front of him.

"Fishing again?"

"Yes! It will be much more fun than just sitting around here. Besides, Mama asked me to catch some fish for our neighbors." Artur realized too late what he said was only going to be used against him, and he blushed with embarrassment.

"Do you always do what your mama tells you to do?" The question of his character was no doubt a sneer, as if listening to one's parents was considered anathema by his peers.

"N-no!" Artur couldn't keep from stuttering, and Ronan didn't believe him in the slightest.

"Our parents are overreacting too. Does that mean we shouldn't be allowed to go out and do what we want?"

Artur didn't answer. He only dropped his gaze to the grass to find some relief from Ronan's intimidating presence.

"Let's just play in the field tomorrow…I want to go fishing now."

"Fishing is so boring."

"You're only saying that because you don't know how to fish."

"I know how to fish!" Ronan retorted defensively. He didn't want Artur to have an advantage over him with anything, even if it was true.

The reaction made Artur feel as though he had gained some kind of power, an edge in the conversation for once, and it spurred on a sudden swell of courage.

"Well, then…" He almost didn't finish his sentence, so great was his hesitation, but he pressed forward regardless. "You're probably just too daft."

"Little bastard! Take that back, you Mama's boy!" Ronan attempted to wrestle Artur to the ground, but though he was taller and lankier, Artur was faster and stronger. It was easy for him to shift away from Ronan's outstretched arms, and he took off down the field in a sprint that could not be matched by his opponent.

Kian watched his brother and friend with the utmost amusement, finding it a bit satisfying that Ronan had already given up on trying to chase after Artur. He always stayed out of their playful scuffles, for he would be the one coming out bruised and scraped and running home crying at such times.

Before Artur reached the village, he couldn't help but turn around and shout back at Ronan, "Maybe if you listened to your parents a little more, you would be good at fishing! Or good at something at all!"

It was all in jest, the familiar spat that they often had. But there was satisfaction in seeing the blatant flare of red about Ronan's cheeks. By the next day's playtime, it would all be forgotten. For now, he was eager to grab his fishing pole, and head down to the river for his joyous pastime.

CHAPTER 6

Artur let his line fly through the air. It was the third time he had reset it. The previous opportunities turned out to be fruitless, the river itself teasing as a fish would. There were many days he had no luck, but their frequency did little to lessen the sting of disappointment, especially when he felt folk were counting on him to bring supper to their tables. It was in times akin to these that he concocted a story in his mind that maybe the fish had finally wizened up, refusing to fall for such blatant trickery any longer.

When the pole was secure in the cavity he'd dug in the sand, further fortified by purposefully placed rocks, Artur took a seat by his still-empty bucket, his socks and boots strewn about where he'd discarded them without a second thought. As he had for the past few hours, Artur sat there quietly and watched the clouds pass, witnessing the natural shifting of time, and gazed about the mountains off in the distance. He once again used the opportunity to note new details on those ridges and cliffs, the shifts in the rock faces. There was a beauty to them he knew little about, experiences his young life lacked that made him wonder what standing atop one of those mountains would be akin to. How small the world would look with just a mere tilt of the head. What he would finally see for the first time. How would the wind and sunlight feel about his face with neither tree nor hill to block their path? Would he be able to touch the clouds, as the peaks did? He always imagined they were akin to fur, soft as a bed, even a blanket.

Artur's eyes slowly drifted back to the river as he realized he might never know what it was to be a part of the greater world around him. There was very little he understood of things outside of the forest and the village boundaries…perhaps nothing, really. He believed the rest of Skana lived a life akin to the one he already knew: simple, quiet, and tranquil. Now he wasn't so certain. The Valeriaans fit nowhere in the world he'd constructed in the limits of his understanding and imagination.

What else did he not know? Was what he did know, wrong? Such thoughts made him grow restless; even in the lull which came with fishing he could not find peace.

"She'll never tell me," Artur concluded in a soft whisper from his lips as he brought his knees to his chest.

His thoughts raced as he reconstructed the events from the past couple days, trying to make sense of everything to the best of his capacity, putting together what he remembered of the Valeriaans who had come so eerily close to the village—the catalyst of his quest for answers. Then, his thoughts took a more somber turn. He had heard his mother crying last night, as if she were weeping just beside him, directly in his ear. He had dared to make neither sound nor movement. There had never been a time in which she had failed to comfort him when he needed it most. The times he shed a tear, he had soon found himself wrapped in her arms, within the loving embrace only a mother could provide. Yet he didn't reciprocate.

It brought a rather sickening feeling to the pit of his stomach, nauseating and painful. His father still hadn't come home, and all his mother had was him. In such an absence, Artur felt it was his duty to take care of his mother, and he could hardly do so. He brushed his fingers through his thick, black hair with a frustrated sigh, and he suddenly found himself back on his feet as if the mounting, nervous energy had finally imploded on itself and demanded an outlet.

Back and forth he paced the riverbank, his mind seemingly intent on punishing him with guilt-ridden thoughts emphasizing his failures and inadequacies as a son. Had his father been there, it would've been him Artur would have confided in. Certainly, Thelric would've understood. Certainly, he had gone through the same when he was of Artur's age. But the truth was, his father wasn't there, and it hurt not knowing when he would see him again.

What would you have done, Papa? Artur thought to himself, as if his father would hear his thoughts no matter where he might be. There was no answer, of course, and it pained him still to be alone in his turmoil, lost in a sea of uncertainty.

Artur would have pondered for the remainder of his time there had he not heard the cracking of a branch across the river. The uncommon sound ricocheted between trees and traveled through the forest akin to an echo, searching for his ears and his ears alone. He shivered a bit, a quiver down the length of his spine. The hairs on the back of his neck stood on alert as his body naturally primed him for the potential danger that lurked about unseen.

He had only heard stories from his father of the way the body prepares one for the worst: senses heightening, the mind determining whether one would stand their ground or flee. The forest was a domain he felt he knew well, and besides the story of how Vána's kin had been devoured by the deadliest of creatures found in such territory, there had never been any other concerns. Yet as he touched at the back of his neck, he couldn't help but attempt to decipher what exactly his senses were trying to tell him. It felt as though there were a pair of eyes settling their gaze upon him. Watching, observing. His every move was being examined and scrutinized with the utmost attentiveness. He searched about the all-too-familiar forest that had only been a companion to him throughout the years, and not even the sharpness of his senses, honed in response to potential danger, could apprehend what exactly was lurking beyond the river.

The forest always presented a mysterious charm that was never forthcoming in revealing its secrets, delighting in its own alluring temptations. It was what made it admirable to its inhabitants, folk and beast alike, until it decided to turn against them. Unpredictable and, at times, volatile. Was it now humorously hiding its spectator for the events about to unfold?

Artur swallowed nervously. Heart pounding in his ears, he could feel the vigor rushing through every nerve and fiber in his body, heating both face and chest. The world suddenly stopped around him. There was no sound of the rushing water, no rustling of the trees in the sway of the wind. The animals ceased their vocalizations, suddenly growing silent as if they too feared whatever was lurking out of sight.

"Always remember to stay calm. Panic will get you killed." Artur could hear his father's voice imparting a gentle reminder.

"Predators want to give chase. It's the thrill of the hunt that fuels their bloodlust. Don't give them that. Always keep your gaze on them. Move slowly until you have safely removed yourself from the situation."

With the words resonating in his memory, Artur heeded his father's guidance and kept his eyes about the forest, pinpointing exactly where he heard the rustling, the crack of a branch giving to weight, and he slowly began to back away across the sand in case his would-be attacker panicked, seeing its prey attempting its escape. He only stopped when he felt the cool of the soil touch his heels, the fallen leaves crackling with his delicate movements. He lingered, waiting for anything which would force him to make a decision for the sake of his life.

The time passed by with no mind to the tensions about, and to Artur's relief, he neither saw nor heard anything further. If there was something presenting as a threat, certainly it would have made itself known, made a defining move to either cease its pursuit or carry out its intentions. There was nothing. And the more time passed, the more he became conscious of the sound of the river once again, the wind brushing against his bare skin. Even the forest creatures began chattering amongst themselves once again. His body began to calm as the senses which previously had him on alert went dormant once again.

Eventually Artur himself was convinced that all was well, though he kept vigilant as he slowly made his way back onto the riverbank where his belongings were strewn about. He could no longer feel that gaze. There was such a distinct shift about him that he knew it was gone—a sense of calm returned and serenity restored. Artur couldn't help but let out a sigh of relief.

Artur checked his fishing pole once more. Noticing the line had gone a bit slack, he tugged on it slightly to straighten it and make certain it hadn't snagged on the bedrock below. He secured the pole back in its makeshift mount in the sand and finally took the moment to stretch after a prolonged period of doing absolutely nothing. The lull was becoming more discouraging as the day progressed, regardless of the light left and the liveliness of the forest. He bent backwards at the waist to stretch his abdomen, and rising back did he let out a grunt from the strain. The final release of tension escaped through his lips as a sigh, his eyes fluttering open. His gaze naturally drifted across the river, and as expected, the riverbank and the landscape looked the same as ever. However, he soon realized there was something more than what he knew to be familiar.

At first, he thought it to be a trick of his imagination. Perhaps he had drifted off to sleep and fallen into a strange and capricious dream. But it became increasingly clear it was no dream, nor was it a trick of the mind. Artur could still feel the sands at his feet, the rugged texture against his skin, the warmth of the sun's touch about his arms. This was as much the real world as it ever was. What he couldn't explain was why there was a young girl standing across from him, on the other side of the river.

His mouth went slack, his eyes widening akin to those of a frightened fawn. The disbelief and wonder were obvious about his expression, and yet he was so enamored by the unexpectedness of her appearance. It was only ever he and his father who graced these shores, but she stood there as if she too had always belonged.

Though they seemed to be of similar age, she stood with such grace and poise that it put him to shame. He felt a sudden diffidence, disparaging his own stature and person. He had never been aware of his own body until that moment, realizing the slouch of his shoulders and the crude unkemptness of his overall appearance; it was obvious he had been tussling in the sand and dirt of the field earlier that day. In comparison, she was so clean and neat in appearance. She wore clothes of the finest material, in bright colors, akin to a bird boasting the beauty of its feathers. Her shoulders back, she carried herself with a straightened posture that further accentuated the way she held her head, her pride befitting of her standing in society.

Artur stood there as quietly as she did. His eyes were completely fixed on her as if she were a snake with those tantalizing eyes, ensnaring even the most cunning of rodents. Despite its initial awkwardness, the silence did present them the opportunity to study one another at length, comparing their features. His raven-colored hair to her shining silver. It was short, just as his was, though the textured layers framed her face in a rather delicate and feminine manner. Bangs brushed over her forehead, just above sharp eyes. He couldn't help but notice their beauty too. Underneath those dark, thick lashes they were a stunning violet that glistened in the sunlight, capturing his attention. He was lost in them, transfixed. Never before had he seen such a color, their vibrance making him detest his own dull grey eyes. Even her skin, smooth and pale as ivory where his was peach and sun-kissed, suggested that her standing was well above his own. The milkiness of her skin tone amplified the rosiness of her lips and the flush in her cheeks. It was already obvious, just by her physical features, that she was indeed not from the region. Her clothing, too, was unfamiliar, from her boots to the cleanliness of her trousers, to the long-sleeved white blouse tucked into the high waistline. Artur believed she had to be a gift of the forest, manifested by magical forces unseen, and the fact of the matter remained that she was the most beautiful girl he had ever seen. There were enough girls his age in Trivaden to compare, and it was obvious she was not cut from the same cloth. Looking about her face, which held all the curiosity and caution any stranger would feel in an unexpected encounter, he became instantly, completely infatuated.

Artur noticed not how the heat rose from the center of his chest and flooded his cheeks and the tips of his ears. Not one of the girls in Trivaden had ever produced from him such a reaction. But it was deeper than just the outward appearance. There was something in the depths of his being, an unrecognizable response rising beneath the surface of his own awareness. It kept him there on that riverbank, a captive. The only coherent thought that he could understand amidst the scrambling of his mind was, *Does she feel it too?* Was she as enamored as he was? It was what he wanted to think. To flatter himself. There had to be a reason she too didn't leave.

If only he'd known what was going through her mind as her eyes wandered about his figure. The rose-colored gaze made him blind to the sharpness of her eyes and the scrutiny she placed upon him. He was everything she had heard about the commonfolk—dirty and unkempt, unimpressive in every sense of the word. His trousers were filthy and wrinkled from the bending of his knees. His white blouse was not so white anymore, only partly tucked in at his waistline with seeming carelessness. The only pleasant thing about him was his face, because it was also the cleanest thing about him, surprisingly. Reluctantly she had to admit to herself that she loved the peachiness of his skin, the way his cheeks flushed red. She adored the darkness of his unkempt hair, a trait which was very foreign to her. It was a welcoming change, refreshing to see. Even his eyes—she couldn't help but notice—were much softer than hers, lit with the wonder a child would possess. In the grey of his irises, she could see flashes of blue when the sunlight embraced them.

'Tis a pleasant face, she thought to herself, and the moment she felt a hint of smile begin to form, she let her pride and unwillingness to be enamored of a simple village boy instinctively return. Her expression soured a bit as she configured a reason to detest him, to find some kind of fault to distract her from the feelings developing within her.

No...'tis a daft face, she concluded. *A daft face indeed. And he's nothing but a daft village boy.*

Their eyes finally locked, now that they were no longer distracted by their personal quests of exploration, and they suddenly found themselves about each other's gaze. Artur let himself be taken by the feeling within, while her stubbornness and prejudice were no match against the truth. She felt as drawn to him as he to her, even if she couldn't realize it herself. A sudden and unexplainable compulsion had them both within its grasp, and no tug or struggle was sufficient for an escape.

Unakin to Artur's wide-eyed and curious expression, however, hers seemed almost coy and uncertain. It unsettled Artur to see such reservation. He knew himself not impressive by any means...but he certainly was no threat. The scrutiny of her gaze made him tremble a bit, made him aware of his own inadequacies. The vast differences between them were becoming clearer. Subtly shifting her weight about her legs, she contemplated returning to the depths of the forest, her gaze turning to the tree line behind her. Artur flinched, her intentions made clear with only the shift about her demeanor. He realized then that he needed to do something to keep her there. Yet, there were no words. There was no motion. There was no outward show of his want of her company. Artur felt imprisoned, rendered immobile by his own reticence.

She was not the least bit impressed by the way his mouth hung slack, the pathetic look about his face, when she spared him but one last glance. It was still in the back of her mind to leave. There was nothing of worth keeping her at that riverbank. In fact, she had only come to waste time in a show of open defiance. What held her there, she did not know. But she remained there, her desires at odds, thoughts conflicted.

They were so engrossed with each other that neither realized the wind picked up around them in a most unusual manner. It was akin to a ghostly murmur, making the trees tremble around them, and the forest once again fell silent. There was a transference, a certain heaviness about them—thick with an energy never felt before. Although Artur remained unaware of the change around them, she could not say the same. To Artur's ears, it was just the wind, familiar but inscrutable. For her, it carried a whisper, though it was unintelligible, a combined speech of words that could not be deciphered, but spoken as though they were in complete and perfect synchrony. They graced her ears as if lips spoke softly against them, the sighing of secrets shared only between the two of them. It was terrifying.

Had it just been the indescribable sounds carried about the wind, she would have ignored them and explained it all away as a figment of her imagination. But the whispers invoked something within her. Down in the depths of her very being, it began to stir and awaken with neither remorse nor permission. Traversing the inner complexities of her body, weaving through every fiber, coursing through her veins, did it come forth to answer the ghostly chattering about her. The air of elegance and confidence she'd portrayed abruptly devolved into fear and hesitancy. Her eyes grew wide, and lips began to quiver as she stumbled away with uncertain steps.

Artur remained completely oblivious to her inward struggle, believing her sudden change in demeanor to have something to do with him instead. He stepped forward, reaching forth as if she were close enough for him to grab hold of. He wanted nothing more than call to her, to keep her from leaving him. But Artur had no say in the matter. The girl hurried into the forest without warning, her speed so great that it took Artur a moment to realize she had indeed departed.

Wait! Artur could only think the words he wanted to speak, his lips left slack, tongue stilled. His feet only got him as far as the water's wake before he stopped in his tracks. There was only one way to pursue her, one way across the river. He looked to the path of boulders that endlessly enticed him to test the river's might, and already his parents' warnings came to advise him otherwise. There came the stirring in his feet, a trembling as they ached to move forward. To even grace but the first stone before them. Artur clenched his teeth, his breath harsh. He just...couldn't do it...

Throwing his hands into the air with a loud groan, he paced along the river's edge as he cursed himself for his hesitation, his inaction. Artur wanted to be the one to make that choice. He felt he was old enough to do so. And yet, it was but a memory that made him falter in a moment that was to be his own.

Artur inevitably succumbed after much grumbling and fury, letting out an exasperated breath as he threw his arms down in frustration. He had never been more disappointed in himself than in that moment, and he had been disappointed in himself many times as of late. This was possibly the only chance he would ever have to see her, whoever she was, and she was gone. He wished himself braver, capable of defying his parents' wishes—to not be the good child, the obedient child for once...the, dare he admit, Mama's boy.

When he gazed across the river, he saw only remnants of her existence about the sand, footprints as a reminder she had indeed been in his presence. By the next morning, they'd only be fainter, carried off by the wind and erased forever. A distant memory. Artur bowed his head in defeat, retreating to his fishing pole and belongings to retire for the afternoon with absolutely nothing to show for it but the bruising of his pride.

As Artur began to wend his way into the forest, he felt a sudden chill—a brush against the back of his neck by the ominous wind that had successfully chased the girl away, returning now to claim him next. As it made its presence known once again, Artur became aware of it. His skin crawled in response to its company. It tickled at his ears with the same indiscernible whispers, prompting him to wildly swat at the air as if it were filled with incessant bugs. It proved to be an ineffective remedy. There was a presence in his company, holding him at the riverbank. But as he turned sharply when the winds shifted about once more, Artur found that he was indeed still alone.

Panic began to set in, and an inward battle of rationality against what was being perceived by the senses began to wage. Artur could feel it, could hear it, and yet his mind was trying to convince him that there was nothing there.

The same sensation that had overtaken the girl now welled up in him too—something deep inside of him beginning to awaken, extending its reach about his body as if it were all too familiar with its every intricacy. A warmth. A heat. He could feel it swirling around in his chest akin to a fire. It tickled, uncomfortably so, as though a beast were attempting to clamber about his arms and his legs, consuming him with the uncomfortable prodding of sharpened talons digging into his being. Artur could bear it no longer.

He dropped his belongings and frantically brushed at his body, clawing at whatever it was that attempted to devour him, and when it proved ineffective, Artur saw no other choice but to dart down the path to find some safety within his own home. He paid no mind to the leaves and needles shed from trees and foliage around him, even as they poked into his bare feet unforgivingly.

When Artur reached the cottage, he cared not to call for his mother, nor look for her for that matter. He simply burst through the back door and scurried up to his loft to hide amongst the blankets of his bed. He felt akin to a child again, the way he hid beneath them as if they would provide any sort of protection. But there was some comfort to be found in the absence of the whispers there. He did not feel the unseen presence which had moved around him, did not feel whatever had been stirring inside of him. It was all mercifully and comfortably quiet. Artur decided in that moment he would not speak a word of anything that happened at the river. Not of the girl. Not of the whispers. Not of whatever had surfaced within. Absolutely nothing.

CHAPTER 7

The night was quiet and uneventful. Even at dinner Ygrayne had little to say, exhaustion having noticeably befallen her. She made modest eye contact, put little food on her plate. Her hair, which she always kept neat, was a bit disheveled. She was entranced by the thoughts that clouded her mind, and Artur felt it best to leave her be. The silence was a welcome guest at the table that night, neither mother nor son averse to its presence. After the food was put away, the candle flames extinguished, and the fire burning low in the hearth, Artur found himself lying wide awake in his bed...again. There was no tiredness in his eyes, no quiet in his mind. He could only think about one person even after her presence had left him earlier that day. Her image was as vivid as if she were standing before him once again. His eyes met hers. Those violet eyes—the loveliest he had ever seen. He gave a deep sigh, one of longing and yearning. Artur dared not think about the events which transpired afterwards, for they were unpleasant and terrifying. At least the girl was real. She made sense to him. Everything following was only a distressing trek into the indescribable. So, Artur only thought of her. A remedy to cast out the fear that now dwelt within him.

He would have thought of her all night, had he not heard the creaking of a door outside. Peeking through his open window, did he see Urda's home was not as dormant as the rest of Trivaden. There was a faint glow through the shutters of her window, only open wide enough to show there was still activity in the late hours. Of course, it could all be simply explained away as the faint glow of an active fireplace. After all, there was smoke coming from her chimney.

That is, until there came a sudden, "Aye!"

Artur flinched at the unexpected exclamation and crouched behind the window frame, just low enough for him to still peek over the edge and not be seen.

He couldn't make out any words, but there were undoubtedly whispers emanating from the house. Several of them. Neighbors? No, they didn't much care for Urda, let alone visit her. Travelers? Artur couldn't recall any new visitors arriving in Trivaden. If there were, the village would've made a commotion about it.

As he thought further, Artur recalled catching Urda talking to herself, on many occasions, and she was known for doing things at odd hours of the night... doing many odd things at odd times. He'd observed her venturing off into the forest alone, long after the rest of Trivaden was asleep, from the same window he was now watching through. But Artur had never truly given any mind to it, nor did he care. What business Urda was conducting had never concerned him.

The light vanished and the whispers ceased as suddenly as they had begun. There came the brief sound of creaking, similar to that which had first caught Artur's attention, and once again there was silence. Artur sat quietly in the hope that more odd happenings might transpire, but there was nothing. It was quite unsatisfactory, even as dispassionate as he tended to be where Urda was concerned. But there was indeed something amiss. Artur could sense it.

He settled back into bed and his thoughts immediately returned to the girl across the river. There was something in his very being, every fiber of his self, telling him—nagging him—to return. As though an unseen force was winding the cords of Fate around him and tying knots to this girl. As if they were meant to meet each other, as if they were bound to one another in some way. Two futures woven together.

When Artur woke the next morning, the cottage was strangely quiet, and the smell of breakfast, which never failed to greet him, was absent. When he peered down to the living quarters, did he see his mother still fast asleep. Her arm hung over the side of the bed, her long, raven hair streaming around her. There was a vase of purple flowers on the nightstand beside her bed, ones he recognized from Urda's own garden. Besides these few particulars, there was nothing seemingly amiss, though it was odd that she was still asleep at that hour of the morning.

She hardly moved at all, nor did she make a sound when he crept down the ladder with the utmost delicacy, the most calculated of movements. She looked exhausted, her eyes swollen as if she had been crying all night, no doubt over his father. It was evident Thelric hadn't returned home, or the two would have been found together. He felt a sense of hollowness then, a hollowness only his father could fill. He knew his mother shared the sentiment. With a sigh, Artur carefully pulled the blankets over his mother, a small gesture he felt obligated to do. It was a small gesture that might bring her consolation without awakening the tension between them.

Artur took the opportunity to quietly sneak back to the river. Regardless of the strange things that had happened after the girl had vanished, he couldn't miss his chance to see *her* once more. And to give his mother some time to rest, the space she perhaps needed…that's how Artur justified it to himself. Ygrayne was not to stir. There was very little that would disturb her after such a stressful day.

He took a hunk of bread with him to eat on the way and quickly headed out the back door.

Artur had barely reached the gate when he saw Urda walking up that familiar dirt path, humming to herself as she always did, a basket of herbs and flowers in the crook of her arm. He already knew what was going to transpire. As much as he wished he could flee to the riverbank, he knew she was going to stop him and converse without an inkling of his discontentment.

When their eyes met, escape was impossible.

"Artur! Guid mornin'!" Urda called to him with that chime in her voice.

"Good morning, Miss Urda."

"Where are ye aff tae?"

Artur inwardly groaned but responded, "Going down to the river to fish."

"Is thon whose fishin' rod an' belongings I happened upon doun at the river?" Urda placed her hand atop her chest, surprise crossing her expression.

"…They're mine…"

"Why did ye leave it?"

Just leave me be, woman.

"I got really tired and…f-figured I'd be back tomorrow…so, I left them." Even to himself he sounded so unconvincing.

"Eh, makes sense tae me." Urda shrugged her shoulders and nodded.

She truly believed that?

"Forward thinker." Urda winked at him.

Artur laughed nervously and responded quietly, "I suppose."

"I'm certain you'll have a wonderful day doun thare. But, before ye gae, please tell me, hou is yer mother?"

"…She's sleeping."

"Awe, poor thin." Urda let out a sigh, her body visibly shifting with a discouraged lean. "She's quite exhaustit worryin' ower yer father. An' ower ye, o' course."

"I know."

"I don't think ye dae," Urda was quick to correct him, a smirk crossing her face—or so that was how it looked, prompting Artur to raise a brow.

"Well, ye gae have fun. I'm certain I'll be seein' ye around, young man."

"I will, Miss Urda. You have a good morning as well."

The exchange was nothing short of awkward. Urda didn't seem to mind, however, smiling down at him, unbothered by his aloofness. Artur was waiting for Urda to leave, wishing not to simply depart from her presence so impolitely. When she made no move, he pursed his lips together and averted his eyes in his mounting discomfort, his arms swinging at his side.

Urda finally dismissed him with, "Well, don't let me keep ye. Aff wi' ye."

Artur was elated to go about his day with her permission. Without another word, he hurried down that path while Urda watched on until he disappeared into the thicket of trees.

When he had gone, Urda touched at her face thoughtfully and said with absolute glee, "Such a charmin' boy. Sae polite!"

When the tree line broke and his feet dug into sand once more, Artur came to a skidding halt just at the water's edge. The waves gently lapped at his toes, cold in the early morning hours. The thought that she would be there the moment he arrived was inane, but he couldn't help but grasp onto the hope nonetheless. It made it all the more dismaying when he found the opposite riverbank abandoned. Her tracks were long gone, as predicted, erased by the breeze. He sighed heavily, his posture deflating. The aching feeling of last night couldn't have misled him. He had to be there. She had to be there.

His belongings lay scattered where he had cast them the previous day, but Artur hadn't even given them a passing glance when he sprinted onto the beach. He had a singular determination, and his eyes were fixed on the vacant riverbank that lay before him. His thoughts were his only company again, an exhausting company given their nagging nature. They spoke of what a fool he was to think she would be there, that she would come at all. He pouted, frustrated at the naysaying within his own mind.

There came that tickle in his ear, as though lips were gracing the delicate skin. There still was no physical presence, no being from which those whispers could possibly emanate. But they faded away just as quickly as they came, their attempted conversation interrupted by the rustling of brush in the distance, the pacing of steps, quickly approaching. Artur was prepared now, his eyes already focused across the river. It could very well have been an animal, or the natural shifting of the forest in the wind, but reason did little to keep Artur from hoping. His spirits were high, his anticipation not yet quelled. Akin to a deer bounding across the unpredictable terrain, she emerged. Her figure cast in shadow by the trees above, the girl's movements were elegant and her poise suggested she knew how to navigate the area well. And when, at last, she broke through the tree line and sauntered out onto the riverbank, did she gaze at him. She might as well have had a halo surrounding her entire figure, a glow in the sunlight—serene, divine, an image worthy of such a refined person.

The world once again fell away as Artur stood there in awe and bewilderment. His eyes widened with unbridled delight, mouth ajar with a faint smile playing upon his lips. She didn't appear as ecstatic to be present as he, nor as pleased to see him as Artur was her. Nevertheless, she was there, and there had to be a reason for it.

It was silent between them. In Artur's shyness, he struggled to find the words to speak. It had never proven to be much of a hindrance in his life before. He was more reserved than Ronan and Kian, whose natures were boisterous. Now it was clear to him just how reticent he truly was, finding no courage to initiate a conversation—at least, not quite yet. He found himself intimidated by her still-wary demeanor, suggesting an impending departure. Her eyes prudently watched him with all the shrewdness of a vigilant spectator, assessing the situation at hand, observing the possible risks. Her guard was up, the display of confidence from the previous day now absent.

Oh, how he wanted to say something—anything. He wished the words would pour forth without hesitation, wholly unbridled. But his tongue was trapped—trapped by his own reservations and nervousness. She had left him before without so much as a word spoken between them, and likewise he feared that the introduction of conversation would produce the same outcome. This purgatory was torturous for Artur. Lost in his own introspection, Artur hadn't realized that she was just as nervous as he was, and mutually curious. She too had heeded the urge which compelled her to the sands she now occupied. They shared a want of knowing, an answer to their inquisitiveness. She had come to see him as he had come see her.

He had to speak the first words, to grasp the opportunity he let slip away before. To reward her patience and interest alike. There was no other way. He swallowed hard, made way for breath, allowed his body to relax and call forth the confidence he willed. His heart was racing, the warmth of bashfulness hastening to his cheeks again.

Without another thought, before the shadow of doubt could overcome him once more, Artur finally said to her, "Hello."

CHAPTER 8

Ygrayne finally awoke when she felt the wetness of a tongue lapping at her cheeks, hot breath through moist nostrils. She scrunched her face at the sensation as she endeavored to make sense of what was transpiring in her groggy state. She abruptly sat up, her hair a thick mess around her, and sleepily did she wipe at the moisture on her face, her eyes slowly fluttering open to see the dire wolf sitting before her with an all-too-jovial grin.

"Good morning to you too, Vána," Ygrayne said through a big yawn.

Vána's large, golden eyes beamed at her in delight.

Ygrayne took the moment to brush her thick, long hair, and naturally did it fall down the entire length of her back, thick and heavy. She donned her usual dress, her thigh-high socks and slippers for the day, before she peeked up into the loft to find the bed vacant, Artur nowhere to be seen. She panicked not. There were many mornings Thelric and Artur would leave early to fish when the stock was more abundant, chance in their favor. It was a fair assumption and a correct one, unbeknownst to her, and yet her motherly yearning to know the whereabouts of her child began to present itself. Those pesky instincts.

He's fine, she thought to herself. *He doesn't always need his mother...*

There was a certain sadness in thinking so. There was nothing that truly prepared a mother for the time her child would leave the safety of her bosom to venture out into the world on his own, to navigate the intricacies of life. Artur was only twelve, but she could already see him growing into his own. In the blink of an eye, he'd be eighteen and taking his first steps into manhood. At least, that was how she felt. Such thoughts ran through her head while she tidied up her own bed, picking up a bit around the cottage, with Vána watching quietly until she fell asleep about the floor in a snoring thicket of fur.

Ygrayne became almost lost in the chores a home required. Her hands moved with a deftness and familiarity that needed hardly a thought, sparing her the time to reflect on the past days during which she felt the world was beginning to close around her, eager to share its secrets to all those willing to give a listening ear. Something was amiss not too far from their small village's borders, and the Valeriaans were at the very center of it all. The hope she had of keeping Artur sheltered was beginning to diminish.

Was she to swallow her pride and move past her own fears to reveal the truth? The trepidation was so immense that she hardly wanted to consider it, even still. The longer Thelric was away, the more devasting news continued to flood into Trivaden, and the more afraid she became. They had made the decision to move to this insignificant village to be away from all the politics, from all the travails of the world, from the chaos of an ongoing struggle to right the existing state, and yet it had come striking at her door. She wasn't prepared for any of it.

Ygrayne took a deep breath. Their little cottage was now clean and spotless and there was nothing left for her to do for the time being. She was hardly hungry, her appetite gone since the night before. She had slept better, at least, a bright spot amidst the tears she shed. The remedy which Urda had given her did wonders, the sweet smell of the concoction temporarily putting her mind at ease and bringing calm to her disposition.

It was then Ygrayne noticed the small vase of flowers at her bedside, her attention no longer occupied elsewhere. They were the same purple ones she had seen Urda watering the day before when tending her garden. Ygrayne was puzzled at first. Recalling the day prior, she remembered not if she had indeed brought them home and adorned her nightstand with them. Urda must have visited during the night, or in the wee hours of the morning, and delivered the generous gift.

"Maybe I should go thank her. It's the very least I can do," Ygrayne said to herself. She made her way out the back door, Vána still sleeping soundly on her back, jowls flapping open. Through the garden did Ygrayne amble over to Urda's home.

She hadn't yet reached her neighbor's door when she heard light chatter, wafting from Urda's very own garden. Talking to herself again, no doubt. Ygrayne headed around to the side gate and made her way down the stone path, set by Urda herself as was everything else. When she rounded the corner of the cottage, did she stop abruptly, her eyes wide and mouth agape with awe.

Urda was indeed there, her dress slightly dirty from tending to the garden, her red hair tied back in a heap of locks. But it was the person she was talking to that caught Ygrayne by complete surprise.

The figure looked to her with a slow turn of his head, and Ygrayne found herself gazing into a vibrant pair of eyes—a gleaming amber, a flaring of red and orange in the iris, surrounded by a dark brown limbus. The black pigment ringing the eyes and brow only emphasized the startling colors. The face was completely hidden by a white mask, carved akin to a face itself, with delicate and smooth features. The figure was dressed in a dark grey, floor-length robe that cascaded over a light grey tunic with overlapping folds at the chest, tucked within the high waist of his trousers and fastened with a belt and sash. The trousers were deep grey and tucked into black, knee-high boots. Gaping bell sleeves covered the gloved hands folded at the abdomen, and from the neck of the robe a hood pooled over his shoulders and shrouded his head. With a high collar and head-wrap that covered collarbone to crown, what lay behind the mask was completely hidden. There was not a sliver of this person's skin to be seen, save for what was hinted at beneath the paint.

It was, unmistakably, a *Schiva*. Ygrayne had only ever seen a few in her lifetime, and that had been many years ago when she still resided in Falkhearth.

A fabled brotherhood known far and wide, the deeds of the Schiva were renowned from even the olden days. Beings who devoted their life to the service of others, the Schiva trained and studied their specific crafts in temples well away from the main continent of Skana, on a grouping of islands called Avalon which spanned the Northwestern shores.

The Schiva were well-versed in even the most intricate of skills: medical practices, herbal remedies, childbirth, the arts, building and landscaping, the mundanities of relationships, and practices to improve the lives of even the simplest of folk. Their entire existence was devoted to the good of Skana, to help those who could not help themselves. Many found it intense in its austerity, but the elaborate attire of the Schiva was designed to fit the oath that was made when the Brotherhood was first founded. Adherents were to cast away life's pleasures, to abandon the need for superficial commodities, the celebration of status, the temptations of sexual desire and relational prospects. The helping of others required the disavowal of fame and fortune. Therefore, they hid their faces, so they could be neither recognized nor praised. Their bodies were covered from head to toe to uphold the purest of intentions. They lived nomadically, traversing as itinerants to the farthest reaches of Skana to help anyone they could. From the smallest village to the largest city, there were no limits to their reach, nor was there a being they would not help. They were the most universally revered folk in Skana—so much so that when the purge came at the hands of the Valeriaans, their temples were spared and their libraries left untouched.

But such "generosity" did not come without its conditions. The vastness of knowledge was spared, provided that their teachings and resources were contained within the Brotherhood itself, and that their deeds remained strictly philanthropic. Sharing their knowledge and practices with the commonfolk was well forbidden, and grounds for severe punishment.

It was quite simple to know if a Schiva was in the vicinity. The populace they graced with their mere presence flocked akin to chicks to a mother hen, the buzz of gossip quick to spread the word. There was not a dwelling they could patronize without being recognized and sought after. There had not been a time during Ygrayne's residence in Trivaden at which they had been blessed with such a presence though, and to bear witness to one with her own eyes was almost unbelievable. To her incredulity, he looked just as staggered to see her as she was him. The amber eyes widened with bewilderment; Ygrayne's presence had not at all been expected by him. Similarly, Urda's face could not hide her own disconcert.

A sense of impropriety hung heavy in the air. The three of them looked between each other without a word, waiting for another to speak forth and disrupt the silence. Ygrayne was hardly equal to such a task. She found herself lost, ensnared not only by the enigmatic presence of the Schiva, but by the look in his eyes. Slowly softening from the initial shock, not once straying from her own gaze, those amber eyes peered straight through her, as if observing the soul which lay deep within. It was unnerving, the sensation of having her intimate secrets laid bare by a gaze equal parts mysterious and alluring.

Given that the Schiva did not make any attempt to break the mounting tension, it was Urda who took it upon herself to finally do so. She quickly composed herself, the smile of hers returning to her face, her demeanor playing off the initial awkwardness of having been caught off-guard.

"Ygrayne!" she called to her dear friend. "How are ye doin' this morning?"

"Erm..." Ygrayne could have been drooling for all she knew, the words completely lost on her.

Only when the Schiva dropped his gaze behind a thicket of lashes and slightly turned his head away did Ygrayne feel released. She blinked excessively, as if waking from a trance. She looked to Urda bewildered, searching for the proper words to respond but was only able to muster, "What?"

Urda chortled nervously, her eyes quickly shifting to the Schiva before coming back to Ygrayne.

"How are ye doin' this morning?"

"Oh!" Her head finally cleared. "I'm well! I was just coming over to thank you for the flowers."

Urda was taken aback for a moment, speechless, and Ygrayne was quick to add, "The purple ones you left on my nightstand...though I'm curious as to when you did so."

"The flowers!" Urda exclaimed, clasping her hands before her chest.

"Yes-yes! that's richt." She let out a slight chortle. "I put thaim on yer nicht-stand this mornin' after I met Artur as he wis headin' doun tae the river. I didn't want tae wake ye, poor thin'. Ye finally lookit sae at peace."

"Ah," Ygrayne let out a sigh, relieved to know of her son, of the flowers. "Well, I appreciate it very much. Thank you. And," Ygrayne began to approach, "You mentioned Artur. Was he amiable this morning?"

"He lookit in a hurry, but nothin' out o' the ordinary I wad say."

"Oh good." Ygrayne nodded. Her eyes shifted once more to the Schiva, who returned her gaze again. Silence was still about him, his air guarded, given the closing distance between them.

Ygrayne wondered if she could have misremembered the temperaments of the Schiva. Her experiences were few and long ago, but she could've sworn they were kindly and warmhearted, never fretting over the wave of unfamiliar faces and the perpetual attention. He fit not this narrative.

Sudden guilt overcame Ygrayne. Had she done something to unnerve him? Did her bout of staring only serve to make him uncomfortable in her presence?

"I'm s-sorry." Ygrayne's nerves got the better of her. "Am I disrupting anything?" She looked to Urda with a pained expression, and though Urda parted her lips to respond, the Schiva finally spoke. "Not at all."

The voice was deep but surprisingly as soft as the look in his eyes, not at all muffled by the mask which concealed his identity.

Both Urda and Ygrayne looked to him as he continued.

"I beg your forgiveness for my unwelcoming demeanor. I promise you it shall not happen again."

Ygrayne was surprised by the sudden shift in his disposition, and though the words were genuine, there was a certain playfulness in his voice—a confidence—as his eyes sharpened.

"Oh..." Ygrayne stumbled a bit for a response. "There's nothing to forgive."

"Hm." He hummed. "Ygrayne, was it?"

Ygrayne hadn't at all noticed the snide gaze Urda was giving him in that moment, her displeasure evident. She was preoccupied with the prospect of responding to the Schiva's query with a shy smile. "Yes. Ygrayne Sigurdsson."

"Ygrayne Sigurdsson." The Schiva held out a gloved hand to Ygrayne, and of course, she couldn't help but accept his gesture. His fingers curled around her hand, a gentle squeeze, a delicateness, she was prompt to notice, as they conducted the greeting common amongst strangers.

Had it been a normal introduction between commonfolk, this would have been the moment the man in the scenario would lower his head and grace the lady's hand with a gentle touch of the lips. But the Schiva were different in how they interacted with the masses. Even something as simple as a handshake was replaced by a mere bow of the head and the exchange of verbal pleasantries.

The Schiva were always conservative, never laying hands upon an individual outside of the assistance they offered. Their touch was never more than platonic, never beyond the requirements of their practice. Ygrayne did not resist this unanticipated break in time-honored tradition. This time, however, she noted how Urda shifted about with obvious discomfort at the sight of the exchange happening before her. Arms over her chest, she turned her head with a sour look about her face, gazing sharply off into the garden.

"Pleased to have made your acquaintance." The Schiva's words brought Ygrayne's gaze back to him. The light of a soft smile reflected in his eyes, and Ygrayne reciprocated with her own as she responded, "I would ask for your name, but I assume I will not get an answer."

"Unfortunately you would not." The Schiva snorted, withdrawing his hand to the confines of his sleeves. "You may refer to me as you do the rest of my brethren." He bowed his head slightly, his eyes closed, as he finished with, "I insist."

It was a cheeky addition and Ygrayne admired it.

"Whan the both o' ye are quite done, we dae need tae finish business," Urda finally chimed in.

Neither Ygrayne nor the Schiva had the chance to object before Urda ambled over and locked arms with her dear friend.

"If ye wad excuse us for juist a moment, Schiva."

He bowed his head in acknowledgement and Urda turned with Ygrayne in tow, heading for the side gate of her garden. Ygrayne glanced over her shoulder and noticed the Schiva was regarding the two of them– her specifically—as his figure remained as still as a statue decorating the garden. Embarrassed for their curt departure, Ygrayne's brows furrowed as she mouthed, "Sorry," before disappearing around the corner of the cottage.

She wished she could have seen his response, but it was too late. They were standing in front of the cottage and it was Urda's turn to capture her attention.

"Didn't mean tae interrupt yer greetings," Urda said quietly, turning to face Ygrayne. "But richt now he's helpin' me wi' somethin' o' importance."

"A pretty vague explanation for having a Schiva in your garden." Ygrayne tilted her head slightly, raising a brow. "I haven't seen one in years. What's he helping you with?"

"Oh, juist hou tae encourage faster an' more abundant growth wi' ma herbs. But tell please, did ye need somethin' from me?"

The response was curt, but the guarded demeanor melted away a bit—a hint of her vivacious tone returning in her words. Ygrayne, though, was still taken aback by Urda's unusual frankness.

"I just wanted to come and thank you for the flowers." It was Ygrayne's turn to be wary, though her tone bore no note of caution.

"The Ilyndórs. It's one o' the flowers I usit in the oil I gave ye. The scent helps ye sleep an' calms yer nerves."

"Well, it most certainly helped. I feel more at ease today. Thank you."

"Anythin' for ye, ma dear friend." Urda touched at Ygrayne's arm, a light grasp about the forearm. "Let's have tea this afternoon. Tae make up for this mornin'."

"I say that sounds rather lovely. Fetch me when you're ready?"

"O' course!" Urda clasped her hands together, hopping slightly with the sudden joy she felt. It was then the stiffened figure melted away and there standing before Ygrayne was the friend she had known for years—her body relaxed, and the often-devious smile returned to her lips.

"Until then, tak' care, Ygrayne. I'll send for ye whan I have everythin' ready."

Ygrayne said nothing more, merely gave a small nod of her head, a rather forced smile about her lips, as she watched Urda stroll back into her garden nonchalantly.

Ygrayne let out a sigh. Walking out into the middle of that dirt road, she felt suddenly alone in the village she called her home. To her back was Trivaden, bustling with activity even in the early hours of the morning, the light chatter and commotion of the day's work beginning and the aromas of the morning meal soon to fill vacant bellies wafting out to the road. Ygrayne turned her head and looked to the path which led to the river—the path that would lead to her son. She felt an urge to go to him. To reconcile in some way, to ease the tensions which divided them in the past agonizing days. Yet despite her deepest desire, she believed it best to leave him be. Some time apart would do them well.

She was left to herself then.

She made the unconscious choice to take a quiet walk to the main road, where the forest bled into the valleys which separated them from Falkhearth ahead. Vibrant in all the colors of the fast-approaching spring, they stretched out endlessly before her.

Beyond the shadows of trees and the concealment of the forest, Ygrayne stepped out into the sunlight and let the grass of the fields surround her.

The wind was free to travel around her as she stood, warmed by the sun and basking in the scent of the fields which began to come to life at that time of the year. The strands of hair she'd left loose tickled at her face and the skin of her shoulders. She crossed her arms about her chest in response to the gust, her demeanor sullen. She realized then what had brought her there to the edge of those valleys, out of the confines of the forest she called her home: the hope that Thelric would fittingly come into sight, at first as a faint and insignificant speck against the horizon, slowly inching his way closer until she could see the details of his face and feel the grace of his presence. But no matter the length of time she stood out there, there was still no Thelric. No caravan. Nothing but the shifting of the day right before her eyes. She wasn't certain how long she had been there—how long she waited—but the lovely winter day did little to ease her somberness.

"Ordinarily this would be the moment I would say, ''Tis a lovely day, isn't it?'"

The suddenness of the voice had Ygrayne letting out a cry, and she stumbled about the path as she placed her hand over her startled heart. She turned sharply upon her unsteady legs as the very Schiva she'd met within Urda's garden came into view.

"Yet something tells me such a remark is rather inappropriate."

The cheekiness was not lost on her, even as Ygrayne stood there in a near panic. Only when her breath calmed did she manage to speak. "Schiva! By the gods, you nearly scared me to death!"

"My apologies. I did not mean to frighten you."

"Something tells me you're not at all apologetic." Ygrayne narrowed her eyes at him, and he couldn't help but let out a snicker.

Ygrayne regained her composure, standing straight to retrieve what little air of confidence she still retained. Her pose was a near-perfect mimicry of how the Schiva himself stood before her, with a straight back and his hands folded before him.

"You seem to have a habit of appearing out of nowhere," she stated, again trying to mimic his cheekiness.

"As are my ways." His eyes sharpened with the smirk about his lips, hidden behind his mask.

Ygrayne couldn't help but snicker herself. His sudden appearance was a rather pleasant and certainly welcome surprise. Despite the expectation to abide by oath and service to Trivaden, he had instead come to court her company once more, to Ygrayne's disbelief. She needed no help at the moment, or at least, there was no concern of hers he could indeed remedy. No one would be able to bring her husband back.

She folded her arms about her chest again and conceded that she was curious. The lack of forthcoming conversation only made her speculate as to his true intentions for being there, and now that she could scrutinize him with a clearer mind, he seemed so arrogant watching her fret—amused by her distress, even. The impertinence on his part dulled the fascination that had beguiled her earlier.

"So." She arched a brow at him. "Did you come all the way out here just to frighten me?"

There was a hum again, deep in his throat. His eyes hurriedly swept over her figure to gauge where he should step, figuratively. She felt the need to cover herself with more than just her common dress, feeling so bare, so exposed from the simple glance.

"No," he finally spoke, his eyes coming to rest on hers once again. "I did come for you, however."

Ygrayne's brows furrowed, and she took a step back as he drew nearer, calculation and thought in his steps.

"For me?" she asked.

"Yes—well, I came to see if I can assist you in any way." The Schiva stood before her, and Ygrayne found herself arching her neck just to look up to him, they were so close. "Let me redeem my behavior earlier. If you would allow me."

Ygrayne's demeanor softened. Her annoyance was replaced by her sorrow over the predicament which had no remedy. A solemness came about her once more, and in such a state she replied quietly, "There's no one who can help me." She turned and paced a bit farther up the road. "Not even a Schiva."

She gazed out into the vast emptiness of the horizon, but there was still no Thelric.

"Indulge me."

Ygrayne scoffed. Turning her head, she couldn't help but give him a rather incredulous look. "You're not at all what I imagined a Schiva would be. Was that greeting we shared a farce?"

"And in what way am I disappointing you?"

Ygrayne was startled by his response. Lips parted a bit, her face softened. She wasn't at all disappointed in his disposition. She was surprised—even intrigued—but not disappointed.

"You're not." She spoke quietly. "I just…I always heard of how temperate Schivas are known to be. Humble. Traditional. You—you seem nothing of the sort. But I think it's refreshing. Different. Aside from the frightening me bit."

The Schiva took kindly to her words. A softness came to shape his eyes, hinting at an equally soft smile playing about his lips.

"But it is not false modesty when I say that you cannot help me in any way." Ygrayne looked to the empty path once more. She could hear him this time—the footsteps approaching as he came to stand beside her.

"May I ask why you object to my offer so?"

Ygrayne took in a deep breath. If only it were so simple to ask for what she desired, simple enough that a Schiva would be able to grant it.

"Unless there is some way that you can get me into Falkhearth, there's nothing you can do for me."

"Falkhearth?" It was the Schiva's turn to be startled. "What business could you possibly have that you wish to go there in a time such as this?"

"My husband."

There was only a brief silence before the Schiva uttered, "Ah."

"He went with our village caravan only last week, as they always do. They were supposed to return days ago. But now I hear the Valeriaans aren't allowing anyone to leave Falkhearth. If he can't come to me then perhaps I will have to go to him."

"I regret to inform you, not even I can enter Falkhearth at present."

Ygrayne let out an exasperated sigh. It was exactly the answer that she expected, but the anticipation of it had done nothing to lessen the discontent.

"Not even a Schiva," she said under her breath.

"I don't believe I'd even get past the watchpoint. The Valeriaans largely leave us be, but they will tolerate no insolence from anyone. I'm sorry, Ygrayne."

The Schiva looked to her, and though Ygrayne tried to hide it, the pain on her face was clear. This was no longer time for a jest or lighthearted banter.

"I know it be not of equal bearing…but if it's any consolation, I have many brethren who are imprisoned within the city walls as well. Not even their standing will protect them from what may soon befall Falkhearth."

"You're right." Ygrayne looked at the Schiva and stated curtly, "It's not the same."

The Schiva became guarded. His failed attempt to bring Ygrayne any peace noticeably wounded him. That is, until she smiled softly and said, "But I very much appreciate the effort. I'm sorry that your brethren are trapped. None of this should be happening. No one should be held in the city against their will."

A quiet breath escaped his lips, and the Schiva visibly relaxed.

"This is all a mess." Ygrayne shook her head. "We came to Trivaden to avoid the conflict between the Oathbound and the Valeriaans. Now I find we're at the center of it."

She looked down the road yet again. Still no Thelric.

"You're certain you wouldn't be able to get past any of the watchpoints?"

"I'm quite confident so."

Ygrayne thought a moment, her eyes drifting to the ground as she thought of her son.

"I don't know how I'm going to tell him," she muttered under her breath.

"Pardon?"

It wasn't necessarily intended as a question to the Schiva; rather, she was speaking aloud the thoughts that had constantly plagued her in the past days. When she realized what she'd said, the Schiva was already tempted by intrigue and curiosity. Looking to the Schiva, waiting wordlessly for her elaboration, Ygrayne swallowed nervously. She had hoped the conflict would resolve itself between herself and Artur alone, staying only between the two of them. Yet it seemed the gods, though she hardly believed in them, had gifted her a potential resolution. Someone who could offer more than just a listening ear.

"I..." Ygrayne hesitated a moment. "My son...I haven't told him yet, of the war. Of the things that have happened. I thought I could protect him from it all...at least for a little bit longer. But with everything happening around us, he's begun to ask questions that I...that I am just not ready to answer. I thought I would at least have my husband beside me, so that we might take that step together. But now, I just find myself utterly alone...and afraid. How am I to answer questions I am too frightened to ask myself?"

"Ah." The sigh escaping his lips was one of sympathy and concern. "I see."

"I know you don't, and won't, have children of your own. But if you were to have any, how would you tell them?"

The Schiva averted his gaze a moment, and returning to Ygrayne did he answer, "Children are naturally curious, as terrifying as it may be at times for a parent. Nevertheless, I think it best to encourage such inquisitiveness. To answer to the best of our abilities. But I understand your reservations. This is not a modest matter to approach. I am of the strong conviction, as difficult as it may prove to be, that answering these questions garners their trust, encourages critical thought, and sets the very foundation for the values you wish to instill to prepare them to face the challenges awaiting them in the future. Your son need not know all the horrid details. But he should have an essential understanding of the world around him, conflicts and all. In my opinion, it can only serve for his benefit and growth."

They turned to face each other, a slow swivel about the heels, and Ygrayne asked, "Do you think me a fool, that I have only rebuffed his attempts?"

"No, not a fool." The Schiva shook his head. "I only think you to be a mother who wants what's best for her child. If I were a father, I feel as though I would be guilty of the same. So, how can I fault you so?"

There was a pause.

"Oh dear," Ygrayne let out a small titter under her breath.

"Pardon?" His brows lifted.

"Seems you have helped me in some way after all."

His eyes turned up again. He was smiling under the mask, and despite herself, Ygrayne smiled in response.

"It does no good for you to wait for your husband out here, Ygrayne. Shall we return to Trivaden?" The Schiva gestured to the forest from which they came.

Ygrayne looked down the path once more, holding out one last bit of hope that maybe Thelric would come ambling down that road in her direction. Emptiness, even still.

"I do believe that is best." She finally resigned herself.

CHAPTER 9

They strolled beside one another, the hem of their respective garments brushing slightly. It was a peaceful walk even in the silence between them. Both were contented, at ease. They felt a satisfaction, a fulfillment from one another's company.

Ygrayne had a sense of serenity in having someone to confide in without a bias, to whom she could divulge the battle she had been fighting within herself. The Schiva was only a recent acquaintance, but the words they'd exchanged were enough to make her realize he understood her pain—even if he spoke as a mere bystander, having garnered no experience in the realm of parenthood, of fatherhood.

And as for the Schiva—he was pleased to be in service of another. He had felt the need to rectify the awkward first encounter they had shared that morning, in some way. He had been granted more than he had anticipated. There was no doubt that his antics had provoked the fiery response from the woman; she did not take well to his playful jest, understandably so. Customarily, the commonfolk were quick to forgive and forget; enamored merely by his presence, they would be so willing to overlook a bit of playfulness. But not Ygrayne. She had put a halt to it before he could attempt to push further, and he thought it quite becoming of her.

He took the lull in the conversation as an opportunity to observe her face, to study the features and details that composed it. He noticed the deep blue of her eyes, akin to an abyss—an ocean—that would put at ease anyone who fell into its depths. Her skin was flushed rosy over her high cheekbones. The straightness of her nose led down to soft red lips. Eventually his eyes reached the defined jawline, strong compared to the fullness of her cheeks.

It was all so fascinating—her features, and the resemblance they bore to those with which he was familiar from his historical studies of clans long passed and bloodlines still prominent.

There was one such clan he remembered distinctly—the Heríkssons, identified by thick, raven-colored hair, and deep blue eyes. The clan's insignia was the Myratarí, the Dark Queen of all birds, and its members were known as some of the most feared and frightening warriors in all of Skana. Even the Valeriaans, who were undisputedly their ardent rivals, feared them so. Said to have been birthed from the terrifying Dark Queen herself, the Heríkssons were described as descending into the battlefield with death about their wings, their dark hair an unmistakably morbid omen. It was this ferocity and tenacity in battle which ultimately brought them to the throne in olden ages, where they claimed their sovereignty by deposing the long-reigning Valeriaans. It was a well-deserved, albeit frightening rite of passage into power.

They took the throne from the presiding Allfather with ease. Their only downfall? As with any great, long-standing empire, their once-fearsome dispositions and war practices gave way to the airs of nobility and expectations of marriage to those who possessed neither the passion nor the fierceness that were the Heríkssons' pride. Their bloodline diluted, the clan was but a distant memory now, known only to those amongst the Schiva brethren who were privileged to possess what history of Skana was still afforded to them. The name could be uttered and not a man alive would know of their legends and tales, their lineage diminished to a handful of descendants who could hardly recall their own family's past. But it was the physical traits which kept their heritage alive, however passively.

Just as the Schiva's own eyes were a distinctive trait of a long-forgotten clan, so were hers—or so he suspected. Curiosity was overtaking him. The urge to indulge in his inquisitiveness always triumphed over any other logic present in his mind.

"I appreciate your company," Ygrayne said when they reached the outer limits of the village. The Schiva himself had hardly noticed their arrival, so immersed was he in his own thoughts and observations. She clasped her hands behind her as they slowed their pace, her cottage before them.

"There is no need to thank me," the Schiva responded, concealing his surprise. "I'm pleased to be of service."

He turned to Ygrayne and said, before any unexpected interruptions could come between them, "But may I ask you something, Ygrayne?"

She too turned on her heels and responded, "Of course."

"Are you perhaps a descendant of the Heríksson clan?" He couldn't delay another moment before asking the question, restrained excitement in his tone.

"Heríksson?" Ygrayne's head tilted slightly. "I'm afraid I've never heard of them. What makes you ask?"

"Well," the Schiva took a breath, "I notice you bear the striking features of the bloodline. By physical appearance alone, you very much display the exact qualities they were known for."

Ygrayne was intrigued. "Do I now?" The interest in her voice was unmistakable. "I wouldn't be able to confirm or deny your claim. My maiden's name is Trévorn. I'm uncertain if it was changed after the war or before... Any knowledge of my family lineage has been lost, I'm sorry to say. I wish I could tell you otherwise."

It was just as he expected, which left little room for disappointment. The Schiva felt akin to a child, delving into the conversation in his quest for knowledge, not even the unsatisfying answer deterring his curiosity.

"No need to apologize to me." The Schiva gestured with his hand. "I'm fortunate enough to have studied Skana's history, and the Heríksson clan was as greatly renowned as it was feared on the battlefield in days of old. They were recognized by their raven-colored hair and deep blue eyes, and were said to be the harbingers of death. I've not met anyone with a resemblance as pronounced as yours. Therefore, I thought I might inquire in the hope that I would be fortunate enough to have my assumption proven correct."

Ygrayne touched at her hair as she brought her locks forward and draped them over her shoulder. She had always thought her hair to be boring, dull, surrounded as she was by the golden locks of her neighbors that danced at their backs in the sunlight. While theirs was beautiful and admired, she thought hers insignificant and hardly enviable. Never had she anticipated learning that the very sight of it had once heralded fear and death... Thelric had told her that the darkness of her hair was what attracted him to her upon their first meeting, a touch of serenity amidst the overwhelming warmth. But no one else had ever complimented her hair color, her darker features against an ivory complexion.

She could hardly respond, words absent from her lips, lost as she was in her thoughts. Noticing her apprehension, the Schiva was quick to lighten the mood. "Legend also tells of the women who were as much warriors as their male counterparts. They likened the black of their hair to the wings of ravens, flowing about in the wind wildly as they charged into battle on horseback. It was even speculated that these women were so fierce, they would engage in combat while with child."

"Are you being flippant?" Ygrayne lifted a brow at him.

"Not presently."

Ygrayne crossed her arms over her chest and said, the corners of her lips upturned, "I am still trying to figure out if you're complimenting me or perhaps insulting me. I doubt telling a woman that the color of her hair is a symbol of death is really appropriate."

The Schiva did not respond quickly. He eyed Ygrayne carefully as she gave him a sympathetic look, sensing his embarrassment. What had meant to be a remark of admiration appeared anything but. To rectify the inadvertent blunder, the Schiva cleared his throat and said, "If you are not indeed a Heríksson, you are undoubtedly a Dúlír—the folk that once predominantly resided in Kingstone, descended from the olden clans the Heríkssons once ruled and known for their similarly dark features."

"Dúlír," Ygrayne said, the word upon her tongue as foreign as the Heríksson name.

"Dúlír." The Schiva nodded his head in affirmation.

"A much more flattering description," Ygrayne snorted, and the guarded eyes of the Schiva brightened with a similar smile.

They stood there, their eyes narrowed at one another until he parted his lips beneath his mask to speak, only to be interrupted by a voice off in the distance. "Look there! It's a Schiva!"

Both their heads turned in unison, catching sight of one of Ygrayne's neighbors pointing in their direction directly at the Schiva himself. His voice had certainly carried throughout the small village, as a swarm of residents began to gather in response. If they weren't frozen in awe, they began their approach with eager steps and smiles upon their faces.

"Perhaps this is a conversation for another time," said he, and Ygrayne couldn't help but titter at his expense.

"Thank you again, Schiva." Ygrayne quickly bowed her head. "I enjoyed your company and appreciate your wise words."

The Schiva returned her thanks with a bow in kind, and when their eyes met, they continued their bantering within the silent exchange. They watched each other intently as Ygrayne retreated toward Urda's cottage to evade the encroaching masses. The Schiva, abiding by his oath, turned to the crowd and acknowledged every warm greeting with the patience and finesse perfected only by the Brotherhood.

Ygrayne found herself backing into the awaiting arms of Urda, who had come walking out of her garden when she heard the growing commotion. Urda and Ygrayne stood clear, arm in arm, watching as the Schiva was taken away by the excitable crowd surrounding him, drawing him farther into the village.

Question after question was thrown at him, and as a Schiva would, he handled it with steadiness and grace.

"He'll be entertained for a while," Ygrayne said, a hint of a smirk about her lips.

"For a long while, if the village has anythin' tae say aboot it," Urda responded, and they both giggled.

"I'm sorry about this morning. I hope I didn't make either of you uncomfortable."

"It wasn't ye thon made me uncomfortable. It wis thon damned Schiva. I hardly expectit the overtly warm greetin' he extended tae ye."

"Tell me...are they always so...charming?"

Urda rolled her eyes and said, "Hardly. Ye juist happened tae be a fortunate one."

"Apparently so."

They both peeked from the porch, their movements practically mimicking one another, and they spared one last glance for the forsaken Schiva who was practically being dragged toward the village plaza.

"He was...interesting," Ygrayne said. Urda grabbed her by the arms and asked with an intensity which caught Ygrayne off guard, "Whit did he dae?"

"Well, nothing. I just thought he was interesting."

Urda narrowed her eyes at Ygrayne. The doubt was clear about her expression and Ygrayne was quick to set her mind at ease. Carefully prying Urda's hands from her arms, she chuckled a bit and said, "Truly. Everything was fine. He was very cordial."

"I don't know, Ygrayne. I don't trust him! He seemed a bit friendly wi' ye, an' I will have na man be overly friendly wi' ma dearest friend whan her husband is away!" Urda proclaimed, her finger pointed up into the air.

Ygrayne crossed her arms, her weight shifting to a single leg, and she gave Urda an incredulous look.

"Really now? And what if a man was friendly with me when Thelric was here?"

"Then I'll leave it tae Thelric tae tak care o' ye. I wad provide support, however, if needed."

Their friendly repartee was interrupted when they heard a horse neighing in the distance, hooves pattering against the dirt path. Both Ygrayne and Urda turned and saw the once-empty road now unexpectedly crowded with the caravan returned...or at least, a little of it. The wagon was gone and the numbers which made up the departing party had visibly dwindled. Only one horse, the white mare named Mara, accompanied them. Weary, worn down, and filthy, the men stumbled in as if they were the walking dead, and even the sight of their long-missed home was not enough to lift their spirits.

"The caravan!" Ygrayne exclaimed, running to the approaching group. It was Godríc, who was at the front leading the beautiful Mara by her bridle, that she went to first, and though he looked in no shape to be interrogated, Ygrayne gave no care to it.

"Godríc!" She stopped before him. "You're back!"

Godríc let out an exasperated sigh, his eyes closing ever so tiredly as he replied, "Only some of us."

Urda came to join Ygrayne, primarily to listen so as not to overwhelm the already exhausted neighbor.

"They only let a few of us go from each village. The rest...they had to stay."

"Why? Why not everyone?"

"That I don't know, Ygrayne. I didn't stop to ask questions. I just wanted to get out of Falkhearth."

Ygrayne took a moment to search amongst the somber faces, none of which were the one she was so desperately hoping to see.

Godríc, knowing full well who she was looking for, quickly chimed in, "Thelric is still in Falkhearth. He didn't get the choice."

"But they may let him go? Are they still letting folk out of the city?"

"I don't know. They might be..."

"That means Thelric can still make it out..." Ygrayne said aloud to herself, bringing alarm to both Godríc and Urda's faces.

"Ygrayne...you can't!" Godríc protested, the distress in his tone the only life in his voice.

"But—"

"There were armies gathering outside the city. Who knows what they're planning to do! Going there could get you killed."

It was clear to her exactly what she had to do. There was a chance she could get Thelric back, a chance for the father of her child to return home. Falkhearth was only a few hours' ride away, and if she left immediately, she believed she could make it before anything happened. That some of these men had returned was the sign she needed, the inspiration pushing her to act.

"I have to go," Ygrayne whispered, shifting her gaze to Mara.

Godríc stepped back a bit, pulling the mare with him.

"Ygrayne, you can't! You may not even get past the watchpoint...and even if you did, the Valeriaans aren't going to let him go just because you ask."

"He's richt, Ygrayne," Urda chimed in, her hand placed upon Ygrayne's shoulder. When Ygrayne turned, Urda continued, "Ye are more likely tae be thrown in wi' the lot o' thaim before anythin' else happens."

"But if there's a chance that I can get Thelric out of there, I need to take it. Or else I will never forgive myself, knowing that I could've done something... and didn't." Ygrayne pushed Urda's hand from her shoulder and approached Mara, reaching for the reins in Godríc's grasp. He quickly held them away from her reach, protesting, "Ygrayne—"

"Don't try to stop me! Give me the fucking reins!"

Godríc put up no more fight after hearing the harshness of her words. Her authoritative tone left him meek; the venom in her voice very well would have poisoned him had she been able to bite him with it. It was simple for Ygrayne to tear the reins from him at that point, mounting the startled mare who pranced around nervously from all the commotion.

"Ygrayne!" Urda protested, but Ygrayne would hear none of it.

"Watch out for my boy. I'll be back, I promise you. And I'll have my husband with me when I do."

There were no more protests to be had. Ygrayne kicked at Mara's sides with such vigor that the horse reared onto her hind legs in surprise. Ygrayne then gave a sharp tug on the reins to turn her about, leaving both Urda and Godríc in the dust as the horse took off down the road, a flash of white in the sunlight.

When Ygrayne and Mara had disappeared over the horizon did Godríc turn his head subtly to Urda and say, "Couldn't you have tricked her to stay by casting a spell?"

Urda turned her head, her brow quirked and a smirk about her lips. The question was as unintentionally rude as it was truly innocent, prompted by the many rumors about the "witch" with the red hair, and Urda couldn't help but be amused by the inquiry.

Godríc felt embarrassed for his question when Urda had still given no answer after some time, and he put his hands up in defeat and a silent apology for his misstep. He dropped his head and made his way into the village to join the rest of the men.

Ygrayne's hair whipped wildly in the wind akin to the mane of the mare, black and white banners streaming behind them. The land was but a green blur, the focus of her gaze on the unchanging dirt path which would eventually lead to her destination. It mattered not how afraid she was in the moment. The agonizing days she'd spent envisioning every terrifying scenario were more disturbing than the might of the Valeriaans who held the city ahead of her. Toward them, she felt only fury.

CHAPTER 10

Artur regretted it the moment he spoke, his initial excitement now turning to utter embarrassment. It was evident on her face, lips curled in disgust, that she wasn't at all impressed by their very first exchange. But he wasn't destined to wither in his mortification for long, as at last she spoke.

"'Hello'?" she snickered at him, her voice a wind chime carried across the river between them. "Is that really the best you have?"

It took Artur by surprise, hearing her voice for the first time. But its softness and grace were shadowed by the disgust in her tone, meant to make a mockery of him, sneering at his attempt. Yet, Artur couldn't help but fixate on the pout about her face—the way her nose crinkled and her cheeks expanded when she huffed. It was…comical, amusing.

Artur chortled to himself, surprising her in turn. Her snicker soon transformed as her eyes widened and her lips parted in confusion. She was so expressive, needing no words to articulate her sentiments, or what exactly was going through her mind. Never had Artur met someone with such uncensored expressions, and it made him blush, a sudden giddiness overtaking him. She looked so endearing in that moment.

She wasn't used to being disadvantaged, to not having the superiority in any given situation.

"What's so funny?" she hissed at him, as threatening as a newborn kitten. Artur was intrigued by her accent. It was thick, the words coming across strong and proper, aggressive but for the way her voice softened their sound. Artur wasn't familiar with such an accent in the region. His and most of the villagers' speech was tame and flat to his ears. Not only was it clear that she was not a native of the region, but he was quite certain she had to have come from beyond its borders.

"Sorry." He chortled a bit more, once his wonderment subsided enough for him to bring his attention back to the conversation at hand.

"My name is Artur. What's your name?"

Courage at last found him again, but she didn't answer. Instead, she turned up her head with all the inclination of regality and said, "Why would I tell you that? I don't even know you." She was teasing him.

"Well…" He stumbled on his words a bit, taken aback by such blatant rudeness. "It's only polite to introduce yourself, don't ya think? That's how we can get to know each other."

She scoffed and looked away from him. She wasn't prepared to answer yet, so he moved forward.

"I haven't seen you around here before. Are you a traveler? Where are you from?"

She looked at him from the corner of her eye, violet iris gazing through thick, dark lashes.

"You could say that." She was purposefully vague, insolent.

His inkling was correct at least, but there was apprehension in her tone, secrecy still her companion. It helped not that Artur had never truly conversed with any of the young girls in his village, and thus her behavior was as foreign to him as she herself was to the region.

The boys had their faction as the girls had theirs, and any moment of possible mingling turned into bouts of teasing which ultimately served only to widen the divide between them. Artur wished now that he had made a more concerted effort in befriending at least one of them, to understand them. Maybe then he would have an idea of what to expect from this mystery of a girl.

"Um…" The conversation lulled between them and she began to lose interest in him altogether, her attention turning to the river rocks just below the water's surface. It made Artur's heart sink a bit, but he wasn't keen to relent. His eyes wandered as if searching for anything to revitalize the conversation, to find perhaps a common interest to recapture her attention. He didn't need to look too long before he knew exactly what to talk about.

"Do you want to fish with me?" he asked excitedly, pointing to his pole lying in the sand. She looked to him and then to the pole, and again to him.

"I don't fish. Folk fish for me." She practically spat the words.

Artur only ever knew the men of Trivaden to fish, and he hardly cared what the women and girls did. He suddenly felt silly for asking her.

"Do you do something else for your village? Take care of livestock? Grow vegetables? Oh-oh! Or perhaps, bake pies?" He grinned with delight at the prospect.

She scoffed again, and this time, he couldn't help but feel a bit annoyed. Only he was putting any sort of effort into the dialogue, and in return did she sneer at his every attempt.

"No. Everything is done for me. I don't have to do anything. Especially something as dull as fishing. Why would I want to fish if others fish for me? Or make pies when they're always made for me?"

"Why would you want someone to fish for you when you can learn to fish for yourself?" he retorted, and this only annoyed her further, as she perceived it as a challenge to her supposed position over him. But Artur meant no ill will by his question. It was one of genuine curiosity.

Completely unaware of the exasperation growing within her, he said to her, "I can show you. It's quite easy."

"Fishing looks daft! I'd rather not!"

The dismissal went unnoticed, for the prospect of showing someone a hobby he truly enjoyed filled him with delight.

"No! No! It's not daft! Please, let me show you." Even as he fetched his fishing pole, he failed to notice how uninterested she was as she observed his demonstration—how to cast, how to reel in the line so there was no slack, how to recast, and so forth, until he reeled in the line a final time to converse with her once more.

"See? It's truly that easy."

"Ooh," she said scornfully. "How fascinating."

In this remark, Artur finally took notice of her blatant derision.

The continual disengagement was beginning to dampen his enthusiasm, and Artur let out an exhausted sigh.

"Well, what do you like to do?"

"I like to do lots of things."

There was a pause, as he waited for her to elaborate. She would do no such thing.

"Then…what's your favorite thing to do?" he asked awkwardly.

"Hmm…" She touched her finger to her face a moment, and finally said, "Horseback riding. I have my very own horse too."

"Aye! You have your own horse?" Artur abandoned his pole to the sands and crouched at the banks of the water to hear more.

"I do. My family has lots of horses," she boasted proudly with a lift of her chin.

"Our village only has a few, and they're used to pull wagons and labor in the fields. I've never ridden one before."

"It's probably because your village is too poor to have more horses."

Artur was taken aback.

Poor? he thought to himself.

Never had such a word been used to describe him, and certainly not as an insult. The word was completely absent from his vocabulary. His family and the village weren't poor, at least, not to his knowledge. How would one know if they were poor or not? How would a person even describe such a concept?

"What do you mean by that?" Artur lifted a brow to her.

She shrugged nonchalantly, dismissively. "Everyone I know has lots of horses."

"But…just because I don't have lots of horses, doesn't mean I'm poor," he responded, still not precisely grasping the notion that the word presented. "I'm not poor…" he whispered to himself.

"Yes, you are," she huffed at him. The proclamation was so matter of fact that Artur couldn't help but feel a sense of annoyance. This girl knew nothing of him, or the life he lived, and yet felt inclined to insult it all directly to his face.

"How would you know that? You're not even from around here." Artur's brow furrowed, and there was a certain venom in his tone which even he was not used to hearing. It sounded so hateful, so angry. So counter to his temperament.

"Because my papa said so," she retorted, and had the audacity to stick her tongue out at him.

Artur had reached the threshold of tolerance for her arrogance and insults, particularly given how welcoming he was trying to be to her, a stranger. Every attempt was only rebuffed without consideration. Embarrassment normally shaded his cheeks pink, but now resentment took over the role, staining his cheeks a deep red. Artur had never felt so insulted in his life. Not even his friends were as harsh, as malicious to him as she had been.

Spurred on by the pain of rejection, dejection, and resentment in response to such blatant disrespect of himself and his hobby, Artur could bear it no longer.

With a deep breath, he bellowed what was perhaps the most derogatory formation of words ever to come forth from his lips.

"Well…y-your papa is an arse and it looks like he raised one too!" He felt filthy the moment the words left his mouth, but they were cathartic at the same time. Artur's mother was always certain to sway him away from expletives, but this time, he couldn't help it. In his rage, Artur relinquished the possibility of cordial conversation.

Turning away from her, Artur went about collecting his fishing pole and the belongings he had left behind the day prior. She remained speechless in her shock at his outburst, and the sudden disregard for her presence.

Words fumbled at her lips as she attempted to retort, or to at least chastise him for the harshness of his words. Finally, she formed a shaky, but coherent, sentence. "Y-you can't s-speak to me that way!"

Artur didn't say anything. As far as he knew, the conversation had concluded, and he didn't want to entertain it further. Once he had all his possessions, Artur headed for the trail that would take him back to Trivaden.

"Aye!" the girl shouted. "Where are you going?"

He heard her call after him and turned, unable to resist.

"I'm going back home to my—" Artur made a sweeping gesture to match the mocking tone of his voice, "—poor village."

"You can't just leave me out here!"

"Oh really?"

He had only taken his first step onto the soil when he heard her call to him once again.

"Don't leave me!"

Artur paused. She sounded far away now, despite the little headway he had made. There was no longer a note of condescension in her voice. Instead, she sounded pleading—yearning, almost.

Artur found himself returning to the riverbank, the heat of anger rushing through him upon seeing her again.

"Why shouldn't I?" He was indignant now.

"Because…because I said so!"

"Because you said so?" Artur couldn't believe the words even as he repeated them. "You can't tell me what to do."

"I'm eleven, I can do whatever I want," she declared.

"So? I'm twelve. That means I'm older and you can't tell me what to do!"

She ignored him and instead began making her way down the riverbank. What she was up to, he hadn't the faintest idea.

Stopping before that forbidden trail of stones across the river, she held her hands behind her back and said to him, "Well fine then. If you won't stay, I'll just have to come to you."

Before he had a chance to retort, she leapt onto a boulder just slightly peeking above the rushing water, landing with the grace of a prancing doe. Artur nearly choked as he watched her. After all the times he had been told not to cross the river, he could hardly believe that she was doing it with such ease and without hesitation. A wave of panic overcame him, and his fishing rod and belongings dropped from his grasp to the sands below as he raced over to the other end of the stones before she could proceed further.

"No, don't!" Artur cried out to her. "It's dangerous! You could fall in!"

"The river isn't flowing that fast, nor is it that deep. Calm yourself," she called out to him, leaping from one boulder to the next with the same effortlessness.

Artur was stunned, observing how easily she bounded across. It left him speechless, questioning everything his father had told him about the supposed danger of the river. It looked so simple, even mundane. That he could have crossed it at any point had he just done so without the consent or knowledge of his parents—the thought made him feel so foolish.

Her heel hit the water with a splash, and Artur was back to the present, blinking at the girl moving toward him with amazement. The slip of her foot was hardly enough to stop her, a minor setback in the progress made. When she drew closer, Artur held out his arms, ready to catch her should she fall. She completely disregarded him as her feet finally touched the sands on his side, and she stood there with a triumphant, and rather smug, smile about her face.

"There! That wasn't so hard. Now," she hit Artur's arm with a closed fist, playfully. It didn't hurt in the slightest, but the abruptness of it made him press a hand to the spot.

"What was that for?"

"For walking away!" She furrowed her brows at him. "And for calling me and Papa an arse."

"You were being an arse!" he grumbled through clenched teeth.

"Stop calling me that!" She stomped the floor, akin to a petulant child.

"No!" He pointed a finger at her. "Ever since we started talking you've been acting as though you're better than me. Why did you even bother crossing if you're just going to act like that?"

The question took her by surprise, and with a quiet gasp she quickly fell into silence. Those hard eyes softened as she looked to Artur, and he couldn't help but feel himself soften with them. There had been very few times in his life in which he had been angry enough to yell with such vitriol, and now he found himself regretting it. The feeling was quite dreadful.

"I don't know," she finally said after a moment's thought, her eyes drifting to the ground.

It wasn't much of an answer, but it was all she had to give, though Artur effortlessly perceived it to be a falsehood. It was her bearing which gave her away, the uncomfortable shifting of her eyes.

Despite his desire to press further, Artur decided to leave it be. He hardly wanted her to go running back across the river if discomfort overcame her, for he knew he wouldn't be able to chase her, his limitations set, his boundaries drawn.

All he wanted to do was provide her with the comfort to remain in his presence.

"How about...we just start over?" Artur asked simply.

"Start over?" She raised a brow at him.

"Yes, from the beginning. My name is Artur. Can you at least tell me your name now?"

She looked at him, her expression contemplative, rendering him uneasy.

"My name..." She hesitated a moment, her violet eyes wide, anxious. "My name is Lovisa." The words came out almost trembling.

"Lovisa," Artur repeated out loud, and it was if he spoke some sacred script, forbidden to the commonfolk. He was overjoyed to finally put a name to the girl who had so captured his attention.

"It's nice to meet you, Lovisa." Artur held out his hand to her, a polite gesture as he was taught when meeting someone to make a proper first impression. Lovisa looked at his hand as though it was some foreign entity, with obvious disgust.

When their eyes met once again, she let out an, "Ugh."

And with that, she walked away from him with her head held high and her lips puckered. Had it still been their first encounter, Artur would have been offended by the sneer. Now that he was growing accustomed to her behavior, he found it quite befitting of her character.

"Well, at least you told me your name." He couldn't help but snort to himself.

"This can't be that hard to do," he heard Lovisa say behind him, only to turn and see her with his fishing rod in her hand. He watched in horror as she began to swing the rod repeatedly as if it were a sword, the line flailing about with her erratic movements, the hook dangling ever so close to her figure and threatening to snag her as though she were a fish.

"Aye! Wait!" Artur called out to her as he approached cautiously, evading the fishing line. He remembered the first time the hook had snagged his finger. The removal was a rather unpleasant and painful experience even as his father tended to it as carefully as possible. Only when Artur plunged his hand into the river afterwards did he feel some kind of relief. The last thing Artur wanted was for her to go through the same experience.

"Stop! You're going to hook yourself!"

The statement was so bizarre to Lovisa that she turned around and gave him an incredulous scowl. "What?"

With the rod now still, Artur quickly grabbed the line and pinched at the hook so it wouldn't snag either of them.

"There's a hook at the end of this line, see?" Artur held it up to her, and she stared at it curiously.

"You don't want this snagging you. This is how you catch the fish. They bite it, and you reel them in when they do."

"How do you know if you caught one?"

"You'll see them pulling at the line. But before you can catch anything, I need to show you how to cast."

"Fine," she huffed. Lovisa hated being taught by someone such as him, her pride wounded.

Although learning a lesson about fishing was irritating to Lovisa, Artur was beyond excited to show her. The thought of sharing his passion with someone elated him. None of his friends had ever showed any interest, or even the slightest affinity for the hobby. She was the first person to give him the chance to teach them, even if she showed such willingness in her own odd way.

Artur went about explaining the process of letting the line loose to cast properly, and what to do in the event of catching a fish. He miraculously managed to catch one in the middle of the lesson, a momentous opportunity to show exactly what made the activity so exciting. Lovisa watched with a tame eagerness, daring not to let her inward sentiments be known lest she look as ridiculous as he did.

Artur quickly dropped his newly acquired catch into the bucket he had left behind the day before; they both took a moment to observe it as it thrashed in the water. When Artur looked to her with eagerness, she met his expression with a roll of her eyes. But her feigned disinterest no longer bothered Artur. After demonstrating the entire process a few more times, he passed the task to her.

What transpired thereafter could have been one of the comedy skits that traveling minstrels would occasionally put on for the children in the village. Artur lost count of how many times Lovisa cast and recast—and recast and recast—simply because she wasn't happy with the way she did so each time. Artur stood back to avoid being hooked himself, and to hide his barely contained laughter at her expense. This girl who had once seemed an almost otherworldly being in his eyes, was after all nothing more than a child. With every attempt, she became less foreign to him. They were one and the same—children, young and naïve to the ways of each other's worlds, and just as he was happy to show her the life he knew, she was happy to experience it, even if she wouldn't admit it.

One last cast sent the line traveling farther than it had yet, soaring with a grace that had been lacking in all previous attempts. Artur knew a good cast when he saw one, and he wordlessly watched her very first good cast fall into the water with a loud *thunk*.

Lovisa couldn't help but jump with unbridled delight as she looked to Artur.

"Did you see that? 'Twas perfect! Wasn't it?"

"It was a great cast!" Artur smiled at her. "Now we wait for you to catch something."

Lovisa placed the pole in the makeshift stand Artur built her, and the two sat on the sands to practice the patience the hobby required.

The silence had hardly stretched between them before Lovisa asked, "How long does it take?"

"I dunno...sometimes they bite really fast. Sometimes it takes a couple hours. Sometimes you don't catch anything at all."

"Seems a waste of time to me. Why would you fish all day when you might not catch anything?" She pouted at the very thought that all her hard work could very well be for nothing.

Artur shrugged at her question. It was an idea he hadn't even thought to ponder, as fishing was never a matter of wasting time to him. It was just the way of life he had come to know, while the thought of testing one's patience with what she believed to be a menial task was unfathomable to her.

"Wouldn't you rather be playing with your friends than sitting here all day?" she asked honestly. "If you even have any?" She snickered.

"I have friends, and I do play with them." He shot her an unamused glance. "Some days though...I just would rather fish, especially with my papa..." His voice trailed off after that last word—*Papa*. The man who had yet to return home. The man who should be here beside him.

Artur brought his knees to his chest, hugging them tightly as the grief overtook his delight. Sensing the sudden change in his presence, Lovisa looked at him with genuine worry—an expression which seemed unbecoming of her.

"What's the matter?"

"My papa hasn't come home yet. He's been gone for days. I don't know what's happened to him." He looked to the river, a gaze lost, wandering about without a destination in mind.

"Why hasn't he come home?"

"I don't know." He shrugged. "A lot of the papas haven't come home yet."

Lovisa looked to Artur with those violet eyes of hers, large with sorrow. It was peculiar, sensing a hint of his pain. A first for her. What she felt in that moment wasn't at all on behalf of herself, but someone else. Lovisa wouldn't have believed the two of them could share anything in common as far as the lives they knew, who they were. They were so discernibly different, divided by the sharp contrast of their respective worlds. Yet here was something they did indeed have in common, something which affected her deeply too. Lovisa swallowed, her gaze on the river.

"I don't see my papa very much either. He's often too busy to be with me."

Artur looked to her. "My papa has to go into Falkhearth for trade. Does your papa have to go into the city too?"

"I suppose." Lovisa shrugged. "He travels a lot, or he's busy with other folk. So, when he asked me to come with him to travel south, I thought he would spend time with me. But nothing's changed. So now, I'm left to do things on my own…again."

"Well, don't you play with your friends when he's gone?"

There was a momentary silence. Her gaze still forward, she quietly responded, "You're the only friend I have." The words stung more deeply than Lovisa anticipated, and she felt pitiable for having revealed such sensitive information, hearing it admitted by her own tongue.

"I'm sorry." It was all Artur could think to say, and as simple as the words might have seemed to him, it was an empathetic and genuine sentiment not often bestowed upon her.

Lovisa's breath caught in her throat, but pride would not allow her to display even momentary weakness. Not to him.

"But you…you consider me a friend?"

Lovisa looked to him with a raised brow. "What else am I supposed to consider you?"

Given the hostile events which had transpired between them, and the harsh words thrown at him, Artur's doubts lingered.

"I don't know. You did call me poor," he huffed.

I still don't know what that means.

A "tsk" escaped Lovisa's lips as she said, "Everyone is poor compared to me. It's only the truth."

Artur didn't respond, merely looking at her with large, blue eyes, for words escaped him. It was a concept he was still trying to grasp, unable to determine how to properly retort.

Lovisa sensed the depth of his silence, and it stung, unexpectedly. Rarely had she ever experienced the sensation of regret, of guilt. But given their nearness, the depth of his hurt gave weight to her previous words.

She cared—she truly cared, surprisingly so. The culpability finally overcame Lovisa, and her face softened with the newfound compassion she felt within.

She was careful of what she said next, so that the words came out gently. "But, yes. You are my friend."

It worked as intended. Lovisa could almost feel Artur's spirits rise from the depths of dejection. As much as she didn't want to admit it, it made her feel delighted in return, warmth flushing her face. Such a feeling she could hardly recall ever having before. Perhaps when she ate her favorite candies, or sipped a warm drink on a cold winter's night… It was pitiful in comparison to the joy Artur had expressed. His was undoubtedly pure and genuine. And Lovisa, in everything she had in life, had nothing to compare in worth and sentiment, as embarrassing as it was to admit to herself.

She turned away, flustered, to glance at the pole still propped beside her in a rather dormant state. It was only the soft sway of the river's flow which made the line ebb with a hint of life.

"Are these fish going to bite or not?" she asked, peeved.

"I told you it does take some time. You need to be patient."

"Being patient is so boring!" Lovisa threw her hands up into the air and fell back into the sand, the warmth a comforting touch at her back.

The sky wasn't as blue as it once was. A hue of orange was beginning to set in—the first hint of the afternoon coming to greet them. Artur came to lie beside Lovisa, his eyes following hers to the skies above. She hardly noticed, but he was smiling. Smiling akin to a fool. Looking at her with a tilt of his head, he took in the new details of her face. The curvature of her nose and her lips. The long lashes which nearly grazed her brows. Her violet eyes reflected the gold of the sands around her. The shine of her silver hair shimmering with the vibrant colors about them.

"Your skies are so beautiful. Especially at night," said she, and Artur only listened quietly. "The Nerúnors touch your peaks here. They fade almost entirely where I live. And the stars…I've never seen so many in the night sky before."

"What do you mean?" He looked once more to the sky.

"It's just different where I live."

"How come?"

"I don't know."

Artur pondered this for a moment. It still made no sense to him. He thought the world shared but one same sky, just as they shared the same mountains, the same valleys and hills, the same flowing waters—same everything.

"Well, aren't you staying here?"

Lovisa shook her head. "No. We are just traveling through. We've been stopped for a while now, but we will leave soon…I think. When my papa gets back to our camp, we'll go back home."

"Will you ever come back to visit?"

"Visit you?" Lovisa looked at him with incredulity.

"Yes…wait! No! I-I mean, Trivaden. Come visit Trivaden. You can stay with me, of course. I'm certain since you have to come such a long way, she won't mind. We won't be able to share a bed though, so you can have it, and I can sleep on the floor. I sleep next to a window, and that has the best view of the night sky. You'll love it."

It sounded too good to be true, skepticism giving Lovisa pause. However, her hesitation hardly seemed to discourage the hope radiating from the boy beside her.

"You would want me to come visit?"

"Yes! And you can come any time you want to!"

Lovisa could feel her cheeks flush with that heat again, but this time, she did not shy away from it. There was no urge to hide it away, to put on a farse. It was raw and pure emotion. The feeling of being wanted was nearly overwhelming, and such a thought pooled tears in her eyes.

But Lovisa loathed crying in front of others, especially her father. He'd taught her that it was an indication of weakness, a flaw. Something that your enemies could use against you. So, Lovisa pursed her lips together and blinked her eyes dry before they could even turn pink from the mere touch of tears.

"Then I will come visit. I don't know when, but I will."

A moment of connection. All the frigidness of the first words they'd exchanged suddenly melted away in the heat of the sun. Their differences, known and unknown, no longer mattered. They were on an equal plane of understanding, of friendship, of a greater depth than either of them could conceive.

As they lay there looking at each other with fondness, the breeze kicked up ever so slightly. They paid no mind to its presence, regardless of how much it tugged and pushed at their figures, no matter how much it tickled at their faces.

The only thing which broke this connection was the sudden movement in the corner of Artur's eye. Beyond Lovisa's silhouette, he could see the fishing pole jerking about. It was the indication every fisherman looked forward to, something he always made certain to keep a keen eye on.

"The pole!" He lifted onto his forearms, sand clinging to his backside. Lovisa followed his gaze, but to her untrained eyes, it was merely bobbing as it had before, moved by the touch of the water.

"So?"

"No! No! You have a fish! Go get the pole before it gets pulled into the water!" Artur pointed with his finger, but when she failed to move at the speed he needed, Artur took matters into his own hands and went for the pole before it could join the few others lost over the years to the river's depths. Lovisa followed him and watched on with confusion. She truly couldn't tell the difference in what was happening, save for Artur's drastically changed disposition. The way he pulled on the line, reeling and then tugging so precisely, as if one mishap would mean the end of everything—it was all so intriguing to her.

"Here, take it! You'll be able to feel it pull."

The pole unexpectedly landed in her unready hands, and she became consumed by panic. Something she'd earlier deemed so simple now seemed to be an impossible feat.

"What do I do?" she exclaimed in fright, now reeling in the line as if her life depended on it.

"Hold on! Don't reel it in so fast! You might lose him!" Artur placed his hand atop hers to stop her frantic movement.

"Then what do I do?" she repeated once more, stiffened by the unexpected contact of their hands, his rough to her delicate.

"Ease up. You need reel him in slowly. Then you're going to tug on the line to make certain you still have him. And just keep doing that until you got him."

Lovisa did so with the assistance of his expertise, together. The moment she allowed herself to calm did she feel the difference. It was no longer just the waves which she sensed. She could feel the fish fighting back, pulling and pulling on that hook with great urgency. At first, it was the way she imagined wrangling a wild beast would feel. Then, the more she settled into the motion, did it start to come with ease, as if she were naturally destined for the sport.

When Artur felt she could handle the task herself, he slowly removed his hands and stepped away. She reeled. She tugged. She reeled again and she tugged once more, until finally she could see the sheen of the fish's scales just below the water line, glimmering and beautiful their iridescent shimmer. There was no impeding the smile which spread across her face, for the sheer excitement nearly had her screaming for joy.

"Oh, there it is! Keep going! Keep going!" Artur's cheers only deepened her bliss. It was a dream come to fruition to have any friend enjoying what he loved so much, and to see her succeeding as she was right before his eyes.

When at last the fish peeked above the water's surface and Lovisa pulled it into the air with a mighty tug, it was over. The fish lost its battle to her, left swinging at the end of the line without an inkling of what was happening to it.

"There it is!" Lovisa exclaimed with a joyous tone, one she hardly recognized in her own voice.

"Amazing, Lovisa!" Artur praised her. He grabbed the fish and proceeded to remove the hook from its mouth as Lovisa watched on in awe. The fish refused to submit, however, wriggling around in the crook of his arm as he twisted the sharp hook from its jaw.

"There we go," Artur said the moment the line was released. "You caught your first fish!" He held it up to her, its iridescent scales glistening in the light.

"Aye! My first fish! I caught it all by myself!" Lovisa took the fish in her hands and held it before her.

Artur chortled a bit and said under his breath, "Yes. All by yourself." It could've been taken sardonically, or genuinely.

Lovisa never seen a live fish before. She'd only encountered them lain before her on a plate adorned with spices and other delicious condiments to make a most delectable feast. In the heat of excitement, Lovisa took it all in—its odd smell, the surprisingly slippery texture which left a sliminess on her hands, the way the luster of its scales bounced between head and tail in sequence with its struggle, and the eyes, at once both blank and fathomless, displaying no hint of fear or panic, or even any understanding of what it was experiencing.

Lovisa then held it up above her head and chanted, "I caught a fish! I caught a fi-ish! I caught a fi-ish!" with an uncoordinated swivel of her hips and arms.

Artur couldn't help but laugh, joining her enthusiasm, not only out of delight, but because of how silly she looked. He remembered his first catch very distinctly, and how his father had looked at him with the pride any father would wish to bestow upon their child.

All celebration ceased, however, when the fish decided it had had enough of the cheering and lack of water. Its one last attempt at freedom had Lovisa nearly dropping it to her feet. Sensing her imminent loss of control, Lovisa gasped and exclaimed, "What do I do with it now?"

Artur went to retrieve his bucket, doing so with enough haste that Lovisa was able to release the poor creature into its confines, the water splashing up into their faces as a result. Artur didn't mind it though. It was part of the hobby. Lovisa let out a disgusted groan and wiped the water from her face.

Artur placed the bucket down onto the sand and knelt beside it, seeing that the fish they just caught had to curl at the base of the bucket. It was quite an impressive size, and a remarkable first catch for anyone. This made him, though he hardly knew it then, all the more drawn to her.

"Aye, look at it." Lovisa knelt beside Artur and gazed into the bucket. "My fish is bigger." She smirked at him.

"Eh, I've caught bigger ones than yours," Artur retorted with a wit he didn't know he possessed. It came forth so naturally and without thought, it surprised him.

"Just you wait, I'll catch an even bigger one next time."

Next time.

Would there be a next time? he wondered in silence. *Would she really come visit?*

"Just wait until my papa sees this."

"Do you have to leave soon?" Artur gazed to her.

Lovisa looked to the sky once again. The evening was coming. They would be making supper soon and she hadn't even had an afternoon snack.

"I probably should be going."

"Will you be back tomorrow?" Artur asked, his words tumbling out in a rush. Lovisa looked to him again.

"Maybe. I really won't know until tomorrow."

"Well…I hope you do. I can introduce you to my mama and friends tomorrow, if you would want?"

Lovisa's lips tilted to one side. "Mmm…I'll think about it."

"We don't have to if you don't want to."

"I said I'll think about it," she restated, but there was no malice in her tone. Just an uneasiness which Artur couldn't quite understand. Everyone he knew was nice and cordial. Well, his friends were nice enough, but everyone in the village was genial and hospitable. She would be treated akin to family, and certainly his mother would be interested in meeting the girl who had easily captured his affections.

I've never brought a girl home to Mama before, he thought to himself, wondering what kind of experience that would be.

"Think about it then. Why don't you take the bucket with you so you can have your fish for supper tonight? I'm certain it will make a great feast."

"Is it really all right?"

"Uh-huh. I'll just carry my fish home."

Artur reached in and grabbed his fish by the mouth, plucking it from the waters with no mind to its teeth or its struggle. Lovisa was in awe at first, but quickly regained her composure. The ease with which he performed actions she found so unusual had yet to cease to surprise her. She took the bucket into her arm, admiring her catch once again, the events of just moments ago replaying vividly in her mind. She could hardly wait to boast about her feat.

Maybe for once, he will be proud of me, she thought to herself, a smile crossing over her lips.

"Will you be all right crossing the river with it?" Artur asked.

Lovisa looked at him with such annoyance and said, "Truly? I'm telling you, it's not that difficult to cross. Those rocks are big."

She passed him without another word and headed for the makeshift bridge, leaving Artur almost aghast at the realization that those were to be their final words for the day.

"Well...bye...I guess," he said under his breath, his voice softening with each word spoken. Lovisa stopped at the edge of the water, where one leap would mean her departure.

Artur thought she might leave for the adjacent shores with neither a parting word nor backward glance. It would befit her character, after all. But to his surprise and delight, she turned to him and said, "Goodbye, Artur. I'll see you soon."

Lovisa granted him one last gaze with those violet eyes, a sincere smile—which still felt foreign on her lips—and one final chance to look at her lovely face. The image was permanently imprinted in his memory. A wide smile, with a slight lift in his right cheek, was all he could muster as she bounded away across the strewn-stone path, the bucket hardly proving a burden. In fact, all it did was serve as a testament to her nimbleness and finesse.

When her boots hit the sand of the opposite bank, she bolted for the tree line, her figure swallowed by the depths of the forest akin to a beast returning to the comfort and embrace of nature.

She was gone.

Artur lingered for some time. There was hope, however silly the prospect, that Lovisa would return to him. At least one last time for the day. Of course, the longer he waited, the more he realized it was all for naught. Just as the sport of fishing demanded patience, so too did her eventual return.

With one last glance, Artur smiled and headed up the path leading home. All the while the wind was at his back, a gentle whisper in his ear.

CHAPTER 11

Artur returned down the path that was so familiar he hardly paid any attention to his venture, allowing his thoughts to flit through the heavenly clouds of memory. Etched in his mind akin to carvings in wood were images of Lovisa, as true to form as if she were still standing before him. Her voice was as clear as the wind he had grown to know and recognize. Despite his elation, the memory also brought with it the feeling of sorrow. Fate had been kind to him this day, more so than any other time he could recall. Would Fate be just as merciful to allow them to meet at least once more?

Suddenly, home didn't feel akin to home anymore. Home was back on the riverbank with his friend. Home was her company. Nevertheless, he proceeded until he reached the cottage, finding it as cold and empty as the coming tide of the grief within.

"Mama?" Artur called out into the empty premises, despite his eyes recognizing that the dwelling was indeed vacant. He also peered up into the loft just in case, finding it equally as empty.

She's probably just visiting Urda, Artur thought.

Artur hummed as he went about the normal duties his father had shown him many times before—without the reminder of his mother, he acknowledged to himself proudly. He took a stool to the well pump out in their garden to clean and gut the fish, disposing of the abdominal contents in a pail beside him. Artur did so quietly, the movements the task required as natural to him as breathing.

There was nothing out of the ordinary or amiss, until he felt a shove against his back that sent him falling to the ground. A wet nose pressed to his cheek the moment he had the chance to turn on his bottom, and he was instantly faced with snorts of hot air and subjected to odorous breath that filled his own nostrils.

"Vána! No!" he shouted.

The large and powerful beast was standing over him, sniffing about in search of the river-dwelling prey she knew was close at hand.

"No! Stop!" Artur couldn't help but let out a laugh as he objected, her wiry whiskers tickling him in her determined search. It was a miracle his resolve held strong in the face of such an opponent, shielding the dead catch in the safety of his arms. One bite would mean the end. She would either pull it all from his grasp or shred it to bits in the process, and Artur knew his strength was no match for her natural prowess for much longer.

"Vána, come!" Artur heard Urda call out, an unexpected savior come to his aid. The dire wolf quickly responded by retreating to her side, lying down most majestically at her feet.

Artur recovered enough to see the woman standing within the bounds of their garden and said, "Thank you, Urda. I thought she was going to get the best of me."

"At yer service, dear boy." Urda reached down to pet the wolf's head. "Where have ye been? Still by the river this whole time?"

Artur stood up and brushed the twigs and brush from his clothing, then replied, "Yes. I was there all day. Just returned now."

Urda could feel Vána twitch under her palm at the very prospect of food, but the beast did not lunge for it again. She instead lay patiently and obediently by Urda's side.

"By the gods. I don't e'en know o' a man who enjoys fishin' thon much."

Artur dropped the fish into a wooden bowl that served as a basin through the kitchen window and wiped the remnants of its innards on a cloth he brought out with him. Though odd, it was rather convenient he had encountered Urda when he did. Turning to her, Artur asked, "Where's Mama?"

There was a glint of displeasure in her eyes, before a smile returned and she replied as she normally did in her jovial tone, "She went out today for Falkhearth. She hopes she can gae find yer father."

"Papa still isn't back yet?"

"Unfortunately, na. A few o' the men returned but many are still left in the city. Sae, yer mother took it upon herself to…well…find oot whit is happenin'. In the meantime, she left ye in ma care."

Oh…no… Artur trusted his face didn't indicate the displeasure he felt.

"Oh, all right…" he muttered reluctantly. "Though I'm certain I can take care of myself while she's gone."

The giggle Urda hid behind her hand almost seemed more of a taunt. "Charmin'. I na doubt believe thon ye can tak' care o' yourself. But for yer mother's sake, let's juist be cordial wi' one another. Sound guid?"

"All right." Artur nodded his head.

"Hou aboot, I cook up thon fish ye caucht, an' for dessert, we have some fruit wi' honey an' sweet bread. Wad ye like thon?"

Artur paused a moment before he asked, rather baffled, "…You can make all that?"

"Oh, ye have na idea o' the things I can dae." Urda winked. "I know ye think me odd, but I have ma uses!"

Artur was intrigued. The mere discussion of food was enough to spark an interest in the neighbor he never thought he'd want to know beyond mere acquaintance, as more than someone he simply waved to in passing out of courtesy.

Urda did indeed deliver on everything she promised, and Artur was still rather taken aback. As the rest of Trivaden did, he'd always thought her peculiar and eccentric. But now, given the evening they shared, he didn't think her so bad. Still odd, but not in the adverse way he had been led to believe based on rumors and heresy. Urda pontificated freely on a multitude of topics, her hobbies and activities, and she did so with a passion he likened to the way he felt about fishing. When Artur talked to her about the hobbies he so enjoyed, she responded in kind with keen interest and genuine curiosity, inviting him to elaborate. It was nothing at all akin to the interactions he had been having with his mother as of late. Urda fostered a setting in which he couldn't stop talking. He spilled his heart out without hesitation. The words came forth from his lips as though she commanded them with a beseeching spell. Yet there was no hand waving, no magic jargon being uttered. She simply sat there and listened with a soft smile about her face, her chin propped atop her hands.

There was something warm and welcoming about her home, a place he'd never had any interest in visiting before. It was decorated with candles and adorned with various plants and things she was growing for her tonics and... whatever else it was that she made. Jars of various spices and herbs bedecked her shelves and hung from the ceiling around them. The place smelled of more than one kind of incense, wafting into the air about them in tendrils of smoke from an incense holder. There were many liquids, and stones, and tools he hardly could recognize, neatly organized about various tables. He had stepped into a world so unakin to his own that he thought it enchanting, and he found that what might otherwise contribute to the already sordid rumors surrounding her character, only made her even more fascinating and enigmatic.

When she presented him with a delicious dessert, which Artur couldn't help but stuff his face with, he said to her with a mouth full of food, "Hank you 'o much 'or dinner...an' 'essert."

"Well," Urda gave him a tantalizing smile. "Thank ye for catchin' dinner for us. Haed ye no' been hard at work fishing, we wouldn't have eaten this delicious feast tonicht."

His cheeks flushed at her compliment. In his mind he hadn't worked hard at all. It was mere luck, pure coincidence, that a fish graced his line. There was no meticulous thought nor planning to it. His victory of the day had been his feat of impressing the girl who had captured his affections, the girl he was distracted by for the better half of the day. Just thinking of her, Artur almost looked to have fallen into a trance.

"Whatever is the matter, Artur?" Urda questioned his sudden silence.

Artur recommenced chewing and after he swallowed his food, he suddenly blurted out, "I met a girl down there."

A quiet gasp escaped his parted lips as they went slack, the realization of what he revealed hitting him squarely in the chest. He hadn't wanted to tell anyone about his encounter, at least not yet, not until he knew Lovisa could visit for certain.

"Ye met a girl doun thare?" Urda tilted her head curiously.

"Yes." Artur swallowed hard, his eyes turning down to the table.

"Tell me aboot this girl. Who is she? Where is she from?"

"Why do you want to know?"

"Why don't ye want tae tell me?"

"Hm," Artur hummed thoughtfully.

"In aw ma years o' knowin' yer mother, she has no' the pleasure o' tellin' me aboot any girls her son has met. It pains me tae know I am the first tae have this conversation."

"I just…I just don't know much about her."

"Tell me whit ye dae know then."

Artur looked to Urda apprehensively.

"If ye wish," she added with a reassuring nod.

Artur breathed for a moment, wringing his hands nervously in his lap, his palms sweating. As he had been so forthcoming mere moments before, the words once again spilled from him as a flooded river did over the terrain.

"S-she said she's traveling through the region from far away. We just happened to meet each other when I was fishing by the river just yesterday."

The seriousness shifted to a quick upwelling of delight as he spoke, before he quieted again out of bashfulness.

"What's this girl's name?" Urda lifted a brow, ensnared by her own curiosity.

"Lovisa…"

"Lovisa." Her pitch was high. "Whit a pretty name."

Artur nodded in agreement.

"She's not akin to any girl I've met before. Well...she's kind of mean...all girls are kind of mean, I guess... But I really like her. I'm hoping to see her tomorrow."

"Awe, hou smitten ye are!" Urda clasped her hands together gleefully, taking note of the blush about his cheeks and the grin on his lips—all of which deepened when Urda called attention to them.

"I'm not smitten!" Artur retorted, his voice shaky. "I just think her hair and eyes are lovely. That's all."

"What's sae special aboot her eyes an' hair?"

"Her hair is silver. Her eyes are violet. I've never seen someone akin to her before."

Urda's demeanor shifted subtly. There was still the air of intrigue about her, but her once boisterous temperament found itself tamed, subdued into a caution unbecoming of her.

"Violet eyes, an' silver hair, ye say?"

Artur nodded, completely heedless of Urda's sudden change in bearing. She simply nodded as well. There was so much to be said. So much to reveal. Yet Urda found herself silent, unable to unearth the words which often came to her so easily. Seeing the boy sitting before her did nothing to help—his vitality, his enthusiasm were palpable. He had not the faintest idea of how easily he had swayed her tongue to silence. Little did she want to sully the mood they had been fostering for the entirety of their supper.

Resigning herself to silence on the matter, Urda simply smiled, her posture relaxing, and said, "Well, that's guid. Ye made a new friend."

Artur looked to her with a smile of his own, spurred by her acknowledgement, her enthusiasm over the newfound friendship.

"Would you mind not telling Mama? I was hoping to wait until I can bring Lovisa to Trivaden to introduce her."

"Dear boy, I doubt she'll be back tonicht tae begin wi'. E'en if she were tae return, I'd tell no' a soul. Ye have ma oath."

"Thank you, Urda."

"There's na need tae thank me." Urda chortled gleefully. "Will ye be seein' her again soon?"

"Tomorrow!" His voice rose with excitement. He quickly hid his mouth behind his palm when he realized just how loud he was. "We're going to fish again."

"Very guid. I hope ye have fun tomorrow. Juist be certain tae stay oot o' trouble."

"I will…" Artur found it an odd thing to say.

"But, if ye should ever need anything, I'll be here." Urda flashed him a wink, and Artur simply nodded. He still found the sentiment silly. Even as curious as he was by nature, he wouldn't intentionally put himself into a predicament.

There was nothing left to be said at that moment in the conversation, and Artur used the lull to fill his plate once again with the ever-so-delectable dessert, not at all noticing how Urda's eyes sharpened. Her smile flattened, hidden behind clasped hands before her. She watched Artur keenly, thoughtfully. The cautious air settled about her again, even as subtle as it was.

And when at last Artur did look to her again, they simply exchanged cordial smiles.

CHAPTER 12

Her hair dancing akin to fire in the wind, its darkness a deep contrast to the white mane of her majestic mare, Ygrayne made her way to Falkhearth with the speed of lightning across the land. The Valeriaan breed of horses were known for their nimbleness and stamina, and Ygrayne couldn't have been more thankful a Trivaden villager had managed to find Mara those years ago, alone in a field.

The galloping mare's hooves beat as drums against the trail, accompanied by the steadied breath which showed signs of neither wavering nor fatigue. Mara was young with the spirit to prove it, and this ride would pose no difficult feat. It made the long journey considerably more pleasant.

Falkhearth was but a few hours' ride from their small village, depending on the promptness of the caravan or the preference of the traveler. On the back of a freely galloping horse, Ygrayne was making good time on her journey despite the distance before her, and with each strike of Mara's hooves did Ygrayne feel her heart jump and race, vigor quickening, the thunder vibrating through her chest. Even still, the pace wasn't fast enough. The yearning to see her long-awaited beloved and the rest of the villagers who hadn't come home grew stronger and stronger. It almost brought tears to her eyes, the thought of it, though it was accompanied by a feeling of dread in the pit of her stomach. Those instincts most folk of her time seemed to have long forgotten were ordinarily her saving graces, and from experience she knew that a churning in the depths of her stomach was a sign she could not ignore. Something terrible was upon them.

Over an hour into her ride, Ygrayne felt her breath catch in her throat, her heart dropping. Her face paled when she caught sight, just after a bend in the road around one of the many hills that surrounded them, of one of the makeshift watchpoints she had been hearing about—a settlement of white tents and horses, and weapons of war she could hardly put a name to. The Valeriaan armor glistened in the sunlight, the silver and violet piercing amongst the greens and blues of the land.

"Oh no..." Ygrayne whispered to herself. There was no turning back now.

They had already seen her, and if she so dared to retreat to where she came from, they would pursue her, and she would no doubt be punished for the slight indiscretion. They would treat her as a potential enemy, running to conceal the confidences of the Oathbound. The truth of it mattered little so long as they had an excuse to do with her as they wished—to torture, interrogate, and, given she was a woman, ravish and indulge in other sadistic pleasures.

Ygrayne swallowed hard, pushing aside the growing nervousness, and slowed the mare to a trot in the hope of delaying the inevitable even if just for a moment. As she approached, three of the soldiers positioned themselves in the exact center of the road, giving her no hope of passage. The man in the middle of the frightening trio possessed higher stature and esteem, as evidenced by the intricate designs of his armor and the violet cape draping from his left shoulder.

Mara tossed her head a bit, a nervous whinny escaping through her teeth. Even she could feel there was something amiss. Ygrayne patted her neck and uttered a gentle hush close to the mare's ear to keep her calm.

The higher-ranking soldier held up his hand and called out to her, "Good morning, my lady." It was that thick, heavy Valeriaan accent which Ygrayne had come to resent. The stronger the accent, the stronger the tie to the founding bloodline. It was an indicator of higher prestige, and sometimes, even royalty.

As Ygrayne grew closer, she could see his vibrant violet eyes and silver hair poking out from under his helmet. The two soldiers accompanying him were nothing more than grunts—known as karls, they were lesser members of the royal family, or unfortunate commoner sworn in to military servitude due to past indiscretions or calamitous circumstances. They spoke not a word, nor carried the same air about them as their leader possessed.

Ygrayne brought Mara to a stop before them and said through gritted teeth, knowing it was expected of her, "Good morning."

She bowed her head out of the obligatory veneration she knew they demanded, her wind-brushed hair falling about her shoulders, framing her face. When she looked back to the leader, Ygrayne couldn't help but feel an uneasiness as she noted the smirk on his lips, the sharpness of his eyes.

"I am Commander Reinhardt of the Allfather's First Division Army, and I oversee this watchpoint. Where are you headed at this time of the morning?"

There had been few times in her life that Ygrayne found herself so nervous she couldn't find her words. Unfortunately, this was one of those times. They were testing her fortitude as she looked about the encampment and took in the vast Valeriaan presence that surrounded her. But this was not the time to falter before such an encumbrance.

She took in a deep breath, and though her voice trembled a bit, she answered the commander's initial question. "I'm on my way to Falkhearth… Sir Commander. Might you be so kind as to allow me to pass?"

His lips pursed into a hum and he replied, “I’m afraid not, my lady. No one is to leave or enter the city at this time. Where are you coming from?”

Ygrayne was already annoyed.

“Trivaden, Sir Commander. Pardon me, but a few of our residents were able to return to our village hours ago, but my husband was not among them. I was hoping I could petition in some way for his release.”

She tried to keep the displeasure from her tone, but she couldn’t help narrowing her eyes for just an instant—a change in countenance the commander noticed, snickering quietly.

“You’re some distance from home.” The commander approached. A mere step made Mara pull her head back with a snort. Ygrayne maintained a tight grip on the reins and brushed her fingers through the thicket of her mane to calm the uneasy mare, keep her as composed as a horse could manage. The commander grasped at the cheekpieces of the bridle and ran a gloved hand down the plane of Mara’s face. What normally would be a consoling gesture gave no comfort. Horses were known to have a sense of the folk they encountered, able to feel who they were within and determine their disposition. In turn, they were not shy in showing their displeasure toward those they found unfavorable. The commander was such a man, indicated by the way Mara shifted her weight on restless legs, and in her attempts to turn her head away.

His violet eyes gracefully moved about the mare’s face until they came to rest upon Ygrayne with such perfectly practiced control that it sent shivers down her spine.

“And alone.” There was a smile in his voice.

Ygrayne refused to waver in her stoicism, mainly for the sake of her own pride.

“Sir Commander, with all due respect, I must ask, is there any chance my husband can be released from Falkhearth?”

There could be no trust placed in the words of a Valeriaan, a principle Ygrayne had long ago come to understand and live by. But she saw so much more when she looked into this man’s eyes. It was much deeper than dishonesty, deeper than the weight of justified hatred widely held for his clan. There was something about his gaze which made him seem precarious. Ygrayne kept her eyes fixed on him, for even just a spare moment’s look away could mean her demise. He in turn gazed at her, eyes unblinking.

While she held his gaze for self-preservation, however, he was finding their staring contest mildly amusing. How long would it be before she looked away? Before her eyes lowered in submission to his presence? When she failed to acquiesce, he smiled again and said, "Unfortunately my lady, no one else is to be released from Falkhearth. Orders as I have received them."

He took pleasure in saying so, took pleasure in the fleeting distress he could observe in her expression. "Your husband will just have to bear the might of the Valeriaan Empire along with all folk within those walls."

Ygrayne's lips flattened about her face.

"Even if there were a possibility, I doubt I would grant you the opportunity." The toothy grin that materialized on his face might as well have served to bare fangs.

"Officer Klaus," he called, and the soldier replied immediately, "Commander?"

Without taking his eyes off Ygrayne, he said, "This white mare. From whence does this beast originate?"

Ygrayne didn't want to beg or falter, but she was desperate. Her husband awaited her, needed her, and by all appearances, the situation was more dire than she could've ever imagined.

"Please…Sir Commander…" Ygrayne didn't have a chance to finish before the officer answered, "The white breed originated from the Valeriaan homeland, Commander. From the Valeriaan Isles."

"You hear that, my lady?" the commander, who spoke with such condescension in his voice, was beginning to make Ygrayne's blood simmer as she recoiled in disgust. No longer was she unnerved by the presence of this army, nor the commander himself. She despised being played with, and even more fervently, by a Valeriaan.

"This mare belongs to the Allfather."

Oh, how she had to use every ounce of fortitude in her being not to let the sharpness of her tongue take command.

"You may have the mare, Commander," Ygrayne stated curtly. "I humbly call upon your kindness to allow me passage into Falkhearth, please."

Ygrayne dismounted the mare, holding out the reins to the commander. She could barely contain the contempt she harbored. Her face twitched with the exertion of maintaining its expression of composure. The commander didn't seem to mind the emanating rage. Instead, he seemed empowered by her reaction, basking in the knowledge that he had even a nonphysical power over her. Ygrayne hated to admit to herself that she had faltered. Deep regret pooled in the recesses of her being.

"We will take the mare. My kindness is allowing you safe passage back home, on your own feet. Do not take my generosity for granted, my lady."

"Why are you not letting anyone into the city?" Ygrayne at last gave in to her temper.

"You have no liberty to be asking such questions," the commander replied. It was a warning, liberally granted in his mind, for he could do much worse very quickly.

"My husband has been delayed for days! I beg you, please allow me into the city. I will leave as soon as I find him."

The commander looked at her, apathetic. The blank expression about his face was more frightening than his open condescension, as he wordlessly conspired. She had crossed a boundary, one which often meant punishment, and even death. Ygrayne couldn't help but feel the utter disappointment in herself—not for letting her anger get the better of her, but for the possibility of leaving her son without a mother, knowing his father might not return to him as well. She had unmistakably let down her family.

Ygrayne didn't have a chance to fully succumb to the darkness of her thoughts before she felt the back of his armored hand slam into her cheek with such force that it sent her straight to the ground with a cry. A cloud of dust rose around her, and Mara nearly trampled her in sheer panic. By some absolute providence, the hooves missed her by mere inches as the mare retreated from the sudden confrontation. The commander kept a firm grasp about her bridle, unbothered.

Ygrayne had never felt such pain before. At first, she couldn't really feel the impact, her initial shock and the abruptness of it all holding the awareness at bay. Only when the disbelief finally waned, did she feel the true nature of the impact. Her whole face ached and cried out. Pulsing. Red. Hot. Her lips fell open and yet her scream was silent, not even a hint of a bellow. The warm touch of blood filled her mouth, and dripped to the ground below in thick, ominous droplets. Her black hair fell around her, tangled in the dirt. Her head felt light as a plume on the breeze, her mind unable to comprehend the once-familiar world around her, now beginning to spin nauseatingly. Even the fluttering of her eyes did little to relieve her symptoms. She could hardly feel the hand she placed on her inflamed cheek, only the heartbeat which pulsed with such vigor that it seemed her heart had migrated to that very spot on her face.

"You should have left when I gave you the opportunity." The commander's words seemed so distant, a blurred echo in her ears.

Alas, Ygrayne still had not managed to comprehend the situation before she felt a hand grasping the knots in her hair, followed by a sharp tug which forced her to gaze into those hateful violet eyes again.

"I don't appreciate when my generosity is taken advantage of."

She could barely make out the details of his face, even as close as he was, let alone find the vigor to escape in that moment.

"You really are a beautiful woman." He let out a disappointed sigh. "Truly a shame you have such unfavorable blood running through your veins. I simply don't fuck Dúlír whores such as you."

The commander stood, dragging Ygrayne with him as he made his way over to his subordinates. It was only then she fought and struggled. But the resistance and the crying did little to help her, the tussle only serving to draw the attention of the soldiers from the camp, their rapacious natures awakened to the sound of squealing prey.

The commander looked to the two soldiers and said, "The whore is yours to do with as you please. I'll take the mare to the pen."

He tossed her straight back into the dirt once again, the dust choking her as she gasped with surprise. But that single breath was stolen from her lungs as she felt another hand grasp at the neckline of her dress. The seams of the delicately woven fabric ripped, the sheer force of the gesture pulling her onto very much unprepared legs.

Many a story warned about the tongues of vexed women, telling of their kind who had fallen into disfavor, left to the wrath of the Valeriaan army. Taken against their will by their ravenous abductors despite screams and struggles, never be seen again. What remained was merely the somber pondering of the horrors and pain endured before meeting their unfortunate demise. How they fought. How they struggled. How they cried. They stood no chance. Brutalized, degraded in their final moments. Anecdotes alone were a fright upon the mind, but Ygrayne found herself facing such a fate manifested. If these were indeed to be her final moments, an addition to the morbid tales retold, then she wasn't going to give herself so easily to them.

Her thoughts went to her son. How he would be without a mother. How she would not be there to comfort him in his struggles, to witness the defining moments in his life, the milestones he was yet to reach. How he would miss her loving embrace, the irreplaceable love she would always have for him. There was only one comforting thought which came to mind in the midst of this morbid new actuality—Urda would no doubt take good care of Artur. She then thought of Thelric. Her loving and ever-doting husband of the past thirteen years of her life. Her confidant. Her partner in all the good and bad times. He would undoubtedly think her foolish for attempting such a feat, testing the Valeriaans' might against her own. But he would be proud of her courage, be proud to know she refused to succumb. It was these very thoughts which gave her the vigor she so desperately needed.

At last, her legs found their bearing. As an angered mare would, she dug her heels deep into the dirt and stood her ground. She swung, contorted her body in ways she'd never known possible to escape the clutches she found herself in. Ygrayne could hear their laughter ringing in her ears at what they would deem a feeble attempt, for her strength was nothing in comparison to theirs, honed and refined by their training and battle.

It took but one soldier to overwhelm her own strength, and Ygrayne soon found her arms twisted and forced behind her back. His arm locked around the both of hers, only her legs were left to carry forth the fight in their stead.

She kicked wildly, her dress fluttering about her, prompted to new extremes as they continued to taunt her for the vain effort. The soldiers dragged her toward the camp, cooing and spouting vulgarity at the expense of her character and body alike. Oh, how she tired and ached. How her body wanted to succumb to exhaustion. It was only the thoughts of her family and the sheer force of her stubbornness which kept her belligerent. But as the white tents drew nearer in her sight, Ygrayne knew exactly what was to befall her. She knew every last bit of her mind and soul—her Húgar—was to be stripped away. Her body defiled. Her spirit broken. The humiliation in the final moments. But no. Ygrayne would have none of it. She would fight until the end, perhaps even provoke them further to an anger with no return—an anger leading to her ultimate demise. She would rather be dead than humiliated. Yet she felt herself faltering once more—not by any means of her will, but by the limitations imposed on her physical prowess by injury. The wound to her face was much more than spilled blood and bruising. Her head ached. Throbbed. The waves of nausea and lightheadedness threatened to overcome her consciousness. Everything became a blur around her—a blur of soldiers standing against a field of green, of white fluttering in the wind.

Ygrayne heard the fabric of her dress tear once again. The expertly woven fibers gave way, affording all in the vicinity the pleasure of seeing her exposed breasts. The soldiers sneered with amusement, releasing antagonizing taunts in response to bearing witness to a female figure such as they had not been privy to for some time. Their desires and urges left unquelled, a hunger, a thirst, had become their disposition, had become their motivator.

The commander paid no mind to her screams and struggle. The sounds were all too familiar to him. The years of repetition had made his mind and body numb to the agony that transpired around him. He showed more interest in keeping Mara calm as she watched her rider suffering before her very eyes, the screaming provoking her to fright.

Ygrayne kicked with an exhausting ferocity to deter the soldiers as they so eagerly tried to tease and fondle her breasts. Her efforts proved fruitless until she successfully landed a single kick to the abdomen of one.

It hardly hurt the soldier, stunning him only momentarily. It just served to sour his mood, as the common woman had dared to dirty his otherwise immaculate uniform.

Her persistent struggle was now proving an annoyance rather than an amusement, and the soldier made his sentiments known when he delivered a hard strike to her own gut. At long last Ygrayne fell silent, her breath stolen from her burning lungs, her tussle ceasing in her stunned state.

"If you won't come with us," he said coldly, his voice deep, "then we'll have our way with you here. I'm not particular."

He grabbed her by the arm and tossed her to the ground with such force that she fell away from his companion's hold.

Finally free, Ygrayne was consumed by a single thought: *run*. She knew she wouldn't get far, but she had no choice but to try. And yet, all she could do was grasp at her bruised abdomen, no breath about her lips.

"When you're done with her, I'll have a go," the other commented.

The words echoed with absolute finality in her pulsing ears. Resolution and resignation washed over her simultaneously, two waves racing over the shore, granting her some sort of acceptance for what was about to transpire. Ygrayne closed her eyes, one shallow breath escaping her lips, a gasp forced from her constricted lungs.

"Reinhardt!" a voice rang out, startling all present Valeriaan soldiers.

It was only Ygrayne who was unaware of the sudden interruption, and when she looked about to see why they had stopped the intended incursion, she noticed that her attackers had gone pale, stilled into silence.

She had never seen soldiers, with all the fortitude they were trained to possess, as alarmed as these men looked. Even the commander, though he preserved his composure, turned sharply on his heels, made tense by the sight. Their attention diverted, they hardly noticed when Ygrayne crawled away, scrambling feebly in the dirt. Only when Ygrayne felt she was far enough from the soldiers did she take the moment to peer up and see what exactly was transpiring.

She quickly understood the change in the atmosphere, at least before the faintness once again clouded her mind with nauseating vertigo. Yet just the brief glimpse left her with an overwhelming sense of relief, a hope that her suffering was ended. A second wind had come to give her another chance, the breath returned to her aching lungs. With a grunt, she pushed herself onto her knees and folded the bodice of her dress together to cover her exposed figure. Feeling the torn fabric within the clutches of her hands, she couldn't help but shed a tear, not just for the total disregard of what it took to make such attire, but for nearly having every bit of dignity stripped from her in the vilest of ways. She lowered her head, matted hair cascading around her as a shrouding veil.

As humiliated as she felt, and as brutal as the ordeal had been, Ygrayne couldn't help but look up again at her savior if only for a moment.

It was him. Even through unfocused eyes she could make out the grey of his hooded robe and distinctive tunic, of the horse beneath his saddle.

The Schiva... she thought to herself before she could bear it no longer and closed her eyes.

CHAPTER 13

The Schiva sat astride a majestic, dapple-grey horse with snow-pelted spots that accented the light-to-dark transition of his form. A thick, black mane flowed about his neck and large hooves pranced at the ends of blackened legs. The sheer size of this beast granted the Schiva a most commanding air. The mischievousness and affable inclination he'd previously flaunted with Ygrayne were entirely absent. There was no weapon of steel at his waist, or hiding in his saddlebags, for there was no need for it. His presence alone was his weapon of choice against his armored adversaries.

The Schiva clicked his tongue, and the stallion gracefully started into a gallop down the hill. There was no need to spur or whip the steed. The two possessed an unspoken understanding, a bond of unbreakable tethers forged by years of shared experiences. It became even more apparent when the stallion stopped right beside Ygrayne, their intended destination, with no visible or audible command from the Schiva. This beast of a horse towered over her the way the mountains loomed over the lands below.

The soldiers stumbled away, their hands instinctively grasping at the hilts of their blades, a conditioned response to any perceived threat. But a Schiva never intended to be seen as a threat. The pacifists boasted no prowess in battle, nor did they engage in physical conflict.

It was only the commander, though he too felt uneasy at the closeness of the Schiva, who maintained his composure beside the anxious mare whose reins he held. He was more irritated than alarmed, stewing over the way his own soldiers trembled at the mere sight of their unexpected, but well-known, guest—an embarrassment. Emphasized by the darkness around his eyes, the Schiva's piercing and fiery gaze identified him promptly to the Valeriaans, leaving no doubt as to who was in their presence. His grey robes were recognizable on their own. What was a welcome sight to many, instead made the commander swallow nervously.

Ygrayne turned her head just enough to gaze upon the beast towering over her, watching as the well-developed muscles flexed and glimmered in the sunlight underneath his glossy coat. She only caught a glimpse of the Schiva's boot about the stirrups before sharp pain called her attention once more to her bruised face. With the mercilessness of a needle point, the pain traversed her wounds as waves along a shoreline. Ygrayne couldn't help but draw in a breath, her eyes clenching tight to spare her from the intense gleam of the sun above. The Schiva heard her inhale. He peered down at her with a tilt of his head, his movements subtle to keep tension from mounting.

His stallion, a powerful beast called Onír, let out a snort and lowered the length of his neck to bow his head. He too sensed the distress which emanated from Ygrayne's being, gently blowing air from his large nostrils against the side of her head. She barely felt the gesture in her weakened state.

"I know. I know," the Schiva whispered, patting Onír's neck to appease the concerned beast.

"No need to draw your swords, you damn idiots." The commander's voice did not hide his discomfiture, drawing his soldiers' eyes to him.

"He's not going to hurt you. He's a Schiva after all."

They reluctantly withdrew their hands from their sword hilts and instead held firmly the scabbards at their sides.

The commander tossed the reins of the mare to the ground and marched over as though he were a petulant child throwing a tantrum rather than a soldier with authoritative presence.

The Schiva found it rather amusing to watch the commander huffing and turning red with anger and shame. Had he not worn a mask, he would have been punished for failing to hide the fox's smirk that crossed his lips.

Ygrayne didn't find the commander's approach as diverting. Instead, she felt a wave of fear overtake her once more. She didn't have much fight left, if any at all. This would be his chance to put an end to the woman who had caused a nuisance for his men.

She wanted to scurry away, even if it meant doing so on her hands and knees, yet she still couldn't move. The orders of her mind did little to influence a body too tired and aching to function. Instead, all Ygrayne could think to do with what little strength she had left was to hug herself so tightly that she felt a sense of protection from her own embrace—a makeshift shield at best.

Her quickened breath was a whisper in the Schiva's ears. Panic rose closer to the surface with each step the commander took in their direction.

There was little the Schiva found intimidating, and the commander possessed no such qualities. The Schiva's only concern was the safety of the battered woman on the ground beside his steed's hooves. Ygrayne was not out of peril yet; even he knew so. And Schiva brethren who found themselves in similar predicaments were often killed alongside the victims they intended to protect. Though he was aware of the risk, the Schiva couldn't afford to lose the upper hand he held in that moment. There was a ploy up his sleeve, one he knew he could use to his advantage, regardless of the consequences that could befall him.

Sensing the commander's approach and Ygrayne's fright, Onír pounded his front hooves hard against the dirt road, raising a cloud of dust about his legs. He angled his body to provide a tall, sturdy buffer between Ygrayne and the commander. The show of force was enough to make the soldier slow his pace, approaching with caution rather than fury.

All Ygrayne could feel was the world trembling beneath her, the warmth of the beast's proximity to her. She feared she would be trampled if a scuffle ensued, and all she could do was keep her eyes closed and hope it would not come to be so.

The Schiva bowed his head as he respectfully addressed the commander. "Good afternoon, Commander Reinhardt." But when he raised his head and met the commander's gaze once more, the Schiva couldn't help but throw in a cheeky remark. "I hope you don't mind my intrusion."

"Don't patronize me, Schiva." The commander spat at him with a venomous hiss. "You shan't concern yourselves with my current affairs."

"It was hardly my intention to concern myself with the matters at hand. I simply heard a woman screaming and I happened to find that woman in distress at the hands of your soldiers. A mere, shall we say, coincidence."

"You play coy with me, Schiva. I could kill you where you stand."

"You cannot kill me where I stand, for I am not standing. I am sitting. And the Allfather would not be impressed to know that his cousin murdered a Schiva who was going about his philanthropic duties to the commonfolk."

The Schiva knew he spoke truth, an advantage. Schivas were not killed needlessly due to a certain respect the Valeriaans grudgingly held for them—a notable distinction, given what little respect they had for anyone but their own.

Schivas, compared to the commonfolk, were held in much higher regard. They were revered—even by the highest-ranking royals—for their knowledge and expertise in various practices and studies, many of which the Valeriaans were not themselves versed in. It was for this reason that their temples and possessions, including their extensive ancient libraries and laboratories, where skills were sharpened and studies were furthered, had been spared in the great purge.

This reprieve had been granted under one condition: the Schivas were not to interfere with the Empire and her proceedings. This restriction generally caused few conflicts, given that the Schivas only busied themselves with helping the commonfolk and did not make a habit of concerning themselves with political or military affairs.

There were very limited exceptions. Should a battle or siege take place, and the Schivas be dispatched to all parts of Skana where they were needed, their deaths could only be permitted as collateral. They were never to be seen as a threat or an enemy and were therefore not to be attacked directly. They were often left to rely on their own discretion, even in the aftermath of a catastrophic event.

The Schivas also provided a buffer, taking care of matters which the Valeriaans themselves did not wish to partake in. The Valeriaans cared little for the struggles of the commonfolk, and thus did not trouble themselves with their woes and concerns. The intervention of the Schivas appeased the folk just enough to keep conflict at bay. But this was a different matter altogether. Both the Schiva and the commander knew so as they conducted their discourse.

The commander scoffed as he looked away for but a moment, and when he gazed to the Schiva once more, he responded through a toothy grin, "You Schivas pride yourselves on your 'philanthropic duties' and yet you do nothing about the Empire, or the powers that were. Your kindness is a façade to disguise the cowardice which lies behind the masks you don."

"Empires rise and fall naturally," the Schiva replied calmly. "Your time will come, as it has for all before you, and all that will come after—*and it will be done by your own hands.*"

The commander's eyes, once filled with confidence, now narrowed into a cold and piercing glare.

"I grow tired of your impudence. You're fortunate we hold your kind in such high regard, or I wouldn't have let you live long enough to spout such blasphemy. Sometimes we Valeriaans are too generous."

"But we both know why you wouldn't have." The Schiva returned an equally potent gaze, his eyes narrowed with a confidence and a sharpness undiminished by the commander's icy stare.

It was with little effort that the Schiva completely disregarded the commander's very presence as he dismounted the stallion with grace beside Ygrayne. In one fluid motion, he draped his robe about her and Ygrayne felt immediate comfort, a protection akin to that of a child in the warm embrace of a mother. The robe was soft and warm to the touch, compelling her to pull it tighter about her to preserve the feeling.

"It's all right now," said the Schiva as he knelt beside her, placing a tender hand upon her back.

How Ygrayne wanted to thank the Schiva for coming to her aid, for rescuing her from the gruesome conclusion of her own life. But her lips were quivering, sputtering words akin to a bumbling fool.

"There's no need to say anything," the Schiva whispered to her. "Just stay as you are for now."

Ygrayne trembled as dread for the circumstances against him again rose within her. She looked to him, the tears beginning to well up in her eyes and threatening to spill over her bruised face. She could see it in those soft amber eyes, highlighted by the darkness which encompassed them; he knew of her gratitude.

His own gaze traversed the wounds about her face, determining the extent of the physical cruelty she had sustained. It displeased him so to see her in such a state. The soft gaze he used to put her at ease hid the burning fire raging within. Had he not dedicated his life to the Brotherhood, and forsworn any form of violence, he would have indeed done much worse than direct a few fancy ripostes toward the commander.

"We'll get those wounds cleaned up for you." He kept his voice calm, quiet, the conversation meant only for the two of them. And it would have stayed private, had Onír not lowered his head and let out a breathy snort. The nosy horse heard everything. As the Schiva stood, he playfully pushed at Onír's face and gave a snort. The lighthearted moment would not last, however. There was still the commander to handle, and their next exchange would determine Ygrayne's fate.

The Schiva calmly folded his hands in front of him and approached the commander at a leisurely pace. He wanted the commander to trust that he possessed the authority in the coming conversation, which required the Schiva to take a posture of appeasement, to entertain the rather delicate ego.

"I must request that you release the woman to me," the Schiva said politely as he came to stand before the commander.

"This woman is my prisoner." The commander was quick with his rejection.

"What grounds do you have to keep her?"

"She tried to cross the watchpoint. I gave her plenty of opportunities to walk away with her life and she chose to openly defy me. Such insubordination is often punished with the penalty of death."

"And you thought having your men rape her was a better punishment?"

"It would have been preferable to death."

"You cannot possibly think that to be the lesser punishment. If you do, Commander, then your judgment has been sullied by disuse and ignorance."

The commander's face turned red, his teeth gritting hard in anger. He wouldn't have let the encounter go on as long as it had, to be insulted and challenged in such a manner. But the Schiva was right. They both knew why no such tragedy had taken place. The commander wanted nothing more than to reach for his blade and remove the Schiva's head from his very shoulders. Instead, his fists merely trembled as they clenched together at his sides.

"You would hold your tongue under different circumstances, and I would cut you down if you were anyone else!" The commander pushed his words through clenched teeth. His voice was low but forced, his tone harsh. "I'm aware of who you are. We *all* know who you are."

He took a breath, raising his chin as he straightened his posture to regain his composure. "Ye-es," he purred. "Your reputation precedes you among my clan members. The 'Amber-Eyed Schiva,' they call you."

The sneer on his face could be heard in his voice. "I always thought it to be redundant, but given that such a clan no longer exists, there are only a handful of folk alive now who bear the defining characteristic of the Thórdarsons."

They were both thinking the same—of how and why the Thórdarson clan had long ago perished—but neither spoke a word more about it.

"And only one of those remaining happens to be a Schiva—a Schiva of whom my cousin has grown peculiarly fond." The commander took a step forward until their faces were close. Amber eyes to violet, neither dared break their gaze in the mounting confrontation. Once again, a purr returned to the commander's voice as he said, "The only reason you still stand as you are."

"Then perhaps we can use my standing to your advantage," the Schiva said in a cunning tone, the glint of a smile in his eyes.

The commander's smile flattened into a cautious expression.

"What trickery is this?" he growled.

"No trickery. A proposition."

The commander was still hesitant, as indicated by his prolonged silence; the Schiva elaborated.

"I've heard of you as well, but," the Schiva took a step closer, drawing his masked lips to the commander's ear. "Your cousin is not very fond of you, I'm afraid," he whispered. "Your rank is only achieved by nepotism and pity."

The breath hissed sharply through the commander's teeth as he prepared to refute such a vile affront to his name, but the Schiva was quick to continue. "However, perhaps I can help you change that."

It worked. The commander's words died upon his lips, his curiosity piqued as to the Schiva's next words.

"Let the woman go. Release her to me and I'll speak of your generosity and...professionalism...to your cousin. He values my word and would be most pleased to know that you treated me well."

The Schiva stepped away and took the moment to gauge the commander's reaction, to observe the tense demeanor and the stone-like face harboring guarded eyes that watched the Schiva's every movement.

The commander was deeply contemplating the offer at hand. As tantalizing as a meal sprinkled with the most delectable of spices, it was an opportunity he would be a fool to deny.

The Schiva held his breath. It was a cruel and dirty trick pulled from his sleeve, and one greatly unbecoming of a Schiva. Yet desperate circumstances called for desperate solutions, and he had no choice but to show his winning hand.

"And, while the offer still stands, I will take the mare as well. The breed is no longer exclusive to the Valeriaans, since they were left to roam free across Skana."

The commander knew he had but two choices. Over the course of his military career, he had taken down adversary after adversary. In no single fight had he been bested in battle. He had the rank to prove it, the blood to back it, and the garments to boast it. He had believed himself to be invulnerable. Yet now he found himself bested, his pride insulted by someone he found inferior and inept. It was infuriating. The Schiva offered him a chance to gain favor in the eyes of his cousin—a man he had not known himself to be held in contempt by. This was appalling. The Schiva could very well be merely goading him with his sly tongue, a chanced fib, a bluff. But the commander knew it was no ordinary Schiva who stood before him, and if his cousin trusted this masked silhouette of a man, then certainly this was no bluff.

"You're wasting my time, Commander," the Schiva said curtly, but calmly, pulling him from his ruminations. "Do you take my offer?"

Ygrayne felt her stomach drop.

Offer?

It was the only part of the conversation she could hear clearly, and just from the one word alone she gathered that she was being bid on akin to cattle at auction.

What offer? she thought to herself.

"Very well." The commander exhaled, licking the back of his teeth. "I'll accept your offer."

Ygrayne turned her head, hearing the suspected transaction finalize, and as she gazed at the two men from behind a thicket of fallen hair, they bowed their heads toward one another in agreement. The Schiva then turned on his heel and made his way back to her and Onír. She could hardly look at him as he knelt beside her and rested a tender hand about her back, feeling herself to be the object of a trade she'd had no say in.

"Let's get you back home," the Schiva whispered.

"I can't!" Her voice suddenly burst from her after its prolonged absence, surprising even her.

"Ygrayne…" The Schiva was taken aback. "The best thing for you right now is to return to Trivaden."

Ygrayne hardly cared about her own state. There was no chance she was turning back now, no matter what she had already endured or what lay before her. Her son was safe, she knew that for certain, but now she was convinced something dire was about to happen, and her husband was in the center of that peril. It was clear to her what she still needed to do: she had to get to Falkhearth.

"You do not wish to go back?" The Schiva questioned her objection.

Ygrayne let out a breath and finally the tears began to fall down her face, the cool touch almost a remedy to the pain.

"My husband," she responded, her voice hoarse.

It was just as he had expected, and everything he feared. The Schiva had hoped, given her state, that Ygrayne would make the sensical choice to return to where she would be safe, for there was nothing either of them could do for her husband.

"There's nothing—"

"I," Ygrayne finally turned her teary gaze to him, her eyes wide with desperation and intensity. "Am. Not. Leaving."

Neither the strike to her face, nor the assault she had endured, were enough to convince her of her futility in the enormity of the situation. Just thinking about it so, Ygrayne dropped her face into her hands and wept quietly. No audible cry escaped her—just her heaving breath and her body shuddering in unison with her tender sobs.

The Schiva couldn't help but sympathize with Ygrayne's plight. Over the past few days, he had tended to commonfolk who too were inconsolable, worrying themselves enough to be bedridden as they imagined the worst of scenarios. The situation was worsening, and even his most stoic of brethren were growing apprehensive.

Stubborn, foolish woman, he thought to himself. If nothing else was to appease her, then the Schiva knew he would have to adapt.

"Commander," the Schiva called out, turning to the man who was still waiting quietly for the Schiva to conclude his part of the bargain. He looked dejected, as if he had just forfeited his rank and was now nothing more than a common soldier awaiting his next order.

"May I make a request?" the Schiva asked, approaching.

The commander gave a most displeased click of his tongue and let out an incredulous sigh.

"You've already got what you wanted, Schiva. What more can you ask for?"

"The woman is injured and too weak to make the trek back to her village at present. May I ask that we stay for the day so that I may treat her wounds and allow her some rest?"

The commander tilted his head slightly, and the small smile which crossed his lips evoked concern in the Schiva, whose eyes narrowed as he tried to decipher the enigmatic expression about the commander's face.

"You may stay as guests," he stated sardonically. "But heed this warning—if you stay, Schiva, neither of you will be permitted to leave until I allow it."

"And how long before we are permitted to leave?"

"That is none of your concern." The commander's brows lifted as he smirked. "The both of you may stay, and I promise no harm will come to you, or the woman. That is the most latitude I'll grant you."

"It sounds as though we will be more akin to prisoners than guests."

"I'm doing you a courtesy, Schiva. You will have access to my supplies, and a tent for the two of you to share—with your own beds, may I add. But let me caution you. Neither of you will want to be on the road by tomorrow morning. Now," the commander let out a satisfied sigh, "that truly wouldn't be very generous of me."

Whatever the Valeriaans had been planning these past days was about to come into fruition, and the Schiva knew that he and Ygrayne both were now caught in its midst. The commander's words were neither a favor, nor evidence of generosity. They were a forewarning. A threat. The Schiva knew it was best to withdraw and test the commander's limits no further. All he and Ygrayne could do was hope for was the safety of Trivaden and Thelric's survival through the ordeal to come.

The Schiva snorted and replied, "How generous of you, Commander."

"Be certain to let my cousin know of my hospitality as well."

The Schiva narrowed his eyes at the snide remark.

"He will know of it from letters written in my own hand. You have my oath."

CHAPTER 14

Every eye was on them as they navigated a sea of white fabric and glistening silver armor. Whispers floating about teased at their ears. The retelling of earlier events had the soldiers intrigued and mystified, and Ygrayne and the Schiva were to be the topic on tongues for days to come. Whether it was due to fear or curiosity, the tension amongst the soldiers was palpable, the air thick and heavy.

It was a humiliating walk through the camp, swarming as it was with adversaries. All Ygrayne could do was pull the robe tightly about her and hide her bruised face within the gaping cowl. She felt helpless, childlike, carried within the arms of the Schiva as he followed the commander to the tent that awaited them. Onír walked steadily of his own volition in the Schiva's wake, Mara's reins tied to the horn of his saddle.

"Do not worry yourself," the Schiva whispered to Ygrayne, sensing her uneasiness. "No further harm will come to you."

Ygrayne didn't have the chance to reply before she heard the commander's skin-crawling voice say, "You will remain here."

Pulling aside the tent flap, he revealed two beds with a table between them. It looked more comfortable than expected, warmer and quieter, and the way the sun danced about the outside of the continuously moving fabric of the tent was a rather beautiful sight. It could have been worse, though it was hardly home.

"Should you need anything, please do not hesitate to ask," the commander instructed magnanimously, bowing his head for the sake of politeness and the conservation of his own ego, his standing.

"Clothes," the Schiva said quickly, before the commander left them.

"Clothes?"

"Your soldiers ripped this woman's dress. She'll need a change of clothes."

"I'm afraid we have no dresses—"

"Anything will do. So long as they're decent, and not frayed." The Schiva turned and gave the commander a critical look. "And something for her to eat and drink as well."

"Very well. I'll have my men bring what you have requested."

"Thank you, Commander."

"No." The commander bowed at the waist. "Thank you, Schiva."

The opening of the tent rippled as it fell back into place, the commander's shadow distorting in the folds as he walked away.

At last, the two of them were alone, left to some bit of privacy and peace amidst a sea of uneasiness. The Schiva placed Ygrayne onto one of the beds with such tenderness that she felt neither ache nor pain from her injuries. For a moment, Ygrayne was able to look into those amber eyes of his, and she smiled with what little strength she still possessed. A sigh could be heard from behind the mask, and she could see plainly in his eyes that he was smiling back.

"I need to retrieve some supplies from my saddlebag. I'll be outside the tent just a moment."

Ygrayne nodded and watched in silence as the Schiva proceeded outside to where Onír and Mara were waiting just beside the tent. Once he had removed the saddlebags with the needed commodities, the Schiva divested both Onír and Mara of their tack, so that the horses could rest for the remainder of their stay at the camp. Neither the horses nor their riders were going anywhere presently. This camp was to be their temporary home for the unforeseeable future.

There was a solemnity between the Schiva and his steed—exhaustion, certainly, as well as quiet relief. The triumph they had attained was bittersweet. Ygrayne was alive and would be well soon enough, but they could only speculate as to the horror of the events yet to unfold.

The Schiva didn't want to imagine the worst that could lie ahead for the once-beautiful Falkhearth, but to deny the grim outcome likely awaiting the city would be foolish. The Schiva brushed the palm of his hand against Onír's neck as he thought deeply about it, seeking some comfort against the encroaching despair. The horse in return rubbed his muzzle against the side of the Schiva's own face. They stood there for a moment, reveling in the warmth and comfort of each other's company—two life-long companions relying on the other as they always had.

Only when they sensed the approach of oncoming soldiers did they know that it was time to part for the moment. With a heavy sigh, and one last touch of his palm against Onír's cheek, the Schiva whispered, "We'll be all right. Watch over the mare for me."

Onír snorted and flapped his lips, pawing the ground almost excitedly. The stallion was all too delighted to be in the presence of a beautiful mare with a shining coat of white.

"Behave," the Schiva warned, pointing a finger. "Watch. Not fancy."

Onír huffed defiantly, turning his head to Mara who stood beside him, none the wiser.

The Schiva shook his head with a small snort and returned to the tent just as two soldiers came to fulfill his earlier requests. They brought food and a spare set of the garments they wore underneath their coats of armor: brown trousers and a white tunic with long sleeves. They had done well to find the best fit, the smallest of sizes for the smallest of soldiers, to suit Ygrayne's frame as best they could.

There were no words, no glances exchanged between either party. Ygrayne kept her head down to hide her glare of displeasure at their very presence, and the soldiers could hardly look into the eyes of the man who had made even their commander tremble.

The next few hours were spent largely in silence. The Schiva himself hardly attempted to make conversation. He understood silence was a remedy, a much-needed medicine in and of itself. When everything finally settled, did Ygrayne feel a tremendous weight leave her body, and the rush of exhaustion finally overtook her. All she could do was sit still and quiet as the Schiva tended to her wounds, working with the dexterity and tenderness of an expert caregiver. The saddlebags the Schiva brought into the tent were filled with various provisions and tools for application. Where others would carry comestibles and munitions, his bags were filled with instruments for healing others. She could hardly put a name to anything at his disposal—a combination of creams and ointments that made her eyes water, her senses overwhelmed by the potent scents.

The closest comparison she could make was to the potions Urda would often concoct and distribute amongst the village folk. The Schiva's assortments reminded her of the flora growing in her dear friend's garden. No one really questioned what Urda's bottles and jars contained. All they knew was that her tinctures worked, and for that reason could be trusted.

"Who are you?" the Schiva asked, breaking the prolonged silence between them.

Ygrayne's brow furrowed quizzically, thinking him momentarily mad for asking such a blatantly obvious question.

"Ygrayne..."

"Good," he replied, with no regard for her puzzlement. "Where are you from?"

Again, she was taken aback by the ridiculous question.

"Trivaden."

"And where are we now?"

"Schiva," Ygrayne let out an exasperated sigh. "What are you on about?"

"Checking for signs of concussion," he replied politely, but curtly. "Where are we now?"

"In a Valeriaan camp," she answered, pondering the word she'd never heard before. "What is a concussion?"

The Schiva raised a finger just before Ygrayne's face, drawing her sudden gaze.

"I shall tell you once we are done. Follow my finger with your eyes. Keep your head still."

Ygrayne did as she was told, perplexed further by the procedure at hand. She performed the task with great ease, not a hint of the concerning indications the Schiva was watching for.

"Good. Thank you, Ygrayne," said he as he dropped his hand into his lap. "A concussion is an injury to the head. Or more so, what is in your head. Though I think you have nothing to worry about, I will keep a close eye upon you for the next few days in case symptoms manifest."

Ygrayne reached a hand toward her cheek, her fingers mere inches away before she paused and withdrew her hand.

"Can a strike to the face really cause a…a 'concussion'?"

"It can. Especially when the offending hand has a plate of armor attached to it."

The revelation rendered Ygrayne silent, concerned.

"But you needn't worry," the Schiva was quick to reiterate, seeing the turmoil dancing across her expression. "By all appearances, aside from a very bruised face, I think you will recover quickly, and quite nicely."

He touched lightly at her chin, a glint of a smile reaching his eyes once more. It was a reassuring sight, accompanying equally reassuring words. Ygrayne smiled gently in return.

By the end of her treatment, Ygrayne's lips were cleaned and oiled. Her cheek was slathered with an ointment which stung, annoyingly so, and covered with a patch that stuck to her skin with whatever adhesive the Schiva had applied. The cuts and abrasions she had received in her struggles, from her arms to her legs, had all been tended to and treated with the same gentleness and finesse. It was an overwhelming relief to know her body was mending. But worse was still to come. Tears filled her eyes yet again as she prepared to lower the ruined dress to the floor, forced to change into clothes belonging to the very folk who had nearly brought an end to her life in a most devastating and humiliating way. She hesitated, looking to the Schiva, who already held the tunic open for her. He was quick to observe her reticence, and averting his eyes, he said quietly, "It's nothing I haven't seen before—if it's any consolation. However, if you wish that I remove myself, I will do so without delay."

She felt the need to cover herself, to cast her arms about her chest and hold the torn fabric of her dress closed. The Schiva was no doubt her savior, a man who meant her anything but harm, and yet she felt disgusting. Her body felt defiled, unworthy to be gazed upon. The thought of feeling yet another pair of foreign eyes upon her figure made her tremble.

Ygrayne lowered her head, and with her hair draping around her did she say in a whisper, "…I'd rather be alone for this."

She hated the insinuation, the implied disrespect to his character out of her own insecurities. But the Schiva was neither disgusted nor disrespected. He understood, and wished only for her comfort. He was more than happy to oblige. He simply, without another word, placed the tunic on the bed and quietly exited the tent. Only then did Ygrayne let her ruined dress fall into a pool of fabric at her feet and begin the painful process of donning her new garments. The scratchiness of the fabric made her skin crawl with the sensation of foreign hands all over her body again. She could barely stomach it.

By the end of her ordeal, all she wanted to do was consign herself to her bed and rest. And she did so. Ygrayne curled up under the blankets and closed her eyes.

The rustling of the tent flap alerted Ygrayne to the return of the Schiva. As he had through most of their time together, he stayed silent. He only passed her a glance before he unpacked the rest of his belongings on the table.

He sat there for the remainder of the day and long into the night, the table barely illuminated by the orange gleam of a lantern as he went about organizing his supplies and tending to whatever it was which called for his attention in that moment. His overnight activities did nothing to disturb Ygrayne, as she was too fatigued to notice anything beyond the boundaries of her cot. But the soldiers gave no such mind to her peace.

The premises of the encampment came to life as night fell. The tent canvas itself glowed red from the various campfires surrounding them, the air filled with laughter and chatter. Armored footsteps passed by from time to time, echoing through the aisles of tents as though they were elongated hallways. If anything hurt more than Ygrayne's face, it was her head. Each intrusive vibration of sound had her gritting her teeth and groaning in pain. But she needed not utter a word before the Schiva set about curing what ailed her. He produced a jar from the assortment on the table, and she took without question the contents of the spoon he held to her lips. The bitter taste playing about her tongue caused her some slight regret, which showed vividly in her expression.

She heard the Schiva snort a bit, not at Ygrayne's expense, but because it was always the reaction he received from every recipient of the tonic.

"It's not the nicest-tasting medicine," he said regretfully. "But it will help with the pain."

"You came prepared," Ygrayne replied in a quiet, hoarse tone. "You carry this much with you always?"

"I do," the Schiva answered. "My specialty is medicinal practices. When I heard the Valeriaan army was on the march, I knew I was going to be needed."

Ygrayne fell silent. All the words the commander had spoken came back to her as a haunting reminder.

"They're going to attack Falkhearth." Those words were even more bitter than the medicine. "Aren't they?"

"Yes." He was just as frank. There was no remedy that could lessen the sting of such an answer.

"Why?"

"To kill Oathbound and destroy their stronghold."

Just as Urda said, Ygrayne thought to herself.

She still didn't want to believe it. She wanted the Schiva to disprove it all, to reinforce her own long-held assumption that there were indeed no Oathbound in Falkhearth. There was no stronghold. This was all for nothing.

Without another word, Ygrayne carefully turned on her side to face the tent, and the Schiva retreated to the table with the sound of the chair creaking under his weight.

"There have been no Oathbound in Falkhearth. They'll be killing innocent folk who have nothing to do with this war." Ygrayne knew she was just saying aloud what she wished were true. "I feel as though I would have heard of their presence."

"You haven't heard about them taking residence in Falkhearth because that is precisely what they wanted."

Ygrayne could find no words with which to respond.

"It is a myth that they tucked themselves away on the outskirts of Skana. Most often, they're right under our noses. Hiding in plain sight. I wouldn't be surprised if you have neighbors who are Oathbound." He kept his voice low so as not to draw attention from any wandering ears. "All of this means the Valeriaans were successful in finding one of those strongholds. A rather sizable one, from what I gather."

Just as she had expected—a confirmation of what she knew all along she would be unable to deny. It brought a silent tear to her eye, trailing down her cheek to the blankets beneath her.

"May I ask why you continue to deny it so?"

Ygrayne closed her eyes and took a deep breath. She could already feel the phlegm from her tears gathering at the back of her throat. She swallowed hard and replied, "I want nothing to do with this, well…if you could even call it a war."

Uttering the words made her feel ashamed of her stance. She hated the Valeriaans with a passion, just as any sensible folk in Skana did. Yet she found herself only on the fringes of the world they had created, a world born from fire and retribution.

Not once had she raised an effort to assist those who continued to fight and die for the freedom most saw as long burned away. Many were openly apathetic to the cause, having accepted its futility. Others chose to act as though the conflict did not exist at all. But regardless of any given individual's opinion, innocent folk still found themselves at odds with the Empire, often resulting in needless loss of life.

"Many folk don't. None of you can be blamed."

It was some relief to hear it spoken from his lips, the validation that her bitterness toward the whole conflict was justified, commendable even.

"My husband may not come out of Falkhearth alive. The same may be said for your brethren because of all this." Ygrayne thought she would feel an overwhelming sense of sadness at the very thought, and perhaps at one time she would have. Now she just felt leaden, almost numb to the revelation. She opened her eyes to release the tears she could no longer keep at bay. "May I ask you something?"

"Of course," the Schiva replied.

"Why is it that you Schivas do nothing?"

Ygrayne knew why. Everyone was aware of the Schivas' oath to maintain a pacifist lifestyle. Never in their history had they risen up in the face of the corrupt and tyrannical empires of olden ages. They had continued going about their good deeds while the world burned around them, just as they did now. And yet, it was still believed they possessed the resources and influence to turn the tides of any conflict should they choose to no longer remain passive.

The Schiva folded his hands in his lap and replied, "Because we are a brotherhood, not an army. We are conduits of knowledge, not perpetrators of war. Our duty to Skana is to help all those we can with the resources we have—to teach, to aid, to guide. We do not concern ourselves with governments, imperial affairs of grandeur. We leave that up to the natural change and balance of the forces guiding the constant turning of tides in the world."

Ygrayne once again found a companion in silence. She couldn't think of an adequate response.

"I know such an explanation is hardly sufficient," the Schiva noted. "It's not the answer anyone wants. But I can promise you this." The Schiva gazed at the lantern, at the flickering flames confined behind glass and iron, the chair creaking as he shifted his weight. "History consistently shows us that empires are finite. They cannot withstand the test of time. The world has seen the dawn of the Valeriaan reign, and it will one day witness its bitter end all the same."

"How long before that happens? How many more folk must suffer and die before that end?"

"I guess it depends on the forces at hand, and the folk behind it."

"That's not very comforting."

"The truth most often isn't."

The Schiva stayed awake most of the night, watching with great care and vigilance over the battered young mother—one of many who had, over the course of history, found themselves in such a dire situation, but amongst the few who survived the ordeal. She was as dormant and lifeless as the dead, having finally succumbed to pure exhaustion with the assistance of the medicine he had given her.

Come the next morning, the camp began to stir early with customary routines. Soldiers cast their shadowed specters across the fabric of their tent, their armor clanking, boots stomping the ground. But there was something erratic in their behavior, hectic even. The atmosphere in the camp didn't spell an ordinary morning—something was happening, amiss. Ygrayne still hadn't stirred with the commotion about them, and the Schiva concluded that she would be safe within the confines of the tent while he went to investigate what exactly was happening. No man there would dare place a hand on her now. He quietly slipped out of the tent and was met with the sight of fully armored soldiers trudging with their weapons at their waists, banners flying high on their staffs, and horses clad in battle attire.

They marched in an organized formation down the road: a long line of pairs walking shoulder to shoulder, the mounted cavalry breaking the pattern at several points. Their faces were stoic, their erect posture honed by years of training, mimicking the stillness of statues. Just from that sight alone, the Schiva knew what was transpiring—they were preparing to march to Falkhearth.

The Schiva's heart sank. He hadn't predicted that their plans would be put in motion so soon. He dropped his gaze in contemplation, thinking of the inhabitants of Falkhearth and his brethren who were about to endure an unstoppable onslaught. If anyone survived, it would be either the result of the Empire's indifference to their existence, or a sheer miracle. The Schiva shook his head, his eyes blinking rapidly in disbelief, his thoughts continuing to wander until suddenly he felt a presence approaching, a most unwelcome one.

"The time has come," the commander announced, pride ringing in his voice. "I can't tell you how long I've been waiting for this to happen."

The fully armored leader of the regiment stopped beside the Schiva with a clinking of metal, one hand firmly upon his sword hilt while the other held his helmet in the crook of his arm. The Schiva merely folded his hands before him in his robe's gaping sleeves. He took a moment to regain his composure, to hide the distress that would have otherwise resonated in his tone. At least he could withhold that satisfaction from the commander.

"A little sooner than expected," the Schiva stated nonchalantly.

"You Schivas, of all folk, should know how fickle war can be. Unpredictable. Ever changing. We must be on our toes."

The commander hoped for a response, but the Schiva remained silent, quietly observing all of which was unfolding before him, surmising what was about to take place.

The commander shrugged, dismissing his failed attempt at baiting, and tried a different tack. "How is the woman?"

The Schiva was surprised to hear the question, but deduced it was merely for the commander's own benefit. He would keep his word if it meant his praises would be whispered in his cousin's ear.

"She is resting. Will be for a while." The Schiva's answer was curt.

The commander let out a satisfied hum. "And you, Schiva?"

"I am well. Thank you, Commander. How kind of you to ask."

The two stood in the mounting tension, their silence frigid as waves of glinting silver passed before them, the barking of orders echoing in their ears and the horses crying out in anticipation. Then, the commander turned to the Schiva and said, "Walk with me."

He proceeded forward before the Schiva could even respond or nod in acknowledgement. He simply followed until they were walking shoulder to shoulder, skirting the readying forces who paid them no mind as they carried out their duties. They marched the length of the line in the finishing stages of gathering, a purposeful trek to boast the might and standing of the commander's forces.

"I wish we had met under different circumstances," the commander said in a genuine tone that took the Schiva by surprise. "I would've loved to have a drink and trade stories with you. I hear your kind is rich in the knowledge of tales of old."

"Circumstances be what they are, Commander," the Schiva responded, "I would've enjoyed hearing your own tales. I'm certain they are rich as well, given your career's many war endeavors, trysts and…let's just say, frisks, perhaps?"

The commander couldn't help but let out an amused laugh. "You have a spirit that burns akin to the fire within your eyes. I must say, I prefer you so. It's what I hear most about you."

The commander fitted his helmet to his head before he continued, "I thought you were going to be frigid the entire morning. Would've been such a shame to leave on such a bitter note, wouldn't you agree?"

"Truly unfortunate." It was a snarky response, but it was what the commander was beginning to appreciate about the Schiva. He had grown bored of the rather subdued and well-mannered behavior of the members of the Brotherhood. It was a nice change to encounter one with such wit.

"Perhaps we can meet for drinks when the battle is over? To celebrate our victory, of course." The commander turned to the Schiva, and the two stood before one another. "Though I must warn you. Us Valeriaans do much more than drink when we celebrate."

"I'm sorry to inform you that I must decline your offer for two reasons," the Schiva huffed. "One, on principle, and two, I'll be busy cleaning up your mess. My sincerest apologies."

The commander was most amused by the answer, knowing full well the rumors that this particular Schiva did not adhere completely to the stringent oaths that had been proclaimed upon the Brotherhood's founding. It was suspected that he had a habit of delving into that which was forbidden to them in secrecy. The Schiva standing before him was already testing the Brotherhood's norms and expectations just by mere association with the aforementioned cousin.

"If you proclaim so, Schiva."

Through a narrowed gaze, the Schiva watched as the commander mounted his armor-adorned stallion standing between two attending bannermen, their flags waving high above, whipping in the wind. Once he situated himself comfortably in the saddle, reins in his hands, did the commander peer down at the Schiva and say, "You are still my guests in my absence. I have arranged for a group of my men to stay behind and tend to you and that woman, should you require anything."

"And when will we be permitted to leave?"

"When the catapults have stilled and the cries have quieted." A toothy grin spread across his face. "I'll be certain to send a messenger your way to confirm your release. Until then, have a pleasant stay, Schiva."

The commander flicked the reins and the horse started into a walk, a powerful and commanding stride which displayed the might of the beast carrying such armor with evident ease. The bannermen kept pace at the commander's sides, and the line of soldiers behind them followed ever so loyally, a show of their rigorous training. Their organization was both fearsome and enviable—arms moving in unison, boots hitting the ground with a beat which meshed seamlessly. The line of gleaming armor almost seemed endless, spanning across the plains, leaving trampled fields in their wake where their heavy footfalls pressed the grass into the mud at its roots.

For a time, the collective march and the sound of armor shifting interlaced together in an echo across the land, making it quiver with anticipation of what was to soon unfold. When the river of silver dwindled to a trickle and the last of the soldiers marched past, the fading of the echo provided only a modicum of relief. The river appeared to be swallowed by the horizon as it disappeared in the distance.

Only then did it grow quiet. Even the few soldiers who remained at the camp didn't make a sound, stunned into silence by the display that had deafened the ears and overwhelmed the senses. The atmosphere left in the army's wake was thick and heavy, the pressure of everything happening and still to happen lingering in the air.

The Schiva looked about the path forged by readied soldiers as the warm winds brushed past him, his waving robes mimicking the graceful movement of an ebbing tide. He took a deep and sorrowful breath in a preliminary bout of mourning for the wave of death about to crash. It wasn't just the folk for whom he felt, but for his brothers and sisters seeking only to bring some semblance of hope and goodwill to those who needed it most—brothers and sisters he had known for many, many years. When the time came to rummage through the carnage of what would be left of Falkhearth, would he find their bodies amongst the dead?

CHAPTER 15

Artur looked out through his window to the night sky above, his eyes growing heavier, a full stomach lulling him to calmness and contentment. The Nerúnors above were a soft-flowing lullaby stretching across the sky, the waves moving about in serpentine patterns. His mother wasn't there that night, and had it not been for Urda's comforting presence down below, he never would have been able to sleep for thinking of her. It was hard enough coming to terms with his father's ongoing absence, but he had hardly expected to experience any child's worst nightmare.

The soft glow of a candle drew his eyes to the figure climbing up the ladder and creeping quietly over to his bedside. She was unmistakable, if not by the distinct silhouette, then by the way the flames glinted on the waves of fiery red hair. Urda placed the candle on his nightstand with a gentle tap, the shimmer of light illuminating the features of both their faces. Artur gazed at the qualities of her countenance in an almost intimate manner, as if it were the first time he had ever seen her. Never before had he taken the time to commit her face to memory. Now that she was kneeling at his bedside, in the silence and permissiveness of the night, he was able to realize how beautiful she truly was. The creamy tint of her smooth skin drew attention to her full red lips, button nose, and sun-spotted cheeks. The green eyes under dark brows. It was fascinating how her red hair cascaded about her face, appearing untamed and purposeful at the same time. Gazing into her emerald eyes, all Artur felt was comfort and a vibrant burst of life. A friendliness. A companionship he felt he lacked.

He could see why someone would admire her. His mother only ever spoke well of her, commenting on her abilities with reverence and her nature with affection, and after sharing such a hospitable night, he couldn't help but agree. Even Ronan and Kian admired her, albeit for...other reasons. On many a day he had caught them both gazing at her bosoms when she was seemingly unaware of their gawking, and before her attention could transfer to them, they skidded off in giddy delight for having gotten away with their shenanigans. Artur himself could not deny that he himself had let his gaze linger a time or two, but how Ronan and Kian were able to keep their eyes in such an area for so long, he still did not understand. He would only get a glimpse in before he felt ashamed and dropped his gaze with a heated face, a deep red he feared would absolutely give him away. And if his mother ever caught him, all the forces in the world would not protect him from her wrath or spare him the humiliating apology he would no doubt have to give Urda.

There was no such temptation that night. All he could see was who Urda was. Who his mother saw. Behind the beauty and admirable assets which made up her figure, she was a kind and generous woman who had no qualms about caring for him in his parents' absence. Still, nothing compared to his Lovisa. There was no woman, or girl, who could compare to her beauty. But that was a thought for another time.

In that moment, Artur thought of his mother. How she had left without saying a word to him. How he had come home to find the cottage quiet and empty. He even preferred the awkwardness of their supper to the heavy air of her absence. Had it not been for Urda, he would have felt completely lost.

"When do you think Mama will come home?" he asked.

Urda smiled gently and replied, "I wish I could answer thon. I don't know whan she or yer father will be back."

Artur nodded. It pained him to think even Urda could not enlighten him so.

"She's been acting odd lately. I think there's something wrong, and she's not telling me what it is."

Urda folded her arms on his mattress and rested her chin in the crook of her elbow.

"Why dae ye think she's actin' odd?"

"Probably because Papa has been gone a long time." Artur let out a long sigh.

"Has she told ye why yer father hasn't come home?"

"No." Artur shook his head. "Maybe it has something to do with the caravan I saw a couple days ago. Ever since I told her about them…" He paused a moment and said, "Maybe I shouldn't have." Artur dropped his eyes a moment and thought about it, the distinct shift in her demeanor once the word "caravan" had escaped his lips.

"I wish she would tell me more things. She says I'm too young to know what's going on but…I'm twelve years old now. I'm not a kid anymore. Why am I not allowed to know things?"

Urda found his disgruntlement amusing, but she answered before a chortle could escape. "You're growin' intae a big lad. However, thare are still many things ye are no ready for."

"I am ready to know whatever it is that's going on!" Artur scowled at her.

Urda propped her chin on her hands and looked at him with a tilt of her head.

"I think if she found oot I telt ye anything, she micht no' trust me tae care for ye anymore."

Artur beamed at her with hopeful eyes, mirroring her posture.

"I promise I won't tell her! I want to know what's going on. Please! Please! Please!"

"Artur—"

"I just want someone to tell me. I'm tired of not knowing anything!"

"Honestly, aw I wanted tae dae wis tell ye goodnicht before goin' home." Urda let out a breathy chortle. "This story micht keep ye up tonicht."

Artur sat up in his bed, legs crossed, and beseeched her once more, "Please, Urda. I won't tell Mama. Please tell me what's going on."

Hou persistent ye are, Urda thought to herself.

Everything was telling her not to. It could be a betrayal of the trust of her dearest friend. Then again, the rush of defiance was running through her veins, and she knew she could trust Artur not to speak a word of their forbidden conversation.

She smiled and, akin to a child herself, hopped onto his bed and copied Artur's stance. He couldn't help but let out a laugh when the bounce of his cot made him tip over slightly.

"In order for ye tae understand what's gaeng on, I need tae gae back a long time ago. Ye certain ye can handle thon?" she asked, touching her finger to the tip his nose.

"Urda, if I can survive my mother's lectures, I can survive anything."

"Fair enouch, lad," Urda couldn't hold back the chortle this time. Then the lightheartedness seeped out of the conversation, and the anticipation of the story she was about to tell set in. She took a slow, deep breath to calm her excited nerves.

The mood about them became suddenly somber. Artur could feel it—the warmth descending ever so slightly, the light growing dimmer. It was almost frightening.

But Artur wouldn't—couldn't—withdraw from the opportunity now. He was so close to receiving the answers he had been seeking for what seemed akin to an eternity. Without even noticing, he grabbed his pillow and held it close to his chest. He was ready to listen, ready to bear it.

"It aw startit two hundrit years ago in the ninth age," Urda began, looking to him, her green eyes seeming to glow in the flickering light.

Artur hugged his pillow tighter with growing anxiousness, anticipation. The story had hardly begun and he was already instinctively reaching for comfort.

"Clans were beginnin' tae take up allegiances after the last empire fell in the seventh age, with two prominent sides forming: the Valeriaans an' the Lodbróks. Skana soon found herself in the very grips of a terrible war, fueled by ancient grudges an' resentment. It wis a long an' terrible conflict, aye it wis. An' whan the war eventually came tae an end…let's juist say, the Valeriaans were the side the folk didn't want tae prevail. They aw paid the price. Valeriaans an' her allies slauchtered aw those who sidit wi' the Lodbróks. No' a soul wis sparit. Whan the bloodshed finally came tae an end wis Skana herself set afire. Her lands an' folks alike were cast tae the cruel flames in whit wis then called the Black Dawn. It is said the fires burnit sae bricht thon the nicht never came, an' the day refusit tae break. In the tales wis it telt thon Skana herself wept in despair at such a sicht. Wept for aw her folk. Towns, cities, villages—gone. Expanses of soot an' cinder. Livelihoods completely uprootit."

Urda paused a moment to gauge Artur's reaction. The boy was terrified, evident in the way he was clutching the pillow, his hands gripping at the fabric with trembling tension. But it was what he wanted—the truth, after all.

Unakin to Ygrayne, Urda was not averse to speaking the truth when asked, no matter the recipient.

"Ye have been coddled, Artur. Yer mother an' father did a great deal tae protect ye. At least, for as long as they could. Beyond our borders ye won't find the haven thon is our village. We are fortunate tae live the life we dae—away from the ensuin' conflict. We're able tae rely on Skana an' aw she has tae offer. Others, the majority o' thaim, are no' sae fortunate, an suffer to this day. Yer mother had the best of intentions. But I fear very soon ye won't have a choice but tae see it for yourself. Thae soldiers who passed by here a couple days ago—they're no' here by coincidence. Ye will see firsthand, whit the Empire is."

Artur had sunk his chin into his pillow, the look of horror plain on his face. Urda looked at him with concern and said, "It got a little bit dark i' the end, didn't it?"

"At the end?" Artur let out an exasperated sigh. "The whole thing!" he exclaimed, his pillow collapsing into his lap as his arms extended into the air. "I-I didn't know about any of this! The war…the-the…Empire! The Black Dawn! What even is going to happen?"

"Ever since the Valeriaans won the war, thare has been an ongoin' rebellion. Folk wha' continue fightin' against thaim." Urda gently caught Artur's wrists and lowered his arms back to his sides. "Oathbound, they call themselves. An' there has been talk that they found an Oathbound stronchold in Falkhearth."

Artur paused, his voice catching in his throat. A small gasp escaped parted lips, his expression growing solemn.

"That's why Papa hasn't come home..." His voice was quiet. "Isn't it?"

"That's richt." Urda nodded, her brow twitching in the sorrow of such a revelation. "They haven't let anyone else oot of Falkhearth in case they're part o' the rebellion."

Artur dropped his gaze into the unseeable void before him, and a quiet whisper escaped his lips. "Is he an Oathbound?"

"I don't know," Urda answered honestly.

"Is Papa...going to die?"

"I don't know, Artur. Na one knows what's aboot tae happen." There was no sense in evading veracity, even if it saddened her to answer so.

"Will they come here—the soldiers?" Artur looked back to her.

"If they believe they have a reason tae, they will." Urda sighed again. "But na one here has given thaim a reason. We should be safe."

"If they do come..." Artur hesitated a moment, his voice trembling. "W-will...I die?"

Urda narrowed her eyes. "No," she stated bluntly. "I made an oath tae yer mother I wouldn't let anythin' happen tae ye, an' I always keep ma oaths. Me an' Vána will protect ye."

Artur grew silent, pondering, deliberating, turning over all the information he had been given. And when he finished dwelling in that silence, did he whisper, "I don't know what else to ask."

"Ye don't need tae ask any more questions tonicht." Urda placed her hand on his shoulder. "But if ye ever have any, dae no' hesitate tae ask me."

Artur nodded solemnly.

"Will ye be able tae sleep tonicht?"

Now that the tale was told, Urda did feel guilty. What young mind would be able to sleep after realizing the world he thought he knew wasn't real, and the truth offered no consolation? The threat of impending bereavement, the uncertainty of the future, the safety of childish naïveté shattered—it was a lot for one to bear.

"Yes," Artur whispered. The shortness of his response was a sign he was ready to end the conversation. Urda nodded, removing her hand from his shoulder.

"Well, me an' Vána will be downstairs if ye neit anythin'."

She decided it was best to stay should he be so wrestles.

"All right," Artur replied simply.

Urda slid off the bed, as Artur got himself as comfortable as possible under his blankets in silence. Once he settled, he said in a quiet voice, "Goodnight, Urda." She grabbed the candle from his nightstand, and said as softly as she could, "Goodnicht, Artur."

He didn't look at her. He diverted his gaze to the window, hoping that he could find solace once again amongst the Nerúnors still gleaming above. Hoping that they would lull him to sleep as they so regularly did.

Urda pursed her lips. She truly did feel guilty. Her affinity for storytelling often swayed her into the dramatic, the passionate. Not even the morbidity of the tale for the evening had tempered her flair. She looked down, disappointed in herself, and when she looked to Artur once more, she said in all sincerity, "Don't worry tae much, Artur."

He still did not look to her.

"A lot of thae events happened a very long time ago, an' I believe if yer mother has anythin' tae say aboot it, she'll be back wi' yer father soon enouch."

She managed to coax a small nod out of Artur, but there would be nothing more for the night.

He listened to her footsteps descend the ladder, the touch of light on his loft slowly dimming until it disappeared completely down below. He could hear Vána let out a concerned whine, and he felt his chest clench in response—her pain his, as his was hers. He knew she felt the turmoil dwelling within him. Had she the physical capability to do so, she'd join him at his bedside for the night.

Footsteps echoed dully about the main quarters until there came the low groan of his parents' bed shifting under Urda's weight and the brief light pattering of Vána's paws against the wood-paneled floor as the dire wolf took her spot beside the bed. Once Urda's soft breath extinguished the flame, the house grew silent. Hauntingly quiet. Still, the knowledge that he would not pass the night alone gave him some small measure of relief.

Artur was wide awake, the story fresh within his thoughts, his imagination left to wander and envision the war Urda spoke of. Artur could hardly conceive of it. He had never seen a battle, let alone a conflict that lasted countless years and laid entire villages to waste. There was but one other thought which truly terrified him more than the prospect of war: his mother and father never returning home. They too could be caught up in whatever turmoil was to ensue.

And Lovisa…maybe she didn't know what war was either. Artur could feel a deep pain in his chest from the contemplation. He closed his eyes tight to keep the tears from falling down his face. For the first time in his life, he felt hopeless.

"Papa…Mama," he whispered to himself, stifling the sniffles building in his nostrils. "Lovisa." The name escaped his tongue unexpectedly, but it was true. He had only known her for a short time but the fondness he had for her was undeniable, even if he didn't fully comprehend what it all meant.

The wind howled suddenly, a piercing sound akin to the dire wolves of old. It battered at his window, the unexpectedness spooking him exceedingly. A gasp escaped his lips, the heat from his chest suddenly rushing to his face. The cottage itself trembled around him, easily set to quivering by even the gentlest breath of nature. In a moment of panic, Artur quickly closed his window and pulled his blankets so tight around him that it seemed he would never be able to unwind from their clutches.

The wind howled and howled that night, demanding the mountains bow before its ferocity and the clouds flee across the skies. It stirred uneasiness across the otherwise smooth surface of flowing waters. As the grasses danced wildly, and the trees hissed in unison, their branches creaking and leaves rattling, even those who reveled in the night they claimed as their domain took refuge wherever they could find it. The only entities that proved not to be dissuaded by the presence of the wind were the reoccurring Nerúnors bursting across the night sky. The shifting waves of light seemed to sway and curl with the direction of the winds as if they had made a cordial pact. An unnamable and ominous presence floated about, as if the phantoms of the past were answering a summons, their tales once again spoken on the tongues of their descendants.

Their manifestation made the land tremble with the threat of misfortune to come. Something terrifying was brewing—terrifying and great. Skana herself was preparing, for the land had seen tragedy before and recognized the signs of events soon to repeat.

CHAPTER 16

It was a ruthless night. Every bump and noise caused by the wind scared Artur wide awake. No matter how far he drifted into the depths of sleep, did he still wake at the faintest of disturbances. He felt as though at any moment a Valeriaan soldier would burst through his door and burn down the place he called home. He feared the flames would consume him as he slumbered, none the wiser to his own demise. Would he feel the pain? The burning of his flesh? The sting in his lungs from the poisonous smoke?

Morning brought little relief. The fatigue from the night prior left its mark on him. Not even the smell of breakfast put his mind at ease. When Urda announced the time to eat, Artur hesitated to leave his loft. The cot provided some comfort, however little it was. Yet with enough coaxing, Artur finally mustered up the effort to go down to the table to eat. The whole time he was silent, barely picking at his food when he normally would be scarfing it down as fast as he could to go outside and play with his friends.

Urda looked at him sympathetically from across the table, marking the bags under his eyes, the paleness of his skin, the wilting posture.

"I knew I shouldn't have telt ye thon story." Urda let out a sigh, propping her chin atop a closed fist.

"I'm fine" were the first words Artur finally muttered with a deep long breath. "It was just…really windy last night."

Urda hardly accepted such a fib, but she let it go for the sake of his pride.

"It wis rather windy, wasn't it?" she said after taking a bite. "Oddly strange given the time o' the year. I only woke up a couple times durin' the nicht myself."

"Even you had trouble?" Artur looked to her with a start.

"Yes." Urda nodded to him as she gave Vána a piece of bread. "Unusual weather is aw." Artur looked at her a moment. What he didn't say was how it wasn't just the unrelenting wind which kept him up all night. Artur knew, and Urda did as well, that the story of the war had brought about haunting thoughts to plague his mind and leave him to ruminate on a concept he was still trying to grasp and understand.

He looked to Urda, her expression undecipherable as she too gazed at him, and he gently pushed his plate away from him and said quietly, "Can I ask you something?"

"Of course." Urda tilted her head, her lips moving subtly as she chewed.

"How is it you're able to sleep knowing those things happened? Knowing…t-that they still happen?" It almost pained him to stay it out loud, and he fought to keep from folding in on himself.

Urda looked away for a moment to ponder her thoughts, to choose her next words carefully to spare him any more grief. When she came to a reasonable conclusion, she looked back to Artur and said, "I think it's juist somethin' ye come tae accept as a part o' life. A part o' the world. It doesn't dae ye any guid cowerin' in fear. Ye live yer life as best ye can wi' the hand you've been dealt. Ye don't have tae like what's going on, an' ye can disagree wi' it aw ye want. Either ye dae somethin' aboot it, or ye keep on livin'. There's na shame in the course ye take regardless."

Artur simply stared at her. He wasn't expecting such a deep answer, especially when he was still wrestling with everything from the night before.

"I'm just…supposed to live my life? How is that even supposed to help me?" He hardly masked the annoyance in his voice, unsatisfied with her response.

"I think you'll understand whan you're older." Her lips turned up in a corner.

Artur gawked at her. "When I'm older? I want to know now! Everything you told me last night, I'm just supposed to accept it? What…why? I could die! My parents could die! How can I just keep on living when the world around me sounds akin to a great pile of shit?"

Urda kept silent, calm, while she let him rant and rave, hardly flinching at his sudden outburst. She stifled her smile. Hearing the young boy curse was amusing, given that Ygrayne would have never tolerated such foul language.

"Exactly as everyone else has," she responded calmly. "I've done ye a favor, Artur. As I says, ye don't have tae like it. Hardly a time anyone daes. But don't let it stop ye from livin' yer life. Ye were gaun'ae find out one day. Better ye found out sooner than later. Tak' some time tae think aboot it, come tae terms wi' it. Then, if ye want tae talk further, we can."

Artur glared at her for a moment. As much as he wanted to go on whining, he had to concede that he had gotten exactly what he asked for, and he couldn't fault Urda for that. She had been the only one willing to indulge him. For that, he was thankful. Now he realized, however, it was a lot more than he bargained for. It was best he give up on the conversation, throwing his arms up into the air and retreating from the table. As he climbed up his ladder, he called down to Urda, "I don't know what's more frustrating: my mom not telling me anything, or you telling me too much!"

Urda was further amused, unfazed by the verbal frustrations thrown her way. She merely pet Vána atop her head nonchalantly, the beast calmly sitting at her side listening to the entire conversation as if she too were a part of it. They both could hear Artur rummaging upstairs, dressing himself and murmuring more frustrations under his breath. When Artur came back down, he looked to Urda and said, "I'm going fishing. Thank you for making breakfast."

The words were forced, but the politeness his mother had instilled in him ran too deep to be forgotten even in his distress.

"You enjoy yourself then. Ye know where tae find me if ye neit anythin'." Urda winked at Artur as he left out the back door in quite a hurry. She removed herself from the table and peered out the kitchen window to see him scurrying down the path and out of sight. She smiled, touching her finger to her chin.

"Fishin', he says." She looked down to Vána, who returned her gaze. "He's going fishin'. Dae ye believe thon, Vána?"

Vána merely snorted.

Trudging down the well-worn path, Artur was still heated from the exchange over breakfast. He sulked, blood rushing to his ears and flushing his cheeks. It was more than just Urda's story last night and their morning conversation which truly frustrated him. It was the lack of understanding, the impossibility of grasping the revelation of the world around him. He'd been offered a partial history that lacked complete context, and until that moment the true state of the world had been purposely kept from him, sheltered as he was in the confines of a village he saw as nothing but peaceful and perfect. The entire illusion had been shattered to pieces in a moment, the falsities and lies in shards about him.

Before he knew it, Artur found himself at the riverbank, nearly tripping down the drop-off where the path ended and the sand began. It was only then he heard the river, the soft coos of the birds about the trees, felt the touch of the sun. The awareness of his surroundings filtered in through the haze of anger, his body no longer relying upon its familiarity with the environment to guide him of its own accord. Artur looked about the river excitedly in search of the face he most hoped to see. Of course, there was no sign of her.

Disappointedly, his eyes drifted to his feet with a heavy sigh, and then something peculiar caught his attention. Right beside his own foot he saw a footprint pressed into the sand, one much too small to be his own—never mind that it was pointing in the opposite direction from the one he'd taken himself. There was a trail of prints, emerging from across the riverbank, originating from the rocks bridging the two shorelines. Artur was struck by how distinct they were—pointed toes and a pronounced heel of a boot. Before he had a chance to investigate further, what could only be described as a prepubescent attempt at a war cry rang out from the heavens and a blur of a figure sprang from the tree branches above, tackling him into the sand. The breath whistled from his lungs upon the impact of the weight now shifting atop him, and he barely grasped what just transpired before another shriek rang through his ears. "Ha! I got you!"

It was Lovisa, cheering loudly into his ear, and the next thing he knew her figure was standing over him in a triumphant pose, silhouetted with a ring of light from the sun.

Though stunned at first, Artur found himself admiring how divine she looked basking in the sunlight. He couldn't help but laugh, out of both embarrassment and happiness. She was there—just as he had hoped.

"Do you know how long I was up there waiting for you?" She placed her hands on her hips in a show of indignance. "Lucky for you, I'm quite patient."

"Says the girl not patient enough to fish." Artur scoffed at her once the breath returned to his lungs. He stood, brushing the sand from his clothes.

"Maybe at first," she huffed. "But! Then I did wait patiently, and I caught a fish bigger than anything you've caught before, eh?" She prodded his chest with her finger, proud of her little jest. Artur arched a brow at her. Fighting a smile, he retorted, "How long did it take you to come up with that?"

"I thought of it right on the spot! I'm so clever, aren't I?"

Artur shook his head, his gaze dropping to the sands as the corners of his mouth fell. She was full of excitement and energy while he could hardly force a laugh. If only she had been as amiable those first couple days as she was now. Lovisa too noticed the shift in both of their demeanors. She'd half-expected him to retaliate in some playful manner, and now she found herself rather disappointed. She studied his cast-down face and noticed how tired and unkempt he looked, hardly the boy she remembered from the previous days.

She titled her head to the side and asked, "What's the matter? You look… horrid."

It startled him that she noticed. He hardly wanted her to worry, lest it put a damper on their time together. So he shrugged and indifferently replied, "I didn't sleep well last night. I'm a little tired, is all."

It wasn't a lie, but he didn't know how to tell her the whole truth. How would she react to everything he had learned just the night prior, when he was still trying to understand it himself?

"Awe, what's the matter? Did you have a big scawy dweam?" Lovisa mocked him with a squeal in her voice, her arms pressed against her chest as she faked a shiver.

Artur was used to her taunting, only rolling his eyes and responding, "No. I just didn't sleep. It was windy last night."

"You felt it too?" Lovisa's eyes widened, a gasp escaping her lips.

"Well, yes." Artur was taken aback. "It was very strong and loud. Who wouldn't have felt it?"

Lovisa paused a moment, unable to find the words to answer. Instead, she scratched at her chin in a deep moment of pondering, turning her back to Artur.

"What's wrong?" Artur stepped towards her, reaching for her shoulder before she faced him once more and said, "You're the only one who seems to know about the wind. No one else I asked did. Why do you think that is?"

"I don't know." Artur found it peculiar. He'd felt the unbridled might of nature, and Urda herself even commented on it. Why would it be that no one else could?

"It's odd, that's what it be. Your land is very strange, and different. I don't know how you stand it here." Lovisa flicked Artur's nose and darted away. Artur flinched.

"Regardless of whatever happened last night, I thought we could do something that's actually fun today."

"What?" His voice was muffled as he pressed his hand to his nose. "You didn't enjoy fishing yesterday?"

He spun on his heels to watch her walk about the river's edge, inching closer and closer to the makeshift bridge of rocks across the body of water.

"'Twas fine…I guess." Lovisa shrugged her shoulders. "But now, I'm going to show you what I like to do."

She twirled gracefully to face him, hands clasped behind her. There was a smirk about her lips, a rather devious one at that. It made Artur equal parts excited and nervous.

"But," she added, wagging her finger. She was up to something, and judging by her current course of movement, it no doubt had to do with the forbidden bridge.

"If you want to come with me, you'll have to cross the river."

His heart sank into his stomach with a jolt of queasiness.

"B-but…" He could hardly speak.

"But! But!" Lovisa mocked him once more, leaning towards him at the waist. "No buts! You come or you don't. I'm not going to hold your hand!"

Artur didn't appreciate being openly ridiculed, but Vallar's wrath come for him if he told her the real reason he wouldn't cross the trail of rocks that spanned the river. The feeling of dread overcame him. The battle of desires and good judgment waged in his mind. Of course, he wanted to accompany her, to have a glimpse of the life she lived, even if it was for but a moment.

"Never cross the river, it is forbidden." As always, his parents' warnings came to mind from the mere pondering of it. Artur had to look away from Lovisa to hide the guilt and shame he was feeling for even considering disobeying his parents.

"Come on, Artur! I'm not going to wait here forever."

Still, he hardly budged.

Lovisa rolled her eyes and strode over to him before he had a chance to make up his mind. She grasped at his hand and pulled him along, rendering Artur unable to protest, overcome with shock and seemingly losing all control of his own physical functions. All that came to Artur's mind now was how warm and soft Lovisa's hand was. He had never touched a girl's hand before, let alone held one. He thought maybe they would be as rough as his, but hers were anything but. The delicate skin of her palms had never seen the labor of household chores nor the roughness of the wilderness. The skin felt almost perfect in comparison to his worn and callused fingers.

Artur was so entranced that he hardly noticed they'd already reached the first boulder until Lovisa chimed, "Ready?"

Artur blinked, the river and the path laid before him once more coming into focus. He was mortified at how close he was, after never once breaching the invisible barrier he had set for himself in his mind. He shook his head vehemently in protest, lightly resisting Lovisa's grip on him.

"Come now, Artur! It's easy," Lovisa protested in return, trying to pull him closer to the water's edge.

"I can't, Lovisa."

"Yes, you can."

"No, I really can't."

"Yes! You can!"

"No, you don't understand—"

Lovisa rolled her eyes once more with an irritated sigh and quickly interrupted him, "Yes, you can, and you will! I demand it!"

"You can't demand anything of me, you damn brat." Artur narrowed his eyes.

Lovisa let out a whine, stomping her feet against the rock and pleading, "Please, Artur? Please come with me!"

It was the first time she'd ever sounded sincere when saying the word, and the very melody of her voice nearly made him melt, his cheeks flushing red with heat. He couldn't possibly say no when she asked him in such a way.

With each passing moment his parents' warnings grew less fruitful against the overwhelming desire to please the girl before him, their words in his mind sounding fainter and fainter as if carried away by the wind itself. A mere echo. The desire to please her and to satisfy his own curiosity had grown strong as the flames in a hearth. The other side of the river was an entire mystery, a whole other world that was begging to be explored with the girl he held in such high regard.

The restraint and will that had once held him back relinquished their grip on him, and soon Artur found himself crossing that forbidden bridge, rock by rock, step by step, hand in hand. If Lovisa said anything to him in that moment, he didn't hear—too preoccupied he was with the roaring river licking at his feet, spraying his legs with a cool and refreshing mist, revealing a whole world of colors of rocks and sand akin to a mirage beneath the surface. The moment his feet touched the adjacent riverbank was as though he had stepped into a different world—the feeling, the sounds, the smells, even the way the sun touched him seemed so new and foreign. The way the trees contoured, the shrubbery about the forest floor, the colors making up the palette of an environment soon to be explored. It was beautiful in a haunting way—enticing and terrifying.

"That wasn't so hard now, was it?" Lovisa teased him.

"I guess not," Artur answered with arrested awareness, looking high above him and admiring how the sun shone through the leaves of the trees.

"Well, now that you're over here, are you ready to see the surprise?"

Artur looked to Lovisa then. Even through the shading of the trees did he see the glimmer in her eyes, the excitement welling up inside, the same she'd had when she caught her first fish.

"Yes, show me!" The smile on his face was genuine.

The rest of the way was traveled in silence. Their hands hadn't parted since they first came together, each of them finding a sense of comfort in the gentle touch and intertwining of their fingers, in the way their palms fit together. The sun-warmed sands turned into a serpentine trail which maneuvered carefully through the forest, concocted to follow the curvature of the forest floor. The rush of the river gave way to the subdued sound of the wind through the trees, the mysterious fauna all around them chirping and cooing away, not concerning themselves with the presence of folk. The two companions hadn't traveled far before the narrow trail became a defined path where the sunlight warmed the colors of the clearing into lively, glowing hues.

What completed the beauty of the scene was the stunning white horse standing on the trail, adorned with a golden-brown bridle and saddle with a long and shining white mane cascading over its neck. Artur couldn't help but gape at the beast standing there majestically, patiently. The stallion seemed born of elegance and grace, almost mystical in the way it captured the essence about them.

"Ama-zing," Artur gasped in awe.

"He's beautiful, isn't he? And he's all mine," Lovisa boasted proudly.

"He really is… What's his name?"

"Thyraen. I've been raising him since he was a foal." Lovisa patted his firm breast and the stallion let out a snort in acknowledgement, his head rocking as if nodding in approval.

"That's incredible." Artur stayed cautiously behind her. "Our village only has a few horses, even a white one akin to your horse. But I've never ridden one before."

Artur reached out and touched Thyraen's shoulder, finding himself pleasantly surprised at how soft and clean the coat was, gleaming akin to a pearl. Even the gem itself would be envious.

"You've never ridden a horse before?" Lovisa was genuinely shocked by the revelation. "I thought all the commonfolk knew how to ride horses. Everyone I know certainly can."

"All the adults ride them and use them for labor in the village. I've never been given the chance to. My family doesn't own one. I'm poor, remember?" Artur rolled his eyes with a click of his tongue. He still didn't truly know what that meant, but he could throw her words back in her face at the very least.

Lovisa stuck her tongue out at him and retorted, "Well, I'll show you how then. I ride a lot, so I know what I'm doing."

Lovisa grabbed the reins and began to lead Thyraen down the road, observing keenly the landscape around her. It didn't take long for her to happen upon a very conveniently placed tree stump a little way into the tree line, exactly what she had been looking for. She brought the patient Thyraen to a halt just beside it, the horse following her lead without restlessness or opposition.

"See this?" She reached out and grabbed the stirrup. "Step up onto this stump and put your foot here. Then, pull yourself up by the horn." She pointed to said part of the saddle.

It seemed a near-impossible feat. The horse was so big, Artur's stature paled in comparison. From his vantage point, there was no chance he would be able to throw his leg over the beast's back.

Lovisa noticed his hesitation and said, "Don't worry. Once we find something for you to stand on, it's not as bad as it looks. It's easy."

Of course, that was simple for her to say.

"I don't know…" Artur said quietly.

"I trusted you when showing me how to fish. Can't you trust me with my own horse?"

"Yes, but…fishing is much different than handling a whole horse."

"I will handle Thyraen." Lovisa groaned. "Just get your arse into the saddle! I don't have all day!" Standing beside the tree stump, she held out the stirrup at an angle that would make it easier for him to place his foot inside.

Artur still hesitated a moment, but seeing the intensity in her eyes made him realize he needed to act, and act very quickly, or he might not be returning to the village that day.

Artur nervously stepped atop the stump, as if to present himself before all eyes dwelling within the forest unseen, calling attention to the event. It made him blush with discomfiture. He lifted a quivering foot to the stirrup, feeling the heat rushing through his body, compelling him to leap for the saddle still high above him. He grabbed ahold of the horn in a near panic, his arms assisting him when his legs could no longer. Artur found himself plopped onto the saddle on his stomach, looking more akin to a recent kill than a dignified rider. His legs kicked wildly behind him as he fought to find purchase, to maneuver himself about the saddle correctly without embracing the ground with a painful kiss. Had it not been for Lovisa grabbing hold of his legs, turning him about the saddle until his abdomen aligned correctly and he could finally sit erect, he would have most certainly fallen in a most humiliating fashion. It was already terrifying, how high up he felt, how far away the ground seemed. His nerves frayed, his body stiffened, he could hardly hear the snicker that escaped Lovisa's lips.

Thyraen let out but a single snort, shifting his legs in response to the sudden arrival of weight on his back, though largely unbothered by the boy who felt as though he had struggled for his life. But the movement typical of a horse made Artur stifle a cry as his body stiffened again, corpselike. He had witnessed folk get bucked off a horse before, and of the pain that lasted for days. The thought crossed his mind that Thyraen was preparing to cast him from the saddle, and he gripped that horn as if his life depended on it. Had Lovisa not maintained a firm grip on the reins, keeping Thyraen calm as she patted his cheek, the horse's natural movement would have scared Artur to death.

"How does it feel?" Lovisa asked.

Artur sat there and pondered a moment. The saddle was more uncomfortable than he'd anticipated, but there was a certain feeling of control he seemed to gain as the horse willingly submitted to his presence. And Artur couldn't deny that the view was beautiful, a different perspective on the world around him. The entire experience was sensational.

Artur looked to Lovisa and said, "It's good."

"Just good?" She looked at him incredulously.

Artur nodded at her and she let out an exasperated sigh. "Slide back. I'm coming up."

Lovisa hopped on the stump, grabbed the horn, and was already lifting herself up into the saddle before Artur had the chance to respond, her leg nearly connecting with his face as it swung over Thyraen's back.

Artur moved back in a panic and before he knew it, she was seated in front of him, the saddle surprisingly large enough to fit them both. Lovisa was so close. He could feel the warmth of her body, the scent of whatever aroma she may have used, even the softness of her hair as it brushed against his face. She was completely unaware of his growing nervousness, wholly ignorant of how his heart was racing.

"All right," Lovisa nodded. "Are you ready?"

"Where are we going?"

"Wherever I want to go." Lovisa shrugged. "Put your arms around my waist."

Artur was thankful Lovisa wasn't facing him in the moment, for he blushed up to his hairline at the very request.

"Wh-what?" Artur stuttered, inwardly kicking himself from not been better at hiding his nervousness.

"Put your arms around my waist." It seemed more of a command the second time around, Lovisa annoyed she had to repeat herself.

"But…"

Lovisa shrugged again and said, "Suit yourself."

With that, Lovisa gathered the reins and clicked her tongue, and Thyraen lurched forward into a gentle walk. But to Artur, it seemed more akin to a sprint. It forced his hand, startling him into throwing his arms around Lovisa's waist just as she had suggested he do.

He pressed his cheek into her back, eyes shut so tight they would have to be pried open, his arms coiling snakes tightening around her waist. She hardly minded it. She knew Artur need only to ease into the unfamiliar motion.

It felt as though they were floating over the land, the movement comfortably predictable. Thyraen's hooves beat the ground in a steady four-beat tempo. The wind through Artur's hair reminded him of the breeze by the river, crisp and lively as it flicked about his locks.

Artur relaxed himself, and his eyes eventually blinked open to the view of the world around. He could still see the details in the trees, in the brush, in the rock formations meshing within the land, and he couldn't help but admire it—a whole new perspective revealing itself to his virgin eyes.

"Quite done being scared?" Lovisa snickered at him.

"I wasn't scared," he hissed back, blushing.

"Who are you trying to fool?"

He could see her looking at him from the corner of her eye, head slightly turned to reveal the upturned corner of her lips.

"Well, if you're so confident, here." She grabbed Artur's hands and passed the reins into his grip.

"What are you doing?" The panic was beginning to set back in.

"Calm yourself. He'll do most of the work." She was quick to comfort him, placing her hands over his to provide some stability. "He'll follow the trail. You just need to let him know you're there. Hold firm, but not too tightly."

Artur swallowed nervously but did as he was told, adjusting his grip on the reins. It was surprising to him how easy it was. Thyraen hardly seemed bothered or even aware of the handoff.

"See? Not so hard, is it?"

"I suppose so," Artur said absentmindedly. He was busy focusing on the trail ahead, keeping control of the beast now at his command.

"If you want him to turn left, move your left rein away from his neck. If you want him to turn right, move the right rein. If you want him to stop, you pull back. Gently."

"What if I want him to go fast?"

"It depends on how fast you want him to go." Lovisa narrowed her eyes, suspicious of the question. Still, she answered, "Flick the reins and tap his sides with your heels to ask him to trot. Tap again and maybe let out a call to ask him to canter. If you want him to gallop, squeeze your thighs against the saddle, kick his sides and hold on. When he starts running, make certain to lean forward. One of my uncles was riding with me and Papa once, and when he made his horse gallop, he was leaning too far back and he tumbled right out of the saddle. He was out cold—the idiot." She couldn't help but chuckle to herself. "But you're not ready for anything akin to that."

Something ignited inside of Artur. Where he normally would turn the other cheek and not relent to the taunts of others, he took her words as a challenge—one he was quite inclined to accept. She had outshined him the day he taught her to fish. Now, it was his turn. If only she could see the smile across his face. She would know exactly what he devised.

Artur did as he was instructed—he tightened his legs about the saddle, and without another thought, he kicked at Thyraen's sides and let out a loud "Hah!"

The pearlescent beast gave a sharp whinny and sprang forward with all the power his well-muscled hindquarters could produce, and the three of them took off down the trail with the speed of the wind and the force of thunder. In her surprise, Lovisa cried out, falling back into Artur from the sudden shift in pace.

"What are you doing?" It was almost a shriek. Her years of practice and execution had her reflexively reaching for the reins, regaining her composure. Artur couldn't help but laugh, never minding that he nearly fell off the back of the horse as well. Pure vigor now was keeping him in control, hands clasped tightly on the reins. It was just as Lovisa said. Thyraen was doing the rest of the work, following the trail. The landscape now disappeared behind them in a compacted blur of greens, blues, and browns. Though initially stunned and furious for being taken off guard, Lovisa eased herself into it. Artur's laughter was contagious, and she couldn't help but join him.

CHAPTER 17

The two traveled on and it didn't matter where. The thundering hooves echoed through the forest, bouncing off the towering trees, vibrating through stone and ground, rattling the brush around them. Artur imagined that to the world around them, they were nothing but a white distortion shimmering from the lightest touch of sunlight, a sudden flash of lightning traversing the land itself, cast down from the heavens.

The path brightened ahead with a ring of light where the trees formed tall pillars and then fell away from the trail, a break in the forest line. They passed the stately tree columns into the clearing, stepping into another world in which the winter air caressed their skin and welcomed them to a lush valley with a view of majestic mountains standing tall in the distance. The river they exchanged greetings with followed them through the rest of their journey, eventually transforming into a slow-moving, shallow stream through the open fields.

Artur pulled on the reins gently with Lovisa's assistance, and Thyraen eased through his paces until he arrived at a walk once again. Artur steered him off the path and down the grassy plain which narrowed between the bends of the river.

"You could've gotten us hurt," Lovisa commented playfully, nudging him with her elbow. "Falling off horses can be, as my father says, 'life changing.'"

"And yet, we're fine." A newfound confidence radiated from Artur as he comfortably steadied the reins.

"Fortunately. You're quite good, almost natural. You certain you haven't ridden a horse before?" Lovisa turned her head to peer at him over her shoulder.

"I'm certain."

"Liar."

"I'm not lying. I just did what you told me to."

"Hm, I guess you're right. If you mounting a horse is any indication."

When they reached the sandy riverbank of the stream, Artur handed the reins off to Lovisa and dismounted, sliding down the side of the saddle and plopping to the ground below, landing on his bottom.

"Ow," he commented, rubbing his rear as he stood.

When he turned to help Lovisa dismount, she had already thrown her leg over the saddle and slipped down next to him with the grace of a practiced rider. She walked about the sands, taking in the new surroundings around them, and Artur followed, quietly joining her side.

He had never left the confines of the forest, let alone traveled miles beyond them. Urda spoke about the world as if it was full of darkness and cruelty. He'd half expected there to be clouds of smoke, akin to the plumes that rose from chimneys in Trivaden, cascading over the entire sky. He'd pictured sand the color of ash, and water tainted with a coat of grey. Yet here he saw anything but. All the newfound landscape did was remind him of home—the beauty, the tranquility, the sense of peace it brought to the mind.

There was a relief which overcame him. An ease. It was still just as he had once believed it to be.

"It's beautiful." Lovisa's soft words brought Artur's gaze to her, and he nodded in silent agreement. This was the real world before him, and it was nothing akin to the one he'd conjured in his mind from the stories he'd been told.

"Yes, it is," he whispered. As he looked to her, Lovisa's delicate ivory skin glowed in the light of the sun. Just when he thought she couldn't get more stunning, she continued to prove him wrong.

"Lovisa." Artur spoke her name, and she looked at him with those violet eyes of hers. "Thank you." He blushed. "I'm grateful for today."

He figured she was going to have something sardonic to say in return. Lovisa, however, stood there quietly, listening. She knew this was not the time to jest or take his words lightly.

"I kinda...woke up this morning feeling as though I don't know anything anymore. And what I thought I did know, was all probably just a lie. It's... scaring me."

The revelation hit him deeply again, and he felt as if a hole in his chest was beginning to open, aching and hurting. He dropped his gaze to the sands below.

"I feel the same way," Lovisa admitted, and when Artur looked to her in utter disbelief, it was her turn to look away, her eyes focusing on the faraway mountains.

"Papa tells me all the time that I'm not supposed to associate with folk akin to you. He tells me...bad things. A lot of bad things. But...you're not akin to that at all. And from what I've seen, your world is beautiful. Odd, but beautiful. You're fortunate, Artur."

Artur couldn't believe what he was hearing. She'd spent the better part of the previous trying to convince him that he was the unfortunate one, given his circumstances. Dealt a cold hand in life, poverty-stricken. Now, she was proclaiming something akin to envy for it all.

"What does your papa say about us folk?" he couldn't help but ask.

"I cannot say." Lovisa only shook her head. "But it's terrible."

Artur followed her gaze and looked about the mountains, their snowy peaks receding upon the onset of spring, their coat of white flowing down to the lands below.

"Is it really beautiful, or are you just teasing me again?"

"It really is beautiful." Lovisa was taken aback at his skepticism of her proclamation. "I haven't seen much of the world. It's my first time traveling this far. But everything I've seen is beautiful. Truly. And the things my father has said about you…I don't know how it could be true anymore."

She inched forward until the toes of her boots barely touched the ebbing water at the river's edge. The river was slow enough that she could make out the silhouette of the mountains and the clouds in the sky, her reflection staring back at her in the clear waters.

"I firmly believe that even parents can be wrong at times. They act as though they're always right about everything, but I know for certain that they aren't."

"Yes, I suppose you're right. But who are we to question them?" Artur tried to lighten the tone a bit, even as he spoke, he felt a sense of dread creeping over him. Lovisa couldn't help but smirk.

"I guess they don't understand what we see anymore. As I said before, beautiful, but odd," she said quietly.

Arthur tilted his head and asked her, "What do you mean by odd?"

"Don't you feel it? I feel it when I'm in your forests. As though…there's something watching me, always. As though there's always something there."

"Well, there are a lot of beasts in the forest. They stay hidden most of the time. Papa says it's in our nature to sense when we're being watched." Artur came to stand beside her once more.

"No, it's no beast. Maybe a person? It just feels much different. I really don't know how to explain it."

"I haven't felt that at all and I've lived here all my life. There's no one else in the forest besides me and the other village folk of Trivaden. Oh! And we have a dire wolf too."

"You have dire wolves in your forest?"

"I only know of one, and that's Vána. She lives with us in the village."

"Hmph." She was impressed, but hid it with smugness. "Dire wolves are extremely rare these days. I only know a few folk in my family who have one as a pet. But it's no dire wolf that I sense either. I don't know how else to describe it, but it feels as though there's something always there, just out of sight."

"Sorry, Lovisa. I don't know what you mean. I guess I'm just used to the forest. It's my home after all."

"Perhaps you're right." Lovisa sighed. "Still though, it feels pleasant out here. I haven't had that sense since we left the forest."

"Well, what do you want to do?"

Lovisa let out an audible hum as she thought, tapping her finger to her lips.

"This is the kind of place where I would want to read a book," she said thoughtfully.

"A what?" Artur raised a quizzical brow, and she looked at him incredulously. But her slack jaw quickly resolved into hardened lips, her own brows furrowing. His question would have seemed so ridiculous, had laws and circumstances not been what they were. She remembered her many teachings about the commonfolk: their illiteracy, their general lack of education and skills beyond those useful to the trade that even the Empire could not be without. She had always been so indifferent to their supposed plight when she had everything, feeling only pity for the unfortunate circumstances they were born into. If not for this boy beside her, she would still have thought no different. But seeing the genuine ignorance about his expression now, she could only feel sadness, heartache. It was wholly forbidden, what she was contemplating. But as defiant as she was by nature, it was a gift she was more than happy to bestow upon him.

"Wait here," she said to him, and she hurried to her saddlebags. From within them did she produce the item in question and bring it to hold before Artur, allowing him a glance at what was otherwise prohibited to him—rectangular in shape, a most intricate cover of patterns and symbols, pages of valuable vellum bound with leather.

"This," she spoke softly, "is a book."

Artur observed it with all the candor and curiosity within him, admiring the cover—blue with shimmering gold accents and letterings.

Artur was hesitant, warily taking the book within his own grasp. He felt the weight of the object, the vellum pages curling gracefully with age and wear. When he opened the book, he found those pages filled with script he could hardly comprehend, much less begin to decipher in all his illiteracy. His longing showed on his face. But he loved the smell of it—the smell of the history of its existence, its longevity.

As Artur studied it, enamored, Lovisa felt a twinge of pity for her friend once more. Simple commodities such as books were abundant in her way of life, one of the most easily accessible forms of knowledge at her disposal, and she'd hardly ever considered that someone could exist without knowing how to read, without ever having held a book. But the past few days had her thinking otherwise. Lovisa looked at the world with a renewed pair of eyes, looked at folk with new understanding. There was no doubt that Lovisa's family could afford the privileges that had been handed to her from birth, and at one point she would've jested about Artur's ignorance at his expense. Now, it was just dismaying.

"I don't know anyone in my village that has a book," Artur said under his breath.

"None of the commonfolk do," Lovisa answered brusquely. "It was prohibited by the Empire a long time ago."

"Why?" Artur looked to her.

Lovisa only shrugged her shoulders and responded, "They just did."

Artur's brows furrowed, his lips flattening as puzzlement befell his expression.

"How...how come you have one, then?"

Lovisa was silent a moment. There were a few moments during their interactions that she believed Artur humored her simply out of flattery, or perhaps to hide his fear—seeking to appease the Valeriaan in his presence lest he find himself punished. He played it off well enough, if her assumptions were true. But the truth was, as revealed in this very interaction, that Artur truly hadn't an inkling as to who she truly was. Every moment of their time together was genuine, void of any biases and prejudices. Unaffected by the world around them. Lovisa nearly blushed at the thought, relieved that she hadn't been played for a fool.

"Because I'm allowed to have them," Lovisa answered honestly. She wanted not to reveal herself, for fear that it could end what she had come to appreciate deeply.

Artur was perplexed still, but sensed Lovisa was purposefully being vague in the way she answered. He decided to prod no further, returning the conversation to the book itself.

"What exactly are they supposed to be?"

"Um..." Lovisa scratched at the back of her neck, looking away. She took a moment to think about it and then said, "Books tell stories. Or they teach lessons. Retell of olden times. Many, many a thing. They're all different and they are countless in number...at least where I'm from."

"What kind of stories do they tell?"

"All kinds. Romance stories, adventure tales, historical accounts, terrifying lore, scientific discoveries. Out of all of them, I love romance stories the most," she responded readily. "The one you're holding is my favorite book. It's about a mortal warrior and a goddess who were in love with one another, and who were torn apart by a great cataclysm—a war waged by a malevolent and resentful god. I shan't spoil too much, but it is a delicately woven tale filled with conflict, romance, friendships. I love all those themes so much." The more she talked about it the more excited she became, reciting the contents of the pages she had read over and over again. Lovisa paused when she realized Artur only looked more confused the longer she went on. He had asked but a simple question of what a book was, and she blushed with embarrassment for allowing herself to be carried away with the retelling of her favorite tale.

She fumbled a bit with her words until a coherent sentence finally formed. "Well...do you want me to show you?"

To her surprise and delight, Artur promptly perked up at the offer.

The two sat on the warm riverbank, toes scrunched into the sand, their shoulders touching. Lovisa slowly read aloud the words on the pages, and Artur followed along with her the best he could by sounding out what Lovisa uttered first, her fingers trailing the lines between the sentences of text. Every word, every letter seemed so foreign, and yet it was the language he conversed in every day. It seemed impossible that he could speak it so easily without reading it at all.

Lovisa remained patient and persistent with him, going as slowly as he needed and repeating if prompted. Eventually, Artur grew quiet, entranced by her voice speaking the words on the page. He was content simply to listen and immerse himself in the world that unfolded. Lovisa didn't at all mind being the storyteller for the time being. She too was absorbed in the pages, as if it were her very first time reading the tale. Unnoticed by them both, Lovisa rested her head on his shoulder, and they nestled in closer to each other.

That winter day was unseasonably warm and the temptation to wade into the water pressed its way to the forefront of their minds. Taking a break from reading to stretch out cramped limbs and long-stilled bodies, they dipped into the cool river to refresh themselves with its frigid touch, the product of the snow melting from the peaks of the mountains around them. Artur didn't mind the temperature. He had grown used to its chill over the span of his life and gave it hardly a second thought. Lovisa had to adapt. The sudden drop in temperature was something she wasn't quite accustomed to. She tended to enter only bodies of water sourced from natural hot springs and directed into pools and baths. After much whining and hesitation, she eventually gave in to Artur's coaxing and tiptoed her way into the waters to join him. To her surprise, her body adjusted easily to untamed nature as she plunged below the water's surface. The two began to enjoy their time together—playing, cheering, partaking in friendly competitions of chase and splashing. It helped that the water was shallow. They could run about more easily and relax in its midst without the concern of being swept away.

When they eventually had enough, they both flopped down on the riverbank in the warm sand and enjoyed the thawing touch of sunlight.

Rested, they explored the shores around the bend, searching along the riverbed and in the watergrass for anything of interest. At one point, Artur found a frog, small and wide-eyed with icy-blue skin and white feet. He showed not a hint of fear as he picked it up with his bare hands and showed it off to Lovisa with enthusiasm. Lovisa wasn't nearly as amused and did not hesitate to voice her disgust. She did what she could to get away from the disgusting creature, only for Artur to chase her, further encouraged by her screaming and cries and the peeking smile she tried so hard to hide.

Only when she began to plead with him almost angrily, growing tired of the ongoing chase, did he at last relent and release the poor creature back to the waters from which it came. It scurried off into the duckweed to escape the traumatizing event.

When they took to the waters again, they searched amongst the pebbles and rocks for treasures below. The riverbed was a mesh of dark burgundies, greens and greys, with the occasional silver and crystal-like minerals whose luster set them apart from their dull neighbors. Something glistening especially bright amidst the dark tones caught Artur's attention. He had to be standing at just the right angle for the sun to reflect and reveal its location, an encounter brought about by chance.

Artur let out an audible "Aye," as he reached into the murk of the sand and pebbles and shoveled the stone into the palm of his hand.

"What is it?" Lovisa called over, though Artur hardly acknowledged her, being too preoccupied with his finding. He brushed the sand and pebbles aside to reveal a gem he had never seen before, one that captured the light in its sharp edges and changing planes. Artur could see his palm, distorted through its translucent shape. The stone shone with an array of iridescent colors so beautiful they rivaled any rainbow. And it wasn't gleaming simply because of the effect of the sun's rays upon it, Artur realized. The stone was glowing of its own accord. Akin to a star winking in the night sky, it shimmered in his palm with a quiet and ethereal hum, glinting in his eyes, colors dancing about the soft peach complexion of his skin.

"What?" Lovisa gasped once she too caught sight of the stone. "You found a Mírén stone!" She nearly grabbed it from Artur's palm to hold it for herself, but Artur was quick to pull his hand away and hide the stone within the confines of a closed fist.

"Aye! Let me see!" Lovisa demanded, reaching once more for his hand only for Artur to turn away from her.

"I found it first," Artur said, continually turning just enough that Lovisa missed each time she attempted to grab hold of his arm.

"But I want to see it! Give it!"

"You could at least ask nicely. Don't you have any manners?"

"Why do I have to ask nicely? Just let me see it!" Lovisa huffed at him. When her many attempts to take the stone from him failed, she stomped her foot and trudged through the water to the shoreline where she sat and sulked petulantly.

The whole ordeal was so ridiculous that it made Artur laugh for a moment. He remembered throwing his own tantrums. But those had occurred in his younger years and had come to a quick halt once he realized neither of his parents would have any of his behavior—especially his mother. All she had to do was say his name in full and he knew it was all over for him. He wondered if Lovisa had experienced the same growing up. Seeing as how she was pouting for not getting her way, he doubted she had ever been disciplined at all. Or at least, there were enough folk in her life who had always been more than willing to please her.

"I was going to let you see it, you brat." Artur scoffed as he made his way to her.

Lovisa was too busy grimacing to say anything, and when he sat next to her, she made a point to look away from him, turning her body so that her back was to him.

"Lovisa," Artur sighed, trying to stifle a bout of laughter at her expense. "You can look at the stone if you want. I was going to let you see it."

He held it out to her, the glowing stone still illuminating his palm with those beautiful colors. It was so bright, Lovisa could see it shining in the corner of her eye, feel it shimmering across the delicate skin of her face as she peered over her shoulder. It was far too tempting to continue her fit for long.

But she hesitated a moment, looking to Artur cautiously for any hint that he might take it away from her once more. When he showed no signs of doing so—in fact, he encouraged her by drawing his hand closer—she quickly snatched it from his palm.

"What did you call it again?" Artur asked.

"We call it Mírén stone. We have a whole bunch of these back home. Big ones too," Lovisa replied, in awe at the sight within her own grasp.

"Oh." Artur looked away as he thought of how this was yet something else she had that he would probably never acquire himself. "This is the first time I've seen anything akin to this before." He pursed his lips, preparing for the inevitable jest at his expense.

"Really?" His lack of things she knew as common continued to amaze her. "My goodness. We use it for a lot of things back home: light, remedies, jewelry, such and such. We mine it up north where we're from. But I didn't know it could be found here, and so far away too. If we knew Mírén stone was here we would be mining this land for it. Maybe it came down with the water from the mountains? During the snow melt?" She was speculating for her own sake more than trying to give him an explanation for its unexpected appearance.

"What's so special about them?"

"Mírén stone is unakin to any other stone that's been discovered. I've heard that folk can feel an energy from it, and that the energy can possibly be harnessed. But we don't know how to do that yet. Or maybe we forgot how to? I don't know. It's been described in books from a long time ago, from what I hear. The folk in olden times said to have experienced weird phenom... phanominans...phenominas...phenomimons... You know what I mean."

"Uh...a what?"

Lovisa paused a moment. Of course, Artur wouldn't know the word if she herself could hardly say it.

"It's a word that means strange events which can't be explained."

"I guess I wouldn't know, huh?" Artur smirked.

"I guess you wouldn't." Lovisa tossed her hair. "Just know, we haven't been able to unlock its energy as it's been described in books, and even then, those reports are very vague, and rare. So, for now, we use it for more...er, material and medicinal purposes, I guess."

"Sounds awfully fancy. We don't have anything akin to that back home."

"I'm not surprised," Lovisa teased, though her expression of pride for possessing such a commodity was not intended to be malicious. "But if I'm going to be honest," Lovisa dropped her voice, a blush coming to her cheeks.

She hardly believed that what she was about to say was even leaving her lips to begin with.

"I've never seen anything raw akin to this before, and…nothing near as beautiful."

Lovisa gazed once more at the Mírén stone as it sparkled across her face. Artur admired her thoughtfully. He knew exactly what she was feeling—the warmth of basking in curiosity and awe upon such a discovery. He'd felt the same upon first seeing the book.

"Would—" he paused a moment, a blush coming to his own face. "Would you want to have it?"

"You would give this to me?" Lovisa turned sharply toward him.

"Mhm," Artur nodded. "If it really makes you that happy, then I want you to have it."

Lovisa nearly said something but caught herself, pressing her lips together. Instead, she crawled along the sands to where she had discarded their belongings, and when she came back to Artur, she placed her most cherished book into his hands without hesitation and said, "Then you can have this."

Artur was shocked. He looked down at the book as she had done the Mírén stone, with complete awe and wide eyes. It was hard to accept that she was giving something so precious of hers, to him.

"But…" The gold letters shimmered in the sun. "This is your favorite book."

"Yes, but you're giving me the Mírén stone. Besides, you need to practice, and I can always get another one back home. You can't…so, you have it."

Artur smiled at her, never minding that the innocent remark she made could have otherwise been a snide comment on his lack of fortune in any other context.

"I'll practice so next time we meet, I'll be able to read it to you."

It was a most delightful thought. But even such delight could not last long. She was taking a great risk with this gesture, and she felt the need be forthcoming regarding such perils.

"I must tell you, speak about this to no one. You can get in…a lot of trouble if the Valeriaans find this book. You'll be punished…your family, your friends, your neighbors, they'll all pay for it."

The ominous warning was not lost upon him. But certainly, if his mother had done so well in hiding so much from him, he must have inherited some of her skill. He could not resist such a precious gift from an equally precious girl.

"Knowing this, I will understand if you don't—"

"No," Artur interrupted her, "I won't let anyone know of this. I promise."

Lovisa had the stone cupped within her palms, the light so bright it could be seen through the gaps between her fingers. Artur had the book pressed to his chest, his heart beating against it. They smiled at each other, the silence of their unspoken happiness stretching comfortably between them. Neither of them needed to say anything. They both knew they were thankful, for they had exchanged something they would forever be able to cherish.

When orange hues began to span the sky as the later afternoon crept in, did they decide to make their way back to their meeting place—across those endless fields and the ever-flowing river, to the forest's edge where the towering trees seemed to absorb the sunlight over the path. Reluctantly they returned to the world they'd left momentarily behind.

Thyraen pranced lightly between the columns of trees and immediately they felt the warmth of the sun disappear from their backs. The cool shade of the trees brought about an unexpected feeling of comfort. This could be the last day they would be together, for all he knew, and with that possibility in mind, Artur pulled on the reins and brought the horse to a walk to draw out their time together. Thyraen let out a snort as he obliged loyally to unspoken commands. Lovisa, whose turn it was to sit at the back of the saddle, peered over Artur's shoulder and questioned the unexpected change in pace.

"Why are you making him walk?"

"Just thought he could use a break," Artur replied without a hesitation, hoping she couldn't detect the deception in his voice. "…A-and the view is nice."

He could feel her narrowed eyes scrutinizing him with skepticism. He kept his gaze forward and body still so as not to let his nervousness betray him.

"You live in a forest." She smirked. "What more is there for you to see?"

"Uh…well…" He chuckled nervously. "I haven't been to this part of the forest before."

Lovisa hardly believed it, but she didn't mind. It just meant she had more time to spend with him. She relented and wrapped her arms around his waist as she rested her head about his back.

"If you insist," she whispered.

Artur could feel a smile spreading across her face, her lashes batting as she closed her eyes to rest after the exhilarating day they had shared together. They walked on in silence, Thyraen's hoofbeats pronouncing a steady rhythm in the air not filled by words, aligning with the beat of Artur's heart reacting to their closeness, to the physical, and even warm, touch. Just thinking about it made his face flush and his heart quicken. He did what he could to distract himself, to keep from getting too flustered. And so, he looked about his surroundings which indeed seemed so familiar to him, as comforting as home. The sounds, the smell, the feeling. It was all a part of him.

Thinking back on the previous conversation, Artur wondered once more what Lovisa meant when she said she was feeling "watched." He could think of only one instance in which he could relate—when she had no doubt been the one watching him from the cover of the forest preceding their first meeting. He could think of no other remarkable occurrence. The village folk of Trivaden shared the forest with many unseen and mostly harmless beasts, and it was only expected that they would be as attentive to them as they were to their neighbors.

The way Lovisa explained it seemed haunting. Unnerving, even, to feel as though a pair of eyes were piercing through the forest from deep in the unknown and beating down on upon you with a probing gaze. Yet no matter how much he looked about and tried to "feel" this sensation, he detected nothing but the usual forest activity. The birds were still twittering up high, the bushes still rustling as rodents and other wooly beasts hid themselves away from the presence of man. It all felt the same. Artur could only conclude that perhaps it was a sensation unique to a foreigner, the feeling of being away from home. To be out of place in a world that was so unfamiliar. Artur wondered if he were to ever visit her homeland, would he feel just as out of place there as she did here?

When they reached the riverbank on which he had spent many a day, Artur commanded Thyraen to come to a halt, and he sat there quietly, contemplating whether to disturb the resting Lovisa. It was predominantly out of respect for her, with just a trace of his own selfishness. They would have to part again for another day and he wasn't ready for that. Unfortunately for him, that wasn't up to Artur. Lovisa had awakened as if she subconsciously knew they had arrived at their destination. The cessation of movement roused her from sleep.

"You all right?" Artur asked. Glancing over his shoulder, he could feel her arms tightening around him.

"I can feel it again." She took in a sharp breath, her voice low. "Someone's watching us." Her eyes were fixated on the river, to the origin of whatever was prompting the unexplainable sense.

Artur followed, looking about the river and the tree line for anything that could confirm her wariness. Still, there was nothing.

"Are you certain?" Artur asked. Lovisa didn't reply, her senses all at work, in focus.

"Lovisa?" Artur prompted her again, after some time of silence.

When her eyes were done darting about, she blinked a few times to direct her focus back to Artur. With a deep breath, she replied, "I'm never certain. But I don't think there's anything there. Maybe there has never been anything to begin with."

"The forests can be scary for folk who aren't used to it. Maybe that's all it really is—just you getting used to it."

"Perhaps you're right." Lovisa sighed, disappointed with not only herself, but also the notion that nothing was amiss.

"Time for you to go home, I guess."

It was hard for Artur to hear, but she was right. It was time for them to part, though hopefully only temporarily.

"Time for you to go too."

Artur dismounted first, and to his surprise, Lovisa allowed him to help her down from the saddle though she hardly required assistance. She was comfortable with Artur, trusted him. The way he grasped at her waist was tender and gentle, just as she expected. Once her feet were on the ground, did she smile at him and find great amusement in the bashful flush overcoming his face. Lovisa patted Thyraen's neck, and Artur too ran his hand over his glistening coat as a way of saying goodbye—and thank you—should they not meet again.

Artur retrieved his new but already beloved book from the saddlebag, clutching it closely to his chest as the two bounded across the river on the pathway that was now nothing more than a line of rocks and boulders caught within the clutches of a most unintimidating river. No fear, no hesitation. Lovisa, of course, was the first to arrive on the beach, and she patiently waited for Artur to join her with a triumphant smile on her face.

That is, until she heard the sharp crack of a tree branch breaking behind her. With a gasp, Lovisa turned around just as a large grey object smashed against the side of her head. The force of the impact made her cry out in pain, and falling to the ground, did she clutch at the wound already spewing red. Blood dripped between her fingers, staining the sleeve of her once-white blouse.

The aching and dizziness overcame her almost immediately, the pain rippling from the wound to encircle her head. Her eyes clamped shut as the world started to spin, nausea setting in as her vision blurred. Lovisa gritted her teeth against the pulsing pain, and the last thing she heard before the void of unconsciousness overcame her was Artur's voice shouting her name.

CHAPTER 18

Watching from only a few feet away, Artur was horrified—nearly tripping off one of the boulders, so taken off guard by the incident transpiring before him was he.

"Lovisa!" Artur hurried the rest of the way until he skidded to a stop beside her on his knees, his cherished book crashing to the sands below without a second thought.

He saw the glistening blood staining and mingling with the silver of her hair, the strands sticking to her rapidly paling skin. He watched with dread as the crimson liquid dripped down her face, traversing the curvature of her cheek and jawline to the sand beneath her.

Artur's hands were quivering as he reached for her bloodied hand, wanting to see the severity of her wound, to take her home and help her. Yet all he could do was kneel beside her, helpless in his panic. His mouth ajar, his breathy attempts to speak were nothing more than incoherent sentences.

"Artur!" He heard a familiar voice call out to him.

To his horror, did he see Ronan breaching the forest line and stomping his way down the riverbank in their direction. There was a look about his face that Artur had never seen before on his friend, and it was apparent in his face, in his eyes, in the way he breathed, that Ronan was fueled by a hatred and an anger which had never surfaced until that moment. His expression was one of determination—a look to kill.

"What the fuck are you doing?" Ronan's voice was strengthened with a fury Artur had never experienced himself. "I haven't seen you for a couple days, and when I do come looking for you, I find you with this witch?" Ronan pointed a trembling finger at Lovisa.

Artur couldn't even find his words, his breath quickened and shallow in response to the fright spreading over him. Thyraen was crying out on the opposite bank, the horse rearing and pawing at the ground in distress at the unfolding turmoil.

When Artur didn't reply, it only heightened Ronan's anger. He shouted once more, looking for some kind of vindication from the boy he considered his best friend.

"Say something! Why are you with a Valeriaan?"

Valeriaan. The word hit him right in the chest, where it hurt the most. A name he had only just learned the night before. A name weighted by malice on the tongues that dared speak it.

Artur looked down at Lovisa, silently writhing in pain, struggling to stay conscious long enough to grasp the situation herself. If there was one thing she did indeed understand, it was fear—the fear of what could befall her in her most helpless state. There was no chance she was going to be able to fight in her condition.

Her fate lay in Artur's hands.

But now that he knew the truth of who she was, she feared her odds did not fall on the good side of favor. Yet she also hoped that Artur's kindness, even in the times she had treated him unfairly, cruelly even, would allow him to disregard her identity and be her friend, her protector. At least until she regained her bearings.

"Ronan..." was all Artur could muster in a weak and shaky voice.

"You know what? I don't care! I'm going to kill her and that's one Valeriaan we'll never have to worry about!" Ronan's words cut as mercilessly as a knife, cold and unfeeling, and without hesitation he charged for Lovisa.

Everything appeared to happen so slowly, as if time itself was attempting to lend a helping hand. Artur watched as Ronan became no more than a raging assailant about to end its quarry, his eyes crazed and wide with anger.

Artur felt all the color drain from his face. That the friend he'd had for his whole life could end the life of the girl who held his affections was a likelihood he could not comprehend. How he wished that it was nothing more than a dream, transpiring as he dozed out in the open fields—that he would awaken just before the worst part of the nightmare unfolded. But the truth was this: it was all real. Happening before his very eyes.

He had only an instant in which to decide what he was going to do, what side he was going to take. Looking to Lovisa, he had never seen her so afraid. All traces of her characteristic pride and confidence had vanished. She was too stunned, in too much pain, to run. She could only watch as the window of her life narrowed with each stride Ronan took. When Lovisa looked to Artur with terrified violet eyes, he could plainly see the unspoken plea in them—she needed him. Was begging him to come to her assistance. She would've yelled out her pleas, had she been capable.

Ronan was his friend, a friend he'd grown up alongside from the days they were but infants. The many shenanigans and scrapes they had gotten themselves into flashed before his eyes. Ronan was one of the few village folk he could say he was close to. Then he thought of Lovisa, the girl he had unexpectedly befriended, with whom he had enjoyed every moment they were able to share, brief though their time together had been. Regardless, Artur cared deeply for her, more deeply than even he understood. The last thing he wanted was for harm to come to her—let alone death, as Ronan so boldly threatened.

With Ronan's feet pounding against the sand, echoing dully in Artur's ears, vibrating through his entire body, he felt his heartbeat accelerate as heat flooded his veins. The surge brought warmth back to his body, initially frigid with fear. Artur clenched his teeth, his hands closing into quivering fists with an anger provoked. This was his only chance.

Just as Ronan lurched towards Lovisa, Artur threw himself between them, his body a shield over hers. There was no time for Ronan to react, nothing he could do to divert the momentum propelling him forward. He collided directly into Artur, and as the two fell back their arms coiled around one another, their breath forced from their lungs as they crashed to the sands below. Both were stunned a moment, stilling as they tried to regain their bearings, to understand how the circumstances had suddenly changed.

It was Ronan who first realized what happened. Lying there next to him in the sand was not his intended target, but his friend. Artur, who willingly made the decision to stand between him and a sworn adversary. He could hardly believe it. The realization that he had been betrayed by the boy he called a friend stole the breath from him anew.

Ronan looked to Artur in disbelief, searching his eyes for some hint of familiarity before circumstances could deteriorate further. He found only an unrecognizable gaze of blue, one that conveyed Artur's determination, that made plain his willingness to throw their years of friendship away for this girl—this enemy.

The collision was only a suggestion of Artur's strength, surprising in its magnitude. Ronan would never have believed that Artur possessed such prowess. Regardless, Ronan was determined to end the Valeriaan cowering behind Artur, and the unexpected betrayal only magnified his rage.

Ronan yelled out a battle cry, meant to instigate physical conflict, as he scrambled to stand. Artur followed suit, meeting Ronan before either of them had even risen onto their feet.

They collided once more, Ronan shoving Artur back with a hard punch to the gut. It stunned Artur long enough for Ronan to pin him to the ground with his own weight, unleashing a barrage of punches that did not cease even as Artur cried out, nor as he tried in vain to shield himself. With his arms stretched out to his sides under Ronan's knees, he could not retaliate.

Lovisa finally managed to focus long enough that her vision cleared and witnessed the terrifying brawl of blood and strength beside her. She struggled to her knees, the nausea and dizziness seeming to shift the ground beneath her. Her head throbbed in response to any movement she dared attempt. Lovisa clutched her head once more, hunching until her hair cascaded around her face and brushed the sand, hiding the tears as she dry-heaved from the pain.

"Lovisa!" Artur's call made her whip her head around, which she immediately regretted when it screamed out in pain once more.

In the same moment, Artur finally managed to free an arm and get a strike in amidst the unrelenting barrage, a fist right to the side of Ronan's face. Now with Artur's arms and legs coiled around Ronan, the two struggled about on the ground, rolling to and fro in a fierce battle for dominance. The sand sprayed around them, the sound of their clothes tearing mingling with their cries and grunts. Flecks of blood appeared on lips and seeped from abrasions dealt by hands, feet, teeth, and the detritus of the forest floor.

*Artur...*Lovisa thought what she was unable to say, unable to scream. How she wanted to jump in and help Artur overcome her assailant. To save him as he was saving her. They could stop Ronan together. Only, she could hardly move. Couldn't find the resolve to act upon her desires. Her feelings of ineptness brought tears running down her face. All she could do was watch the boy she truly cared for take strike after strike on her behalf. Every punch or kick he received made her flinch and cry even harder.

When Artur finally managed to pin Ronan beneath him, did he finally look to her. "Run, Lovisa! Run!" he exclaimed, his voice strained.

The sight of him made her sob harder. His soft and affable face was bloodied and bruised. His clothes were torn and bloodstained from the altercation.

She didn't want to leave him, regardless of how much pain she was in. If he were to suffer even more greatly on her account, she would never be able to forgive herself for abandoning him.

"Lovisa, please! Go!" The desperation in his voice was heartbreaking. Those strained words, forced out as he was struggling to maintain the upper hand, were hardly what she wanted to hear, but she knew it was the only thing she could do now.

As she turned toward the path across the river, Ronan managed to elbow Artur in the face and escape the bind he was in. With Artur momentarily stunned, Ronan scurried to his feet and made a charge for her once again.

Lovisa was stepping on the first rock when she realized Ronan was right behind her, reaching out to her with determined, battered hands. She cried out, fearing that her attempted escape was about to be thwarted. His fingers were mere inches from her blouse before Ronan was heaved away from her, pulled back down into the sand as Artur pinned him once again.

Time stopped as they looked at one another, the hurt of betrayal plain in both of their gazes. They knew this was the defining moment of the fight, the turning point of their relationship. Neither threw a fist nor made a move, both waiting to see if the other would be the first to do so. The boys were exhausted, wounded physically and emotionally. Tears glistened in the corners of their eyes. Neither of them was to relent. Neither of them would concede the victory.

Then Ronan's sorrowful expression twisted into contempt and anger, his arms resuming the struggle once more, and Artur let out a choked breath and quickly swung his fist right into Ronan's face. It was more forceful than he intended. But his strength was amplified by the vigor of the fight, a release of energy through a closed fist. He could hear the breath leaving Ronan's lips as his head turned sharply, his cheek pressing into the sand. The dizzying, head-spinning strike sent a flash of white cracking across Ronan's vision even as his eyes closed. He was too stunned to fight back, to pursue Lovisa further.

At last, her chance had arrived, and though she stumbled on weak and unbalanced legs, Lovisa made it across the riverbank to a very panicked Thyraen. The beast was in distress, prancing in place until she pulled herself into the saddle with what little strength she had left. Lovisa sat there, nearly slumped over in her saddle, watching from afar the fight she believed would continue to rage on in her absence.

She could only hope Artur would come out the victor, for her continued presence would only prolong the conflict. With a cry, Lovisa kicked at Thyraen's sides and the horse bolted down the trail, disappearing into the abyss of the forest.

Artur caught a glimpse of the horse and rider vanishing into the thicket of trees, and a wave of relief overcame him.

Only then did Artur finally relent. Releasing Ronan, he crawled away across the sands, rough and coarse at his knees and palms, his breath quivering, his body shaking. He knelt there for a moment, and turning his hands before him he could see just how bloodied and battered they were, the open abrasions about his knuckles, the bones and muscles screaming in pain when he dared try to flex them even slightly. He touched at his face. The tips of his fingers had hardly grazed his flesh, where the skin had torn at his cheek, before he had no choice but to stop. It was too excruciating to bear.

He might have won the fight, but he did so at a cost. Lovisa was hurt, and she was gone. Forever, most certainly. His cheek, eye, and brow were so swollen that he could practically feel the purple hue of the bruise staining his complexion. His lips were twice their normal size and numb, but he could taste blood on his tongue, could feel it dripping down the length of his chin. Even his nose, Artur could feel, was clogged and bleeding, the droplets trickling down to his lips. Ronan's onslaught had been relentless, and Artur now began to comprehend the extent of the damage. Peering down, already was there the formation of bruising about his abdomen, past the clothes nearly in tatters, dirtied, stained with both of their blood—*Ronan's blood.* That's what stood out in his mind. Artur looked to the boy who was moaning in pain, rocking about in agony. Struggling to catch his breath. Suffering just as Artur was.

It was done. Over. They both possessed no more fight within them. Ronan didn't bother throwing another punch, his arms weakened and tired. There was no amount of hate left in him that could give him enough vigor to resume his rampage. Instead, Ronan turned on his side, facing away from Artur. He couldn't bear to look at the one he once considered a friend.

Artur himself had no words, his vigor drained away. If Ronan did try to reignite the conflict, he simply wouldn't be able to retaliate. That he had gotten into a physical altercation in the first place was something he was still coming to terms with. He'd never gotten into a fight of such magnitude before—nothing more than playful scuffles amongst boys. Never had he drawn blood. Never had he fought to what he felt akin to the death, and for his opponent to be none other than Ronan still seemed unbearable.

The weight of the situation finally began to settle upon his shoulders, and the immense wave of guilt made him realize that he had just turned his back not only on his friend, but also on his family and the village. He had chosen what he now felt to be the wrong side.

He had put a Valeriaan, descendant of the most hated and feared clan ever to rule in Skana, the object of disdain amongst the commonfolk, above his own friend. But in the heat of the moment, it hadn't been about them and a Valeriaan. It had been about saving his friend, saving Lovisa. To Artur, she wasn't a Valeriaan. She was...Lovisa. Was that so wrong?

"You're a fucking traitor." Ronan's hoarse words hit Artur as though they were another punch to his already-tender abdomen, and he couldn't help but gasp and recoil with disgust at himself. "How could you?"

Artur turned as Ronan slowly rose to his hands and knees. His body was shaking and quivering as the vigor slowly lessened and the aches deepened. Ronan raised his eyes to Artur's, scowling with the hatred once reserved solely for a single kind of folk.

"You chose a Valeriaan over me."

It was true. Artur couldn't deny that he had willingly chosen Lovisa over Ronan, with little hesitation.

Artur's breath quickened as he prepared himself to finally speak.

"She...s-she is my friend...Ronan—"

"I was your friend!" The sharp volume of his voice made Artur flinch. "Valeriaans aren't, and never will be, our friends! Don't you know what they've done to us?"

"But—"

"I don't want to hear your excuses!"

"I couldn't just let you kill her—"

"The only good Valeriaan is a dead Valeriaan! You're a traitor! Traitor! Traitor! Traitor!" Ronan's voice quavered as tears began to run down his face. Artur had never seen Ronan cry. It was a disturbing sight to see.

"Traitor." The word rang so deep and true in his mind that it made Artur hurt all over again. He felt a searing tear fall down his own cheek, something he had never allowed in front of his friends for fear of evoking a volley of teasing. Neither of them had enough dignity to hold back at that moment. Everything was laid bare, entirely uncovered. There would be no teasing, no friendship to fall back on.

"You're going to pay for what you did," Ronan hissed through gritted teeth.

They said no more to one another. Ronan silently wept, unable to find the strength to get to his feet, as Artur relived the conflict in his mind repeatedly. He didn't know how, but he managed to find a bit of strength to stand, and looking across the waters did he see the empty bank.

Lovisa was gone. Gone for good. There was not a chance she was coming back after what had transpired. He could only hope now, that at the very least, she would be safe and taken care of. He fought back more tears at the very thought of it, as it dawned on him that not only was he a *traitor*, not only had he lost his closest friend, but he had also lost her.

Artur went to Ronan, and in one last attempt at some good grace between them, he reached down and gently pulled at Ronan's arm to help him up.

"Don't you fucking touch me! Get the fuck away from me!" Ronan shouted as he pulled away sharply.

The voice was so jarring it nearly startled Artur off his feet, and he stood frozen as Ronan, granted a second wind, climbed to his feet and bolted down the path back to the village, quickly disappearing from Artur's sight.

Artur let out a breath, his eyes closing. Fearing once Ronan caused a stir with his bloody and disheveled appearance, the whole village would hear of what happened. Would know of his rapport with a Valeriaan. The rumors to encircle him would render him a pariah, an outcast amongst the children and folk of Trivaden. What he had thought was the right in the moment now felt so, so wrong. The revelation of it all was so overwhelming to Artur that the tears fell in cascades as he retrieved his book and made his way home, one slow and painful step at a time.

CHAPTER 19

The home was vacant and soundless. Urda was nowhere to be found when Artur returned early that evening. It felt so unfamiliar, as though even the steps he took through the living quarters were a habit that didn't belong to him. Artur wiped at the tears falling about his face, disregarding the pain, and made the slow climb up the ladder to his bed where he collapsed atop his blankets as his body went limp. Sprawled out across the cot, with the book just beneath his palm, he lay there for some time to weep quietly in his loneliness. The window he left closed, the lantern dull and unlit at his bedside. There was nothing but the darkness to accompany him in his sorrow, and it was hardly a consolation in such despair.

It was then he realized the extent of his pain—from head to foot, Artur ached and trembled terribly from the tiredness of his muscles, some of which had never been called to action in such a way. Now they were bruised and strained, protesting the damage they'd sustained in the scuffle. And even through all the physical pain he was in, Artur soon felt the onset of hunger, the cries of an empty stomach ignored for too long. Still, starving seemed the lesser of two evils if he could avoid making the trek back down the ladder and being reminded of the pain all over again. He had neither enough vigor to leave his bed, nor the desire to satisfy his hunger. He felt he didn't deserve it—not to feast upon a delicious meal, not to come walking back home with the dignity of victory. He expected the whole village to come barging through the front door at any moment to reprimand and disown him for his iniquities. Yet the silence, sweet and welcome, persisted for what seemed akin to an eternity. Early evening passed into night and it all felt the same to him. The cottage grew darker and remained just as empty, until he heard the heart-stopping sound of the front door opening with a slight creak of wood, followed by hesitant footfalls. Artur froze and grew silent. Hoped that whoever intruded upon his home would think him absent and leave the premises. But the claws clacking against the wooden floor revealed the identity of the intruder to be none other than the kindly neighbor he was growing fond of.

"Artur," Urda called out. "Are ye here?"

Artur wanted to respond, to call out to her, and yet he was trapped in the silence surrounding him. All he could muster in response were hushed sobs that wracked his body.

He listened as she went about the house, Vána following. He heard objects shifting on surfaces, the tapping of wood tossed into the hearth which then caught flame with a crackle and a hiss, filling the cottage with light. Then Artur heard the groan of the ladder rungs, shifting under weight, and as Urda made her way up to the loft, Artur quickly pushed his book under his pillow. He buried himself beneath his blankets, through all the pain that screamed about his body.

"Artur?" Urda called to him again, finally peeking over the loft. "What is wrong, child?"

Upon his continued lack of response, Urda made her way across the loft to Artur's bedside. Making out the figure beneath the blankets, she gently placed her hand about his shoulder and Artur only tightened the blankets around him. He couldn't bear the thought of having Urda see him as he was, knew he wouldn't be able to stand it.

"Artur," she spoke with a softness that was unexpected yet warming. It was almost as if she were his mother, and he her child, the way she spoke.

"Come now. It's gaun'ae be all richt." Her hand gently caressed his shoulder. She spoke as though she knew exactly what had transpired, exactly what he was feeling.

How could she? If only she knew… But maybe it didn't matter. Maybe she would provide the kindness he so wanted, even if it wasn't what he felt he deserved. He wanted more than anything to have someone understand the turmoil and grief consuming him. To listen. To help him come to terms with everything that happened, without a bias muddling their perception, without retaliation in response to their own prejudices. To provide words of wisdom to one so naïve and ignorant as himself.

Artur relented when he felt Urda gently pulling at his blankets, slowly unveiling the battered body beneath. Artur gazed at her with teary eyes. The anger and hatred that would have been justified were not to be seen. She merely looked at him with compassion, her eyes surveying the wounds of his face and the tattered remains that were his clothes, assessing his overall condition. There was no judgment. No words spoken. Just tenderness and silent understanding exchanged between two neighbors. Artur couldn't help himself in that moment. He turned to Urda and embraced her with his arms tight about her, face buried deep in the crook of her neck. He sobbed, harder than ever before in his life.

Urda reciprocated with her arms wrapping around him, her hand cradling the back of his head. She let him cry. Let him weep until he was taken by sheer exhaustion, until there was nothing left but the heaving of absent tears, his cheeks left red and damp, nose clogged.

When his breath finally calmed, Urda placed her hands tenderly at Artur's jawline and gently lifted his gaze to hers.

"Come. Let's get ye cleaned up." Urda smiled. Whether it was one of sympathy or pity, Artur didn't care. He didn't care how haggard his overall appearance was. In that moment he had needed only to release everything, to have that literal shoulder to cry on.

Urda would have led him down from the loft at his own pace, had she not been given pause, the expression stiffening on her face. Someone was approaching the cottage. The energy about them was incensed, the footsteps forceful. They were approaching with a rage begging to be unleashed, and Urda knew who the intended recipient would be. There came the sound of pounding at the door, the anger behind each hit radiating through the entire cottage, the structure itself trembling in the unexpected visitor's very presence.

"Artur!" A woman's voice shrieked from outside. "Artur, come out here right now!"

It was Petra, Ronan's mother. If there was one parent Ronan got his vigor and temperament from, it was her. She had a reputation for being loud and belligerent when she was angry or drunk, never mind how unreserved and boisterous she was otherwise. Loud-mouthed, and often unabashed and blunt in conversation, Petra was one that the folk of Trivaden had to look out for. And when she was angry, the recipient of her rage might as well dig their own grave and suffocate under the weight of the soil rather than deal with her. Artur had only heard so in passing, and secondhand when her voice reverberated through the entire village in one of her tantrums. There was a whole new fear knowing she was coming directly for him.

Vána was the first to react to the hostile presence. Submitting to her protective instinct for the sake of her boy's safety, she bared her teeth, hair standing up along her spine. She went to the door with a low growl deep in her throat to make known the danger that awaited Petra, should she present herself as a threat. It didn't matter that it was a folk she had known for the entirety of her life. Vána was not about to let anyone hurt Artur or Urda in her presence.

They're coming for me! Artur thought to himself.

He nearly started crying again, had it not been for Urda, who put her finger to his lips and quietly shushed him. She was to handle the situation, to handle Petra. Petra was hardly intimidating to her—more of a nuisance than anything. There were very few folk Urda disliked greatly, but Petra was one of them. She despised loud-mouthed individuals who had nothing of substance to their character beyond uncensored and uninformed declarations meant only to attract attention.

With Vána at her side, Urda—the only obstacle keeping the dire wolf from lunging the moment the perceived threat came into view—answered the door before more furious knocks could take it down.

There, standing before them, was the very angry Petra. Red in the face, steam nearly coming out of her ears. At least, that's what Urda imagined to amuse herself. She stood there indifferently, as if she didn't have a beast of a woman glaring at her.

"Guid evenin', Petra. How can I help ye?" Urda gave a courteous greeting, knowing it wouldn't stop the verbal tirade that was about to come her way.

"Where is Artur?"

"'Guid evenin' tae ye too, Urda! How are ye?'" Urda mockingly acted as Petra when she failed to return the pleasantries. "I am well, thank you for askin'," she answered herself in kind, a smirk crossing over her face.

"Don't give me your attitude right now, you bitch! Where is Artur?" Petra hissed at her, spit flecking from her lips akin to a rabid beast. Petra had no qualms about cursing at Urda. She was one of the many women who didn't fancy the odd woman living at the edge of their village, very much believing her to be one of the witches spoken about in the legends of old.

"Why dae ye need him?"

"Do you know what he's done to my son?"

"Do ye know whit yer son has done tae Artur? The poor boy has been distraucht since before I got here."

"He almost beat my boy to death!" Petra nearly lost all control, just saying the words out loud. "Apparently, they got into an argument and Artur started beating on my son!"

"Really?" Urda raised a skeptical brow at Petra. "Artur wis the first tae beat on yer son in an argument?"

"Yes!"

"Repeat whit ye juist says, an' then tell me if thon still sounds believable."

"Why would my son lie about that?"

"Come now, Petra." Urda crossed her arms about her chest. "Considerin' hou fickle yer son is, ye don't think he's the one thon startit the confrontation? I'm certain he conveniently left oot his responsibility in the matter."

Petra was taken aback for a moment, speechless. She really couldn't put it past her son to skew the truth. He was a known hothead, a troublemaker in the village, although usually his antics were harmless enough. But the moment she had seen the state he was in, she could only see red. That was her boy. She was his sworn protector. The motherly instincts compelled her to action.

Now that there was a pause in the conversation, as Petra's wrath waned however momentarily, Urda asked her calmly, "What wis the argument aboot?"

"I'm not certain." Petra looked away. She hadn't even thought to push for more detail once she heard there had been an altercation. "I just know that they got into a fight. Are you certain Artur hasn't told you anything?" She looked to Urda once more.

"Why would I lie aboot thon?"

"I am aware of your wicked ways, and the deceit that spills from your tongue, witch. I will not be deceived so easily!"

Urda let out an exasperated sigh. She still could not understand how her knowledge of well-known and long-studied procedures, and widely practiced medicinal concoctions, made her a witch compared to other specialists and physicians in her field. Sometimes she relished the old tales and the history of those possessing her physical attributes, while other times they were just a nuisance. Artur was in trouble. This was no time to defend her own character from skepticism and prudishness.

"Perhaps the truth will reveal itself soon enouch, Petra. For now, ye an' I both have children we need tae tend tae. Artur didn't come out o' the conflict unscathed either, an' he's in na condition tae bear the brunt o' yer wrath. Gae home. Be wi' yer boy, an' I'll be wi' mine. We can discuss this later if ye wish, but it will no' be tonicht."

"But—"

"Good nicht, Petra." Urda couldn't hide the smirk in her voice as she closed the door right in Petra's stunned face.

Her dismissal did little to tame the wrath of a mother scorned, and the pounding and screaming commenced once again to Urda's amusement. Even Vána, who had done well in keeping herself from attacking, couldn't help but snort at the woman's tenacity.

"She'll tire herself out," Urda commented to Vána, who looked up to her with perked ears. "Just give her some time."

"I can hear you, you bitch! I'm not finished here!"

Urda placed her hands over her mouth to keep the chortle begging to taunt Petra from escaping the confines of her lips, despite the curses and slander being thrown her way. Though Urda was more than capable of handling such a verbal barrage, the neighbors would not be keen on listening to the confrontation at this hour of the night.

One such neighbor, Anderson, who owned the tavern just a little down the way, poked his head out of his window and shouted, "Will you shut the fuck up, Petra! We can't hear the bard over your screaming!"

"Don't tell me what I can and cannot do, Anderson!" Petra's rage was easily directed to the next closest target, when she realized she was going to get nowhere with Urda. Her heeled boots clattered across the wooden porch until her footfalls were muffled by the dirt path, and she began arguing in earnest with Anderson, who was just as unlikely to back down as Petra was.

Their argument diminished to white noise, and Urda couldn't help but giggle to herself as she went back to her cottage to retrieve some needed supplies—an assortment of ointments, tools, and bandages to tend to Artur's wounds. When she returned to the Sigurdsson cottage, she put a pot of water over the fire.

Once everything was organized, she peeked up the loft at a very terrified Artur, who had pulled his knees up to his chest and buried his head within the confines of his arms.

"You'll be alricht, Artur," Urda called to him. "Come doun an' we'll get thaes wounds cleanit for ye. An', how's aboot some supper, hm?"

As Artur found the strength and courage to make his way down from the loft, the screaming match outside finally subsided. Anderson finished the argument with, "No wonder your kid got his arse beat—when he acts akin to you!" His door slammed and Petra stormed off back home, cursing all the way there.

CHAPTER 20

Fortunately for Artur, Urda had brought a pot of stew home with her from another neighbor, still hot and smelling heavenly to a ravenous stomach. Urda offered to tend to his wounds first, but Artur was famished, only shaking his head in objection and sitting at the table quietly until she brought him a bowl and a loaf of bread. She didn't mind waiting patiently as the poor boy ate as though he'd never had a meal in his life, stuffing his face until his hunger was spent and his belly was full. Even Vána, far and away the most ravenous eater in Trivaden, watched in absolute awe at how much Artur consumed. She could hardly pry her eyes away from the sight to enjoy the raw cut of venison lying between her paws.

When the meal was finished, they sat before the fire and Urda began the slow and tender process of nursing Artur's injuries. Artur flinched and groaned a bit, even from the gentlest of touches, as she cleaned his open wounds and wiped away the dried blood and dirt from his skin. She had nursed enough folk to know when she could ignore their objections and whining. There was a task that needed to be done, and if she allowed herself to be foiled by every little protest, it was only the patient who would suffer. Given that most of the ointments and medicinal creams she applied in her practices often delivered a sting even as their healing properties began to take effect, Urda had to move quickly and with as much finesse as possible. She deftly operated her tools with one hand while the other simultaneously handled the application of her creams and salves, a technique she had spent a lifetime perfecting.

Beyond the pain and the mild inconvenience that came with it, Artur was pleasantly surprised at how much better his wounds began to feel. Every time Urda applied whatever was neatly organized in her jars, the injury almost immediately felt noticeably better, practically numb to the point of nonexistence. Urda applied gauze to his newly cleaned wounds, and wrapped his knuckles, knees, and anything else that needed protection from outside elements, as the final touch.

Artur sat there surveying the great quantity of bandages that covered everything that had been done to him, taking stock of how battered the fight had left his body. There was a soreness still, something no amount of medicine was going to be able to fix, something his body would have to heal on its own. Throughout Urda's procedures the two had basked in the silence, a remedy in and of itself. Now that he could see the magnitude of Urda's help and generosity, she didn't deserve just silence, and though Artur wanted to weep again in pure thankfulness, he held back those tears.

With a deep breath, Artur finally uttered his first words of the night. "Thank you, Urda."

"There's no need tae thank me, Artur," she said with a smile, gently nudging his chin with a closed fist. He couldn't help but smile back.

Urda's work wasn't done. She needed to sterilize her tools and clean the cloths she used to wipe the blood away. The pot she kept on the fire was waiting for such a moment, along with a bottle of vinegar, which had been sitting patiently on the kitchen counter. She stood and went about finishing her processes, while Artur looked to the fire beside him, lulled into a trance by the dancing flames that warmed him. He continued to watch until Vána let out a whine from where she lay beside him. The flames released him, allowing him to engage in patting her between her ears where she adored it the most. Vána too played her part in his healing process. Her loyalty and concern for his well-being were more appreciated than Artur could put into words. Not once had she left his side while Urda was tending to him, and she remained long after his wounds were bound. Looking to the fire once more, Artur hoped Lovisa had made it to… wherever she currently called home in a foreign land…safely, and was being cared for as tenderly as he had been: the blood clean from her silver hair, the tears no longer falling down her face, and her terrified expression softened to one of calmness and peace.

Before Artur could delve too deeply into his thoughts, too deeply into the memories of recent events, he heard a loud blast in the distance. It rattled the entirety of the cottage and sent vibrations emanating through his already aching body. Hardly a gasp escaped his lips before the explosion proved to be only the herald of what was to come: the beginning of a continuous barrage that reverberated through the forest and the village both.

Urda too had no choice but to put down her tools as her attention was pulled toward the commotion, her head turning sharply and her eyes darting about the cottage trembling all around her. Artur was already succumbing to panic. A quick glance showed her the terrified boy curled up with his hands over his ears. Vána herself had jumped to her feet with a start, the hairs along her spine standing at attention once more, her ears tilted back as she let out a concerned whine. She refused to leave Artur's side. Should he be in danger, she was going to be there to defend him.

"Urda…" was all Artur could mutter as he turned to her with a horrified expression on his face. She didn't reply, only looking to him with her brow furrowed in concern.

"They're coming for me!" he exclaimed, his voice as trembly as the cottage.

Urda quickly went to his side and cradled the poor boy in her arms as tenderly as she could, mindful of his still-fresh wounds. The boy shuddered within her embrace, his tears soaking her blouse anew.

"They're coming! And it's all my fault," Artur repeated, distraught.

"No one is comin' for ye, Artur." She tried to soothe him, her hand caressing the back of his head.

"Yes, they are! I did something terrible!"

"Artur, whatever is goin' on has nothin' tae dae wi' ye, I promise."

"No, Urda! You don't understand!" Artur pushed away from Urda just enough that he could meet her gaze. "I saved a Valeriaan!"

The stoic expression about her face did little to soothe him.

"The reason me and Ronan fought was because I stopped him from killing her! My friend is a Valeriaan!" He pushed the words out through the sobs beginning to resurface. "They'll know we hurt her…I turned my back on everyone—"

"Artur, hold on now—"

"No! No! This is all happening because of me!" He once again buried his face against her shoulder and wept.

Urda felt for the boy, truly she did, but he was beyond hysterical and would only prove a detriment to himself if they were indeed under attack. Urda highly doubted their village was in imminent danger, at least for the time being. The continued explosions were too far off in the distance for her to conclude that Trivaden was affected by what was transpiring. No—it was no doubt Falkhearth. Whatever had been brewing in the past days was finally beginning to unfold, and Falkhearth was the first victim of such an onslaught. Urda's main concern now was to keep Artur from completely losing himself to the panic consuming him. She hated what she was about to do, but she had no choice. It was no time for coddling. Urda grasped Artur by his shoulders and held him firmly before her. He could look nowhere but right at her.

"Artur! Ye need tae calm doun an' get a hold o' yourself."

"I can't—"

"Yes, ye can. An' ye will. Richt now. You'll be worthless tae e'en yourself if Valeriaans were here."

"But—"

"Deep breaths," she interrupted before the excuses could ensue. "Dae as I dae."

She inhaled and Artur tried his best to imitate her through his weeping, and when she exhaled, he did so as well, nearly spitting phlegm on her.

"Again," she said, and they repeated the process until Artur quieted down enough to slow his breathing and stop his tears. He was a mess still, but at least he was manageable.

"The last thin' ye want tae be is a danger tae yourself, Artur. Especially if it could mean yer life. Cry an' feel guilty aw ye want afterwards. But richt now, ye need a level head. Understand?"

Artur only nodded to her and wiped his puffy, red eyes.

"Now, I'm gaun'ae gae outside an' see what's goin' on. Stay here an' stay quiet."

"No, Urda..."

"Yes, Artur. I need tae see what's happenin'. I'll come richt back for ye once I can, alricht?"

Artur shook his head in disagreement, but Urda gave him a firm shake and said, "Good boy. Now stay here."

She couldn't let herself be stalled any longer. Disregarding his objection, she left him sitting there in bewilderment as she exited the house, a very agitated Vána staying behind to continue guarding him.

Urda wasn't alone in her curiosity. The other village folk gathered just at the edge of the forest to look out upon the vastness of the plains before them. The endless darkness that visited them nightly was interrupted by a faint glow of orange upon the horizon. The unrelenting explosions echoed through the emptiness of the air about them, a deep thudding felt in the chest. Even as the village folk whispered to one another and shook their heads in disbelief, no one dared speak aloud what they knew to be transpiring. They all secretly wished someone would be the first to say it, to break the tension.

Urda paid no mind to any of the conversations around her as she pushed past the crowd until she reached the very front of the group. She could feel the cool breath of wind through her unkempt locks, the disturbance in the air caused by the bursts reverberating through the land. While the others looked on in fear and sorrow for those caught in the midst of the event, Urda's lips pressed together into a hard line as she fought the scowl begging to cross her face. She worried deeply for her dear friends. For Thelric. For the brazen and foolish Ygrayne, who had thrust herself into harm's way for his sake. Urda could hardly blame her. To have someone you love so much you're willing to do anything for them—that was rare and admirable in equal measure. Were they doomed to perish? Would it be her fate to take Artur under her wing in his parents' stead? The thought was almost unbearable.

"They're attacking Falkhearth." Svend, the resident smith who owned the forge in Trivaden, broke the silence.

"Will they come here?" Revna, Svend's wife, asked, and the query evoked a flurry of questions and worries as the panic over the unknown possibilities grew to a crescendo. Some of the women filled the air with cries and hysterics for their husbands who were still trapped within those walls, for the fathers and sons who had yet to return to them safely.

All the comforts, all the words of sympathy and empathy, they all merged into a meaningless murmur. There was no truth, only speculation of what had befallen Falkhearth. History showed that the Valeriaans left nothing to chance. They would burn down and destroy everything they thought necessary to secure the longevity of the Empire. If it did prove true that there were Oathbound in Falkhearth, then Oathbound could also be residing in the surrounding region, even as far as Trivaden and her neighbors. Urda was the only one amongst the village folk who cast her mind to the future rather than lingering on the concerns of the present. The carnage wasn't going to stop in Falkhearth. Urda had suspected ever since the small band of missing villagers had returned that the Valeriaans were not demonstrating generosity. Kindness wasn't in their nature. Every action was deliberate, and she feared this one would lead to grim consequences. Otherwise, those few would have been kept in Falkhearth, doomed to die along with the others.

Urda turned to the weeping crowd and searched amongst the faces belonging to the caravan, wondering to herself, *Whit is goin' on?*

Urda couldn't present such questions without a basis. All she could do was suspect, and the panic and rage her speculations might provoke in the crowd weren't worth the risk or the headache. The village folk were already in distress. Even the boisterous Petra, who just earlier had been the embodiment of rage and indignation, was trembling at every rumble.

What if her caution was unfounded? Or ignorant, even?

"Everyone," she called out over the voices. It took a little more coaxing before they quieted enough to listen to what she had to say.

"As far as we know, the Valeriaans are only after thaes in Falkhearth. We've aw heard the rumors o' thare bein' Oathbound in the city. Thon doesn't mean they'll be comin' for us. Never mind the fact we haven't given thaim a reason tae."

She once again scrutinized the faces for their reactions, to see who had grown visibly uncomfortable, nervous. Who would avert their eyes at the mere mention of Oathbound? There were a few shifts here and there, but Urda was well aware of how disciplined the Oathbound had become over the years. They were taught to remain composed under duress, to choose death rather than give anything away. If there indeed were Oathbound in Trivaden, uncovering their identities would be difficult. Or perhaps, there truly weren't any? Urda hardly believed the latter, but there was no way she would be able to pry out the truth when they were so adamant about keeping it hidden.

"Don't be so certain of that, Urda," someone chimed in. "They could think we have Oathbound here in Trivaden."

"If they thought that, they would be here already," said another.

"And they're no," Urda pointed out calmly. "However, if any o' ye are truly worried aboot it, ye can leave. Na dout they'll have watchpoints up an' doun our roads, but if ye believe it tae be worth the risk, I suggest ye tak' it." Her eyes surveyed the folk before her once more.

There's your way out, Urda thought. *Oathbound or not.*

"Maybe the best thing we can do is stay here and wait it out," said Cenric, a neighbor and the bard of Trivaden.

"Wait for them to come and kill us?"

"I already telt ye ma thouchts an' suggestions. If any o' ye have any other ideas, I'm willin' tae listen." Urda crossed her arms over her chest.

Silence fell over the crowd, as the village folk looked between each other for some kind of indication as to the correct course of action that should be taken.

"So, until one o' ye has a better idea, we better keep our heads doun. There's nothin' more we can dae."

No one wanted to admit it, but the assumed witch was right. There was nothing they could do. Cattle turned out to pasture or cattle lined up for the slaughter. In the end, still cattle.

After contemplating and weighing the options before them, the village folk eventually dispersed, some back to their homes and some to the tavern to find some sort of comfort in the songs of the bard and the company of drink. All they could do in their situation was hope that war wouldn't arrive at their doorstep.

Urda watched from her neighbors' porch for her dear friend in silence, her shadowed silhouette leaning up against the column of the cottage. She'd said her piece. Now the decision was left to the village folk. In the distance she watched as the lanterns that usually spilled light through the windows and under the doors of the active residents, were dimmed or extinguished altogether. The residents of Trivaden sought comfort and protection by blending into the night, becoming as inconspicuous as possible so as not to draw unwanted attention to themselves. Only the tavern showed signs of life. The hearth inside burned warm and bright, and the bard could be heard singing and strumming at his mandolin. His voice, which brimmed most nights with vigor and eccentricity, was melancholy.

Urda retreated into the cottage and immediately felt the exhaustion of the whole ordeal finally taking its toll. The night was hardly over, however, and there was still someone who needed her. She took in a deep breath, pulled back her fiery tresses, and straightened up her posture to project a sense of togetherness, however feigned. She approached the fire, where Artur sat with a blanket wrapped tightly around him, having retrieved it sometime during the commotion. Urda took a seat next to him on the floor and he let out a startled gasp, eyes widening. The blanket folded and wrinkled in his lap, purposefully covering the hands he had pressed again this abdomen. Urda had moved with such stealth that he hadn't at all been aware of her presence until she was sat next to him, taken aback by her sudden appearance.

Urda's brow furrowed, a smirk crossing her lips as she found the astonished look about his face rather amusing, as well as curious. She couldn't help but inquire, "Whit dae ye have thare, lad?"

"Nothing!" Artur was quick to answer, his poor attempt at innocence only proving that there was in fact something.

"Why dae ye no' wish tae tell me?"

Artur's lips only hardened, his eyes lowering from her gaze which glistened brightly in the touch of the fire as if her eyes emitted a glow as vibrant as the flames beside them.

"If it's a secret, it shall ne'er leave ma lips. Ye have ma oath."

Artur hesitated, considering. If their interactions had revealed anything, it was that she could be trusted. Her word was her word. Her intentions were well meaning. But would such integrity be fair to expect with a revelation so alarming? Artur had already gambled with fortune by retrieving his now most prized possession when events called Urda's attention away. When enough time had passed in his continued solitude, he'd thought it reasonably safe to do so—thought he could return it to secrecy before she graced him with her presence once again. But unakin to the many times he'd heard her saunter across the living quarters, this time she had approached with an almost unnerving soundlessness. As though her feet had never touched the wood-plank floor. Not even Vána had given any indication of her approach as she lay still beside him. Having been caught in an action meant to be discreet, Artur saw no other choice but to relinquish the truth to her and hope she would take the admission well enough.

Sorry, Lovisa... He thought of the promise he made earlier, and how easily he was compelled to break it.

As the blanket unfurled from his lap, Urda saw it: the dull sheen of brown pages in the fire's light, rustling as they turned.

Urda managed to stifle a gasp, but could hardly stop her eyes from widening in surprise. "Where did ye get thon?" She was almost breathless.

"Lovisa gave it to me," Artur whispered.

When Urda reached for it, Artur held it away from her. He stared at her in confusion and mild irritation. She could see how tired he was, more exhausted than she was herself. She determined it best to withdraw her hand, letting it fall in her lap as to not further aggravate him.

"The Valeriaan girl?" she asked calmly.

Artur only nodded and returned to the pages filled with words he could hardly recognize without Lovisa's guidance.

"She was showing me how to read but...I don't really remember how to." He looked to Urda. "Lovisa told me that books are forbidden. But why? Why can I not have a book? How come I never learned to read?"

The fire crackled as if laughing, mocking the poor boy and his ignorance for asking such a question.

"When the Valeriaans won the war, thare wis a great burnin o' any an' every type o' literature. It wis made illegal tae have anythin' o' the sort. Artur, if anyone saw ye wi' this, they could turn ye in. Or worse—if a Valeriaan caught you with that book..." She paused.

"But...she gave it to me."

"Despite her knowin' o' the laws... Artur, you'd best burn that—"

"No!" Artur snapped at her, holding the book against his chest. "I'm not going to! You can't make me!"

"It wad be for yer own guid."

"No! It's the only thing I have left of her." Artur choked a bit, and Urda held back her response. "I'm never going to see her again..."

Urda let out a sigh and said quietly, "All richt."

She would get nowhere trying to persuade him otherwise. Instead of taking the book away from him by force, she could at least arm him with the knowledge he needed to keep himself safe.

"Artur, if you're determined tae keep it, ye have tae make certain na one knows aboot it. No' e'en yer parents."

"I told you though..." He eyed her cautiously.

"I won't speak a word o' it. Yer secret is between us. I swore an oath on it."

"What even is an...oath?"

"It's a promise. A promise never tae be broken. Back in the olden ages, whan one made an oath, they wad bleed on it. Should they break it, they were tae pay for it wi' their life."

Artur stammered to find the words for a moment. "D-do they still do that?"

"Na, dear boy." Urda chortled to herself. "That wis a very long time ago. Folk don't swear their lives tae it anymore. Which is probably why sae many folk break their promises these days. But I digress. Whit I'm tryin' tae say is, I swear an oath tae never speak o' it."

"Thank you, Urda." Artur dropped the book into his lap, cushioned within his hands.

Urda nodded her head and looked once more upon the book, this time admiring the beautiful blue of the cover, the delicate stitching along the spine, the way the lettering shone of gold. Apart from the sentimental value, she could see why it would be a waste for it to be discarded. Such beauty hardly deserved to be demonized simply to enforce a preposterous punishment.

"Why is reading forbidden?"

"You tak' away a folk's past, they have na future. An ignorant population is a controllable population."

Artur looked to her. He wanted to know more. To hear her speak unfettered in his presence, to know of the world around him. Urda knew this, but she hesitated. The last time she spoke of such a world she left him trembling, and she feared that to say more would only worsen his already fragile state. Artur wasn't about to relent. He continued to look at her with obvious, unwavering eagerness.

Urda took a breath, and she nodded her head in resignation.

"The commonfolk only have a limitit understandin' o' writin' an' readin' tae allow them tae trade an' conduct commerce. But as far as readin' books, an' havin' access tae knowledge o' the ages before us, thon we're na longer permitted, tae learn o' tae teach. This is by Valeriaan design. They want the folk tae be simple. Tae rely upon thaim without question or opposition. Tae no' have the masses possess the knowledge tae tak' up arms against thaim. Folk, without the most basic o' education, are easy tae keep under control. Thon is why ye cannot read. It's why yer parents cannot read. Nor yer friends, nor anyone in Trivaden."

Artur looked to the book in his hands, wondering how something seemingly so simple and unassuming could be so threatening. And opening it so delicately, he wondered what exactly it contained that made a stack of pages so valuable. There was beauty in its simplicity, an alluring gentleness. Perhaps if he ever learned to read the script upon the pages, he would truly understand why the Valeriaans kept the ability amongst their own ever so selfishly.

"This Valeriaan girl," Urda spoke when Artur didn't reply. "She truly is yer friend, isn't she?" And then she thought to herself, *Why else would a Valeriaan gift something so forbidden?*

"Was my friend." Artur sighed. "Ronan…hurt her…hurt her badly. That's why we got into a fight. He was trying to kill her and…I-I stopped him." Artur's voice quavered, admitting so out loud. It was hardly the whole truth, but he hesitated to continue to speak upon it. He trusted Urda, but there was much uncertainty in what he was about to say next.

Ronan was one of his best friends, and he had turned on Artur so easily in the right set of circumstances. Who was to say Urda wouldn't do the same?

"She's gone," he said quietly. "Now I feel…as though we were never supposed to be friends. That I was supposed to hate her as everyone else hates her. But…but I just don't. Is there something wrong with me?"

The boy sniffled, wiping at his face.

"Ronan called me a traitor, and all I was doing was what I thought was right." He sat there crying softly, awaiting Urda's harsh words and disparagements, his wrongdoings thrown in his face once more. They did not come, however.

Urda simply placed her hand upon his shoulder ever so gently, and said kindly, "No, Artur. There's nothing wrong wi' ye."

She carefully lifted his face by his chin and brought his gaze to hers.

"The world will tell ye hou ye should feel. Hou ye should act. Predetermined by its own hatrit. But once in a while, thare comes along a small exception thon shows a glimmer o' licht in aw the darkness thon has consumed the world. Ye an' yer friend are thon licht. Settin' aside such expectancies, the two o' ye found somethin' thon is beautiful. Perhaps the world has been blindit for sae long, it hardly recognizes whan thare is somethin' blossomin' richt before it—a beauty thon the world needs tae see once again—needs tae feel. Sae don't be ashamit o' yourself. Cherish whit ye haed. Remember it aw. Ye cared for her for who she wis, no' whit she wis. An' na dout, she afforded ye the same courtesy."

Despite all the turmoil and commotion of the night, Artur managed to fall asleep and sleep soundly. The stress and exhaustion finally took hold and dragged the boy down into the depths of slumber, holding him there until the light returned with the morning. Though the sky wasn't as blue, nor the air as clear that day, the beauty of the land tainted by the acrid touch of smoke and brownish clouds, at least it had grown quiet. The air smelled of fire, of destruction, of anguish. A light dusting of ash blanketed the land, easily stirred by the slightest touch. It served as an awful reminder that, though the explosions had ceased, the worst was certainly yet to come, and a sense of doom hung heavily over the village. Where there was usually chatter and the bustle of everyday life, now there was only silence. Neither conversation nor the commotion of labor could be heard throughout Trivaden. The village folk found solace in the confines of their cottages, accepting willful ignorance of the happenings around them in the hope that the events they feared would not come to pass—so that life in the village might go on as it was.

When Artur awoke, he found the cottage empty and quiet, the fire long burned out in the night. His parents' bed was neatly made, a fresh flower in the vase on the nightstand, purple akin to the one Urda had previously gifted his mother. As he descended the ladder, he became acutely aware of the pain his body was in. No longer was the vigor present to ward off the aches, the ointments' effects similarly dwindled away. He struggled to grasp the ladder with his swollen hands, wincing and whining quietly to himself until his feet touched the floor. Urda had already helped herself to an early breakfast but had left some laid out for him as well—a simple one of bread, cheese, and milk. Artur took the remaining loaf and munched on it on his way out the back door, discovering how deathly quiet it was as he emerged from the cottage. Not only had the village grown quiet, but so had the birds, and the wind and the beasts within the forest's domain. It was almost haunting, yet Artur didn't seem to mind. He wanted no one to lay eyes on him, wanted no one to be aware of his existence for fear of being interrogated regarding the previous day's events. He hurried along the path to the river as quickly as his aching body would allow him, and when he reached the riverbank did his memory begin to remind him of what transpired. The sands remained disturbed and ravaged from the confrontation. The damp, cold sediment beneath the surface was visible in several divots, the imprints of bodies telling the story of the fight. There on the first boulder in the river was a bloodied print of Lovisa's hand, dried and darkened in hue but unmistakable. Artur swallowed hard and rushed over to it, dropping his book in his haste.

He couldn't bear to be reminded of how she had been hurt, and he quickly poured handfuls of water over the spot in the hope of washing it away. What little good it did. The handprint seemed now a part of the rock, embedded in its textured surface. What began as sorrow soon turned to anger as his efforts proved futile. He kicked the rock with a loud grunt, hoping it would turn on its side and tumble deeper into the water. And when he failed once more, Artur stepped into the water and grasped the underside of the rock. With all the strength he had left, he pulled at it until he succeeded in dislodging it, and watched it sink beneath the water's surface.

Artur trudged back to the riverbank and collapsed to his knees, holding his hands before him as they shook and trembled with pain. The exertion proved too much for him, and his fingers stiffened as they curled towards his palms to find some kind of release, some kind of escape from the abuse. In that moment Artur would have begun to cry, had he any tears left. He had spent them all the previous night. Instead, he sat there pitying himself for his outburst, realizing how idiotic it truly was in his physical state.

With a long hard sigh, he sat back on the sands to wait. Deep down he knew Lovisa wasn't coming back, and with everything that had transpired the previous day, and the injuries inflicted on his body, it wouldn't be a wise decision to go forth and look for her. Instead, he looked to the skies to see they had further soured since he had arrived at the riverbank, bringing the reality of the terrifying events all the closer. He shuddered at the thought. He didn't even want to think about what might be happening in Falkhearth at that very moment.

To drown out the wanderings of his imagination, Artur opened his book to the first page and once more gazed upon the script that was still so foreign to him. He tried hard to remember how Lovisa had sounded out the words, how she'd taken care to go slowly so that he could keep up, but his mind drew a blank each time. He just couldn't read it. Not without her.

With a sigh, Artur closed the book and held it out before him. His inadequacy didn't take away its beauty, and at least he could admire it for what it was: his beautiful secret, and all he had left of his dear friend.

CHAPTER 21

Earlier that day, in the Valeriaan camp...

For almost the entire day, Ygrayne slumbered. When she awoke, she hardly remembered where she was. The medicine had done well to make her groggy and put her body at rest to heal. Disoriented, she expected to wake in the comfort of her own home but was met instead with the strange tent that comprised the only barrier between her and the adversaries surrounding her. Only when she looked about the tent and saw the previously occupied table now vacant at the center, and the adjacent bed hardly disturbed, did Ygrayne remember where she was. With a solemn sigh, she touched at her head tenderly, the flush of soreness through her face resurfacing upon contact. She wished she could return to sleep if it meant keeping the pain at bay for just a while longer.

When she lay back down, she found herself too uneasy to drift off again. There was an uncomfortable air about her, and for a while she couldn't quite place why. She lay in isolation, confined to her temporary shelter, and then it occurred to her—it was silent. Even when she had first lay down to rest the night before, the camp had hardly been ready to settle in for the evening. The soldiers were boisterous as they conversed by the fire and drank to their hearts' content. There was none of that in the present moment, the camp enveloped in the kind of silence she might find solace in, under a different set of circumstances. Even the Schiva, who had tended to her needs throughout the night, had vanished.

Thus began her search for the truth, for the companion who had recently become her savior. Unkempt and still adjusting to her unflattering attire, Ygrayne left the tent and carefully went about the disconcertingly empty camp. She wandered through the sea of abandoned white tents, passing only a handful of soldiers who did nothing to hide their snide glances and the smirks about their faces. She noted, however, that the soldiers, who she knew to be more than comfortable in committing acts of viciousness against the vulnerable, kept their distance from her.

At first, Ygrayne believed this to be the result of the commander's orders. And perhaps it was the bigger part of the reason, but it wasn't until she heard a snort, and felt a breath of wind on her neck, that Ygrayne realized she wasn't alone. It wasn't the Schiva who accompanied her, but his loyal companion of a horse, Onír.

He had been following her since the moment she left the tent. Never once had he left her side out of a sense that it was as much his duty to protect her as it was his master's. He was her armament in the Schiva's absence. Startled, Ygrayne let out a cry before her hand could stifle it. Onír let out a whinny, which she could only interpret as a chuckle at her expense.

"I'm glad someone is amused," she commented, and Onír flapped his lips in a horsey grin.

"You think you're so clever, don't you?" Ygrayne was entertained by the horse's seemingly sharp awareness in the way he responded, tapping the ground with his hoof and snorting another hot breath as he dipped his head.

"Well." Ygrayne raised a brow at him. "If you're so clever, why don't you show me where your master is?"

She needed not say more for Onír to do as she asked. The horse turned in a completely new direction and toward an aisle of tents she had not yet wandered down.

Very clever indeed, she thought to herself as she followed him.

Ygrayne was truly impressed by how perceptive Onír was, responding to conversation and expressing himself without words. It reminded her of the only other beast in her life who had been observed to possess such ability—Vána. Interesting indeed, but only ever observable, not explainable.

When Onír came to a clearing in the encampment, he picked up an excited trot, sparking a sudden tension in Ygrayne. There was no way she would be able to keep pace with the beast, even if her body were sound. Only when Onír turned did she see the Schiva before him, arms full of provisions she could hardly identify at a distance.

He had been out collecting food for supper, to eat while she slumbered so as not to give away his face, and to provide something immediate for her to consume should she wake up ravaged with hunger. He was surprised to see her. "You're awake."

"I'm awake." Ygrayne nodded, her eyes shifting to Onír as the beast nibbled on the Schiva's shoulder. The platter the Schiva carried was loaded with the most delectable-looking food, one item of which Onír was particularly interested in—the red apple on one side of the plate.

"I thought you'd still be asleep."

"Should I be?"

"If I'm going to be honest, you slept longer than I expected, and have awoken sooner than I had…well, expected. I thought in the meantime to bring you food. I'm certain you're hungry by now."

Now, as Ygrayne observed everything on the platter—a mix of meats, cheeses, fruits and bread—she could hardly be convinced that she was truly hungry. On the contrary, Ygrayne felt she had no appetite. The turmoil of yesterday's events had subdued that natural urge.

"I appreciate the kind gesture, but I'm really not hungry at present."

"You should eat," the Schiva was quick to insist. "Your body heals faster when it is properly nourished."

"Truly, I'm not hungry."

The Schiva blinked at her, those amber eyes accentuated by the black paint around them, and Ygrayne wondered whether he was measuring her conviction, or if he was just as unwilling to relent as she. Reaching for an apple, he proved the latter.

"At least eat this." He held it out to her, and Onír maneuvered his head around the Schiva's arm with lips pulled back and teeth bared to take a bite. "This is not for you!" the Schiva protested, pushing at Onír with an elbow. "You already had your apples!"

"He can, by all means, have the apple. At least someone wants it."

Onír was all too happy to hear this, but his master remained unmoved. "Get on with you!" The Schiva nudged at him again and Onír threw a silent fit, turning his ears back and trotting off in disappointment.

The Schiva held the apple out to her once again and said, "Please. At least the apple for now. It will make you feel a lot better."

There was a hopefulness within his voice, and Ygrayne could see that the eyes behind the mask had softened with the second request. To her, it sounded more of a plea for his own sake as well as hers, for his peace of mind. How could she say no to something so endearing?

Ygrayne took the apple and immediately saw the light of satisfaction within his eyes. "Thank you," she said.

"No. Thank you," he replied. "Besides, you know the saying about eating apples."

"What exactly is this saying?"

"Nothing. Just eat the apple." He snorted as he laughed at the ridiculousness of his jest, and Ygrayne only reciprocated out of awkwardness.

"I see where your horse gets it," she commented with a huff. "The both of you think you're so clever."

"I fancy a jest now and again."

"You should practice more often because that was truly horrible."

The Schiva's amusement was in the deadpan delivery of the nonsense itself. Often, his words were met with a laugh of pity or sheer confusion from the recipient. After some time of continued, and consequently failed, attempts, he had decided to change the tactic so if no one else enjoyed his jests, he could at least take pleasure in them himself. In this moment, he had succeeded doubly—he'd had a good laugh, and Ygrayne was eating the apple.

She took a bite, the fruit so crisp and succulent even she was surprised. It awoke in her a hunger she had thought completely diminished, one she didn't want to admit to in front of the Schiva after so adamantly rejecting his offer of food. As inconsequential as it was, Ygrayne was embarrassed to be wrong. From beneath the thickness of her lashes, she gazed up to the Schiva as inconspicuously as possible, only to find herself discovered as he had been looking at her for the duration of her pondering. When their gazes met, she watched as his eyes narrowed ever so slyly, and she knew he was pleased with even such a little victory. She imagined the smug smile hidden behind the mask, noting the delighted glint in his eyes before he turned his head away.

When they returned to the tent, Ygrayne felt a bit uncomfortable being the only one eating, especially given her previous protests. The Schiva did not touch any of the food as she ate. Deep down, Ygrayne had hoped he would join her so that she might catch even the slightest glimpse of the face that belonged to the man beneath the robes and the mask. Even an event as mundane as a Schiva eating would have been a fascinating sight to behold. Alas, it was not one Ygrayne was to be permitted to witness. The Schiva busied himself with his notebooks and healing implements about the table while she ate, and when she finished, he set about reapplying the medicines and gauze to her wounds once again. The commander's gauntlet had hit hard and cut deep into her cheek, and it was the most tender injury of them all; the rest of the bruising was more of a nuisance than it was painful.

"What is your name?" the Schiva asked, his eyes not once straying from the task at hand.

It was a shameless reminder of the previous night, and one which had Ygrayne smirking. Certainly, the Schiva knew of her clear cognizance after their interaction earlier.

"Ygrayne," she answered, and before he could ask the next predictable question, she was quick to add, "We are in a Valeriaan camp, and I am from Trivaden."

It was just as she expected. There was a smirk in the way he glanced at her for but a moment, before returning to her mending.

"I just wanted to tell you," Ygrayne said as the Schiva gently turned her head up to observe the bruising on her jawline. He let out a "Hm?" in acknowledgement, as he was deep in thought.

"Thank you. For saving me. For tending to me. I don't know how I can ever repay you."

"There is need neither to thank, nor to repay me." He applied a cream that was cold to the touch, something which penetrated the skin deeply and soothed her muscles and bones alike.

"You saved my life. My son would no longer have a mother if it weren't for you, certainly."

"That does not mean I require a thank you."

"So, you will not accept my thanks and gratitude?" Ygrayne's brow furrowed.

"That is correct."

"Even though you saved my life?"

The Schiva finished and looked to her, and with a tilt of his head, he replied, "Even though I saved your life."

"Do the Schiva not accept 'thank you's?'"

"We take nothing in return. It is our duty and pleasure to be at the service of others."

"Which one of you—a long time ago—made that a part of the oath?"

"I am uncertain," he answered. "But certainly, someone very bitter, who wanted everyone else to be as miserable as they." He snorted to himself as he retreated to the table with the remnants of the supplies to reorganize and store them.

Ygrayne only smiled at him. Whether she felt a deeper sense of gratitude or pity, she couldn't decide, but what she did know for certain was that such a predicament seemed wholly miserable and unsatisfying. To not even be able to accept something as simple as a "thank you" seemed to her to reek of self-denial and false modesty. And as she thought about it, Ygrayne was left to wonder once more, *How did he convince the commander to let me live?*

The Valeriaans' courtesy extended only begrudgingly to the Brethren, and never to the commonfolk. The Schiva must have been able to offer something the commander wanted—something of great magnitude, possibly requiring some kind of self-sacrifice. Ygrayne's wanderings of mind soon brought her back to the observations she had made earlier that day—the camp was empty and unnervingly quiet. Most of the soldiers were gone, a departure Ygrayne had not been conscious to notice.

"May I ask you something?"

"You may ask me anything, and I will answer almost anything," he said teasingly, his eyes still trained on the work before him.

"Where are the soldiers?"

CHAPTER 22

That is how Ygrayne found herself atop the hill just at the camp's border, overlooking the endless void of darkness which stretched its gaunt hand across the land that night. It was a darkness so complete that even the Nerúnors were too intimidated to make their elegant appearance, and the moon with her kin of diamonds declined to peek over the mountains. It was deathly quiet. No wind could be heard, no sounds rising from the bonfires below. The soldiers, reposing around them, kept an eye on her as they had been ordered to do, a task made easier by a staff fixed with a lantern right beside her. The soft glow illuminated her face, and the braid resting about her shoulder glistened with a sheen of silver. The only hint of life and civilization was the faint glow in the distance where Falkhearth stood, its towering buildings visible even above the hills. Ygrayne didn't know what she was expecting to happen as she waited in silence. Perhaps it would be nothing—a false hope all in its own.

"They departed in the morning for Falkhearth," the Schiva had told her, and that was all the information she needed to know the city's fate had been decided.

Since that moment, Ygrayne had kept her post throughout the night, waiting for the validation of her nerves and senses telling her something was indeed about to transpire. She had hardly even granted the Schiva a response before starting off for the hill, and she had half-expected him to follow her in the hope of dissuading her. Yet he didn't. The Schiva left her alone for some time to ponder, and perhaps making some progress in coming to terms with it all. She was grateful for such an unspoken understanding—he knew when and where to step, doing so carefully with great thought.

After some time, Ygrayne heard the quiet footsteps and the rustling of the grass bending beneath the weight of a figure. She cared not to look, fearing she would miss something the moment she took her eyes away from Falkhearth. Unakin to the heavy footfalls of a soldier, the steps were calculated and almost tender, leaving no lasting imprint in the grass.

"May I join you?" the Schiva asked.

Courteous, even as he knew he was a most welcomed companion. She said nothing, and he didn't need her to. He took a stance beside her and used the moment to observe what she saw—a most dormant landscape, shrouded in darkness and yet to be disturbed.

"You've been up here for hours," the Schiva finally commented. "Perhaps you should come rest."

Ygrayne shook her head and replied, "I have rested enough for the day."

The Schiva could not refute her response, and so he let it go.

"What do you hope to find, being up here?" he said, instead of trying to persuade her to abandon her post.

"I don't know," Ygrayne admitted honestly. "Maybe I just wanted to be out of that camp. Maybe…I'm hoping the citizens of Falkhearth will be let go and I'll see my husband coming down this exact same path. Maybe I just want to see something happen, whatever it may be."

Was *something* happening better than *nothing*? Nothing could mean that Falkhearth was safe for one more night. Ygrayne feared that if there was to be any kind of event that night, it would be a disastrous one. The only source of reassurance she had was the man standing beside her, her saving grace on such a dark occasion, a source of compassion and comfort. One who could ease her mind should she need it—and she most certainly needed some ease to her darkening thoughts, her ingenuity already conjuring visions of the worst of outcomes.

"Do you think they'll attack the city tonight?" How her eyes wanted to look to him, to gaze into the amber irises and find comfort in the warmth of their hue, the fire of their color, to seek some promise that all would be well. She struggled so, but kept her eyes fixed on the city ahead.

"I do," he answered, and Ygrayne could feel her breath trembling as she exhaled. "Considering how organized and efficient the Valeriaan army is, I wouldn't be staggered. It's the reason they are in power, and why they won the war," he continued, and Ygrayne felt her brows attempt a scowl of contempt upon hearing the repulsive name about his tongue, spoken almost with partiality. She felt her temper rising, a response neither friendly nor cordial. Ygrayne did well to contain it out of respect and gratitude for the Schiva, yet she couldn't help but say in that moment, "You speak as if you're fond of them."

"Not fond," the Schiva was quick to reply. "It is the mere truth. I did say the truth can be cruel. That is what you wanted, wasn't it?"

Ygrayne could feel his eyes on her, but still she refused to look at him.

"I do not bandy false pleasantries to ease minds when doing so will only prove to be harmful."

"I'm not asking for falsehoods, Schiva. But I would hope you would share some empathy considering we both have loved ones trapped inside those walls."

"Do not think me lacking in empathy." The Schiva's voice grew quiet. "It is best to remain calm in times as dire as these. Erratic emotion can cloud the mind—make us react too quickly and without proper thought. But you are a fierce woman. Calmness wouldn't become you."

"Are you mocking me?" It wasn't a serious question laced with malice, more so one born out of curiosity as to how he regarded her character.

"It is a good trait to have," the Schiva said, with a hint of a teasing scoff. "Someone akin to you brings vigor back into a world that has grown submissive to the circumstances. Though for that, no one could hardly be blamed. Nevertheless, it might do you some good to put aside that anger you have for the Empire. Such resentment almost had you killed."

She lifted a brow to him, a smile threatening to cross her lips.

"I still cannot tell if you are trying to compliment me or insult me in jest."

"Perhaps both," he had to admit with a shrug. "Given the circumstances you put yourself in, it would be wise to heed my words. The world would've been awfully duller without you in it."

"The circumstances I put myself in? I was only trying to get into Falkhearth."

"A city that is otherwise inaccessible. What made you think they were going to let you pass?"

"They released some of the men…s-so I thought." She stopped a moment to consider this statement, and now as the Schiva presented his perception, she could find folly in her judgment, in her actions.

"What would you have done differently?" Her voice began to rise with emotion before she caught herself.

"I would've left. You have no power against the Valeriaans. You must know when you are outmatched. Know when you are to be beat—know your enemy."

"Know my enemy? I know who they are!"

"No, you do not." He pointed a finger at her. "You hate them, that's not the same as knowing them."

Ygrayne was gaping at him, stunned. What was once a calm quiet night now crackled with tension, the air around them thickening. Neither one of them was inclined to back down in their conviction.

"Why are you saying this?" Ygrayne breathed.

"I don't want you to suffer any more than you already have. I do not condone the actions of those soldiers, the way they hurt you—most vile and reprehensible. With horrors fast approaching and our relative peace deteriorating, you must learn how to protect yourself in a world that will not protect you." The Schiva reached out and placed a hand upon her shoulder, and although the desire to cast it away was strong within Ygrayne, she refrained. The gut that had always guided her was now telling her to listen, to hear the man out even if it cost her some pride.

"Your hatred is warranted," he said quietly. "I will not argue that matter. But please, listen when I say this—you must learn to navigate circumstances that are not weighted in your favor. Ygrayne, you need to learn to play the game to your advantage."

Ygrayne thought for a moment, recounting the events that had nearly cost her her life. She realized, and reluctantly had to admit, that running off in pursuit of Thelric hadn't been the wisest decision to make. Even after being granted the chance to leave with her life in hand, she had let her hate and rage get the better of her, refusing to be bested by a Valeriaan. The urge to disobey no matter the circumstance had won out over her common sense.

The Schiva was right, Ygrayne hated to admit it. She had played her hand wrong, surrendering with no contest when she had other pieces at her disposal. Ygrayne refused to voice her wrongdoing, but inside she accepted it so, and it ate at her akin to a ravenous parasite. She thought about the ease and finesse with which the Schiva had handled the situation. How he had the commander eating out of his hand before he had even dismounted his steed. There was no doubt that he possessed more influence in the situation, playing his pieces just right with moves ever so calculated, knowing well what to say. As a result, she had escaped with her life.

"Akin to you," Ygrayne said. It was the closest she would get to admitting defeat. "You knew exactly what to say to him. Knew how much leverage you could pull."

"Precisely." His eyes turned up with a smile. "I have more experience with them—I know how they act, what their desires are. If there's anything I've observed in my years of studying the Valeriaans, and any knowledge I may impart to you, it is this: Valeriaans, especially those of noble status, such as our commander, and those with high military rank, pride themselves on their manners and bask in an air of superiority. It's how they separate themselves from the, as they say, 'uncultured.' The low dwellers, the commonfolk. That is, until they're provoked." He emphasized that last bit to her with the upturn of his tone. In light of the knowledge being bestowed upon her, Ygrayne allowed it.

"Crudely put," he snorted lightly, "stroke their ego. Use it to your advantage. Play them."

Ygrayne understood his meaning but could hardly think what she might possess that would influence them in such a way the Schiva could—and had. She was no Schiva herself, and the commander had done a thorough job of reminding her how lowly she was. Before she could frame such a question, the Schiva was the one to answer, as if he could read her very thoughts of doubt.

"If I may say, as platonically as possible." He paused a moment, studying her, assessing whether his next words were inappropriate or unwarranted. Ygrayne was eager to hear what he had to say on the matter. If she was going to learn, she knew she needed every bit of advice he could offer.

"You're a beautiful woman," the Schiva said carefully, as to not insinuate anything beyond the wisdom he wished to impart. "Had you not resisted as you did, I do not doubt the commander would have taken you himself. If a commoner could enchant someone such as the commander, imagine who else you could wrap around your finger, ensnared by your feminine wiles."

Ygrayne scoffed gently, prying his hand from her shoulder. He concealed it once more in his cavernous sleeves.

My feminine wiles, he says, Ygrayne thought to herself, quite taken aback by the concept. She never thought of herself as being attractive to anyone but Thelric, and to think she could entrance another was an almost impossible concept, far from her capabilities of imagination.

"I think you hold my physical qualities in too high regard, dear Schiva." Ygrayne dropped her gaze in self-consciousness.

"Or perhaps you don't think highly enough of yourself."

"You are right about that." She sighed, and looking back to Falkhearth she could only imagine what the armies were up to, how the folk were scrambling in panic at their arrival. "I doubt feminine wiles could do anything against an army amassing in anticipation of battle."

"I did not say that it is a power without limits. 'Tis best you to stay far away from a battle, at the very least. But should the circumstance befall you, I would expect you to make the most of what you have."

"If only I could use my supposed charms against the Allfather." Ygrayne smiled and the Schiva snorted.

"I regret to inform you that you would not suit his tastes, and the Allfather himself is not easily fooled or persuaded."

This rather piqued Ygrayne's interest. There was more than mere speculation in his words—they carried something akin to familiarity.

"Have you ever met the Allfather?" she couldn't help but ask.

"I have," the Schiva replied, and Ygrayne found herself rather surprised. She could not imagine the Allfather, or how she might feel in his presence, given the very little she'd heard of the man beyond the shared sentiments of the Valeriaans.

"What is he akin to? Is he a frightening man?" The opportunity presented itself, and she felt she would be a fool for not inquiring.

"He is." The Schiva was only too willing to indulge her curiosity. "But not for the reasons you might think."

"Tell me then."

"As you wish." The Schiva nodded, surprised and impressed all the same by her eagerness despite her obvious loathing. "Beyond the Allfather's reputation for cruelty and mercilessness, he is incredibly cunning. Pleasant and well spoken, convincing without commanding. It's easy to see why he is the Allfather upon a single meeting, not given his birthright, but because of the air about him. It's compelling enough to forget the brutalities he's committed. But when he's provoked, his bouts of anger are equally frightening, however few and far between they may be."

He fell silent for a moment. Ygrayne tried to conjure an image of the man based only upon the Schiva's words, and still she could hardly picture him. She was mystified by the way the Schiva spoke, with something akin to partiality, deferential to a man who, in her mind, hardly deserved such service. Or perhaps that was the warning beneath the wise words of someone who spoke with honesty and frankness.

"He does sound frightening," Ygrayne said quietly. "I hope I never have the displeasure of meeting him."

"I wouldn't worry so—"

"Because he leaves the dirty work to his soldiers." It was a jab at herself, given that she couldn't imagine the Allfather himself would have bothered with her as the commander had. She was too far beneath him.

"You speak ill of yourself?" The Schiva easily understood her meaning.

"But it's the truth," said she. "The commander made that clear when he said he doesn't lie with 'whores' such as I. I hardly think the Allfather would give me even the courtesy of his scorn."

"Never mind what the commander said." He dismissed the notion with a wave of his hand. "If you ask for my opinion, I say he was intimidated by you."

"You think otherwise?"

"I wouldn't do you the dishonor of agreeing with one such as he." The Schiva smiled beneath his mask. "You are a frightening woman to behold, and the commander knew so simply by your refusal to acquiesce to his orders."

"But in the end, I still had to be saved." Ygrayne gave a self-deprecating chuckle.

She took the chance to peel her eyes away from the landscape below and gaze at the Schiva, who was looking at her intently with those amber eyes of his, emanating the warmth of fire. Eyes which looked as though they might glow amidst the darkness, akin to the eyes of a feline prowling in the night. Whether they were lit by the lantern light, or something else entirely, Ygrayne couldn't ascertain. They looked beautiful regardless.

"I know you say I do not need to thank you, but the truth is, I do."

"Ygrayne—"

"Let me speak," she was quick to say, this time holding her finger to him.

"Yes, my lady." His amusement rendered him compliant to her order.

"Thank you, for saving my life, and for so much more. Your kindness, your generosity in sharing knowledge, your company. Even if I nearly knocked your head off, you were right...about everything."

"There's no need to thank me. It's what I—" the Schiva stopped mid-sentence when a scowl crossed Ygrayne's face—a very terrifying scowl—and there would be no convincing her to see his perspective. It was unbecoming of a Schiva to even receive such words of gratitude, and they were looked down upon should they do so. But the Schiva knew he was beat, that Ygrayne would not take his rejection as absolute, and he decided it was best to give her the triumph this one time.

"I mean—you're very welcome."

Her scowl immediately transformed into a tender smile, and the Schiva knew he'd been had.

"I know you Schivas follow your mantra of not indulging in personal pleasures, or gratification, but I doubt it would sully your reputation so to at least humble yourselves to accept a simple 'thank you.' The gods know you deserve it, and so much more."

"I humbly accept your gratitude. Thank you, Ygrayne."

The tension between them disappeared, replaced by mutual understanding, mutual respect. The Schiva wanted to speak further, but their moment was stolen away by the jarring and terrifying sound of a blast in the distance, followed by a barrage of explosions that, once begun, followed a nearly regular cadence.

They fixed their eyes on the once-dormant city as a fire was cast to the sky—the consequence of catapults and trebuchets let loose, their launched projectiles wreaking untold havoc upon the city and her populace. The skyline blazed with red and orange, the colors beautiful even as they foretold of death.

Ygrayne let out a cry before she clapped her hands over her mouth, preventing the release of a horrified scream. And as she trembled, so too did Skana at her feet, the blades of grass set to dancing by the echo cast through the land. A foul breeze blew, carrying with it the scent of fire, smoke, and ash—a city set alight.

"By the gods..." the Schiva was almost breathless by the time a second round of staccato bursts rent the air.

It was expected—this reckoning. They could hardly speak to one another, the air filled with the booming sounds of impact, of the rain of debris and shrapnel. Though all Ygrayne could see was an attack in her rudimentary understanding of war, the Schiva knew full well what was transpiring beyond what their eyes could not perceive from a distance. It was a military tactic. The Valeriaans would bombard the enemy stronghold at night so their foes would find themselves unable to sleep, unable to spare a moment for rest lest they be caught in the flames cast upon them from the heavens above. Come morning, the people of Falkhearth would be already exhausted. If the bombardment continued long enough before a siege attempt began, the enemy would be too tired and weary to fight back effectively and would capitulate easily.

The Schiva maintained his composure as the scenario played out in his thoughts, appearing unshaken to any observer. Deep down, however, the heat of anxiousness flooded his body. He thought of the screams, the blood, and the carnage this night alone would produce—the aftermath a morbid foretelling of what was to come until the Valeriaans inevitably claimed victory once more.

Ygrayne fell to her knees when at last her strength withdrew from her. The force of her collapse made her injuries ache, though she hardly cared. Her pain was nothing compared to the fate those caught in the crosshairs of the conflict were suffering. She didn't bother trying to hide, didn't stop the tears flowing down her face, her sobs completely silent behind gritted teeth. Her hands trembled against her cheeks as she watched the endless barrage helplessly. Her thoughts immediately went to Thelric, how he could perish at any moment at the impartial hands of unfavorable odds—a cruel and terrifying end. How Ygrayne wished she could see him one last time, wished she could share parting words, wished she was there bearing it all with him. She hoped the "I love you"s they had exchanged before he left for Falkhearth were enough, that he truly knew how much she loved him. She remembered their final embrace and wondered if it too had been strong enough to physically show him the depth of her affections. The regret of not saying or showing it as if it were their last time weighed heavily on her mind.

The Schiva knelt beside her and wrapped his arm about her shoulders in a sincere attempt to comfort her, and covertly, even to seek comfort himself, for he too feared for his brethren and the innocent lives being lost. They didn't look at each other. There wasn't a need to. Even the slightest touch was enough for them to know that they weren't alone in their grief and their anguish. They were there for each other.

CHAPTER 23

Several days passed by and Ygrayne's nerves grew more strained by the hour. Her mind traveled to very dark places never reached before, dwelling on the morbidity of the battlefield, and the devastation she imagined taking place within the walls of Falkhearth. Anxious days and restless nights were taking their toll, and the physical and mental exhaustion gave Ygrayne the appearance of an empty shell of a husk walking through the camp. Had the Schiva not been her company, her whole being would have collapsed altogether; he was her only hope of sanity, an anchor amidst a storming sea.

The days and nights bled into one another. The natural transitions began to blur, hidden behind the smoke and ash that clouded the sky with a brownish coat. The once-green hills greyed and dulled, and the smell—so terrible, so putrescent. Ygrayne soon found herself choking and coughing on what could've been the particulates of a decimated structure or charred flesh. She tried to no avail to force those thoughts away, nearly gagging on several occasions. In the dead of night, there was the always-present orange-red glow of fire, which only grew fiercer with the progression of time. The nightly bombardment was a slow torture, the deprivation of the body's most vital of necessities. Ygrayne hadn't realized at the outset that she too would be under its cruel influence. The barrages were relentless, and many a time she found herself flinching at the cracks and reverberations of the fiery explosions. The high spirits of the soldiers around her only amplified her angst; oftentimes she felt they carried on intentionally to test her nerves, to provoke her so she might give them a reason to retaliate against her. How she wished she could slap the smirks off their faces, drown out their laughter with the sounds of her cries, burn away everything they cared for just as Falkhearth was burning now. But she refrained, staying the intense fire of anger burning so ravenously within her breast.

The Schiva calmed the fire with the mere breath from his lips as he spoke wisdom into her as he always did. Only the somber and gentle company of her companion could soothe her. They had built a rapport with their jests and banter, but the calamitous events before them truly brought them together. No one wanted to be alone in the face of such malevolence, even if it meant calling to the gods above, setting aside one's beliefs in the hope of being heard, being the recipient of a sign or an omen.

"It would serve neither good nor purpose," the Schiva said to Ygrayne when he stopped her from marching over to the lot of soldiers to berate them for their enjoyment of the decimation of the innocent.

"If anything, they'd only derive a sick pleasure from it. Do not give them such satisfaction. Instead, why not share your grievances with me? For I do take pleasure in conversing with you so."

Ygrayne concluded to herself that his exaggerated charm and tenderness was a result of their tense conversation the fateful night the bombardment started, but she also knew the Schiva was right. Her words would be lost on the soldiers, and the Schiva was much better at conversation than they ever would be.

But alongside their many conversations throughout the days, they also abided some time in silence, merely basking in the corporeal company they provided each other. Whether it was their fearfulness, or their exhaustion, there wasn't much to say for a time beyond the words they had already spoken.

Silence became yet another companion, and a welcomed one at that. How Ygrayne wished, however, to know what the Schiva was thinking, to know what was going through his mind, to hear her own feelings reciprocated and validated by someone revered and held in higher standing in the eyes of the commonfolk and Valeriaans alike. What was the experience of a Schiva in distress? Did he feel as helpless as the rest of them? But she kept her inward desires to herself. Were he to ask her the same questions, she too would feel unobligated to share her own sentiments beyond those she had expressed many times before.

Most nights, while lying in her bed in a futile attempt at an ordinary and restorative slumber, Ygrayne observed the Schiva writing tirelessly in his journal at a table only dimly lit by the lantern. All his thoughts and secrets, scribbled on pages she wouldn't be able to read. The deepest and darkest of thoughts, the feelings he hid well behind that mask, all finding release in ink on vellum. One of these nights something peculiar happened, leading Ygrayne to believe the Schiva was up to more than he was willing to let on.

Her back was turned to him, and she was nearly at peace enough to get some sleep after another exhausting day of waiting, when her ears heard a strange sound—the fluttering of wings against the tent fabric and the affable coo of the bird to which the wings belonged. It was rather talkative as it flew into the tent, becoming almost aggravated when it perched upon the shoulder of the Schiva. Ygrayne would have turned around to see what the commotion was about, had it not been for the Schiva's whisper, just loud enough for her to overhear.

"Hush now, Hrafna. The lady is sleeping."

It seemed impossible, but Ygrayne felt strongly that the bird comprehended the Schiva's command, its response a coo that sounded oddly akin to the word "sorry," followed by a low and resonant hum.

She hardly knew what followed. How long the Schiva and the bird carried on in silence and craftiness before she heard the flurry of wings once again as the bird flew out of the tent and away to the skies from which it came, she could not say. The bird hadn't returned since that night, but it was enough for Ygrayne to confirm that the Schiva knew, and was delving into, more than she could possibly understand.

A few more nights passed by fitfully but uneventfully. On one such night Ygrayne found herself waking up from a deep slumber in darkness and silence. To her surprise, the chair usually occupied by the Schiva throughout the night was vacant, and the journal he busied himself with, closed. It was unnerving, how empty the tent felt without his presence. Moreover, there came no crackle of soldiers' fires outside her tent, no murmured conversations or laughter. Ygrayne felt a chill down the length of her spine, and she wrapped the blanket tightly around her for some sort of comfort.

She left the tent with the blanket about her, climbing the hill on which she and the Schiva had spent many a night, keeping watch as the battle raged in the distance. As she expected, there he was, standing quietly beside the fixed staff and lantern.

"Do you hear that?" asked the Schiva, quick to make conversation as she came to stand beside him.

"Hear what?" she asked.

"Precisely."

It took Ygrayne a moment to understand what the Schiva was meaning, and it hit her with the force of a catapult once the revelation dawned upon her.

The quiet of the tent and the camp had been unsettling, but she hadn't noticed the absence of explosions. Ygrayne had grown so accustomed to the sounds of war that they had nearly become white noise, constant through the nights past. Now that she became aware, Ygrayne feared for the worst.

"What does this mean?" she whispered, turning to the Schiva.

"It means they're storming the city now."

Ygrayne swallowed and her mouth fell open in disbelief.

"Though beset with fatigue and vastly outnumbered, it matters not. The Oathbound will not concede. They will give the Valeriaans a fight."

Had it been the first night, and her sensibilities still green to the circumstances, Ygrayne would have found those words repulsive. But now, it was a part of her reality—a truth she could neither ignore nor weep over.

"They'll take the city within the next few days," Ygrayne said, speaking her thoughts aloud as a way for her to accept the outcome.

"It would be a mercy if it were so quick. But I think it will not be so."

Ygrayne looked to him, and he gazed back with the concerned but guarded look in his eyes with which she had grown so familiar. It was all the answer she needed before they turned back to the city once more.

Five more days passed, and the silence weighed heavily on the land, accompanied by uneasiness and foreboding. Ygrayne again woke from a deep night's sleep, and this time found the Schiva asleep at the table. The journal lay open beneath his masked face, his chest rising and falling slightly with his gentle breath, the pen still in his hand awaiting the master to give it orders. Never did she think she would have the pleasure of seeing such a sight—a Schiva, asleep—and she couldn't help but look upon him with awe and wonder, and relief. Ygrayne knew well he had hardly slept since arriving at the camp, so committed was he to ensuring her safety. Seeing that the Schiva had finally succumbed to exhaustion and the invitation of slumber gave Ygrayne a reprieve of her own.

He looked so vulnerable, reminding her, despite their great achievements and reputation, that the Schivas too were but men. She couldn't bring herself to wake him, gently draping a blanket over his back to bring some comfort in the cool of the morning. Ygrayne made her departure from the tent so that he could continue sleeping peacefully, for she was nowhere near as capable of moving about gracefully and quietly as he was, and though no welcoming sights awaited her outside the tent, removing herself was best.

The sky was still tainted brown, but the blue of the sky was peeking through in places. The fires from Falkhearth did not burn as bright as they once did, though they were no less ominous.

Ygrayne took her spot on the hill as she always did and looked out to Falkhearth, or whatever was left of it. Smoke was rising from beyond the walls, a thwarting hand reaching to disgrace the air with filth. The complete consumption of the sky's blue hue was not enough for its ravenous appetite. The putrid cloud looming over Falkhearth called to mind swirling vultures, waiting to feast on death, on the bodies littering the city streets. Ygrayne shook her head at the very sight, terrified by everything she didn't know, of what was happening out of sight. With a sigh, she resigned herself to the ash-stained grass, and she prepared herself for yet another day of watching in suspense, left to wonder what horrors were taking place.

The Schiva woke with a start, surprised at himself for falling asleep. He was met with the delightful surprise that was a pool of saliva within the confines of his mask, dribbling down his chin the moment he sat up. The blanket about his back fell from his shoulders in a pile at his feet. He glanced down at it, and then to Ygrayne's bedside, finding it astonishingly, but thankfully, empty. He felt there cause to question his dignity should she behold the sight of his saliva dripping out from the bottom of his mask.

He blinked his exhausted eyes and instinctively wiped at his chin as if the mask were non-existent. When he realized its smooth surface was all that his sleeve brushed against, he let out an exasperated sigh at such an amateur gesture. He recalled first donning the mask, and the time it had taken to adjust to the notion that his face was but a façade. Many mishaps had constantly reminded him of that—from trying to drink to rubbing at his face. He attributed the lapse in competence to weariness.

The Schiva cleaned his mask and reapplied the black around his eyes, which had been swept away by the sweat and oils of his skin. He straightened his robes, brushed the wrinkles from the fabric to replace his haggard look with a more refined one. He and Ygrayne had grown too comfortable in each other's company. They had no room for concerns about physical untidiness between the two of them when their minds were occupied with much weightier matters.

It was late morning by the time he left the tent after tidying up, and he could see Ygrayne sitting atop the hill at their makeshift lookout. The Schiva paused a moment before moving to join her. There was a different air about the camp. The soldiers who passed by still hardly acknowledged his presence, but they were getting restless, longing for the battlefield they were trained and prepared for, chafing at being left behind to mind their prisoners. They thirsted for blood, and would have eagerly spilled Ygrayne's, given her role in their absence from the conflict in Falkhearth. There was a growing resentment, a desire to act upon their mounting rage and hatred for the common woman who brought them boredom and grief; the commander's words were all that prevented them from doing so.

The Schiva absorbed the new attitude in the camp, assessing the tenor of animosity and the possible danger. He proceeded through under the benign guise of simply fetching a breakfast to share with his companion, while scrutinizing the soldiers closely from behind his mask. They treated him as they always did when under his observation—with the respect and politeness his standing afforded him. But the Schiva perceived with inconspicuous attentiveness their honest gripes when they believed they had escaped his gaze.

Upon reaching the hill to join Ygrayne as he always did, he finally relaxed and bestowed upon her a platter of breakfast. She greeted him with a warm smile.

"Good morning, sunshine."

The Schiva took a seat beside her, dropping the platter between the two of them, and she added, "So, the Schiva is a man after all."

He couldn't help but snort. Such a sentiment was expressed more frequently than the commonfolk would imagine.

"The Schiva have always been men. Man made the Schiva Unman."

"Did you at least sleep well?"

"I did." The Schiva nodded. "I…I needed that."

It felt difficult to admit, perhaps because of the high regard in which they were held—oftentimes an unachievable standard. He truly wished that he could do all that Schivas were thought to be capable of—that he could be that godlike figure, faultless and unwavering. He let out a defeated sigh.

"I guess when there's hardly any commotion in the distance, you tend to sleep better." Ygrayne let out a sigh of her own and her eyes turned to Falkhearth. "It's been pretty quiet over there for a while now."

"From over here it seems so, but…" He needed not speak more on it for her to understand what he was alluding to.

"Please, eat. At least."

She obliged, having not eaten since the night before, though she had taken but a single bite of bread when she realized she was yet again the only one to eat between the two of them. She looked to the Schiva, and when he felt her eyes upon him, he looked to her as well.

"Is it not to your liking?" he asked, eyes widening with question.

"You're not eating again."

"I ate already."

"Liar." Ygrayne narrowed her eyes at him.

"How—"

"Because I know you to be kind enough to bring me food and hardly think of your own well-being for the sake of not eating in front of me."

He couldn't retort, for she was right and would not be persuaded otherwise.

"Schiva, I think we are quite comfortable in each other's company. And if this morning proves anything, it's that you shouldn't deprive yourself for my sake any more than you have. Please, eat. I'm certain you can without removing your mask, yes?"

She could tell he was smiling beneath his mask, for he still could not refute her claims. She was correct. He hadn't eaten that morning, and he hadn't planned to do so until he had time alone later in the day. In response, he obliged—taking a few of the berries from the plate, carefully maneuvering his hands so that they moved his mask the least bit, and just enough that he could slip the berries into his mouth.

Ygrayne gawked at him throughout the moment, the bread still held before her own lips. She watched the spectacle before her with continued awe, hearing the movement of his mouth, witnessing such a rare sight. The Schiva looked to her, taken aback by her unwavering stare. "Pardon?"

"You're eating."

"You…told me to."

"Yes but…you're eating." She couldn't help but chuckle at her own silliness.

"You are easily entertained by the most minute things, it seems."

Ygrayne only tittered more.

The two fell into a comfortable silence as they had so many times before. However, it was not to last. The slow rumble of thunder mounted in the distance—a thunder not as jarring, nor as intermittent as the catapults they had become accustomed to. No, these were hooves, pulsating against the land in a most intimidating rhythm, a consistent gallop that grew ever closer. Both wondered if the soldiers were returning, and yet as they watched it became clear that it was only a few horses. It was too soon for the army to return. But Ygrayne and the Schiva's discomfort was not completely unwarranted.

They watched as two mounted soldiers came around the hill and into their line of sight, making their way down the well-trodden path. They declined to stop at the camp, passing straight through. It was obvious their destination was the very hill the Schiva and Ygrayne occupied. As the two horsemen ascended the hill, the Schiva was quick to his feet and did well to step in front of Ygrayne, to use his body as a shield should the worst befall them. Ygrayne was slower in her response, only getting to her feet when the soldiers brought the horses to a screeching halt. The two beasts' coats shone with sweat, stained with exhaustion from the gallop.

"Schiva," one of the soldiers said with that thick accent, his violet eyes glaring down at the two of them. "I bring orders from Commander Reinhardt. You and the woman are free to take your leave back to Trivaden."

"Falkhearth—"

"Only Valeriaans and the Schivas are permitted to enter the city. The woman is to return home."

Ygrayne suppressed an anxious gasp. She hadn't come this far to be turned back yet again. Before she could speak, she noticed the sly movement of the Schiva's hand, gesturing her to silence. He was to handle the situation.

"Very well." He bowed his head respectfully. "I will take the lady Ygrayne home and return to assist in Falkhearth."

He could feel Ygrayne's eyes upon him, her restlessness and urge to protest. He was impressed that she held her silence to let him continue to speak on her behalf.

"The commander would remind you of your part of the bargain."

The Schiva reached into the inner breast pocket of his robes and produced a letter, adorned with a red wax stamp to seal it.

"I have not forgotten," said he, holding the letter before him. "The Allfather will hear of his cousin's…generosity." The Schiva withheld the attitude from his tone with effort, struggling to conceal his opinion of the mistreatment of Ygrayne.

"I will pass on the news to the commander. Take your leave, both of you." His parting words were hardly cordial, and the Schiva couldn't resist reciprocating with a gesture of his own.

"My regards to your master."

Disdain overcame both the soldiers' faces, the urge to spit back at the Schiva suppressed through sheer will.

The Schiva grinned, narrowing his eyes—a sly fox left to cackle at the fools it bested. One of the soldiers reached down and pulled the letter from the Schiva's grasp without breaking his gaze, and he and his companion wheeled their horses around and set off for Falkhearth. Their affairs were far from concluded, though the battle itself was over.

"I can't…" Ygrayne paused. Her convictions and sentiments throughout the entire ordeal fought within her. The desire she had to find Thelric was still very much present, but now she considered what the Schiva had warned her about some time ago, contemplating both how Artur would be affected should she not return and the impossibility of getting into Falkhearth now.

The Schiva's influence and sway could only grant her so much amnesty, and it would hardly stand should she try to defy the commander yet again and enter the city. There was only one course of action before her, and that was to return to Trivaden, to Artur.

"Shall we go then?" She spoke quietly, hardly acknowledging the Schiva as he looked to her.

"We shall."

Ygrayne choked back the sudden onset of tears.

"I'm going to take you to Falkhearth." The words were not what she expected, and Ygrayne's eyes darted to him in utter disbelief.

"You heard what that soldier said," she protested, though it pained her to do so. "I-I can't get into—"

"You can't get into Falkhearth as Ygrayne," the Schiva said quietly, holding his finger up to quiet her. He drew closer to her until their faces were aligned.

"So, I shan't take Ygrayne into Falkhearth. I'm taking a fellow Schiva into Falkhearth."

Ygrayne took a moment to ponder exactly what he was implying—the prospect of assuming the guise of the revered robed Brethren had certainly not occurred to her. Indeed, she thought he would agree with the soldier's directive, rather than advocate for her continued pursuit of her original objective.

"But…you can't." She didn't want to state the obvious, but she could not resist pointing out the gravity of what he was suggesting. "It's forbidden. What would become of you should I be discovered?"

"True, 'tis forbidden to don the garb if one does not call themselves Schiva." He nodded, a slight sharpness in his eyes. "But leave such outcomes to me, should there indeed be a need to do so."

The Schiva pulled his hand back into the sleeves of his robe, and Ygrayne stepped back but held him in her incredulous gaze.

"You were the one who chastised me for even trying to get into the city. Now you're going to escort me into Falkhearth yourself?"

"I am." The Schiva nodded without hesitation. "We've come this far together, haven't we? I intend on seeing this through until the end with you."

Ygrayne still looked to him, speechless.

"I make an oath to you." He stepped forward, closing the distance between them. "I will see to it that you return to your son. You, and your husband alike. And should I fail, let the cost be my own life."

"Schiva…" Ygrayne breathed. "I can hardly let you make such an oath…"

"Whyever not?"

"I cannot be responsible for your demise should I bring about my own. Especially—" Ygrayne paused a moment, thinking back on everything that had happened, how she had already inconvenienced him so.

"I think it too late to consider that, don't you?" The Schiva read her mind again. "I fully intend to keep my oath, if you are truly so concerned. I rather enjoy living. I believe I'll continue doing so a little while longer, at the very least."

A quick smile flashed about Ygrayne's face, and when she looked to the Schiva, she could tell that he too was smiling. It was his turn to be stubborn, and he presented a very attractive offer with comparatively little danger.

"If you are so certain, then may I make a request?"

"Was my oath not sufficient enough?"

"No," she protested. "It was plenty good. I just…want to make a slight change to it."

"Very well." He was intrigued.

"If neither I nor my husband should return, it is not your life I ask for. I wish for you to care for my son. To watch him grow, to guide him. To take him under your wing. Please…"

The moment of contemplation stretched out between them. Ygrayne feared she asked too much, something too personal, but it was a moment of desperation. She knew her mistakes, caused by her own misjudgment and ignorance, and she felt this was some little way she could rectify them, to put her son's well-being first this time.

"I make an oath to take care of your son." The Schiva bowed his head, eyes closing. "Should, gods forbid, both you and your husband not return."

It was all she needed to hear to be convinced to move forward with his proposal.

"But I must warn you, Ygrayne—"

"I already know what to expect." She held up her hand to silence him. Ygrayne did not need to be reminded of the carnage that awaited them.

"No, you don't." The Schiva gently grasped at her shoulders and looked her straight in the eyes. "There are going to be unimaginable sights. They'll make you realize the extent of the horrors war permits. Should at any point you need to turn back, do not be ashamed. No one should have to see what we're about to."

Ygrayne looked deep into those amber eyes of his, and her resolve hardened just as his had.

"I need to find my husband. Are you ready?"

There was no turning back.

CHAPTER 24

In the morning, Ygrayne and the Schiva made a show of riding away from the camp and toward Trivaden, but when they were out of sight, and enough time had passed that they would not give themselves away, they left the road and started off into the pastures. On the ash-riddled plains, they came across a still-flourishing tree, though its beauty and color were as tainted as the land around it. But the figures beneath the tree were what drew them toward it.

There were two Schivas: one who wore a cream-colored overtunic and robes, and another in brown. Beside them was a brown horse, whose vacant saddle quickly attracted Ygrayne's attention. That was to be her steed, her accomplice in the plot.

"Brother," the cream-robed Schiva called out as Ygrayne and the Schiva approached. Both held up their hands in greeting.

"Brother," he said in response, his hand raised in the same gesture.

"We have what you asked." The other made a motion to the saddlebags secured to the saddle of the awaiting horse.

"Much appreciated, my brothers."

The Schiva and Ygrayne brought Onír and Mara to a stop. He turned to her and said, "Let us get you prepared."

Ygrayne only needed to don the overtunic and the robe, and she soon found them to be rather comfortable but heavy. She was already perspiring in response to the extra garments, her body not yet used to them as the Schivas' were. The Schiva adjusted the garments according to the particularities of the Brethren, all while the other two brothers looked to one another with an air of caution.

They knew that this scene before them could have dire consequences, that their brother-in-robes was stepping well beyond the bounds of the oaths he had made, and they themselves were willing participants. Yet, no word of it would ever leave their mouths. They would never speak it into another's ear. As far as they were concerned, nothing was happening before their eyes.

Within the headwrap Ygrayne tucked her braided hair, while the Schiva pulled up the hood of her robe to ensure the wrap would not come undone in the wind during their ride. And thus came the final touch. When Ygrayne saw the Schiva produce the mask, she felt her pulse race—the last piece of the puzzle, the completion of the transformation essential to her ploy. She looked to the Schiva with nervous anticipation, a strange yearning, and as he drew the mask to her face, Ygrayne closed her eyes as if it were about to anatomically mesh with her own being. The cold, smooth interior of the mask pressed against her skin. She let out a quiet gasp, her body stilling as the Schiva fastened the ties atop and at the sides of her head.

It was only when she heard the Schiva say, "There," that Ygrayne finally opened her eyes.

She felt as though she was looking to the world with a new pair of eyes. What was once forbidden to her, the outsider, was now granted, though with the utmost caution. She was hardly one with the Brotherhood, and yet she could already feel the burdens they carried about their shoulders, weighing heavily upon her own. A burden to maintain their rigorous standards, reach the highest expectations.

Ygrayne let out another breath to relax her body as it grew tense with its new appearance. She would have preferred to take some time to prepare herself, but the Schiva placed his hands on her shoulders and said quietly, "You're going to be all right."

She nodded nervously to him and listened as he continued.

"You'll be protected by the shrouds, but that protection will come with its…conditions, shall we say. We'll do whatever we can to find your husband. However, there will be folk in need looking to you for help, for guidance, sympathy, reprieve. Ignorant, of course, of who you really are. And you will be obligated to carry out the duties of an oath you yourself did not swear, nor have any allegiance to. These are the stipulations, the drawbacks, of the offer I have given you. Do you understand this?"

"I do." Her voice was quiet.

The Schiva withdrew his hands to his sleeves and took the moment to search for any doubt or hesitation within Ygrayne's eyes—for something to give him any inclination she might not be suited to the task. But what he saw was a determination that had not yet wavered—as present as it had been since the day she left Trivaden. They were both in agreement, and they were ready.

Ygrayne had only a moment to bid farewell to Mara—to the mare who had accompanied her through her strife. With a gentle caress of her face, Ygrayne whispered into her ears, "Thank you." Though Mara possessed not the cognizance of Onír or Vána, she could sense Ygrayne's gratitude. The mare leaned into Ygrayne's palm in acceptance of the merits given. At long last, Ygrayne was ready to depart for Trivaden.

And after the Schiva helped Ygrayne onto the brown horse and mounted his own, they parted ways with the Brethren, who went in the opposite direction.

They did not speak another word on their way to Falkhearth, and when they reached the watchpoint which previously served as their prison, there was hardly a protest, only a slight acknowledgement as they passed by. It was all the affirmation Ygrayne needed to know the ploy was nearly infallible. The Valeriaans, the commonfolk, would never know the truth of who she was beneath the robes—so long as she acted in a manner that upheld the ruse.

The horses followed the path, imprinted and beaten into a road by the lines of marching soldiers. The closer they drew to the city, the grimmer the reality became. The darkness surrounded them akin to a shroud, even in the morning hours of the day. The ash and the acrid stench of the smoldering remains of Falkhearth were nearly suffocating. The smoke appeared thicker that day, as if a monstrous fire had burned all throughout the night and was ever so eager to greet them with a menacing, fanged smile. Had there not been the strong odor of something foul overtaking their senses, they might have believed they would find only a pile of ash awaiting them at the end of the road. The stench made Ygrayne recoil and gag, her body rejecting the absolute vileness in the air that threatened to taint her own body. She brought her horse to a halt so she could regain her bearings and adjust to the sudden onset of the odor.

"Ygrayne?" the Schiva called to her, stopping just ahead of her.

"What…what is t-that smell?" She suppressed a cough.

The Schiva paused a moment, looking to her with sympathy. It was exactly as he had warned her, and it was but a taste.

"Death," the Schiva said plainly.

"I've never smelled this before."

"Well, I would hope you hadn't yet endured the stench of burned flesh."

Ygrayne paled. It was more than the mere statement his lips uttered, but the realization that the foulness she was breathing in and choking on was much more than just the ash of destroyed architecture and the detritus of a battle's rage—it was the burned carcasses which plagued her lungs.

Ygrayne had thought she was prepared to face the devastation, but now she was beset with doubt in her own iron comportment. The very thought was sickening to her stomach, and it turned and twisted in knots of agony and warning, begging for release through her lips so that it might find some reprieve. But she swallowed hard and held back that urge to retch, trying to disperse the very thoughts from her mind.

"Ygrayne." The Schiva called to her again, coming alongside her. "Perhaps this was too much to ask of you. If you wish, you can return to your boy, and I can look for your husband in your stead. It would at least spare you an encounter with such devastation."

Ygrayne took a deep breath of the foul air once more, and this time she forced herself to stomach it. She knew it would only grow worse from that point, and it was necessary to push her sensibilities aside and refuse to let it intimidate her.

"No," Ygrayne said firmly. "I can do this. I will not turn back now."

She allowed the Schiva no chance to persuade her otherwise before she kicked at her horse's side and lurched forward into a canter. He followed behind her with reluctance.

As they rode, the ash-riddled plains disappeared behind them and their surroundings were soon dotted with yet more camps of the Valeriaan army, festooned with evidence of war: weapons, armor, and those dreaded catapults whose barrage had been the scourge of all the tranquility and bliss that had once existed in Falkhearth.

The Valeriaans themselves paid them no mind. They went about their business in the aftermath of the battle—celebrating such a victory over the Oathbound, treating their wounded, and taking care of military affairs. It disgusted Ygrayne to see them cavorting about akin to children, and it required great effort to not glare daggers at them—to not react to their taunts at the expense of fallen Oathbound, whose bands and garb, embellished with their symbol, were burned and defaced with the utmost disrespect. As Ygrayne and the Schiva drew closer, they brought their horses to a walk and traveled for some time more before at last their eyes were cursed with the sight of the carnage that had taken place in the city while the pair had passed tense days and sleepless nights in the Valeriaan camp.

Lining the road to Falkhearth, crosses with blackened wooden limbs had been erected, each adorned with the body of a Oathbound fighter. The burned carcasses were left as an offering to the ravens circling above, excited by the presence of death, for it portended a feast. They had wasted no time in satisfying their appetites, as was evident when gazes fell on the ghastly remains of those who had fought bravely. If their eyes and tongues had not been burned away in the fires, they were pecked greedily from their orifices and digested to fill ravenous bellies, leaving only gaping holes in place of the defining features of their faces—faces warped and twisted by the screaming agony of their final moments. Wrapped around each of their necks were ragged blue sashes, torn and defiled, the white insignia stained with darkened blood. This display served as a grim warning for all those who passed through, to dissuade and intimidate the allies and sympathizers of the adversaries of the Empire. A clear message that Oathbound and commonfolk alike were mere pests beneath the Valeriaan boot, and would be crushed accordingly.

Ygrayne had already begun the practice of steeling her bearing and nerves, to strengthen her will as iron in a forge. But all the tenacity she could muster still did not adequately prepare her for the horrors which awaited her.

Her thoughts turned to contemplations of their final moments—all the pain they had suffered through, fighting all those days knowing what their fate was regardless of the ferocity of their struggle. To know how it was all to end—how terrifying a thought. What it would do to one's mental fortitude. Ygrayne had never seen an Oathbound before, nor had she imagined this was how she was going to acquaint herself. This sight was forever etched in her memories—the terror frozen on the faces of the warriors brave enough to stand against the Valeriaans.

Ygrayne felt the Schiva's hand brush her shoulder, a gentle and tender touch to show he was still there as she was nearly consumed by her inner thoughts and grief. It was enough to pull her back from the darkness surrounding her.

She blinked her eyes to clear the blur from her vision, drawing her focus back to the road ahead. The endless rows of crosses only grazed the corners of her vision as she made every effort to spare herself from so much as another glance at their mangled faces, their stiffened bodies, their insides exposed where their flesh had burned away, their blood congealed in dark splotches. The cries of ravens rang in her ears and for a moment she wished she weren't at all intimidated by the sights as they were, wished she could feign indifference to the bodies left as mere perches for the ravens that feasted on them.

The horrors only grew darker. However, Ygrayne was more prepared for the revulsions awaiting them. The time spent slowly proceeding to Falkhearth allowed her to reinforce her nerves, to grow numb. She felt guilty for refusing to feel anything, for conditioning herself to believe it was the custom for the sake of her own sanity and to maintain her composure. But when the walls of Falkhearth finally came into view, her newfound indifference was immediately put to the test.

The city's walls, which once stood a testament to its grandeur and esteem, were decimated. Their remnants were strewn across the ground, a disemboweled beast whose entrails had been left exposed. The gaping holes revealed a glimpse of a war-torn city whose towers had crumbled, whose streets were littered with the debris of the assault. The stone-pocked streets were blackened not just by the scourge of flames, but by the pools and splashes of crimson long turned cold and dark.

The Valeriaan army still boasted a heavy presence just beyond the wall. Groups of them paraded about, watching over the bested city. Along the base of the wall were rows of bodies, neatly placed side by side as they were collected from inside the city by the Valeriaans rummaging through the rubble.

To one side of the gate were the fallen Valeriaans. The battle had left their once-glistening armor muddied and stained, showing evidence of where blades had pierced through, and where the material gave way in combat. On the other side were the folk of Falkhearth, fallen victims of the onslaught who had never wished such carnage upon the place they called home, never had any stake in the conflict between the Oathbound and the Empire. Regardless, they had paid the price. Even death had not proven a mercy. Their bodies were left to decay in the open air. Many of them were missing limbs, their bodies ripped apart, their clothing soaked in blood—so much blood. They could hardly be recognized as man at all, so barbaric was their demise. Their bodies tossed carelessly aside, left for the living to remember them in their darkest moment. Unakin to their Valeriaan counterparts, whose remains were handled with reverence and care, they were handled akin to mere cattle, already slaughtered, carcasses for the market and the ravens. Body stacked on top of body, to be discarded without another thought—waste to be cast into the depths of the great bonfire, whose life depended on the continued supply of cadavers.

Tossed to the greedy and gluttonous fire, the bodies tumbled lifelessly until they found a final resting place, nestling in awkward crevices formed by their fellow citizens' contorted and gaunt figures.

And the soldiers sneered as they went about their cleanup, making light of their work while they disposed of what they thought of only as unintended, but expected. None of these dead were Oathbound. Most of them were elderly, women, and children of various ages—from juveniles to toddlers, to offspring who had not yet outgrown their nursing days.

Children. Ygrayne's heart sank as her gaze fell upon one such child, still wrapped in cloth, thrown to the fires. Motherless. Alone. Cold. Its last moments doubtless filled with fear, a memory of terror accompanying them into the great Vallar.

She thought of her own son, almost picturing him amongst those bodies so cruelly treated, before she reminded herself that Artur was far away and safe back in Trivaden. But she grieved for those children as if they were her own, crying in place of the mothers and fathers who were lying amongst the bodies themselves or now left childless, sentenced to spend the rest of their days in agony and grief.

Ygrayne drew her eyes down, and then forward, before she could lose the composure she was trying so hard to maintain.

The soldiers at the gate scrutinized them intently. Their keen eyes peered through their helmets, their colored irises moving in sync as they allowed the two Schivas through without so much as a question. Ygrayne held her breath until they passed the bounds of the gate and the horses' hooves clacked against the tarnished stones.

She turned her attention to the Schiva, who had been just as quiet as she for the duration of their ride. His silence wasn't provoked by disgust or horror. He had had the great displeasure of seeing such sights on previous occasions. It was out of respect for Ygrayne that he discouraged the prospect of conversation, to allow her the time to adjust to everything around her without the menial distraction of curt words.

Ygrayne could hardly see his eyes. She had no gauge of his response to it all. He remained silent, still. It was almost unnerving how much he didn't react. But it wasn't completely unbecoming, considering that the Schivas had cleaned up after the Empire before.

When finally he turned to her, she could hardly recognize the amber eyes behind the mask. The softness she had come to associate with them was completely gone. Now they were hardened, cold. He nodded his head and led them over to one of the first buildings they came across—a tailor's shop whose curved windows were once decorated with assorted garments on wooden frames—a shadow of its former self, gutted by flames and left a barren shell where once stood an ornamented threshold. As she dismounted, Ygrayne could still feel the heat of the embers, the structure's beams still glowing faintly red in the brush of the wind, crackling, popping.

Ygrayne took another look at everything around her as she stepped forward, vividly recalling all these buildings surrounding her—how beautiful and regal they once had been, how the streets had buzzed with life, all the smells of the fresh-baked goods and the colorful bolts of fabric and the sparkling jewelry. The variety of faces wreathed in smiles and the laughter which had filled the air alongside the songs of the traveling bards and the strumming of instruments. Though poverty proliferated in the darkest parts of the city, and the Valeriaan reign could hardly be called fair, it was the commonfolk who fostered the feeling of home in the city, who inspired many to stay rather than seeking their fortunes elsewhere. Ygrayne could feel none of that vibrance anymore. The life of the city had crumbled akin to its walls and towers, strewn across the ground to be cast away as dust and debris that the wind would carry off until all the particles were dispersed across the land. If it weren't for the crackling of the embers and the continued erosion of the remaining structures' integrity, the streets would have been completely, uncomfortably silent.

Ygrayne left the structure and walked, maneuvering around the rubble and the bodies that still littered the street, too unimportant even to cast to the flames—the utmost humiliation. Under Valeriaan rule the commonfolk had lost most of their customs and traditions, and the beliefs which their families continuously passed down were tarnished by the loss of so much history. But there was one tradition that persisted, because the Valeriaans too participated in it: the burning of the body when one passed on.

The mass grave at the wall was hardly respectable. In fact, it was rather blasphemous according to the old tales that had managed to survive the city's conquest. Traditionally, the departed were placed upon a pyre, fashioned in the rough shape of a platform, and the body was dressed in the person's finest clothing, and accompanied by items they so cherished in life. With family and loved ones present to give a final farewell, the woodpile was set ablaze and the deceased would be sent upon the journey to the hereafter. To the paradise, as they called it, where all who had no peace in life would now find only peace, happiness, and the loved ones who had passed on before them. They called it Vallar, the Land of Folks Passed. And it was said what awaited the dearly departed was a beautiful golden hall with an endlessly bountiful feast, and ale that never ran dry, in a world of ever-blooming beauty that did not know decay.

The question, as Ygrayne walked amongst the dead, was this: would these folk too be able to find their way to Vallar? What a disgrace it would be if they should be found undeserving of such a paradise simply because the folk who remained in the realm of the living cared too little to give them a proper farewell. They were left to rot without a second thought, growing pale as their bodies gave way to the natural decay of death. Eyes staring lifelessly behind a layer of white film. Mouths agape, dried blood streaking from their lips and other orifices. Many, if they had not been afforded a quick death by the blade, had fallen prey to the debris of the buildings above, their bodies now buried beneath the rubble. By now, Ygrayne was all but used to the smell, but the cries and screams of those around her, whether their wails were a testament to their bodily pain or the horror of the death all around them, now challenged her composure and reminded her of the fear she harbored for her own family.

And there they were, more than she had ever seen—Schivas, working tirelessly to aid the wounded, assisting the living citizens with finding their lost loved ones, searching amidst the chaos for those who had long left this world. Unakin to their Valeriaan counterparts, the Schivas treated the dead with the utmost care—lining the bodies about whatever empty space they could spare, folding their hands about their chests, closing their eyes to the world around them. Ygrayne noted with disbelief that the Schivas were accompanied by citizens who still had the will to carry on through all this, the strength to lend to others who had none. They were all dirtied and exhausted, their efforts ceaseless since the beginning of the onslaught. Nevertheless, they were determined to press forward.

"Sister." The Schiva's sudden appearance beside her nearly made her cry out. But whether from the need to protect her identity or by some imagined effect, the robes granted her a sense of strength and power. Ygrayne subtly turned to him and he held up his hands as to not cause any alarm.

"Didn't mean to frighten you," said he, quietly. "But I was calling you for some time."

She hadn't heard a thing beyond the turmoil, and she was simply not used to be addressed so formally by a most informal acquaintance.

"I'm sorry." She blinked at him. "I…didn't hear you."

"Understandable." He nodded. "How…how are you?"

Ygrayne looked about the aftermath once more and said nothing. The Schiva understood and pressed it no further.

"Shall we start looking for…?" He was certain to keep his voice low, his words ambiguous. There were Schiva about who had keen ears and were just as keen to pry should they be given the opportunity.

"I feel as though I shouldn't pull you away from the folk who need you." Ygrayne let her eyes meet his.

"You need me—"

"No, I don't." She said so as gently as possible and hurried to qualify her sentiment.

"I just…I don't need you as these folk do. I'm in good enough health, and I can wander about on my own without worry. I can't say the same for them." She gestured to the scene before them. As much as she wanted the Schiva at her side, to be with her in her own turmoil, what the citizens of Falkhearth had gone through, and what they continued to go through, outranked her own personal needs. And looking to the Schiva, Ygrayne could see that he too did not wish to part from her side, the apprehension apparent in his gaze. But Ygrayne was right, and the Schiva sighed with solemn resignation, nodding his head.

"If you wish it so."

"I want you to be at my side, truly." Ygrayne touched his shoulder. "But I can't help these folk as you can, and I should be safe on my own at this point. Being separated may aid my search as well—we'll cover more ground. And, if I do need your help, I'm certain you'll know, somehow."

There was a slight smile about his eyes, albeit a dejected one.

"Tread mindfully," he whispered, ending the conversation with a wink and a, "Sister."

Ygrayne couldn't bear to say another word to him, worried it would tempt her to change her decision.

As she went about her way through Falkhearth, Ygrayne wrestled with her lack of understanding as to why the parting felt so painful. Was the bond they now shared stronger than she had thought? Or was it because she was terrified of what she might find and being left alone to handle it?

CHAPTER 25

Thelric!" Ygrayne called out as she traversed the city, her voice growing tired and hoarse from the perpetual inhalation of smoke and filth in the air.

Her cry echoed through the streets and alleyways as it mingled with all the other cries rebounding about. Her robes allowed her to move unnoticed amongst the Brethren as she found herself climbing over rubble, dragging through the muck and the debris at her feet. Her arms and legs ached as they worked and pushed their limits to turn over large mounds of wreckage. Ygrayne persevered, the objective too precious to be deterred from.

Thus far, her ventures only produced more bodies—the commonfolk of Falkhearth, as well as Schivas themselves. Hardly had she expected to see them, the most revered of folk, torn and shredded and left for the ravens—simply unintended consequences of war and its propensity to consume all within its vicinity. Ygrayne experienced an entirely foreign feeling when she could see their eyes gazing at her from behind their fractured masks, their faces revealed against their oath and will, death stripping away the mystery. If their demises proved anything, it was that even the revered Schivas were just man, capable of the same errancies and susceptible to the inevitability of death.

There they lay amidst the rubble, stripped of their dignity and taken from the world as they sought to fulfill a duty to a folk they had sworn to serve.

At least, for the time being, none of the bodies were her husband's, though the lack of discovery hardly brought a reprieve. The perpetual silence which met her calls made her weary with uneasiness, and the aspirations she had at the beginning of her endeavor were holding on by a thin and very weak thread.

As the Schiva had warned her, her search was stalled by the destitute and vulnerable, by those who sought help and guidance amidst the chaos.

"Please." One woman came to her in hysterics. "I can't find my son! Have you seen my boy?"

Ygrayne would have helped the grieving mother, had it not been for a fellow Schiva coming to her aid rather quickly, almost as if he were prepared, as though the Brotherhood was matching her every step. There were still so many folks who had yet to have their wounds tended, looking to her for something to assuage their pain until more sufficient service and medicine reached them. Ygrayne did what she could, using strips of fabric torn from her own robe to bandage wounds, craft makeshift slings, fasten crude splints with the debris about—any task she could perform within her limited capabilities. When she had done all she could, Ygrayne advised them to make their way to the plaza closest to the gates where all those alive were gathering and the Schivas' presence was the strongest.

Before their departure, the folk bestowed upon Ygrayne the most heartfelt of recognition. Often accompanied by tears, they grasped at her hands with their own battered ones, bowing their heads in a show of respect. Ygrayne, in return, mimicked her companion's mannerisms—the tenderness of voice, the gentlest of touches, and the sincerest of words. She hardly had his wit or his temperament, but she did what she could.

Regardless, it seemed Fate, with her cruel sense of humor, was all too happy to test Ygrayne's prowess in a situation that completely displaced her from her natural realm.

It was not the cries of a child, not the wailing of a grieving parent which caught her attention so suddenly. As sharp as a knife cutting through skin with ease, a frightening scream reverberated around the remnants of the city as if they repelled it—for they had seen and heard enough. Denied absorption, it then fell upon Ygrayne's ears, compelling her to find the reason for such verbal distress. She felt an unspoken connection, akin to the sudden urge she had when hearing her own child cry out to her. Ygrayne was overcome by the motherly instinct to tend to whoever was so undoubtedly in need of help.

Ygrayne scurried around the wreckage that surrounded her, using the wailing as a compass to her destination. The louder and more terrified it became, the closer she was drawing. She passed by the stricken faces of those who had not the will to respond to a fellow citizen, and instead remained as they were in what little comfort they could find within the wreckage of the places they once recognized. When at last Ygrayne turned a corner and the street opened into the former site of a market, she caught sight of the source of the horrendous screaming.

It was a girl, hardly an adult from the looks of her through the dirt, grime, and blood that coated her once-flawless skin. Her face was reddened from struggle against the four soldiers antagonizing her with amusement and nonchalance. It was a game between the four men—tearing at her already-shredded garments to slowly reveal the fragile body beneath the once-beautiful dress. Every attempt she made at escape was thwarted. Should she attempt to fight, her efforts were rebuffed with the simplest efforts of those who were bred and trained to handle such circumstances, hardly bothered by a child who had never seen deadly conflict.

The rage Ygrayne felt could hardly be described. What she saw before her was herself not too long ago, thrown to the dire wolves to be devoured most agonizingly within drooling jowls. To be teased and humiliated and reminded she was nothing, helpless prey left to squeal as one last breath escaped her lips. The fear this girl felt—Ygrayne knew. The anger this girl felt—Ygrayne knew. But whereas Ygrayne had been granted a bit of mercy by the powers that be with a savior come to her aid, this girl had no one of the sort. Looking about her, there was no Schiva, nor anyone in sight to help this poor girl. It was she herself who was there—who was the only one to answer this girl's cry. As unqualified as she was, Ygrayne hesitated. She could not match the strength of four fully armed soldiers. She did not have the Schiva's bravado to glare back at the violet eyes without flinching. It was not a wound she could quickly mend, not a fear she could speak reassurance to. Under the robes she was no one—and Ygrayne knew that. But the soldiers didn't.

Ygrayne let out a shaky breath. They would never know she was no one. What they would see before them was not a common woman without merit. They would only see a Schiva. It was the robes themselves that would come to her assistance. And although her entire façade could dissolve if she gave in to her own fears and shortcomings, it was a chance Ygrayne knew she needed to take for this girl's sake. She took a deep breath, straightening her posture and squaring her shoulders to give the appearance of a broad and intimidating stature. Once her wits were about her, Ygrayne approached as though she truly was worthy of the robes swirling around her.

It was the clacking of her boots which first captured their attention, and with confident smirks about their faces, the four soldiers looked to her with the expectation that she was just another citizen they could torment for their own pleasure. Their lips flattened as their stomachs dropped when recognition set in. Ygrayne felt some satisfaction knowing her very presence had such power over them—the power of a Schiva, the one folk the Valeriaans revered…and possibly feared.

The soldiers halted their rapacious antics in their disbelief, and the sudden cessation of their efforts left the girl to tumble to the rubble with a loud thud. The force of her collapse raised a cloud of dust and debris around her filthy figure as she wept. She would not be permitted to leave if she attempted to, and she knew it. Instead, she lay in the waste to await all which Fate had prepared for her.

Ygrayne had them, at least for now. She had not yet revealed herself to lack the verbal intellect to capture and maintain their complete attention without sowing seeds of doubt as to the validity of her identity.

Ygrayne stopped before one, the nearest soldier, and his eyes locked with hers as though they were two predators fighting for dominance, and neither one was willing to relent. It was frightening, being as close to a Valeriaan as she was, and had it been under different circumstances she might have surrendered to the tension. But Ygrayne couldn't afford to do so now. This girl's life, and her own life, depended on her fortitude.

"I will be taking this girl with me," Ygrayne proclaimed. Curt and concise—that was how she was going to get away with her façade, as well as both of their lives.

"This doesn't concern you, Schiva," the soldier hissed, and Ygrayne could feel the venom in his breath as it brushed against her. Her skin might have melted had it not been for the shield her mask and robes provided.

"T-the well-being of the commonfolk always concerns me." Her voice faltered, shaking as she attempted to nip back with her own venomous fangs. The soldier's eyes narrowed at her opposition.

"You have the city." She gestured to Falkhearth. "You have your victory. Enough."

The truth was—it was never enough. It would *never* be enough.

"This girl has suffered as it is. Leave her be."

The soldier snickered and took a single step in her direction. Ygrayne nearly flinched. How she didn't, she hardly knew.

"What are you going to do about it, Schiva?" The soldier placed his hand upon the hilt of his sword, the metal of his gauntlet clashing with the metal of the pommel. Ygrayne's eyes flashing to the area but for a moment was all he needed to feel the balance of power tilt in his favor once again.

Would he really? Ygrayne thought to herself.

As revered as the Schivas were, even in the eyes of the Valeriaans, would they really raise a blade to them? Death as the result of a battle, such as the one that razed Falkhearth, was treated as expected. There was no avoiding it. But his threat bore clear intention, for his blade to cut through her skin. Ygrayne saw it for what it was—a bluff. Such an unprovoked act would be frowned upon, and she could use such knowledge to her advantage.

Ygrayne folded her hands before her, as she had observed the Schiva do many times before, and those gaping sleeves cascaded about them as a waterfall spilled down over rocks.

"I will rely upon your good judgment to do what is expected of you.

Swing your blade if you must. I'm certain you'll have an adequate justification for your Allfather as to why a Schiva died by your own hand."

The soldier hesitated. Ygrayne had made a wager and in the pause that followed she knew she'd won the hand. She'd be dead otherwise.

Her victory, however, would be a short-lived one should she give him the time to challenge the verdict, and she was not about to allow such. Without another word, Ygrayne quickly, but calmly, retrieved the girl, who followed her lead without objection. For when one was in the hands of a Schiva, there was no need to fret.

They proceeded away from the area under the watchful gaze of the soldiers who scrutinized them as ravens did a corpse, only escaping those piercing eyes when finally they rounded the corner of the nearest building. A flood of relief overcame them both. The danger was not yet gone, but it was far enough away that they could finally catch their breaths.

They said not a word to one another—they didn't need to. There was nothing to say. Ygrayne was still coming to terms with the fact that she had looked a soldier right in the eyes and lived to tell the tale, had been spared by her own audacity. With the relief came the sheer weight of exhaustion. The vigor which once flowed through her veins in such a fraught situation had now run dry and the fatigue left her trembling.

Ygrayne and the girl came to a main road where a few Schivas were assisting a group of commonfolk who needed immediate attention. Their deft hands worked diligently to tend to the gaping wounds dripping crimson.

They only nodded to Ygrayne as she and the girl approached—an acknowledgement for her presence as they were occupied elsewhere.

Ygrayne gently settled the girl upon the debris of the building beside them. Expecting her work to be done, she bowed her head and attempted to make her leave. The girl frantically grabbed at her gloved hand and Ygrayne paused for a moment, turning to the girl.

The last thing she expected was for that girl to plant a kiss upon her knuckles before she bowed her head and wept in all the gratitude she could spare for the Schiva who saved her. Ygrayne blinked, watching this girl weep as her hands clutched Ygrayne's own.

"Thank you," the girl sobbed, her voice quiet and meek. "Thank you."

Ygrayne knew what the Schiva would have said, had it been him—"There is no need to thank me."

But Ygrayne was no Schiva, and she was bound by neither their oaths nor their customs. She knew, being that she had once been in the girl's place, that all she would have wanted to hear was acknowledgement of her gratitude.

And so, Ygrayne placed her hand upon the girl's head and whispered back, "You're welcome."

It was not just the girl whose ears heard such words. The Schivas within the vicinity also heard the response, and their heads turned slightly in Ygrayne's direction in disbelief at the utterance. Ygrayne paid them no mind. She cared not for their incredulity or disapproval. She had done what she believed was necessary. With such confidence in her conviction, Ygrayne took her leave.

CHAPTER 26

Ygrayne resumed her search, immersed once more in the carnage. As she began to traverse the residential quarter of the city, she was met with sights quickly becoming all too familiar.

The folk here were too overcome with fear to leave their devastated homes, the rubble they found themselves seeking refuge in, confining themselves to the battle-made ruins. Even her presence, that of a Schiva, wasn't enough to coax them from the shadows. Instead, she was met with frightened and weary gazes. The sounds of weeping emanated from sources out of sight—lending credence to the notion that perhaps it was the cries of those who had passed, mere phantoms and memories who were keen to share their bereavement with the living.

Ygrayne was all the more indebted to the mask she'd donned, for it hid her own tears, muffled the soft sobs that escaped her lips. When she turned into an empty alley, and was certain no one could see her, she ducked into an archway to weep and calm her breath.

How imprudent she now realized she was, thinking she was strong enough to handle the brutalities of war. How they laughed at her foolhardiness. The death and the carnage she understood, but what Ygrayne had not expected was how much it affected those who were still alive, condemned to forever retain the memory of the events that had displaced their entire livelihood. They were left with the pain that those granted the release of death would never bear, and while the victims of the offensive went to bask in the peace Vallar had to offer, the living would toil on in the absence of such amity.

And so, she wept—wept until her legs gave way and she collapsed to the fractured cobblestones, seeking comfort in the boundaries of her own body as she drew her knees to her chest. The likelihood that Thelric was alive was dwindling greatly as time passed, and the concern as to whether she would be able to find him at all persisted. Given the grim circumstances around her, it all seemed hopeless.

Tucked away comfortably in Trivaden, she had been ignorant to such injustices, and willingly so. She hoped the expanse of Skana would keep her and her family safe, and yet she still could not avoid the great reach of the Valeriaans. And while she was hiding away from it all, she had willingly turned her back on these folk, past and present, denying their familiarities and adversities. The Oathbound gave their lives for Falkhearth and her folk. Ygrayne had, at one time, thought them foolish and daft in efforts she considered futile. Now she realized the extent of their endeavors, what they were trying to avert, and who they were trying to protect—this. Everything which lay around her. Who, truly, was the more foolish of the two?

Ygrayne concluded her weeping, wiping at her face with her torn sleeves, and stood once more. She patted down her robes before pressing further into the city.

She made it to a courtyard at the heart of the residential area, the gathering place of the folk who called this part of Falkhearth home. The wide-open space was encircled by shops and various food stalls that had been the most popular amongst the denizens. The once-beautiful center was now littered with debris from the catapults, the laid stone now a sea of rubble and craters. It took her breath away, an exhausted breath. Yet the memories remained.

The festivities which took place within the courtyard had been a sight to behold—the way the expanse lit up at night with lanterns strung overhead in various colors. An ideal location for dancing and mingling, it was where she first met Thelric. At the time, they were barely eighteen, and Thelric, along with several other young men, had come from the village she now called home for a short stay in Falkhearth. She could see it as if it were happening right before her eyes, the manifestation of a dream. This time, she was a spectator watching affection blossom between two young and naïve lovers, their awareness of the world around them fading as they became each other's world. There he was, holding her in his arms and dancing terribly, as he always did. He hardly knew what he was doing, but she loved that he tried in an effort to impress her. His friends taunted him from the fringes, unwilling to dance themselves into a mockery. She loved how his golden hair shone orange in the light, how his green eyes glimmered with wonder at the activities around them.

Ygrayne was looking into his eyes once more, witnessing the life they had all over again. And that smile—his smile of absolute fondness beamed at her.

Ygrayne took a step toward that young couple before her, and in all her exhaustion and fatigue from the weight of the day, she realized too late that the ground was unstable as it gave way under her foot. She went tumbling down into one of the craters, landing with a hard thud amidst the sharp debris at the bottom.

Her ankle screamed out to her in pain, but the robes spared her flesh from the hostile touch of the rubble beneath her. She let out a bellow, muffled by the mask over her face, and she cursed herself under her breath for not being nearly as graceful as her Schiva companion, who would have never fallen victim to something so avoidable. She turned herself over with aching arms and touched at her ankle with the gentlest grace of her fingers. Even through the thickness of her boot, she felt the searing pain flush through her entire leg. She flinched, a breath escaping through gritted teeth. Greater still was the sting of embarrassment, her pride wounded from such a preventable mishap, and in a moment of despair, she lay gingerly on her back, staring up at the looming clouds of smoke above and resigning herself to the rubble until her strength returned.

"Sister." Ygrayne heard a voice, and her eyes shifted just above her head to see a familiar mask with an unfamiliar being behind it—a Schiva, attired in dark brown robes. Alongside him were two men—citizens of Falkhearth, for they wore no robes of their own. One man's clothes were in tatters. The other had an obvious wound on the side of his head, dried blood streaked down the length of his face.

The Schiva came down to her with the grace she didn't possess, his movements so nimble even as the dust kicked up under his feet.

"Can you stand?" he asked, reaching his hand to her.

"I think so," she groaned. "But my ankle is injured."

Ygrayne took his gloved hand into hers, and he gently pulled her to her feet. He then threw his arm about her shoulders to relieve the injured ankle in question.

"Quite the tumble you took there," said he, with subtle but unmistakable amusement in his tone. "But you needn't worry. I can inspect your injury once I get you out of here."

Though initially taken aback by the Schiva's response to her mishap, Ygrayne let it be for now. They nodded to each other and the Schiva pulled Ygrayne up into his arms with a movement as graceful as his descent and made his way back out of the crater. The two men grabbed at his arms once he was within reach, pulling him over the edge with strained grunts. Even the smallest exertion was physically exhausting in their state.

The Schiva placed her atop a mound that was once a part of a building bordering the courtyard. He inspected her foot, carefully turning it about to gauge its mobility and flexibility. Ygrayne only winced, doing well to hold back any cry as her body tensed.

"Your ankle isn't broken, fortunately." The Schiva looked up to her. "Just sprained—" His words came to an abrupt halt when his brown eyes met her blue.

Ygrayne watched his calm eyes narrow to suspicious scrutiny—as if he could see well beyond the mask and the oddity of her eyes instantly gave away who she truly was. The Brethren had a sense between them which she could hardly understand, rooted in their familiarity with one another. His head tilted slightly to the side, just as Vána always did when she was listening to someone talk directly to her. Ygrayne held her breath. Was the Schiva about to expose her identity? Her deception?

"Brother?" She addressed him as a Schiva would, hoping it would stay his suspicion. All it seemed to do was bring amusement about his eyes, prompt a scoff under his breath. It was evident he wasn't fooled, but he spared her any interrogation she would have otherwise deserved for his own, unspoken reasons.

"You need to refrain from walking on your foot for a while to let it heal properly." His voice finally broke the tension and mounting apprehension, but this sent a whole new wave of panic over Ygrayne.

"No! No!" she exclaimed. "I'm looking for my…for someone! I cannot stop now."

"But Sister—"

"My ankle will have time to heal. Just not now. I must find this man first. It is of the utmost importance."

"Then, pray tell who you seek?"

"Thelric Sigurdsson," she answered. "He was trapped within the walls before the battle started. Have you happened upon him?"

She looked to the other two men, hoping their faces would give her some hope, and though they glanced at each other wearily for a moment, to Ygrayne's disappointment but not surprise, they shook their heads.

"Neither of us know of a Thelric." The one with the bloodied face spoke. "If you haven't seen him yet, he's probably *dead*."

The other looked at him appalled, and the bloodied man just shrugged.

"Don't give me that. We just survived a fucking battle, for the gods' sake. What did you want me to say?"

"I believe your friend thinks you lack tact." The Schiva spoke, ending the conflict before it could continue. "As do I."

He went about bandaging and reinforcing Ygrayne's ankle with splints as the others waited in silence and she in her mounting uneasiness.

"What my abrasive associate was trying to say was, you may want to prepare yourself for a grim outcome." The Schiva carefully slipped Ygrayne's boot over her foot once more.

"I'm fully aware of that," Ygrayne said through gritted teeth.

The Schiva snickered once more, entertained. She stood, testing the weight-bearing ability of her injured leg.

"You should at least rest a moment," he recommended, but Ygrayne paid no mind to his suggestion. She lightly applied weight until the pain was unbearable, finding the limits of her newly constrained mobility. She would need to be light-footed, keeping most of her weight on her operative foot.

"I don't have time for that," she replied. "Not to say I'm not grateful to you, Sch…Brother… But I know what I need to do. Thank you—all of you," she gestured to the two companions with a nod of her head. "For your help."

The Schiva stood and bowed his head to her with departing words.

"Best regards to you, 'Sister.'" He put emphasis on the term, and they were both fully aware at that point, that he knew the robes to only be a disguise. "And I hope you find this Thelric Sigurdsson."

She did not care for the men's skeptical looks, their doubt in the wisdom of her endeavor that could also be translated as pity for her plight. It mattered not to Ygrayne. She was determined to carry on, even at her own physical detriment.

It made things more difficult, but Ygrayne knew she could manage. To her fortune, there was plenty around to support her—as depressing as that was to admit. Eventually as she progressed through the residential area, Ygrayne turned down a narrow alley that was blocked off by what had been upper apartments that collapsed when hit by catapult fodder. A slab of one of the walls was still intact, sitting horizontally over a mound and creating a surface to climb over an otherwise impassable section of wreckage.

Ygrayne carefully crawled her way up the length of the slab without losing her grip. When she reached the summit, she could see more bodies down the rest of the street, which had yet to be discovered by either Schiva or Valeriaan. Unakin to most places she had wandered, there were clear indications that a fight had indeed taken place here. Commonfolk, which she could assume to be Oathbound, and Valeriaan soldiers littered the alleyway where they fell in battle, mingling together where they clashed, their armor stained, swords still held in their hands which had not loosened their grip upon death. It would only be a matter of time before the Valeriaans would come to collect their dead and dispose of the rest. If these men were indeed Oathbound as she suspected, they'd be dispersed to the crosses or discarded in mass bonfires. She greatly feared the latter.

Ygrayne lay atop the slab to survey the cumbersome descent awaiting her on the other side. Had she not been injured, it would have been an effortless task. With a wounded ankle, everything looked to be an obstacle testing her ingenuity—where she could climb, where she could step without overexertion or risk of further injury.

The slab seemed intent on disposing of her—it shifted under her weight and slid backward ever so slowly before coming to a stop due to its sheer weight alone, mere inches from the ground. A cloud of dust flew up around her and Ygrayne would have let out a gasp had someone else not done so in her stead. She paused in the silence following the unexpected cry. When no more noise followed, she climbed slightly higher up the slab and peered down into a newly formed fissure.

She hardly expected to see large, fearful eyes staring back at her.

"By the gods," she whispered to herself. *A...a folk?* Ygrayne gingerly climbed the rest of the way over the slab and then very ungracefully dropped to the other side.

Her body ached and her ankle cried out in protest, but she ignored her own pain as she lowered herself to her knees before the fissure and searched the darkness. To her disbelief and dismay, the eyes belonged to a child. The poor boy was bloodied and dirty from everything that had collapsed around him. Two trails of tears akin to rivers through sand marked his dirtied cheeks, his eyes still red and flooding. He quivered—the poor thing—so badly that Ygrayne could hear his teeth chatter as he groaned in trepidation.

What was just as dreadful, and even more dismaying, was the lifeless body of a Schiva, whose arms curled around the boy. His body almost completely covered him, his last good deed—using his own body as a shield to protect the boy from the falling debris. His back was battered, and the way his arms lay slack showed they were mangled. Ygrayne swallowed hard. This sight awoke new distresses within her as she thought of her nameless companion, her confidant. How it could've so easily been him instead. And the poor boy, who in a different life could have been her son.

But now was not the time for such self-pitying thoughts. Ygrayne blinked away her tears and reached down to the boy, calling out, "Dearest, give me your hand!"

But the boy did not move. Instead, he continued looking to Ygrayne with those wide blue eyes that no longer beamed childish naïveté. They were aged and weary from what had befallen him, bestowed a wisdom he was not yet prepared for. There was a fear—a fear that tainted the ability to recognize friend from adversary, Schiva from Valeriaan. It was self-preservation, the way he remained silent though the tears started slipping down his face once more. The way he never blinked as he held Ygrayne's gaze. If the child wouldn't come to Ygrayne, then Ygrayne would have go to him.

She set her hand against the slab wedged above the fissure, and a sudden strength rose up from the depths of her being. She firmly pressed her palms to the jagged edge of the slab and pushed, pushed with all her might against an object that should not have budged. But the slab began to shift, and the slight movement motivated her further. Through her grunts and cries of strength, the slab continued to shift at her will until it finally could move no more, wedged against another obstacle.

Ygrayne nearly dropped the slab with the sudden loss of motion. She tried once more, but the slab was still not budging, and Ygrayne's failing strength meant she wouldn't be able to continue alone. And so, she called out to the child once more in the hope that she could convince the boy of her benevolence, a hoarseness in her voice scratching at her throat. Even her lungs seemed exhausted, her voice nearly failing her as it cracked with fatigue. Her pleas, however, would not go unanswered.

"Sister!" A familiar and rather welcome voice sounded in her ears.

She couldn't help but let out a sigh of relief as her strength faltered, her arms quivering. Only her will kept her from failing entirely.

"There's a little boy under here," Ygrayne called back. "And…" She paused, contemplating whether to deliver the news of their fallen brother, or let him discover it with his own eyes.

The Schiva, her ever-missed companion, was immediately at her side and relieving her of the sole responsibility of shifting the slab.

It took but a glance to realize the severity of the situation, and they were soon joined by another—the same Schiva who had set her ankle. Following him was yet another Schiva, arrayed in a creamy-white set of robes.

"By the gods." The Schiva in white gasped—a woman.

"Who is it?" the other in brown asked. He too peered down before anyone could answer. "Unfortunate," he added flatly, the final word on the matter.

"The slab is lodged on something on the other side." Ygrayne said.

"Never mind that," said her companion. "We're here now."

It was so comforting to hear his voice again.

The sister bounded over the slab, akin to a deer in all her agility, and took position on the other side with an equally graceful landing, leaving the three of them to push once more. It was remarkable, how easily the slab moved with a combined effort. Ygrayne knew not what the sister did to shift the slab from its rut, but it dislodged with such ease that Ygrayne wondered if her efforts simply faltered as a result of her own shortcomings and lack of strength.

The slab moved without any more resistance, though the little boy flinched at the sound of the stone grinding across the ruins. His body tensed now that she was completely unprotected.

"I shall tend to the child." The sister spoke curtly, mincing no words. Her brothers nodded to her in response.

"Shall I send for anyone?" asked she.

"Only if anyone can be spared," responded Ygrayne's companion, as his sister stepped down into the pit and gently pried the stiffened body off the child, rolling him onto his side and taking the boy into her arms.

Still the boy hadn't spoken a word, his face rendered expressionless by distress. He gave all appearances of hopelessness despite the folk around him who wanted nothing more than his safety and well-being.

They labored together to pull the sister from the fissure, and once she was free, she leapt from the slab and made her way down the alley with the child in her arms. The boy's head rested on the sister's shoulder, arms and legs wound tightly around her frame. The two departing figures grew smaller in the distance, and when they finally rounded the corner, Ygrayne felt the tension leave her muscles, the vigor now gone.

"I'm sorry about your brother," Ygrayne said exhaustedly to the Schiva and his brother, catching her error a bit too late.

The two Schivas looked at each other wordlessly for a moment—exchanging a silent agreement of secrecy and understanding that would not otherwise be questioned. The brother who knew not of the specifics looked to Ygrayne with that unchanged delight in his eyes.

"Kind of you, Sister," said the Schiva, his own amusement audible in his voice. "But we knew this would happen. He's not the first, and he certainly will not be last."

She was thankful her misstep was not brought into question, preferring to hope that it had gone unnoticed.

The two Schivas gazed down at their fallen brother and silently mourned the loss of yet another. The mask's eye openings were completely black, blood staining red tears down the curved white cheekpieces.

"I'll retrieve him," said the fellow Schiva. "There's plenty of others who need to be sorted through." He spared a quick glance for the trail of bodies just behind them, and the Schiva knew what he was insinuating.

"We'll tend to them," the Schiva responded. "However, there is another matter I must address first."

The brother chuckled and leapt down into the fissure to do as stated, while the Schiva went about helping Ygrayne down from the mound so that she could rest upon a protruding part of the wall. She let loose another exhausted sigh as her body slumped, the full degree of her fatigue now dawning on her through the pain in her body, the numbness of her overused limbs.

The Schiva knelt before her, and spared her a moment to gain her bearings before asking, "How be you?"

Ygrayne laughed anxiously at her continued failure, her gaze dropping to her hands folded in her lap.

"I still haven't found Thelric...a-and I've sprained my ankle." It was hard for her to admit, embarrassed at how clumsy and careless she was to fall into a pit she would have easily noticed had she only paid attention. "So that's making all this a little more difficult than I wanted. How have you been?"

"Those fortunate enough to survive are suffering greatly." The Schiva sighed, sounding equally exhausted. "Not just in body..."

"Such as the little boy." Ygrayne finished for him when his voice trailed off in reflection, and she looked up at him when some bit of confidence returned. She gazed into his eyes and saw just how tired and worn they were. There was some bit of comfort knowing that she did not struggle alone.

"War scars more than just the body." He spoke in a near whisper.

"I'm starting to understand that myself." Ygrayne was equally quiet, as if the weight of her words physically sat about her shoulders.

"You look exhausted," he commented.

"You're looking quite unkempt yourself."

They both laughed behind their masks.

"Perhaps we should consider turning in for the evening."

Ygrayne was taken aback by this, and she looked to the sky only to realize that night was upon them. How quickly the daylight had faded without her awareness of it.

The Schiva stood, the rubble falling from his trousers. He held out a hand to her, but before Ygrayne could take it, or protest, she heard a loud thud behind her.

The Schiva didn't flinch, but Ygrayne turned around to see what the sudden commotion was about. The other Schiva stood atop the slab, their fallen brother within his arms. Without another word, he quietly took his leave and walked out of sight.

"But—" Ygrayne now objected as she turned back to the Schiva.

"The best resolution you can make for yourself, and your husband, is to rest. Give yourself newfound vigor, the fresh eyes to resume your search tomorrow. You would hardly want to miss anything because of your fatigue. And...well, he won't be going anywhere either way..." It was grim, but it was the truth, and Ygrayne was too exhausted to argue further.

She took his hand, begrudgingly so, and the Schiva swept her up into his arms in one smooth motion. Ygrayne didn't even let out a yelp.

"You don't have to do that." She looked to him. "I can still walk." She pushed at his chest in objection.

"Rest your ankle now so that you may walk tomorrow."

"Fine," Ygrayne groaned under her breath.

He snorted, but she ignored it. Ygrayne appreciated the sentiment though, welcomed it even, but it made her feel weak and incapable, regardless of the validity of that truth—she didn't want to admit her limits had been reached.

The passageway itself was determined to leave them with a grim reminder of what would await them in the morning, and Ygrayne's gaze was drawn to the pale faces that called to her from somewhere beyond. The Schiva maneuvered the grim passage with respect for Oathbound and Valeriaan alike. They mingled together, their blades stained with the blood of the other, their wounds evidenced by darkened blemishes on garments and armor. Despite their untimely demise, these soldiers seemed more at peace where they lay—unakin to many of the dead that Ygrayne and the Schiva had encountered through the day. Their deaths appeared to have been rather swift than torturous, their faces relaxed, cold and pale. It was a melancholy sight, placid in a morbid way.

Ygrayne observed the sea of death at the Schiva's feet emotionlessly, until she caught sight of one face which made the warmth drain from her body and the color leave her face. The Schiva too felt the shift in her mien, the stiffening of her body. His concern for her prompted him to pause a moment amongst the bodies.

"What troubles you?" he asked.

CHAPTER 27

Ygrayne did not answer, hardly hearing his question. Her gaze was fixed down below on the unmistakable sight her mind refused to accept. Eyes that no longer radiated a beautiful green, open but lifeless, made milky by the white film death produced. The warmth of the skin faded to a dull hue, peach turned grey. There was nothing—nothing behind the gaze, nothing of the man she once knew.

"P-put me down..." Ygrayne's voice was trembling, hardly able to produce the simple request.

"Ygrayne—" the Schiva tried to protest, still ignorant of her discovery.

"I said, put me down!" This time it was nearly a shriek.

She flailed about as a fish gasping for air, akin to a beast desperately trying to free itself from a trap—pushing against the Schiva, kicking her legs wildly despite the pain the movement caused. The Schiva had no choice but to put her down as she so demanded—clumsily, but gently nonetheless. Ygrayne did have graceful moments in her life, but this was not one of them.

The moment her boots touched the ground, did she stumble over an armored soldier as she tried to scramble to her feet. Her grip slipped down the slick chest plate, smearing the blood on the surface. When she found no success in getting to her feet, she resorted to crawling over the bodies at a frantic pace, stricken with panic, the tears beginning to well up in her eyes as she pulled at her mask so that she could see his face without impediment. Ygrayne tried persuading herself that it wasn't so, her mind eagerly producing excuses—she was merely exhausted, her eyes were playing cruel jests on her—this, alas, only a trick of the mind.

The Schiva called to her, though she neither acknowledged the call nor heard it clearly in her ears. Whether he was following her, she did not know and she did not care. She forced the mask from its binds, tossing it amongst the bodies beside her. Her hands desperately grasped the statuesque face that lay cold and stiff beneath her palms, unmoving to her cries, to her touch, to her very presence.

"No..." Ygrayne was breathless, touching her perspiring and dirtied forehead to his in a last attempt to breathe life into the man before her.

Still, there was nothing.

"No...No-no-no..."

The word poured from her lips repeatedly as she held the face of the man she called her husband. Despite the truth before her, Ygrayne hoped those green eyes would come to life once again and look deeply into hers as they always had. That a smile would turn his lips up to parade the love he still held for her.

"Ygrayne..." whispered the Schiva, now recognizing the reason for her distress.

He knelt beside her, doing well to avoid the bodies, and gently placed a hand about her back. His words, his touch, once again went unanswered and unnoticed. Ygrayne pulled her face away, tears falling to Thelric's sunken cheeks. She brushed her hand over his forehead and through his golden hair. The locks were still so soft to the touch, even dirtied as they were by the debris of conflict. Her eyes then traveled down the length of his body, noting what had brought about his untimely end.

His tunic was torn, and soaked by the blood spilled from his abdomen, a gaping hole in the fabric all the evidence that remained of the blade which had decided his fate. About the rest of his body, the marks of former quarrels with the sword—abrasions to the skin in various stages of healing—told stories of failed attempts to end his life sooner.

Ygrayne touched at his wound with quivering fingers, though she couldn't explain why the urge suddenly overcame her. It seemed almost instinctual. She needed to feel it for herself, needed further convincing that there was a reason to his end—to come to terms with the reality of his death. She felt where the skin was torn open, the muscles and innards exposed. It was then she withdrew her hand, for she could bear it no longer.

When her gaze traveled back to his lifeless face, she finally became convinced he was truly gone. Those eyes she'd once gazed into so lovingly now stared back with a disheartening blankness up into the sky, unaware of her presence. Never again were they to look at her. They held only emptiness.

Placing her palm over his eyes, she gently closed them to grant him peace, and herself some reprieve. She fixed the memory of his vibrant green irises, his gaze full of laughter and love, in her mind.

And at last, she lifted his head to the crook of her neck to weep her loss in full, uninterrupted sorrow.

"My Thelric." She wept. "I'm so sorry."

Her eyes closed so tightly she feared she would never be able to open them again, and a part of her hoped she couldn't. How she wished she could go with him. If it wasn't for their son, she would have followed him to Vallar. To be forever at peace, forever happy, forever in paradise alongside him.

But paradise was not calling for her yet.

"Ygrayne." The Schiva spoke.

There were no condolences, and though this angered her, perhaps that was for the best. She didn't want them, and there was no conceivable way he could truly understand the loss of someone she loved so dearly—the pain that wrought devastation throughout her being. Schivas weren't allowed to love, and thus could never have someone to call their own. What could he say that would comfort her?

The Schiva's arm came forward to reach for Thelric, the movement enough to coax Ygrayne's eyes open. How quickly she wished she hadn't.

The Schiva produced a cloth band wrapped around Thelric's arm, blue in tone—similar to those of the Oathbound—and left to disintegrate with the rest of his tattered clothing. Ygrayne paled all over again. Had it not been so stained with blood, she would have seen the blue color, the mangled white insignia.

The Schiva looked to Ygrayne for some sort of enlightenment, but she herself was mortified and perplexed. A cry rose in her throat, and the Schiva promptly placed his hand over her mouth with startling quickness.

"They haven't discovered these men yet," he whispered. "If they should happen upon us now, with your husband unmistakably an Oathbound, and you equally unmistakably his wife, they will have you executed. You must remain silent. I will dispose of the band, and we will make haste from this place by way of the alley. Do you understand?"

Ygrayne sobbed against his hand, what little fortitude she had left crumbling akin to the debris around her. She could hardly usher forth a response.

"I know you're in agony," he sighed. "But please, for the sake of yourself and your son, stay silent. Nod your head if you understand."

Ygrayne did so.

The Schiva slowly removed his hand from her mouth and Ygrayne mustered the last of her will not to wail in mourning for her husband. Though she wanted to scream until she had neither breath nor the strength to produce such a cry from her lungs, she restrained herself.

Instead, she resorted to a subtler, and more intimate, parting gesture for the time being. She caressed Thelric's cheek one last time and gently kissed his cold lips. For the short moment they touched, Ygrayne remembered fondly how warm they once were, how passionate and yet gentle they could be.

The Schiva averted his gaze, giving Ygrayne and the late Thelric some privacy in their parting. It pained her so, but they could not linger.

She couldn't possible carry Thelric. The Schiva would take him in her stead—or would have done so, had the brother not appeared in the alley along with the two other men who had accompanied him earlier. It appeared as though her cries had been answered by the divine will of the gods after all.

The Schiva stood, tucking the band into the recesses of his tunic as the three figures approached.

"We heard a cry," the brother said.

"Are there soldiers about?" The Schiva held his breath, though he did not believe them to be so far into the city quite yet.

"Their patrols ceased only recently," came the response. "We have until tomorrow afternoon, I would wager."

"I need to escort her out of Falkhearth and to our camp," the Schiva nodded to his brother, "along with her husband."

They both looked to Ygrayne, who buried her head against Thelric's chest.

"So," the brother cooed, not swiftly forgetting Ygrayne's deception. "The truth reveals itself in time—always."

They looked to each other and the Schiva said simply, "I made an oath, and I intend to keep it."

His brother shook his head with a snicker and a sigh, but questioned it no further—for he cared not.

"I'll care for her husband," said he, his eyes narrowed. "You take the woman. I shall meet you back at the camp."

"Another setback," the Schiva interjected, holding his finger in the air. "These men are all Oathbound."

"I have so observed." The brother sighed, exhausted. "I'll have the others relieve them of their bands and remove these men before the Valeriaans arrive."

The fellow Schiva looked to his two companions, and they nodded in acknowledgment. They knew what was needed of them, and went about the task with deftness and haste.

The two Schivas bowed their heads to one another and went about their separate duties.

"We must depart." The Schiva returned to Ygrayne and spoke quietly in her ear. "My brother here will retrieve your husband."

Ygrayne could hardly feel herself moving, hardly felt Thelric leaving her embrace. But as the Schiva took her into his arms again, her eyes remained fixed on her husband, even as they proceeded down the cobblestone path. Peering over the Schiva's shoulder, Ygrayne gazed upon her husband's face as the brother lifted his lifeless body. He carried Thelric over the mound and out of her sight at last. Ygrayne pressed her face into the Schiva's chest, shrouded in the folds of his robe, and wept quietly.

CHAPTER 28

There was no peace come nightfall, though the survivors were taken to a camp on the outskirts of Falkhearth, far enough away to escape the notice of the Valeriaans and provide a reprieve from the city whose sight only brought them sorrow. Falkhearth was still flushed with an ominous red and orange, the remnants of pulsing embers illuminating the dark blanket of the night sky. It was a grim reminder to all that the wounds were still fresh, and painful to the touch. The horrors were alive and well in both their memories and the present.

The camp echoed with cries of despair and pain, while Schivas worked tirelessly to tend to as many as they could as speedily as they were able. Their night was spent relieving the gravely wounded of mangled and unusable limbs, cries of agony mercifully subdued by a sleeping tonic. But all the remedies in the world could not spare them the grief of parting with irreplaceable physical assets. Their amputated limbs were promptly tossed into a fire, long before the patient could awaken and search fruitlessly for what was lost permanently. Others' injuries required only but careful suturing to sew skin back together where it had been torn, bandaging with the utmost tenderness, splinting, dressing with herbal ointments, and the administration of tonics to prevent infection and ease unbearable pain.

Most simply wept throughout the night, now that they could afford the tears. They gave into the pain of loss, grieving for everyone, and everything, that the flames and battle had taken from them. They reverted to almost childlike states, incapable of doing anything for themselves, broken in will and spirit, their vivacity gone with those who had passed on into the great Vallar. Others, despite the tremendous odds stacked against them, were persistent in their search amongst the survivors for their loved ones. They shouted names into the air, where they mingled with pained groans. Eyes scrutinized both the familiar and the unrecognizable faces. Their voices grew hoarse as they strained, their bodies exhausted and trembling. Still, they would not cease their endeavors.

The Schivas, and those with the strength to carry the burden for those who couldn't, worked tirelessly through the night. Their sacrifices hardly ended when the battle ceased, bound by duty to care not only for the living, but also for the dead. Unlike their Valeriaan counterparts, who disposed of bodies as though they were nothing more than rubbish, the Schivas took great care in giving the deceased a respectable valediction. They laid the bodies in rows about the field to allow loved ones to claim them. Once identified, the bodies were wrapped in cloth and set ablaze atop a pyre of stones and lumber neatly stacked together as a provisional altar. Given that folk had little more than the clothing on their backs, they could hardly procure the trappings of an elaborate funeral, but at least they could do something to honor the dead, to bestow upon them the dignity they all so deserved.

Ygrayne was settled at the outer limits of the camp, farthest from Falkhearth, where the darkened plains and the faint silhouette of the mountains provided a welcome change of scenery. There she found respite from the weeping and solemnity of all the others, sharing her final moments with Thelric in peace and solitude. It was a small mercy to have privacy in such delicate final moments before he too would be given to the flames.

With a blanket about her back, Ygrayne cradled Thelric's head in her arms as she touched at his face, ran her fingers through his hair. Not even the fire could bring the color of life back into his pale complexion, restore the peachiness of its former tone. His skin lacked the warmth she remembered so well, having relied upon it during cold nights when the fire's heat proved insufficient, or when the rain brought a damp chill to the air. At least his hair still shone of pale gold, an ever-present luster moving through the locks akin to the sunlight on a river's surface.

Through her tears, Ygrayne gently wiped at his face with a damp cloth to rid him of the dirt and blood which stained his pearly skin. She wanted to see him in the way she remembered, in his full glory and beauty.

As the man she knew as her husband slowly began to reveal himself, Ygrayne couldn't help but remember the day they'd unknowingly said their last goodbyes, to be parted from each other forever.

Thelric had given Artur a kiss to his forehead while their boy was still sound asleep, only stirring slightly when Thelric brushed through his hair with his fingers and whispered in his ear, "I love you, Son. Take care of your mother while I'm gone."

Thelric always did this before he took leave of them for Falkhearth, and he hardly needed a response in such early hours of the morning. The show of affection was enough to grant peace to his mind. Ygrayne always waited for him at the bottom of the ladder and then accompanied him out to the porch.

"I love you," Thelric said to her as the two stood outside their door. The fateful morning was upon them, the rising sun banishing the blanket of darkness to the ends of the world so that it could reclaim the sky for its own, peeking slowly over the horizon. Its rays pierced through the trees, bathing Thelric and Ygrayne in golden light. They held each other close, for it was cooler than expected, and they basked in each other's warmth.

"I love you more," Ygrayne teased.

It was a constant skirmish between the two of them, albeit a playful one. Thelric laughed, pushing aside a strand of hair that fell over her face.

"I'll let you have it for today," he responded with a smile. "Only because you put up with me being gone, and you always wait so patiently for me."

"Maybe that's just because I love you more." She smirked at him.

"Hm." He gave her a skeptical look. "Still arguable. But we can revisit that another time."

The rest of the men who would accompany Thelric to Falkhearth were riding up in their wagons. Both Ygrayne and Thelric looked to the others momentarily and then once more at each other, completely unaware that this was the last time they were ever going to peer into each other's eyes. The last time they would hold one another and share sweet nothings.

"Time for me to go."

"Be safe." Ygrayne nodded solemnly. "And come back to me." It never got easier for her to watch him leave them.

"You know I will," he responded in kind. "You and Artur take care of each other while I'm gone."

The two shared a tender kiss. Ygrayne remembered Thelric felt especially warm and flushed in that moment, and how she wished they'd never parted knowing what she did now. How she wished she'd told him again how much she loved him, and heard him utter those very words in return. She wished she'd held him tighter, longer. Wished they'd shared those moments as if they were indeed their very last.

It was the biggest regret which weighed heavily in her heart now. If she could go back to tell him over and over again, she would. To be certain there was nothing left unspoken. Perhaps to persuade him to stay home. To spare him from the fate that befell him in the end.

Through her regrets and hypotheticals, Ygrayne couldn't help but feel anger rise inside of her. She had believed that Thelric shared the sentiment she held, the desire to be away from the war, to have no involvement with the Rebellion. When she saw the blue cloth, he died to her again—the man she loved was gone, but how well had she really known him? How long had he hidden this other loyalty from her? Why had he hidden it so? She wasn't certain what angered her more—that he'd been an Oathbound, or that he'd kept it from her. Regardless, it was too late.

"Damn you, Thelric." Ygrayne cursed under her breath, dropping her forehead against his to cry once more.

Her shaking hands touched at his cheek as she contemplated all the possibilities, all the unsaid things, all that could have been. She had at one time seen a clear future ahead of them—one in which they lived out the rest of their lives in Trivaden, grew old together, and passed on everything they had to their son, doing everything they could to provide him the best of futures. Now everything was dark, unknown. She couldn't imagine a damned thing. Ygrayne eventually collapsed from exhaustion and curled her body beside Thelric's, and after gazing at his pale, unmoving face for some time, she closed her eyes at last.

Ygrayne hadn't realized she drifted off to sleep until she awoke to the sound of footsteps. She opened her eyes just enough to see a shadowy figure standing before her. The fire had all but burned out in the absence of tending, and in the darkness she at first believed herself to be dreaming. She closed her eyes once more to spare herself the tricks of fatigue, and had every intention of drifting off for the remainder of the night if it weren't for the sound of breath giving life to the dormant fire, the flames resurging with the crackle of wood. Ygrayne felt the warmth once more upon her face, a warmth that banished the slight chill in the air, the cold emanating from the damp soil and grass. The commotion was enough to rouse her to scrutinize what was transpiring.

"My apologies." It was the Schiva's voice, his dark silhouette now illuminated by the fire, the smooth surface of his mask exaggerated by the harshness of the shadows dancing across it. His amber eyes glowed softly in the fire's touch, amplified by the mask's dark planes.

"I hardly meant to wake you, but I believed you to be in need of some warmth."

Ygrayne rubbed at her sleep-heavy eyes and said with a weary voice, "You didn't have to."

The Schiva snorted and said, "Not a matter of me wanting to. It's especially cold tonight. Best to have a fire going."

He knelt beside her, and Ygrayne could see how exhausted he was even behind his mask. His eyes, usually full of spirit, looked as tired as hers. The black paint ringing his eyes and obscuring his brows glinted with the sweat and oils of his skin. Even his bearing wasn't as steadfast as she was accustomed to, slumped as he was over the fire.

"Perhaps an imprudent question." He looked away a moment, thinking, and then asked, looking back to Ygrayne, "But...how are you?"

"Worse than some..." Ygrayne looked to Thelric. "Better than others..."

"Brief, but concise." At least his wits were intact. "Mind if I keep you company for a bit? I've been relieved temporarily."

"I thought you didn't rest." She said this in jest, but the words lacked all the spirit and playfulness that her tone would have otherwise carried.

"Well, it's hardly wise to conduct such critical procedures when plagued by exhaustion. We find it best to operate in turns. It would be rather unfortunate to cause preventable bodily harm."

"Of course." She sighed, as he took a seat beside her.

Silence stretched between them. Neither knew what to say. What was there to say in such circumstances? It was a tender moment as they searched for some peace in the comfortable company, remembering that they were not alone.

The Schiva contemplated how he could console her in her loss. With such tenacity in her pursuit, the unexpected—or expected—end, the worst of outcomes, was all the more difficult to accept. And her reaction when he'd produced the Oathbound band—how stunned and taken aback she had been. Ygrayne hadn't had the faintest inkling. Not only had she found her husband's body, but she had also made the grim discovery of a life kept hidden from her. The Schiva could hardly imagine the turmoil, the confusion, the anger that was coursing through her.

He looked to Ygrayne, but she did not return his gaze. She stared blankly into the fire, completely unaware that his eyes were upon her. Against his better judgment, but spurred on by his curiosity, he assessed that there wasn't anyone close enough to hear the conversation that might ensue before asking her quietly, "Did you know?"

Ygrayne didn't answer promptly, sitting still as stone, and the Schiva nearly cursed himself for his lack of sense and tact.

Only when she shook her head did he feel relief. She spoke a single word, quiet and curt: "No."

It released something inside of her, and the Schiva soon found himself the recipient of a barrage of words he had not anticipated. He presented himself as a much-needed vessel for the sentiments that were clamoring to be heard, to be understood.

With a deep breath, her eyes closing, she said to him, "I don't know how I didn't know all these years. I feel as though I should have...but how could I? I only knew of his dealings in Falkhearth from what *he* told me. Not once did I suspect…" Her voice trailed off, her breath shaking with the threat of tears. Ygrayne took a moment to swallow and regain her composure before she continued, "Maybe it was best I didn't know. I…I-I really don't know anything anymore. It just makes me wonder what else he lied to me about."

"I don't think he lied to you about anything else," the Schiva said quietly.

"How would you know?" She looked at him with disbelief. "You've never had a loved one lie to your face for years. Someone you trusted. Someone you believed wholeheartedly."

The Schiva grew silent, his eyes straying to the fire. Ygrayne contemplated the venom in her own words, the hurt they might have caused. She was disappointed in herself for using his lack of familiarity against him once again. The Schiva had given up the possibility of ever having what she had possessed to serve the whole of Skana, and it was a grand sacrifice her own experiences could never measure to. How painful it must be, to know one could never have such happiness, such pleasure in life. It was nothing she could sneer at or insult.

"I'm sorry." She dropped her eyes in shame.

"Don't be," the Schiva said gently, as if she hadn't been so abrasive. "You're in pain."

"It doesn't give me an excuse to speak in such a manner. If anything, I should be more thankful for everything you've done for me…for all folk."

"Then will you flatter me with a listening ear? It would mean more to me than a 'thank you.'"

She cowered under his gaze. How could he stand to look at her after such an insult? Ygrayne nodded, though she struggled to look to him as he to her.

"Many spouses conceal the truth of their involvement with the Oathbound from their partners—their families. 'Tis not done out of mistrust or ill will. Hardly. It's merely to shield their loved ones from the wrath of the Valeriaans. The burden of such a secret is to be theirs and theirs alone. Do not fault your husband. Do not think ill of what he trusted to be right. From what I've come to know of you, it's undeniable that the two of you loved each other—very much so. I imagine it pained him to leave you, to deceive you even with the best of intentions. But find solace in the notion that he knew the two of you to be safe, due in part to your ignorance."

"He would have never perished had he not been a part of the Oathbound." Ygrayne sighed.

"You think it an offense that he gave his life fighting?"

"I don't know…"

"Even if such an endeavor was for a future in which you and your son are free?"

Ygrayne held her tongue. She could feel the tears in her eyes again, but she was done crying, exhausted of it.

"I suppose...I really can't fault him for that." Ygrayne touched at her eyes, observing her damp fingertips with disbelief. How did she have tears left to shed? "I just hope..." She took a deep breath, paused a moment, and at last finished, "He knew how much I loved him. Because only now do I realize how much he loved me..." She thought back to the playful feud of greater affections and said in a whisper, "Maybe he did win."

"Pardon?" The Schiva titled his head slightly.

"Who loved each other more." She chuckled to herself and wiped away at a tear that dared to spill from her eyes. "I'll let him have this one."

Ygrayne then turned to the Schiva with a despondent, quivering smile and said, "I want to put him to rest now. Send him on his way to Vallar."

At first, Ygrayne thought she'd come to terms with her decision. But when she saw his body awaiting the flames, wrapped ever so carefully in a white shroud, she harbored second thoughts. Ygrayne cupped his face, planted a kiss on his forehead for one last farewell before she pulled the covering over his head. Her hand lay against his cheek, feeling the contours of his face through the shroud, the fabric stretched over his features.

"I love you," Ygrayne whispered, using all the strength she had left in her body to tear herself away from Thelric.

She took a stance beside the Schiva, mere feet away from where her husband would be consumed by flames. She fixed her eyes on the brother who bore a torch in his hand, touching it to the pyre laid atop the stone altar.

Her heartbeat quickened as she awaited the moment the flames would take to the wood doused in oil and resin. She felt she might cast herself over Thelric to prevent the procession. She needed just a little more time with him. But her resolve kept her feet firmly planted. At least she could grant him peace, unakin to so many in similar circumstances. She could still be looking for him. He could've been strung up for the ravens, or cast into a mass grave without thought. Here, she had a choice. She had his body. She had bestowed her farewells. It was more than most folk in the camp could hope for.

The flames of the torch licked at the wood hungrily. Promptly did the fire spread until it finally reached Thelric, his body set ablaze in a glorious and morbidly beautiful display of elegantly dancing flames. Sparks danced and fell akin to tears from the heavens above, and Thelric rose with the smoke to the world beyond—to the great and serene Vallar. Ygrayne hardly noticed the tears falling quietly down her cheeks. What she did feel was her heaving lungs, her shallow breaths. The sight before her was surreal in its finality. Thelric was leaving her sight, his physical form departing for all that was unseen. No second thoughts could be entertained now. There was something inexplicable in the experience of such a finite farewell, when what it meant for her life moving forward was so uncertain. It was overwhelming, powerful. She felt both completely serene and on the verge of panic. It was a moment she fully understood and could not comprehend all at once.

Of course, she couldn't have known the emotions that sending Thelric to the pyre would release, wouldn't have known the grief and mourning had not yet reached their crescendo. A gasp of a cry escaped through trembling lips before her hand swiftly grasped at the Schiva's own. Neither expected it, but only one was aware of the sudden gesture.

He acknowledged it with a widening of his eyes and a slight turning of his head, just enough that he could glance at Ygrayne from the corner of his eye. She only looked forward to her late husband, her composure weakening and her air of moderate dignity deserting her. She was wailing, screaming inside her own mind, calling to her husband beyond the grave. It was the lament of a woman who had just lost the man she loved, of a mother who now faced the responsibility of raising a son all on her own. Her world was collapsing all around her and he couldn't help but feel the utmost sympathy for her strife, for her pain.

And so, he let her be. Where otherwise he would have politely and gently rejected such an intimate gesture, with her he allowed it to continue. If it meant she might feel some sort of reprieve from the despair consuming her, he wanted to give her that.

The Schiva looked about nonchalantly, making certain they were alone. The brother who had come to set the fire had returned to the camp, and everyone else was occupied with their current tasks.

They were indeed alone.

He tightened his hand around hers ever so slightly—to give her the comfort she sought in her moment of desperation and mourning. The Schiva was numb to the sight. Thelric was only one of the many deceased he'd witnessed burning that night. But Ygrayne was watching her love leave the mortal realm before her very eyes, saying a goodbye no one would ever wish for, and she was handling it as well as anyone could.

Just as the Schiva looked back to the fire once more, a flash high above them caught his eye. Though it gleamed with the light of the fire below, it disappeared as quickly as it had appeared, leaving only a slight shift in the air to indicate that it had been there at all. His eyes narrowed, knowing well what awaited him back at the tent.

He would have to be patient. Ygrayne needed him there, and they stayed beside one another until the flames died at last, and all that was left of the body was a pile of ash glinting with red embers. The heat was carried off by the wind. When even the slightest bit of light had faded from the remnants did the Schiva finally look to Ygrayne.

"If you wish," he spoke quietly. "I can give you a jar for his ashes. It's not as elegant as an urn, but it's adequate. He may accompany you back to Trivaden, at least."

Ygrayne nodded her head, her lips pursed to keep from letting out a nervous laugh.

"I would appreciate that." She sniveled a moment, wiping her face. "Besides, an urn wouldn't suit Thelric. He'd want me to spread his ashes around the places he loved…though it would pain me greatly to depart from him yet again."

The Schiva thought for a moment, and said to her, "There is a way."

She sniffled again and looked to him with a furrowed brow.

"A way?"

"For the two of you to remain together. Are you aware that ashes can be crafted into jewelry?"

"Such a thing is possible?"

"'Tis indeed. Would you want that?"

"That would be wonderful," Ygrayne sighed, a weak smile crossing her lips. "Is there anything you can't do?"

"Oh, I most certainly cannot craft jewelry from ash." The Schiva snorted lightly. "Sorry to disappoint. But I know someone, who knows someone… who knows someone—who can do so in my stead."

From her lips came a slight titter and she responded, "Thank you."

"There's no need—" He paused a moment, noticing the disheartened look about Ygrayne's face. He did not want to bring her more pain with his customary modest response. "You're welcome, Ygrayne," he corrected himself promptly, and it did well to alter her dejected expression to one of relief and peace. A smile flashed about his eyes.

He brought their intertwined hands between them, and he gently clasped hers between each of his palms. Only then did Ygrayne realize what she had done in her oblivious state. She blushed with embarrassment, taken aback by her own action and the threat it posed to his oath.

"I'm so sorry!" she exclaimed, breathless in her loss for words. "I didn't realize—"

"Never mind it, Ygrayne." The Schiva kept her hand in his. "I, as a Schiva, am at the service of the commonfolk. Of all the people of Skana. If this was the reprieve I could grant you, I humbly offer it so."

Ygrayne flattened her lips, stifling a small cry and a sniffle as the tears began to pool in her eyes once more. She had no words with which she could convey her appreciation for the confidant standing beside her.

"I think it best for you to turn in for the night," said he. "I'll collect your husband's ashes, and we shall reunite afterward. Be certain to keep your foot elevated while you rest."

Ygrayne nodded, and gently did he relinquish her hand. The two parted ways—Ygrayne to the tent she'd been offered a place in, and the Schiva remaining at the quieted bonfire. Only when he was certain she had departed did he make his way back to his own tent under the pretense of retrieving the jar as he so stated. When he tossed aside the flap of the tent, did he see his brother and sister from earlier awaiting him inside. He could feel a chill about the air. The way they gravely gazed at him in silence made him realize at once that something was amiss. His silver-winged companion, the flash he had seen in the sky, had delivered the solemn news that awaited him, that had rendered the tent utterly silent.

"Brother," the fellow Schiva said as he held up a scroll of vellum between his fingers.

The Schiva took the scroll with a swift swipe of his hand, unrolled it, and read the contents scribbled inside. The note was curt, but it sent a shiver down the length of his spine, his breath taken from him.

"No..."

CHAPTER 29

The explosions in the distance were ceaseless even come twilight, and restless nights they were indeed. The danger posed by Trivaden's proximity to Falkhearth weighed heavily upon everyone's minds. The customary daily activities all but discontinued; folks instead kept to the safety of their homes. Even Artur, who overcame the fears that plagued him the first night to venture out to his fishing spot and see if Lovisa would return to him, promptly lost his vigor and hope. He too resigned himself to the confines of the cottage, his company comprised of Urda, Vána, and the fire when he couldn't sleep.

There was some peace in such isolation and quiet. After the confrontation with Ronan, Artur convinced himself that he would be under the intense scrutiny of the rest of the village folk. They would come barging up to his door as Petra had. But the battle off in the distance dissuaded any such attempts, and Artur suspected Ronan had not yet spoken further of their brutal scuffle.

Day became night once again, and suddenly there was silence.

The bursts that had become a part of the evening routine were halted, and most everyone slept soundly through the night without realizing it until morning conversation brought it to light amongst the neighbors—the first time they had talked in over a week, the first time they stepped out into the open.

What might otherwise be thought a reprieve only provoked more worry. There was a restlessness about, a commotion of thoughts and speculations as to the cause of the sudden peace. In some way, they hoped the blasts they had grown accustomed to would resume, for it would mean the fight was still far away and elsewhere, and the battle being waged was not their concern. They wanted to be left alone, even at the expense of others.

Though the war was far away, the sky was still brown and smelled of smoke. The pine scent of the forest and the untouched nature surrounding them diluted the potency, sparing them from tainted air and suffocating ash. The tavern, ordinarily active only during the night, was occupied and full of folks who wanted to hear the stories of the bard once again. His strumming and melodic vocals did well to placate the masses and lift the stresses which plagued them, if only for a time.

That was what woke Artur that morning: the singing reverberating through his cottage, a pronounced change of sound in the air. The slumber he awoke from had been deep, evidenced by the drool dampening his pillow and the hair plastered to his face. Artur could hardly believe it at first. Such harmonious sounds seemed so foreign, and he gave himself over to sleep for a little while longer. When he woke up once more, the bard was still singing, and Artur was then convinced that he was hearing exactly what it sounded to be. Even so, Artur was not to be coaxed into joining the others. He descended his ladder and found only Vána there to greet him. Her eyes beamed at him, watching his every move until his feet touched the floor, and it was then she went to greet him and lick at his face.

"Good morning, Vána," Artur said to her, scratching behind her ears, and her leg kicked happily at the floor, a satisfied growl deep in her throat.

He looked about the cottage and determined that Urda wasn't present. The bed was nicely made, just as she always left it, and the table was laid with a bit of breakfast for him to eat in her absence. He ate, sparing a bit of food for his canine companion, before casting the dishes to a bucket to take with him outside for cleaning at the well pump. Vána followed and waited patiently as he went about his morning activities, tidying up the cottage in his mother's absence.

It was how he stayed close to her while she was gone. The home was now his responsibility. If he had been asked to tend it only a month ago, he would have voiced his great displeasure for doing such chores, preferring to fill his time with play and outside activities. Now, they'd become part of his routine. Sweeping, washing, picking the vegetables from the garden, pulling out the weeds when he could find them—all obligations his mother would do while his father was away. There was some sense of calm, of pride, in looking at the fruits of his labor once all the tasks had been completed. He had never known such satisfaction before this time when the two most important folk in his life were gone.

When everything was done, and Urda was still nowhere to be found, Artur took to the garden for some solitude outside of the cottage. A blanket under his back, Artur lay about and gazed up to the brown sky above. Vána nestled beside him, her head resting in the crook of his arm so that he could coil his hand around to pet behind her ears. She was in a Vallar all her own, golden eyes closing as sweet bliss overcame her.

He felt a morbid peace looking to the brown clouds, with the unsavory smell of a battle heavy in the air and the bard's voice still filling his ears. There was a welcome isolation in it, at a time he most wanted to be alone—or away from folk, at least. He loved Vána's company. She would never become aggressive, or hostile with him. Her touches were only those of adoration and love, and she listened as well as she could with those large ears of hers. She only cared about him and his well-being.

Artur held his hand above him and observed how well and quickly he had healed—the bandages gone, the cuts mended, and only faint scars left as a reminder of what had transpired. He remembered one of the nights Urda was tending to him once again, replacing his bandages, making certain the wounds were clean.

When she removed them the final time around, Urda was quite surprised at how well he healed, almost impossibly so. All that was left of the wounds were faint bruises or scars of red where the skin had been torn.

"Ye healed sae fast, an' well," Urda commented, turning his hand about as she inspected his condition. "I don't think ye need any more bandages."

Artur looked at his knuckles and he too was staggered by how well his wounds had mended. Even the pain had subsided. Flexing his hand, Artur realized the mobility had returned, and had it not been for the still-visible marks, he wouldn't have believed they were ever hurt.

"Have ye always healed thon well?" Urda asked.

"I never really thought about it, I guess." Artur only shrugged.

"Then it must be yer youth." Urda sighed longingly. "The heavens forbid, if I stand up wrong, ma back is thrown out o' sorts." Urda chortled but Artur ignored it.

It was hard for him to smile, let alone laugh after the day of the fight, which still plagued his thoughts, haunted him in his dreams. It was arduous to focus on anything around him, even before he considered the fact that his mother and father still hadn't returned home. And Lovisa…

He looked down to the floor where his book sat untouched at his side, its mere presence daunting as he still could not decipher the script on those vellum pages. It was humiliating, almost, given that the book was the only remainder he had of her.

"Don't be so hard on yourself for no' bein' able tae read," Urda said, after observing his longing gaze at the tome. "No one today knows hou."

"I know," Artur said. "But…do you think I could ever learn?"

"I think if ye put yer mind tae it, ye could." Urda touched at his nose with the tip of her finger.

"…How would I do that?" Artur blinked, no longer taken aback by the gesture she performed frequently.

"That, I'm no' certain. But I suspect thare is a way, an' you'll figure it out. Though I should nae e'en be encouragin' it tae begin wi'!"

Artur let out a sigh and wondered if Ronan was still in pain, or if he too was healing as well as he had. There was one thing Artur knew for certain: Ronan would still be as cross with him now as he had been then.

Artur dropped his hand to his chest and closed his eyes to rest as blissfully as Vána did beside him, comforted by the softness of her fur and the warmth of her body.

For a time, Artur went about resting serenely without a stir, and Vána was just as quiescent. He remained hidden, unwilling to show his face to anyone else. He couldn't confront Ronan, and not even Petra had attempted to antagonize him again after Urda turned her away at the door. Still, he relegated himself to the garden, with his cottage a few steps away should he need to retreat.

Yet Artur hadn't been as reclusive as he would have preferred to be in recent days—at the insistence of Urda herself, who didn't seem the least bit unsettled by the turmoil in Falkhearth. She managed to coax him out to her garden with her alluring words, in the enchanted way she described everything. It was a place he had previously never set foot in, but if it was anything akin to her cottage, his curiosity was indeed enticed.

As Artur's family harvested vegetables and fruit for the village, he was well acquainted with the plants that yielded the bounty. Entering Urda's garden felt akin to stepping through the gates of another world, enriched by a congregation of flowers and a beautiful tree whose shade cascaded over half the garden. Its branches stretched to the roof of her home, appearing intertwined with its wooden planks. It was a most beautiful tree—so green, so verdant, that it made the forest envious. The epitome of perfection.

There was a family of squirrels that occupied its hollow, having claimed it as their home. Artur had the pleasure of becoming acquainted with two of them, who were not the least bit shy around strangers. They would come skittering down the length of the trunk, spurred on by their own curiosity, taking in their new visitor with wide eyes.

"That's Toska," Urda said to Artur when he first became acquainted with one. She spoke as if they were folk themselves.

"He decidit one day thon ma tree wad be his home. An' he broucht his lover over. They have a few barins now."

Artur only looked to her with a quizzical brow.

"He's quite a chatterbox thouch. He likes tae tell me aboot the village gossip whenever I'm gardenin'." She winked and nudged his chin gently, an amused chortle escaping her lips at both her little jest of a story and Artur's reaction. Whether she was speaking with seriousness or to simply tease him, he honestly couldn't tell.

His look of incredulousness soon narrowed into bewilderment and annoyance, and Urda thought it all the more amusing as she walked away laughing.

"If ye don't fancy squirrels, ye should see the Faelora."

"What are those?"

"Ah! I'm no' surprisit ye haven't seen thaim before. They only come out at nicht an' sleep durin' the day, hidden in bushes an' latchin' onto branches. They're adorable. Let's see if we can find thaim."

Artur hardly knew what to look for when searching the garden, and hardly did he suspect that Urda knew precisely where they were sleeping. She was granting him a chance to find one on his own, to see if he could spot the otherwise elusive creature of the forest. But no amount of peeking under leaves produced any satisfactory results, and after some time spent searching fruitlessly, Artur finally let out an exhausted sigh and said, "I can't find them, Urda."

Coincidently, it was then that Urda happened upon one.

"Come here, Artur. I found ane."

His curiosity piqued, he knelt alongside her before a bush she was gently prying apart.

"Leuk here," she whispered, lifting a few leaves and the twigs that secured them to the branch on which the faelora was sleeping.

He did not know what to expect, and at first, he did not see it. It wasn't until his eyes adjusted to the dim light that he could perceive the transparent little creature hugging the branch it was attached to. No bigger than Urda's hand, it had a round head, with petite ears similar to those of a cat, and a teardrop-shaped figure. The wings at its upper body triangular. Its organs could be seen through the blue hue of its translucent body, an orange glow faintly pulsing within its head and chest.

"You want tae touch it?" Urda asked, though Artur was loath to do so given he had never come across such an…interesting-looking creature before.

"It won't hurt ye, ye have ma oath. Watch."

Urda gently prodded it with the tip of her finger. The faelora let out a gentle coo, its body quivering to life, and the faint glow of orange radiated more brightly as if it were a burning flame. From its core, white shimmers dispersed and floated about the empty space between its abdomen and tail. It only took seconds before it instinctually discerned the time of day and quietly nestled itself back against the branch to resume its slumber until nightfall.

"See?" Urda looked to him. "Ye try it."

Bolstered by Urda's demonstration, Artur too gently poked at the faelora, surprised by how cool and gelatinous it was. The tip of his finger came away with a thin sheen of dampness. Before his eyes the faelora came to life once more—the coo, the radiating color from within, the particles which floated about. Urda and Artur might have been amused, but the creature hardly shared the sentiment. The faelora knew it had been found and needed to search for another refuge to protect itself from possible danger. It detached from the branch and gently floated into the air, its wings waving to and fro in a slow, fluid motion, until it made its way to the adjacent bush where it latched onto another branch and went to sleep once again.

"It's squishy," Artur said, wiping his finger on his shirt.

"I know! Isn't it amazin'?" Her excitement was so palpable that Artur wasn't certain which he was more amazed by.

Urda loved tending to her vast and prospering landscape, the expanse lush due to the fresh water she retrieved from the well at the center of its premises. Carrying pail after pail, she went about and made certain each plant was tended to with the utmost care, talking to them as if they were sentient, as if they could respond. She was lost in her own little world when she was going about her duties, and as of late, Artur had begun to join her. He possessed neither her fondness nor her finesse for nursing, but it was good for his nerves and helped to ease the stresses which had mounted over the past days. And when Artur found no more joy in gardening, he would retreat to her porch, or the shade of the tree, to quietly watch or sleep after yet another restless night.

Once Artur even snuck his book over, not that it was too difficult given that no folk was around to see, and Urda didn't seem to mind when he took to reading it, or attempting to. In fact, never once did Urda mention anything about it, hardly acknowledging its existence after their exchange by the fire.

Artur awoke in his family's garden and realized the morning had passed into the early afternoon. Vána had never left his side, only stirring when he sat up. The two of them retreated into the cottage to find it just as empty as it had been that morning—nothing changed, no indication that Urda had been around during his nap. For the rest of the day, she failed to appear.

Artur was certain he would have heard her singing, or humming, or talking to her flowers. But on their side of the village all he could hear was drunken singing and the melodies of the bard, the festivities growing more raucous as the night approached and village folk gathered to feast around the hearth at the center of the tavern's common area.

He was left to his own once more, and here he struggled. He might have taken to cleaning and tending to the cottage easily enough, but he hardly knew where to begin when it came to cooking. Going into the village proper to fetch some venison or any kind of food was hardly an option for him. So,

Artur resorted to picking vegetables and fruits from his garden and pairing them with what was left of breakfast from that morning. He gave Vána the bigger half of his loaf, coated with honey, and a few of the fruits he knew were edible for her kind. Still, Artur felt it wasn't enough for such a beast.

He opened the back door and said to her, "Go get yourself some more food if you're hungry."

Vána looked to him with large eyes and let out a concerned whine. She did not want to leave him in his time of loneliness and need.

"Go on now, Vána." He dismissed her with a wave of his hand. "I'll be all right."

She was reluctant, but eventually she did as she was told. She could not deny the hunger still present in her belly. She loped off into the forest and Artur went about cleaning up his mess before returning to his loft.

With the window open and a candle at his bedside, Artur delved into the book to see if the script on the pages would suddenly make sense to him. To his great frustration, nothing had changed. The words were as foreign to him as the first time he'd laid eyes upon them, and he was no closer to deciphering their meaning.

With a sigh, Artur proclaimed defeat once again and slid the book under his pillow to put it out of his mind for the time being. He felt he was failing Lovisa, lacking the proficiency to value such a cherished gift to the fullest. Artur wondered for a time if she had made a mistake in entrusting the book to him to begin with. She knew he couldn't read, and it was her favorite book amongst the many she'd boasted about. With a sigh he went to his window to seek the peace he often found when he leaned about its sill. But on this night, it eluded him.

The night sky was still unrecognizable. The beauty it ordinarily boasted lay hidden behind the ugliness of the faraway conflict, concealed by the darkness of the smoke cover. Neither the stars, nor the Nerúnors—not even the moon—came to visit. There was a sense of desolation in the quiet of his seclusion; the peace around him appeared to be tenuous rather than permanent. At least there was the bard's music and the glow from the fire that Artur had set in the hearth—welcome diversions, even if they provided only a flimsy barrier against the worse times to come.

This particular bard, known for the ballads of misfortune and sorrow he delivered in his rather despondent tone, chose more soothing refrains that night. The music was almost hypnotizing, the lull of the melody calling Artur to rest his head in the confines of his arms, let the gentle breeze outside ruffle his hair. The cool air felt pleasant, the smell notwithstanding. He closed his eyes and drifted off to sleep, hoping to find peace in the restful slumber that often eluded him lately.

Though Artur, and all those in Trivaden and her neighboring villages, could not know for certain that the reprieve was not meant to last, they knew not to mistake the silence for safety. Far away down the road, the war reared its ugly head and set its eyes upon them with a raging hunger not yet satisfied, a thirst never to be slaked. The fire and destruction it had cast upon Falkhearth would soon find their way to the forests, to the homes and to the village folk themselves, to scorch and devour with the roar of flames and the thundering hooves of the armies spreading the horrors of war ever wider. It was coming, slithering across the land with a quiet but voracious hiss, determined not to let the night end without the taste of blood about its fangs, its greed fed, and its quest for retribution further realized.

CHAPTER 30

Indeed, it was a peaceful night. Artur fell asleep at the windowsill without the slightest discomfort. The bard was still singing, the festivities were still just as lively as when they had first begun, and they filled the quiet village with an excitement all so desperately desired as they reveled in the momentary peace. Not a soul knew of the danger quickly approaching their doorstep—that is, except for one.

Unseeable. Indiscernible. A force which no one could comprehend, its voice carried on the soft swell of the wind as it brushed through the forest trees, leaving them trembling at the words of warning, across the waters whose surfaces rippled at its touch. The beasts of the forest sought refuge in their homes as it made its way to Trivaden, its target a single boy who slept soundly enough.

Brushing through his hair, tickling at his ears, the hum that traveled about the wind manifested in the softness of a whisper. The words were unintelligible, formless except in the ears of the intended—an admonition, but an elusive one. Artur did not stir, no matter how much it coaxed and prodded him for his attention. He was too deeply asleep, too unperturbed to wake. Artur could have taken it for a dream for all he could understand. And so, as a dream it did come to him to pass on the urgent message before it was too late.

There wasn't much Artur could remember, but what snatches he retained were a true spectacle. They featured a visitor that Artur couldn't completely comprehend, due not only to his own limited experience, but also to how foreign the presence was to the world he lived in. What Artur could interpret, faintly, was a silhouette similar in form to a dire wolf—a very, very large one—whose figure gave off a sort of mist, swirling about before dissipating. The entirety of this beastly form hummed with a brilliant glow, the sea of a pelt devoid of discernible detail. The fur lining the spine was long and wispy, twisting and turning as if commanded by the wind. A tail, akin to that of a horse, lay about in a sea of filaments across the ground. Artur could see no snout, nor jowls, nor the physical traits that would have made this beast more familiar, natural. All he could identify were glowing black eyes, whose irises were gold and as piercing as a sword's edge.

Artur gazed upon this beast just as it gazed back at him, though it possessed a stoicism and presence far greater than Artur's own. He wasn't certain how long they shared the silent exchange, or how much time passed in this landscape that seemed to exist outside the natural world. But there came a point at which this beast tilted its head up to the endless void that was the sky around them and let out a trembling howl. It sounded just as ethereal as it did powerful, a multitude of tones becoming one. The sound was so magnificent, so jarring, that it startled a loud gasp out of Artur.

He awoke with a start and a yelp as his head rose from the crook of his arm. He could hardly recollect what transpired in his dream, but even the faint memory of the apparition left him with a quickened heartbeat and a flushed face. Exhaustion settled over him, the dream having robbed him of an undisturbed night of sleep. With a groan, Artur rubbed at his head and ran his fingers through his tangled hair, his tired eyes blinking to ease the bleariness from his sight.

Only then did Artur see it—a faint glow of orange. Only then did he hear them—the sounds of clattering armor and the thundering of hooves, the cry of horses.

The tiredness fell away in mere seconds, his eyes springing entirely open, his hands gripping tightly at the windowsill. Artur didn't want to believe it. He wanted it to be a dream, he wanted to still be sleeping.

Yet as Artur narrowed his eyes in scrutiny, did he realize the glow was only growing stronger, closer, and he could feel the frame of the cottage shake beneath his grasp, see the candle flickering in its holder. He drew in a sharp breath, his heartbeat pounding in his ears akin to a drum. He held onto the quickly fading hope that it wasn't in fact what he feared it to be, but a definitive answer would be given to him ever so swiftly.

Three horsemen rounded the turn of the road first, banners flying behind them, torches gripped within gloved hands. Following in their wake was a petrifying sight: an army marching in perfect unison, attuned to its leader's behest.

"Oh, shit..." Artur whispered the curse under his breath as he ducked from his window, hoping they hadn't seen him as he had seen them.

He clutched his chest, his heart pounding with rising panic as his body trembled, his eyes closing tight, his teeth gritting. They were coming. Artur was convinced they were there because of him—because of what happened to Lovisa. He needed to act.

Artur crawled across the loft until he could peek over the ledge to utter in a harsh whisper, "Urda!"

He hoped she was there, sleeping soundly after being out and about for the entire day.

"Urda?" Artur called again when he didn't see her in bed, looking about the rest of the cottage before concluding that she was indeed still absent.

"Search the cottages!" Artur heard a voice outside, a Valeriaan Thegn giving his orders. He flinched, fearing that he was already too late, the Valeriaans just at his door. Yet instead of rendering him helpless with fear, this prospect spurred him into action.

Artur crawled to his bed, fetching the book he so greatly cherished and feared would be discovered. As he reached for it, he could see from his window that two Valeriaan soldiers were already at Urda's door. Artur went pale and cold as though he had been caught in a ferocious winter storm. His fear had been realized. He had condemned the entire village, and he had to warn them of the imminent danger—to alleviate the guilt on his own conscience, at least. He couldn't let his choices bring retribution to those who had no hand in them, who knew nothing of his misdeeds.

Artur nearly tumbled to the floor, he climbed down his ladder so fast and so clumsily. After a hurried recovery, he scurried for the back door. As he turned the handle, he could hear the heavy tread of the soldiers' boots on the porch just outside the front door. His stomach sank. He had mere moments left to make good on his escape. The door trembled under the force of a powerful kick, reverberating through the walls and the floor. Certainly, such a fearsome exertion of strength should have smashed the wooden door into pieces with the first attempt. How it didn't falter under such an impact was a true marvel, and a testament to the skill of its craftsman. But even the most expertly made doors could only hold for so long, for their durability would always wane under enough duress. For the time being, the door was Artur's savior. It was holding long enough for him to get a running start, and Artur needed no more convincing to flee after the second kick landed.

Artur swallowed hard and made his escape out the back door, doing well to open it as quietly as possible so as not to alert the soldiers to his presence, hoping they would think this residence too was vacant. He nearly tripped again down the steps as his panic set in, his shaking legs unstable. Yet despite his clumsiness, he built enough thrust to propel himself over the fence in one leap. The gate would have put him in sight of the soldiers.

After another tumble from an ungraceful landing in the dirt, Artur again scrambled back to his feet and sprinted to the tavern. The natural curve of the hill did well to hide his figure from sight, the dip in the landscape an ally in his perilous undertaking.

When Artur reached the back of the tavern, he briefly considered presenting himself at the front door. But peeking around the corner, he could see it was hardly a suitable option if his primary objective was the preservation of his own life. The Valeriaans were already making their way down the road, and their keen eyes were locked upon their next target—the tavern itself. Cursing under his breath, Artur instead went to one of several back windows that belonged to the guest rooms on the lower floor and shook at the wooden shutters with a concerted effort to keep the rattling from emitting too much sound. He hoped the sudden movement on an otherwise peaceful night would catch the attention of those lodging in the rooms. He let out an exasperated breath when no response came, his efforts unequal to the loud cheering, conversations, and singing.

The Valeriaan soldiers were only drawing nearer—Artur could feel their presence upon him, disturbing the air about him. Despite his mounting fright, Artur moved resolutely to the adjacent window for a second attempt, only to find it locked and hardly the warning of danger he'd hoped it to be. To his dismay, all the windows were locked. Artur grunted as he tried with all his might to pry one open, frustrated tears gathering in his eyes. He was scared—terrified—not for himself, but for the folk inside who knew nothing of the threat approaching the tavern. When he heard the Valeriaans walking about the porch, Artur knew it to be too late.

There came the crash of the door—unakin to the door of his family's cottage, a single kick was enough to detach it from its hinges with a loud shriek. What followed suit made Artur's skin crawl, his breath caught in his throat: the folk inside let out their most terrified screams, mingled together as a morbid orchestra that drowned out the jaunty music of the bard. Artur slowly withdrew his hands from the shutters, his breath quivering. He could do nothing but listen to the ensuing chaos, the frenetic commotion transpiring within the tavern. The agonizing cries of those he knew, those he called neighbors, friends.

The war between the Empire and the Oathbound had come to Trivaden.

It was all so tormenting to his ears, his imagination left to envision everything he could not see with his own eyes until Artur caught a glimpse of a faint glow from around the corner and his head turned sharply at the sound of footsteps approaching. He had no other choice but to flee for the trees, for the protection the forest itself would provide. Still, he carried his guilt as he sought the cover of its shroud, of the night, his figure vanishing from sight just before two soldiers rounded the corner and peered around the back of the tavern.

Artur bounded down the hill so quickly he lost his footing—again—and would have tumbled the rest of the way had the rough dirt not slowed his body enough to bring him to a painful stop. Throughout the ordeal, even under the threat of being launched through the air, Artur managed to keep the book within his grasp, holding it closely to his chest. Through the pain elicited by his tumble, Artur managed to gather himself enough to crawl behind the trunk of a tree to rest a moment and to listen once more, to gauge what was happening just out of sight. His mind again raced to piece together events he was still not privy to in full detail. He thought of them—his beloved neighbors. He pictured their petrified faces as he remembered their screams filling the air, mounting, as the Valeriaans made their way deeper into Trivaden. Artur flinched, and had his hand not gone to his mouth, his voice would've been heard through his gritted teeth.

He desired in that moment to possess several more arms and several more hands so he could spare his ears from the sound of the growing turmoil in the village. To spare his gaze from the horrors that required but a single glance to etch themselves permanently in his memory. And at last to cover his mouth, so that he might not utter a cry in horror—a scream so loud the Valeriaans would no doubt find him. Even now he struggled to keep the voice inside, the sound in his throat pushing against his palms so forcefully that tears began to fall down his face, his fingers digging into his skin.

Artur cursed himself for caring primarily for his own well-being. Forsaking the others in his need for survival. Leaving the innocent to fall prey to the enemy converging upon them.

I tried, he thought to himself, tears mercilessly falling about his face. *I really, really tried…*

CHAPTER 31

The cries and screams grew louder and greater in number as the Valeriaans breached each cottage in Trivaden. And if the events unfolding weren't overwhelming enough, Artur's ears were filled with a sound just as horrifying as the screams rending the air about him: it was the soldiers themselves, laughing, cackling akin to ravens encircling a dying beast below. They found pleasure, amusement in the torment of the village folk, cursing and mocking them, making jests of their plight.

It was cruel—all so cruel.

And it was just the beginning. In that moment did Artur begin to understand the true nature of the Empire, of the Valeriaans.

Over an excruciating stretch of time, the cries and taunts began to fade as the soldiers made their way deeper into Trivaden.

Artur wiped at his face and crawled on his hand and knees, cautiously creeping up to the crest of the hill, just far enough for him to peer over the summit. Gazing around a tree, Artur could see the backs of the vacated cottages through the darkness which settled unnervingly over the desolate scene. Noticing that the surrounding area was deserted of both neighbors and Valeriaans, Artur made his way along the tree line until he reached the town plaza—a place where communal dinners and festivities took place, an area he regarded fondly as he remembered the smiles and laughter, the delicious food which had often filled his belly. On this night, the plaza was once again populated by village folk, but for no joyous occasion.

Hiding once more behind the nearest tree, Artur could observe familiar faces contorted by horrified expressions. The merriment which had filled the air in the past was now replaced by the Valeriaans' sustained sniggering and derision directed at the village folk. They had been herded to the heart of the plaza as if they were nothing more than cattle for the slaughter, the wide-open area a makeshift pen in which the terrified livestock fought for space and air in the throes of their suffocating panic.

Artur had never seen them so terrified. Those he might have believed not to possess the capacity to weep were now left lamenting, as vulnerable to the torment to which they were subjected as all the rest. Forced to their knees by harshly barked orders, his neighbors clutched one another for some semblance of comfort and shelter as they knew their captors would not grant them such things. They defied the Valeriaans' attempt to pry them from their physical bonds of comradery. Mothers wept for the fate of the children they cradled within their embraces—the place meant to be the safest for any child. And in return, their children clung to them as they had so naturally and instinctively done since birth—to their support, their protector. Lovers across the ages held onto one another, whispering what they believed to be their last words. If death should befall them, their deepest and truest sentiments would be known, without hesitation or reticence.

Bodies trembled so terribly. Blubbering lips dispersed spittle. Phlegm dripped from nostrils, tears tracked down faces. Weeping. Howling. Artur could feel it all as if it were his own—his own voice, his own debasement. Yet, there was but one that was not amongst them.

Eyes darting the mingled faces, Artur searched for his guardian and dear friend, Urda. She was nowhere to be found about the flushed and dampened faces, but Artur's eyes did stop when he saw Ronan and Kian as they sought comfort within Petra's arms.

"Ronan," Artur whispered. "Kae." Their names were a lament upon his tongue, his lips quivering.

The often-obstinate Ronan could not brave the turmoil, surmount the fear which ensnared him completely. His tears glistened in the fire of the torches, while Kian attempted to spare himself but the smallest of glimpses by hiding his face in his mother's bosoms.

Artur wanted so desperately to go to them, to be at their side in their time of need. But he could find neither the strength to do so, nor the will to act out such a foolish and fatal desire. There was nothing to be done. There were no amends to be made. To feign bravery and act upon impulse was foolishness. Instead, all manner of sense was compelling him to simply run and forget about every folk there, the grim circumstances be what they were. To save himself, for he was the only one left to be saved. There was great guilt in contemplating such a prospect. His fate wasn't yet in the hands of such cruel judges, but he simply couldn't obey his instinct to flee. Artur was drawn to the turmoil, as if in a trance—powerless to do anything but bear witness to a cruelty he was not prepared to face. So he remained, and he watched.

The Valeriaans surrounded the village folk, akin to a pack of dire wolves encircling their prey. Their grins flashing fangs, smirking through the openings of their glistening helmets. They knew what horrors would ensue, unakin to the commonfolk they so looked down upon, and the anticipation made them as gleeful as they were restless. A few soldiers poked and prodded the village folk, causing them to startle and cry out. This made the Valeriaans roar with laughter, whetting their appetite for a brutishness which knew neither bounds nor limitations.

One soldier went so far as to knock over one of the old men with a hard shove of his boot, the heel digging against skin that easily bruised under such duress. Artur recoiled with a gasp when the poor man slammed into the ground with a loud thud, the breath forced from his lungs. He struggled to get back on his knees, and no one made any attempt to assist him in his futile attempts, fearing any undertaking would only subject them to the same treatment.

The village folk bowed their heads in shame, their gazes purposefully averted from the eyes of the man they felt they so failed, as if that would absolve them of their guilt for their inability to act.

But one young woman could stand it no longer—the man's abuse finally provoked her anger to come forth in vocal condemnation of the Valeriaans' actions with imaginative expletives, against her better judgment and all manner of logic. Hurling insults in her bout of rage, she hissed with a venom so potent it could only be born of abhorrence. Those who cowered in their silence and resignation couldn't help but tremble at her behavior. Gawk. Tremble. Although she was braver than them, she was also the most foolish, and they all feared—knew—what was about to befall her.

The woman's sudden outburst only proved to be an amusing challenge for the Valeriaans, one too tempting to refuse. Without a moment's hesitation, one of soldiers grabbed her by the hair and dragged her away from the crowd as she kicked and screamed until her lungs burned. She was no match for the soldier's strength. Her thrashing did little to deter him, only provoking laughter and heightening the already goaded eagerness. A few more soldiers accompanied him, grasping at her dress and tearing it away slowly, teasing and prodding at her legs with the vilest of intentions, even as she kicked madly at them. If these were to be her final moments, she was not going to let them take her without a struggle—and struggle she did, so valiantly, as the village folk watched with shuddering glances, listened to her ceaseless screams mingling with the laughter which arose consequently. The soldiers dragged the woman out of sight, disappearing into one of the nearby cottages. But her screams did not quiet; rather, they intensified as they defiled and tormented the entirety of her being, as they subjected her to a plight of humiliation and degradation. All the while the village folk wept and trembled, knowing well the fate befalling her. The Valeriaans who remained only snickered, the torches glinting within sharpened glances exchanged.

Artur himself had never heard such torment, never knew a woman to be capable of screaming as she did, as loudly as she did. What was transpiring behind those walls, he could neither understand nor imagine. Regardless, her ordeal brought tears to his eyes just as it did to the folk of Trivaden, and as much as he desired for it to cease, it only continued, growing in severity. Her pain and anguish emanated from the cottage, rendering all folk stunned and powerless. In all their cruelty and callousness, the Valeriaans went on carrying out their vile deeds.

It was then the Valeriaan Thegn sauntered over to the crowd upon his armored steed and brought the magnificent beast to a halt, imparting an imposing and daunting stance before the village folk. They were all rendered silent in his presence, their weeping and trembling whines quieted when otherwise thought impossible. The village folk and the soldiers knew when to be hushed, gagged by the mere presence of such mighty authority.

"Your men fought bravely," he announced with a thick Valeriaan accent, a toothy grin spreading across his face. "But foolishly."

Artur recognized such an accent, likening it to the way Lovisa spoke. Their inflection was so distinct from his own he could scarcely miss it. He was taken aback by this, taken aback by how quickly he was tempted to revise his perception of the girl he'd thought to be his friend.

"You all should at least know before…" he paused a second as his expression soured, and following an exasperated sigh, he shouted to his soldiers, "Will someone please shut her the fuck up?"

He was referring to the woman screaming in the distance, an intolerable interruption of his prepared speech. Per his command, one of the soldiers made for the cottage into which she had been taken. Everyone tensed, knowing what was to befall her, of the fate she was so condemned. The screams, which had seemed determined to persist throughout the night, suddenly quieted, cut off in the middle of a skin-crawling shriek. The onset of silence was almost as terrifying. It meant the worst in everyone's minds, the realization of a most unthinkable demise. And so, they quietly wept for the woman known and loved in the small village—the first casualty amongst them, and a grim omen of what was to come soon for them all.

The soldiers returned, satisfied and flushed with the taste of spoils, proudly flashing the hem of the blood-stained dress within their grasp—a trophy between them, the first of their conquests. Artur nearly retched at the horrific sight. To know that one of his neighbors had met such a gruesome end was so sickening, his naïve mind still struggled to comprehend it. Despite his stomach's best efforts to expel what little food he had eaten that night, Artur held it at bay. His partially digested supper lodged at the back of his throat, bile burning on his tongue. He swallowed hard, nearly gagging once more as the fluids forced their way back down.

"That's better," the Thegn chuckled, himself amused.

He looked to the terrified and trembling village folk before him and said, "I should inform you that the rest of your men will not be returning. Those we so graciously allowed to return to you, only served to bring about your demise. You see," a grin spread across his lips once again, "we have been aware of Oathbound in the area, far beyond Falkhearth's borders, for some time. The men relinquished to your company, I must so eagerly inform you, are themselves the disgusting Oathbound trying to tear apart the beautiful empire we have worked tirelessly to build. 'Tis an absolute shame…"

Eyes darted to one another, the village folks' sights focusing on the men they had believed fortunate enough to play on what little mercy the Valeriaans had, only for it to be brought to light that it was nothing more than a ploy. In a moment, neighbors and friends could no longer be distinguished innocent from guilty, commoner from Oathbound.

"They've unknowingly led us right to you." The Thegn snickered. "But fear not. If it's any consolation, the other villages in the region have also been found to harbor Oathbound. You'll all suffer the same fate."

Hurt and betrayal played about faces as the folk of Trivaden realized their demise had been brought about by those they trusted most. A deception. A treachery.

"However," the Thegn's voice drew their eyes to him once again. "I know your village has lost enough already, and I consider myself a generous man. Therefore, to all Oathbound present—if you give yourselves willingly, we will spare everyone else the fate which awaits you."

The villager folk looked to one another again, their gazes converging on those they had been so relieved to see return to Trivaden a fortnight ago. If the Oathbound wouldn't give themselves up, the compulsion to do so in their stead pressed on everyone's minds. They didn't want to pay for a choice they themselves had never made, to be punished for a conflict they had never involved themselves in.

"I also consider myself a rather patient man," said the Thegn, a warning in his tone. "But time is fleeting this evening. To give you more of an incentive—if you do not come forward, we will execute you all without partiality."

The village folk grew increasingly anxious and desperate, waiting for the known Oathbound to come forward for the sake of their own conscience. But none of them had time to decide to act in their stead before every man who had been a part of the caravan stood, their faces stoic, their calm demeanors concealing all fear. Not moments after they revealed themselves, five young women of the village stood up alongside them, terrified and trembling over a decision they had to make if there was a chance of securing the well-being of their friends and kin.

Artur himself couldn't believe it. Not only were there Oathbound in Trivaden, but they were folk of all ages and roles in village life, most of whom would never be suspected—men who looked too old to take up arms, and women so unassuming that no one would think they might pledge themselves to such a deadly cause. It was a wonder so many of the village folk had never imagined that Oathbound could walk amongst them, given how many now revealed themselves.

"Brilliant," the Thegn commented almost proudly, looking down upon all the folk who willingly revealed themselves. "Now you too can die for your 'noble cause'—just as your brethren did in Falkhearth."

There was hardly a moment for them to prepare before they were pulled away and forced to the very front of the crowd, facing the folk they loved and cherished as their final moments dawned upon them. It was as though a ritualistic ceremony had begun, the sacrifices presented to the Thegn. And akin to an omnipotent being, pleased that his acolytes were carrying out his bidding, he watched keenly as the Oathbound were brought to their knees once more, his soldiers readying their hands on the pommels of their swords. It was understood what their sentence was, and the accused accepted it with composure and grace not matched by the horrified village folk.

The Oathbound within each of them, the side of them that had long ago accepted the consequences of the path they'd chosen in life, revealed itself in their resolve. They were to die proud of who they were.

The Valeriaans, in an impressive ensemble, drew their swords. The sharp ring of the blades cut through the air, glints of orange streaking across the sleek silver of their sharp edges, until they rested against each of the exposed necks—cold steel to skin.

Artur felt his breath catch in his throat. He did not need to have witnessed death previously to know it was approaching. Already it was lurking within the village, holding the hilt of the sword to guide the Valeriaans' hands in the fatal strike of the blades. Eyes wide, mouth agape, Artur couldn't help but watch. Even as everything inside him was telling him to look away, the morbid curiosity of it all utterly ensnared him within its grasp. Witnessing death was an enticing experience, even if no one would ever admit it aloud.

When those blades rose into the air, Artur's breath quickened in sharp anticipation. He held it in his lungs when they arced down and through the necks of the Oathbound, as if their bodies were no harder than butter. Artur felt the breaking of bone, the tearing of skin, the separation of muscle. He heard the muffled thwack of metal making contact with cloth and pelt. Felt the land quiver when those heads fell to the ground and rolled in various directions. Felt the air stirred by the bodies as they collapsed slowly and then stilled.

The head of an old man came to a stop mere yards away—blank eyes staring his way, mouth open, his entrails trailing blood. Artur's gaze was drawn to that lifeless gaze almost instinctively. The wrinkles of the face, etched deep by years of easy smiles, were slack. There was silence in Artur's ears, a numbness of body and emotion alike. Even as the villager folks' faces contorted into screams, he could hear nothing. When the soldiers' lips turned up to smiles to emanate cackles, there was nothing. He felt as though he didn't exist, or everything around him had ceased to exist instead. There was nothing—nothing but the darkness creeping around him, its sly tongue well versed in tantalizing whispers. Its tendrils gently wrapped around him, promising the comfort he so desperately needed, a distraction from the carnage which beset his eyes, the carnage which he believed to have brought upon the village. Under the guise of comfort, it sought to claim him. To take him away. To spare him the pain and torture that would eventually befall him. A reprieve from it all was the offer—and tempting it was.

But from the depths of the darkness came a gleam of light, called forth to show him the true way. Artur could see it in his mind: an iridescent light glimmering as beautifully as a Mírén stone. From the silence came the furtive whispers to speak of truth. Though they spoke not in transcribable words, it was clear what their intent was. Artur took a deep breath and blinked his eyes back to awareness. The world slowly began to return around him—the sounds, smells, and coldness of the night now detected by his senses. It was then Artur heard something rather peculiar, new—the clanking of metal and the dull thump of wood echoing in proximity.

When Artur turned his gaze toward the noise, he saw Valeriaan soldiers in the process of boarding up all the windows and doors of the tavern, save for the front door. He could smell the oil that they splashed against the wooden planks, glistening in the light of the torches held by those who watched on. Before he could speculate as to what was transpiring, the Thegn spoke once more, drawing Artur's eyes back.

"I am a man of my word," said the Thegn, rather proudly. "You are spared their fate."

He paused as his soldiers surrounded the villager folk, the pack of dire wolves on the prowl once again. Despite the curses and shouts, the soldiers forced them to move. There was no gentleness, no show of understanding of the horrors they just witnessed. If they moved too slow, they were pushed. If they dared walk too far from the group, they were shunted back toward the others. Some were even forced to stumble over the bodies of the fallen Oathbound, rising with their feet, hands, and clothing stained with blotches of red.

"But," the Thegn tittered, looking down to the meek folk passing before him. "I did not say you would be spared entirely."

He was so amused by the perceived cleverness in his own words that he could not hide his malicious grin.

It was apparent then where they were being taken, and it finally dawned upon the village folk what the Thegn was implying. They felt themselves foolish for believing their lives were to be spared, that he would be so generous enough to reward the Oathbound's cooperation with consideration. They were taken to the tavern and heaved through the door unceremoniously. It mattered not. Even as folk collided and toppled over one another, the Valeriaans were determined to herd them as hastily as possible.

When the last of them passed through the doorway, a loud and purposeful slam of the door shook the entirety of the structure, and the sound of a hammer against nail into wood promptly followed to hold it in place of the broken hinges.

Artur crawled back along the crest of the hill, keeping to the trees and staying low to the ground, being as quiet as possible. Though the walls muffled the cries of the village folk, they could be heard thrashing on the doors and the windows as they sought a way of escape, becoming increasingly aware that they were now barricaded inside.

With torches in hand, the Valeriaans set the oil-soaked exterior of the tavern to flames with but a gentle touch. The fire spread with horrifying quickness, roaring and hissing as it greedily devoured the substance which it hungered for until the entire structure was enveloped.

Built by the hands of the very folk now restrained within it, the tavern was fully consumed within a matter of moments. The cries from within, which once rang of panic and confusion, were now a unified chorus of fear. The village folk felt the heat emanating through the wood, hear the flames eating away at the building as they inhaled the acrid smoke seeping into the air about them. Choking. Coughing. Their throats burning with the heat. The cries turned to screams, the shrieks a testament to all that their bodies were now subjected to, compelled to engage in a battle against a force of nature which was destructive and relentless.

Artur had never heard such agony, such torture. At least with the beheading, it was over within seconds. There was no suffering, there was no interminable persecution—a death brought on by the swiftness of a blade. But this—this was a purposefully slow manner in which folk were made to suffer, to beg for their end. Tears began falling down his cheeks.

Skin charring. Tissue and muscle melting off bone. Bodily fluids pooling at their feet before blackening. Perishing. Dying a most agonizing and prolonged death. The village folk were serving a sentence unfairly brought upon them by mere association, intended by their executioners to convey a message to anyone else inclined to rebel against the Empire. A purposeful deterrent intended to keep the commonfolk disillusioned with those who sought to bring their liberation.

They were all guilty in the eyes of the Valeriaans. The fires with which they set the world ablaze in olden ages were still their greatest weapon. The orange flames dancing in the violet of their eyes were a complement, an aesthetic that suited them well.

Artur wasn't certain how long it took for the tavern to be engulfed by the flames, but the screams came to an eventual end, growing quieter as the Valeriaans went about setting fire to the rest of the village. They would leave no part untouched or unscathed. One by one, the cottages went up in flames. Everything that Trivaden was, every feature of the life the village folk had enjoyed there, was condemned to burn. Artur's own cottage was subjected to the same fate, and had he not been so fixated on the tavern before him, he would have witnessed it blazing in the dark.

The same two soldiers who had raided his cottage earlier were the culprits responsible for its devastation, and the flames swallowed the sanctuary of memories, all the good and bad times, the walls which had kept him safe, given him warmth and refuge from the fury of nature—all destroyed. As those soldiers rounded the back of the cottage, nearly ripping the gate from its hinges, they both realized the grave error they had made earlier that night. Their torches half extended, they paused in their task when the movement of the back door, just slightly ajar, caught their eyes. They would have gone about, unassuming, had it not been for the gentle sway of the wind pushing the door just enough for the opening to be noticeable. One of the soldiers knelt at the base of the steps and held the torch close to the ground to see the distinct imprints of boot marks in the mud. Freshly made, from what he could observe—not at all worn away by the elements or the passage of time. He looked to his companion, exchanging a glance in which they acknowledged that one of the village folks had most certainly escaped prior to their raid.

CHAPTER 32

Artur could take it no longer. In a single night he had watched everything and everyone within his life perish. The numbness which once came to his defense, to protect and spare him a response, receded from his body and left it trembling.

It was a feat in itself that he managed to get as far as he did down the hill in his mental and physical state. He crawled at first, moving deeper into the forest until he felt he was safe enough from Valeriaan eyes to get to his feet. Artur ran down the hill with hardly a trail to guide him, not nearly the visibility necessary to confidently navigate his surroundings. Had it not been for the glow of the fires behind him, Artur would have tripped over something long before he reached the bottom.

He stopped a moment to catch his breath, to allow the shaking in his legs to subside enough to carry him further. He wiped away the tears soaking his face, mourning falling silent and giving way to labored breath. As much as he wanted to surrender, to curl himself against the trunk of the tree and weep all night long, Artur needed to move forward. It was only a matter of time before the Valeriaans decided to search the rest of the area, and he would not be able to outrun a soldier in his current state—or any state.

With another deep breath, Artur stepped forward, and to his dismay, a fallen branch cracked underneath his weight. That single step was all it took to reveal himself, he was certain; the sound of the fracturing wood echoed loudly enough that anyone nearby would have heard it. Instinct told him to freeze. Pretend he didn't exist. But Artur couldn't take the chance, choosing instead to flee for the river. On several occasions did he trip and nearly collide with the various and vast changing terrain, escaping with only scrapes and bruises to his fortune. When he finally reached the break in the tree line and the riverbank came into sight, he leapt from the ledge and crashed into the sands with all the force generated by his run.

He still couldn't stop. He knew he couldn't. Scrambling to his feet, Artur was about to take his first steps into the shallows of the river when he heard heavy footsteps fast approaching. Turning, he was horrified to see those two soldiers coming down the hill, following the very course he himself had taken. They were tracking him, following the evidence left behind all the way from Trivaden.

"There you are!" the one leading shouted to Artur.

Artur let out a gasp and bounded across the river so quickly that he nearly lost his balance on the moss-covered rocks, their surfaces slick and capricious under the water. It was difficult to see with the moon absent and the fire's glow dimming quickly. Artur tripped once more when he reached the far bank, his foot catching where the rocks dipped into the sands. Never before had he felt so clumsy, and in the very moment that his life depended on what little finesse he had. He scrambled back to his feet and took off down the trail into the once-forbidden forest and the hills they shaded. The two soldiers, fueled by their determination, remained upon him.

He pushed himself harder than any other time in his life, amazed to realize he could run so fast, and for so long. He was tired, though his breath did well to keep up with his movements despite how badly his lungs burned. His legs ached, his chest hurt, and yet his body was insistent. Unwilling to submit. The vigor flowing through his veins, giving him fortitude beyond his natural limits, was his only hope against two fully grown and well-conditioned soldiers.

Artur looked back. They were gaining on him, even with the heavy armor they wore. There was hardly a chance he was going to outrun them on a straight, flat path. He needed to make it more difficult, to possibly dissuade them from continuing their chase. Artur ducked into the tree line, still climbing steadily uphill, and made the trek through the trees and natural formations of the land he himself was not acquainted with. The soldiers cursed as they were forced to drastically change their course. Leaping into the forest after Artur, they soon found the unfamiliarity and complications of the new terrain difficult and hindering. Artur looked back once more and saw they were no longer in sight. At last! When the terrain finally flattened, he found himself in a small clearing. He quickly hid behind a tree in the hope that they would pass and continue a fruitless search deeper into the forest, giving him the opportunity to flee for the valley in the opposite direction.

There was silence at first, and then came the crackling of twigs and the squelch of ground giving way under boots as footsteps grew closer. Back pressed against the abrasive bark of a tree, Artur listened as the two soldiers reached the clearing. He closed his eyes, hand over his mouth to quiet his labored panting.

He listened to them breathing. To the light clatter of their armor. To the sound of footsteps fading into the distance. They passed by him entirely.

He waited until there was nothing left to be heard, and peeking around the tree he could see they were nowhere around. For all he knew, it was as good as safe.

Just as he made a motion to proceed down the hill, came the loud stomp of a boot behind him, coaxing a startled cry from his lips. When he turned, Artur was shaken to see one of the soldiers behind him, a smirk about his lips. He had no chance to scurry away before the soldier grabbed the back of his neck and dragged him out into the clearing.

Artur fought and squirmed with all the strength he had, but it was futile. The soldier was too big, too strong. A boy posed no challenge to his physical prowess. His companion came out from the other side of the clearing, and couldn't help but chuckle when he saw Artur, the boy who thought he could outwit two trained soldiers.

It was completely premeditated from the beginning. Given how easily they had tracked him from Trivaden, the soldiers were not easily fooled when the prints suddenly ceased at the clearing. They knew he had hidden himself away within the vicinity, and so they feigned ignorance of his little ploy, countering with their own.

"I will be honest," the second soldier began, crossing his arms over his chest, "you endured quite longer than most Oathbound we fight." It was more a threat than it was a compliment.

"What's in his hand?"

The soldier noticed Artur's arms pressed to his chest, the blue of the book peeking out from the confines of his sleeves. The soldier who restrained him grabbed at his book, and the gesture sent Artur into a flurry of swings and kicks, heedless of the disadvantages stacked against him, his only thought to protect his most prized possession. What a nuisance it all was. A futile attempt as it clearly was. With a roll of his eyes and an annoyed scoff did the second soldier calmly landed an unforgiving punch to Artur's gut.

His struggles immediately ceased. The strike pushed the breath from his lungs most forcefully, and no matter how hard he tried to breathe, it was as though his body refused to accept any inhalation of air to replace what was lost.

The book was pulled from his shaking hands. Once they had what they wanted, the soldier released him to the ground in a most painful and unforgiving way.

Artur wrapped his arm around his abdomen. He could feel his body screaming in agony, pulsing where the impacts took place. His body froze with shock, a whole cessation of even the most basic functions. Curling in on himself, Artur still could not draw in a breath, could not fill his lungs for a needed release. A suffocating panic came over him, a faintness to his head. He couldn't even cry, his body was so stunned.

While he struggled, the two soldiers paid him no mind. He was in no state to run from them now.

"A book?" They looked at each other.

"How does he have a book?"

"What does it matter?" The soldier clutching the prized possession snickered. "We know what that means."

Artur felt a chill run down the length of his spine, and he watched helplessly as the soldier tossed the book away so dismissively, the thud echoing in his foggy mind.

The soldier then knelt before Artur, and with a slight tilt of his head did he say in a low coo, "I'm certain you're aware that it's prohibited to have any forms of literature. A crime—punishable by death."

Artur at last took in a shallow breath, but it was hardly enough to make the feeling of suffocation disappear. His lungs stubbornly refused to perform their designated task. And his stomach, how it hurt! He could vomit from the pain. The very thought triggered that unnerving sensation at the back of his throat, the fluids burning at his insides, the stench filling his nose even before it escaped his lips. A mess of what was left of his dinner and bile emptied out onto the ground in front of him…and onto the soldier's otherwise immaculate boot.

"Aaaaah!" he exclaimed with a most disgusted groan. He scrambled away frantically, nearly tripping over himself as his companion did horribly in stifling his amusement. A hand over his mouth, he turned away and hunched over as a bellow came forth. Laughter mixed with a flood of expletives, the soldier stomped and brushed his boot deep into the soil until most of the bile was expelled from the leather. There was that last bit of damp residue that refused to abide, thickened now with a coat of mud. It would have to suffice for the time being despite how irritating it was.

"You had to make him retch, did you?" the soldier glared at the other.

Only then did he manage to cease his fit of laughter enough to respond, his cheeks reddened and lips nearly sputtering.

"I often forget my own strength."

The soldier groaned, and the glare once intended for his companion then went to Artur—the culprit to the ruination of his leather boot.

He grabbed a handful of Artur's hair and forcefully pressed his face right into the steaming pile of vomit. Artur let out a cry, the sting of the stench hitting his eyes and nostrils, as if the aftertaste wasn't already punishment enough.

"How does it feel, huh? How do you fucking like it?" The anger was palpable, though it did little to stay the howl of laughter from his companion.

But it wasn't just the defiled boot that spurned ire, a reprisal. Artur had given them an unnecessary chase. A superfluous agitator. Cruelly tore them away from the sight and entertainment that was Trivaden. They were going to make him pay for such indiscretions.

It was in this moment that Artur would have cried. Would have crumbled into complete disarray. But the urge wasn't there, nor was it even a thought. The numbness encompassed him once more. Perhaps after everything he had been through, after everything he had witnessed, his body was finally accepting the terrible treatment. The demise now upon him. Having his face shoved in vomit wasn't quite comparable to watching the beheading of familiar faces, nor the extinction of an entire village—hearing their screams as they died a most slow and agonizing death. At least he might only feel the sharpness of a blade as it ran through his flesh as opposed to the burning touch of fire.

When the soldier released Artur with a hard shove, he feebly lifted himself up and wiped at his face with his sleeve. The expelled contents of his stomach clung to and dampened his tunic, once white beneath the stains.

"We should just kill him quickly and return to the regiment. We've missed enough as it is," the other soldier said, countering the proposal to make it savory and unhurried. To calm the wrath of a companion believed wronged. They loved the thrill of conflict, of battle. But this was no soldier. No adversary to match their might, to test their prowess. This was a boy. Feeble. Lowly. There was no need to dwell where they weren't needed, nor wanted to be.

"Fine." The soldier let out a huff, a begrudging agreement. "I want to be the one to kill him then."

"I would dare not to take such an opportunity from you."

It was time. Truly. Unmistakably. Artur resigned himself to his fate and lay quietly on the ground. He closed his eyes. His breath calm. Was at peace… at least, that is how he understood it. Could describe it.

"I'm afraid ye won't be makin' it tae those festivities." A female voice spoke out unexpectedly, and the two soldiers turned sharply in her direction.

Artur let out a quiet gasp. He knew exactly who the voice belonged to.

Urda…

He would've looked to her if he possessed the strength to do so, but his body had ceased to respond to his mind, convinced it was still on the verge of its demise.

Urda came forth from the tree line and into the clearing, her gait a confident strut, her head held high with a smile that easily matched the smugness of the soldiers. She was safe and unharmed, albeit dirty from the travel to reach their location, and her self-assured air made the soldiers uncomfortable just from the very sight of her. Both were silently embarrassed to be caught off guard by someone so unassuming. However, in a show of feigned indifference, they both snickered.

"A woman," one said, the scowl about his face softening to amusement.

"A Keltaes," the other snickered in response, the two exchanging quick glances.

"A witch from the looks of it." The first referenced the locks of red hair pulled back into a long, thick braid.

Urda crossed her arms over her chest, the part of her body which the soldiers had noticed first, and said without a waver in her voice, "Let the boy gae, an' I may decide tae let ye live."

The soldiers looked at each other, the incredulity in their expressions speaking wordlessly. Of course, two highly skilled soldiers wouldn't take her words in earnest, let alone see her as a threat. They had an entirely different intention in mind. A woman as attractive as she, unashamed of her beautiful figure, awakened the baser desires within them, tempting them to satisfy their carnal thirst.

"This one's funny," one of them jeered.

It was just as she expected.

"You really think a Keltaes bitch such as yourself, can kill us?"

"No," she replied sweetly, the corners of her lips perked up into a hint of a smile. "I only plan on killin' one o' ye. Thon bein' says, who thon will be, is up tae the both o' ye."

They laughed, but Artur was horrified. He'd already lost everyone back in Trivaden, and now here Urda was, about to die before his eyes. Artur wanted to stop her. Call to her in objection! Still there were no words to be had, hardly a breath to release from his lips as he slowly forced his lungs to draw in air again. He wouldn't be able to bear it if she perished.

"I'd prefer have your legs wrapped about me!" the soldier who had often found himself laughing during the ordeal found laughter once more in her seemingly jest of a threat. He took a step forward and cooed once more, "Let there be pleasure in your screams rather than pain!"

He brought his hands to his crotch and made the crude jester of stroking, his lips puckering with that abhorrent sound of a suckle.

Urda raised a brow. Where others would have quivered, she found a smirk. When her lips parted to speak did her words come about in a soft chortle, "I heard the Valeriaans are the least endowit amongst the clans. Is thon why you lot speak sae much?"

Both soldiers' faces flattened. Complexions paled and flushed red simultaneously. Silenced. They could handle all manner of debasing expletives, of mutual crudeness. Even their manhood questioned. But to have it questioned by a woman—a Keltaes, at that—was unforgivable.

"I'll kill the bitch." The affronted soldier said, words deep in his throat, as withdrew his sword. "You kill the child."

He began to approach Urda.

The other soldier obliged, letting off a lighthearted taunt through a furrowed expression. "Now, that's hardly fair."

He wanted to be the one to have the witch.

"It is decidit?" Urda mused to herself, her head tilting to the side, finger tapping at her chin. "Sae be it then."

From the darkness of the forest came the sound of thunderous footsteps, beating quick and fierce against the ground. The trembling of the world beneath her paws hardly compared to the growl emitted from the very depths of her throat, pushing through bared fangs which desired to be drenched with the blood of unfortunate prey. A flash of grey burst into the clearing so suddenly that the soldier advancing toward Artur had but a moment to turn in the direction of the sound. Those hungering fangs clamped tight around his neck, an instinctual move to ensure a quick death. Shoved to the ground with such force, the soldier released a garbled scream as the powerful jaws tore his flesh with ease, the armor he wore hardly a concern as the beast dragged him about.

Vána, angered for her boy's pain and torment, her fearsome wrath provoked, was determined to punish her adversary even more. She wasn't going to let her prey die so easily, so quickly. His flailing and cries only excited her, awakening the savagery deep within her. She wanted to watch and listen to him squirm for a bit longer, as he could do nothing but push and shove at her face in fruitless attempts to free himself. His strength was nothing compared to hers. His hands were conditioned to kill with ease, but she was born with the talent. Her jaws and fangs were made for skirmishes akin to this one. When he struggled too much, she gave him a good shake. When he clawed at the ground to pull himself away, she only dragged him elsewhere. Her tail wagged in absolute delight!

Arthur had never been fortunate enough to see her ferocity. Now with hardly any choice but to watch, he was privy to just how vicious Vána could be. Even the tales of her brutality on a hunting trip had not prepared him for what was unfolding before his very eyes.

The other soldier watched the ordeal as if he were stone, stricken with crippling dread as the cries of his companion rendered him useless. It was an immaculate opportunity for Urda to act while he was distracted. She moved with such deftness that the soldier did not acknowledge it, and in mere moments she was in front of him.

She drew her hand to her lips and flattened her palm to reveal a copper-colored powder. One breath sent the entire handful right into the soldier's face. The soldier choked and coughed as his nostrils and lungs filled with its potent sting, his sword dropping to the ground with a loud clatter as he grasped at his neck. While his companion was clinging to the last moments of life, his screams convoluted by the blood welling up in his mouth, he too fell to his knees and struggled to breathe. Urda patted her hands together ever so unconcernedly and watched as her would-be assailant attempted to crawl from the scene, ever so pathetically. She too wasn't going to let him escape so easily, not after everything the two of them had done to Artur, to the folk of Trivaden. She followed him, a hum in her throat, a playful skip in her step.

Vána, in the same vein, grew bored with her prey. With an effortless clench of her jaws, she relieved the soldier's body of its head, which fell to the ground with a loud *thud*, the silver helmet bouncing away until both objects rolled to a stop. Vána, satisfied, licked at her bloodied chops, the fur of her neck stained red, tinted saliva dripping from her fangs.

She joined Urda in stalking the remaining soldier, and though her instincts were telling her otherwise, she refrained from condemning this one. She knew well this was Urda's prey, and so the beast respected it. She resorted to growling menacingly in equal parts playful jest and a warning of what would befall him should he try to oppose Urda once more.

Having crawled as far as he could, the soldier grasped at his breastplate, his fingers slipping against the armor as the toxin reached his innards and began to strangle the last bit of life from within. Urda needed only to gently nudge his shoulder with her foot to turn him onto his back. His eyes stared up to the sky as if they bore no awareness of where he was nor what was transpiring around him, his mouth agape, awaiting a breath he would never receive. A seizure jolted through his body before he finally ceased to move. A final exhale escaped his lips as the color drained from his face entirely.

"Hm," Urda hummed, her head tilting. She was unimpressed by her adversaries, the conflict rather unsatisfactory.

She had expected at least a struggle, but one glance at a dire wolf and it was done. She could've yawned in the soldier's face before he passed, but she felt it would've been too petty of her. She had accomplished what she needed to, and besides, there was someone else who needed her attention more.

The current threat had been nullified, but it still was not safe. The Valeriaans would come looking for the soldiers once they noticed two of their own were gone for far too long, and Skana would burn all over again if they found those responsible for their grisly demise.

Urda went to Artur. Kneeling beside him, she smiled; though uneasy, she wanted to bring some form of comfort to the poor boy as she brushed at his hair and gently wiped the vomit from his face with the hem of her dress.

"I'm sae sorry, Artur." She sighed. "You're gaun'ae be all richt, but we need tae leave. They'll come lookin' for thaim."

"The village—"

"I know." She met his eyes. "There's nothin' left for us thare, sae we need tae gae."

There was no time to exchange pleasantries even if she wanted to, no chance to explain everything. They needed to depart from the area as swiftly as they were able.

Urda brought Artur to his feet, heedless of his readiness. Being forced to stand made him aware of just how much pain he was in. He clutched at his abdomen, hunching over to relieve some of the pain even as Urda took his hand to pull him along. Artur resisted her; the pain was so unbearable he could hardly move.

"I'm sorry, Urda," Artur groaned through clenched teeth. "It hurts…it hurts so much."

"Na need tae apologize," Urda said, ever so sympathetically. She felt for the poor boy. Truly she did. But it was a matter of life and death. If he had made it as far as he did, he could continue on—they had to.

"Lean on me an' Vána," Urda instructed, assisting Artur in throwing his arm around her neck. Vána was there at once, her body keeping him steady as he draped his arm over her back.

"Wait!" As they took their first steps, Artur suddenly remembered his most precious possession. He turned and eyed the book that had been tossed aside with such disrespect, such malice. How it was still as intact as it appeared to be, was nothing short of a miracle.

Urda was the one to retrieve it while Artur used Vána for support, awaiting the return of the only possession he had left.

"Here," Urda said, tucking it in the pocket of his trousers, and the three of them began their slow passage deeper into the forest.

Artur did not know where they were going, but he knew he was going to be safe with Urda and Vána, his two protectors, his saviors. Still, the looming feeling of danger never left them. It was at his back, coaxing him to peek over his shoulder for a glint of silver amidst the darkness, to look about a forest that seemed so unrecognizable, so unfamiliar in the absence of light. The constant apprehension gnawed at him, fraying his nerves and pressing him forward all the same, a constant reminder that the tides could turn against them at any moment.

Eventually, the three stopped. Before them was a thicket of brush, which Urda went to while Artur relied on Vána for support once more. The dire wolf remained next to him obediently.

Urda pulled at the brush, separating the branches and leaves which easily parted into a circular opening, revealing a well-hidden and rather sizable den.

Urda held out her hand to Artur, who hesitantly took it, and the two knelt. It was a welcome reprieve, this moment to rest, to give himself over to the exhaustion and the pain.

"This will keep ye hidden until the soldiers leave," she said to him.

Artur peered into the dark depths of the den. It was even more spacious than he had thought, purposely made by man's hands rather than the ordinary formation of nature itself.

"For the both of us to hide?" Artur asked. To his dismay, Urda shook her head.

"Na, Artur. Only ye."

"But…Urda—"

"It's gaun'ae be all richt, Artur."

How was it going to be all right if she was going to leave him again? He had just gotten her back… She and Vána were all he had left.

"Why can't you stay?" Artur embraced her, completely forgetting the vomit soaked in his shirt.

Urda hardly cared. Artur could have been covered in the worst filth imaginable, and she still would have taken him willingly into her arms to give him the comfort he needed, to show she was there for him.

But their separation was necessary.

"I have tae gae, Artur." She wrapped her arms around him and held him so close to her, she felt as though she were embracing her own child. "But I give ye ma oath, I will come back for ye."

The words stung. Artur never thought he would feel as close to Urda as he did now. Over the course of the days they had spent together, he had grown an affinity for the woman he now knew to be caring and eccentric, a second mother to him in a time he most needed one. He couldn't bear to see her go, to lose her so soon.

"You promise?" He wanted to hear her say it again, to cling to the hope in those words.

"Ye have ma oath," Urda whispered to him, gently touching at his nose with the tip of her finger.

Vána came to him, her moist nose prodding at his face. It was her way of saying goodbye. An impermanent goodbye, but a painful one nonetheless. She licked at his face until his hands came forth of their own accord and he ran his fingers through the fur at her cheeks. Their foreheads touched, and they basked in the familiarity they had built over a lifetime.

Nothing more was said and Urda guided Artur into the den until he had cleared the entrance and was safely inside. The spaciousness of the den allowed him to turn around and look to her one last time, her face encircled by the brush, her lovely features framed. Even Vána gazed at Artur with those large golden eyes of hers, widened with a deep sadness.

Urda gave him one last smile, the tenderness of the expression filling him with a warmth he hadn't otherwise felt that night, but also an unnerving feeling of desolation. The way the two of them looked at him, it was as if they were saying farewell for the last time. But that couldn't be. Urda had promised to come for him again, sworn an oath on it. He would see her soon—at least, that's what he kept trying to convince himself.

"Goodbye, Artur," Urda whispered before she pulled the brush together, concealing the unassuming entrance to the den. Artur couldn't see either of them once the brush came between them, but he could hear their footsteps as they faded into the distance until all that was left was a deafening silence. It was a grim reminder to Artur that he was completely and utterly alone.

He appeared to be safe, and yet he felt anything but. Plunging into the pits of despair, he had no other choice but to listen to what Urda told him.

And so, Artur lay on his side, curling his knees to his chest to ease the pain in his stomach, and closed his eyes. He hardly expected to sleep. He only sought to ease the tiredness of his eyes, to see no more carnage that night.

Through the flashes of events that had taken place before him, his mind went to his mother and father. How he wished to see them, how he hoped they were safe and would come to him soon. All he wanted was to be in his mother's arms again, to feel her warmth, to hear her voice. To see his father and tell him how much he had missed him all the weeks he was gone. It felt akin to an eternity without him, his life marked by an emptiness only a father could fill. Before Artur did indeed begin to drift off to sleep, his mind wandered to the days of innocence and naïveté, living his life unaware of the greater world around him. Spending his days out by the river with his father and in the fields with his friends. How the sun glistened across the river, its rays warming the sand at their feet. They would sit there in comfortable silence, occasionally napping, reposing without a care in the world. It had seemed so simple back then. And when at last the day was done and they left for home, his father would wrap an arm around him and pull him close. They would walk with their fishing poles slung over their shoulders, and his father would say, "Good day, my boy. I love you."

And Artur would always reply, "I love you too, Papa."

CHAPTER 33

It was well into the morning when Ygrayne and the Schiva departed to Trivaden after receiving the grave news that the quaint village was a target of the Valeriaans' ire. The flames that had consumed Falkhearth now threatened Ygrayne's own home. Grief-stricken at the loss of her husband, and now fearful her son would share the same fate, Ygrayne was filled with turmoil as the horses sprinted down the path. They could not move any faster, nor could the village come into sight any sooner to ease her fears and fortify her crumbling composure beneath the mask she had donned once again to conceal her identity from the Valeriaan forces.

Artur... Her dear son's name echoed in her thoughts as snatches of memories teased at her in her grief, the terrifying possibility that these imaginings would be all that remained of him all too real. His smile. His beautiful eyes. His laughter. All of it would be gone.

Ygrayne knew the sight that would await her—the burned corpse of a boy now unrecognizable; that is, if she could even find the body to begin with. If she could sort through the mound of the deceased in the hope that there was something left of his attributes and physical appearance to distinguish him from the others. It brought her to tears on multiple occasions during the ride, and made her realize how wrong she had been to leave him behind. It was impulsive and foolish, as the Schiva would put it, even as he attempted to spare her more sorrow.

You are a foolish woman, Ygrayne, she thought to herself. It was disgraceful how long it had taken her to realize how wrong she had been in everything that had happened. She could have at least been there when the world was collapsing at Artur's feet, when the Valeriaans came barging into their village and pounding at their door. How afraid he must have been. Even with Urda there to care for him in her absence, he would have longed for his mother.

She shut her eyes, one of many times, before cursing herself for referring to Artur as though he had already perished. But it was only the grim actuality of what lay before her. Her son gone—punishment for her own hubris and wrongdoings. Her innocent child the price to pay for her faults. She had ignored them for the sake of her own vanity. Now it only brought her unending remorse.

"Ygrayne," the Schiva called to her.

She hardly acknowledged him at first, but realized that he sought her attention after he spoke her name several more times. She looked to him as he extended his arm outward to signal a halt. Confused, Ygrayne did so, pulling hard on the reins. Her horse let out a snort from the abrupt stop.

With their restless steeds prancing about, Ygrayne asked, "Schiva? What is it?"

The Schiva looked to her, and Ygrayne couldn't help but feel unsettled by the wariness in his gaze. His usually confident and kind expression held a trepidation she hadn't yet seen. Before she could ask what worried him so, the Schiva said, "You wish to know who the Allfather is…"

Ygrayne needed not hear the rest of his words to realize what was to come next, making her blood run cold, her heartbeat quickening with perturbed anticipation.

"Your wish is being granted." The Schiva's head shifted forward, his gaze directed to the still-empty path ahead of them.

Ygrayne followed his gaze, hardly understanding his meaning. Before her, there was nothing. They were alone on a barren road, surrounded by hills long ago stripped bare by the fires. Ygrayne would have protested, urged him to press forward rather than aimlessly lingering for nothing she could see, if a sound didn't happen upon her ears just then.

Faint as it was at first, she could make out the thundering of hooves against beaten dirt, the echo bounding from one hill in the valley to another. She could hardly believe it. The Schiva was right. There was someone approaching—*many* someones approaching. How he had heard it so far in advance, she didn't know, but she now could not deny that his claim was correct.

Crowning the peak of a distant hill were the points of two spears, and down their shafts trailed the unmistakable Valeriaan banners, waving wildly in the wind. And rounding the base of those same hills was the caravan of a frightening cavalry, fast approaching.

There was no doubt in Ygrayne's mind who this was, just by the grandeur of it all. Her experiences were limited to word of mouth, a secondhand introduction lacking all the basic formalities of acquaintance. In the safety of such circumstances, she had been quick and eager to curse him and loathe his very existence. Those harsh words and spite were gone from her, fleeing before the approaching presence to leave her to fend for herself. She felt no hate in that moment, and all words were lost upon her. Her rage was now overcome by a sense of fear.

"Let us maneuver to the side of the road," the Schiva instructed, though he did not wait for her to respond, knowing well the bewilderment that had befallen her, just as it did all others who found themselves unexpectedly in the Allfather's path.

He grabbed at the reins of her horse and did well to guide both Onír and Ygrayne's steed off the road. Ygrayne hardly noticed; her eyes remained fixed on the fast-moving caravan.

Between the two bannermen, the Allfather rode upon a magnificent Valeriaan horse, its glistening coat a blinding white even under the dull sky. It was adorned in armor and the Valeriaan colors, a mighty beast by all appearances to match the master in its saddle. The Allfather's armor gleamed of silver, the finest and most elaborately decorated armor of any Valeriaan warrior, engraved only by the most skilled hands. A cape flowed from his shoulders and the visor of his helmet completely covered his face. The ash scattering under his horse's hooves gave him the appearance of being the fire bearer incarnate, the bringer of the flames that had decimated Skana times before. The thundering caravan set the land to trembling, as if she herself were fearful. Darkness followed the Allfather, blotting out even the dim light and casting the wasteland into shadow. The air shifted, uncomfortably so, growing cold with an uneasiness Ygrayne had never felt in anyone else's company.

"Bow your head," the Schiva instructed Ygrayne quietly, as he did so himself.

She could not hear him through the thunder, and with the Allfather nearly within earshot, the Schiva had no choice but to force her head down. Ygrayne was taken aback, but quickly realized why when the caravan drew up before them. She almost flinched when the Allfather's horse let out a commanding snort, as if it were scoffing at the two of them. She kept her head bowed, hoping the caravan might pass by without paying either of them mind. It was not to be so, however.

The Allfather stopped directly in front of them, and all she could see were his horse's powerful hooves stomping the ground impatiently. Ygrayne gasped. Holding her breath, she was left to the mercy of her own imagination, and every path led to the same conclusion—their demise.

"Pray tell," the Allfather spoke, his voice muffled by his visor. "Is that you, my dear friend?"

Friend? Ygrayne was surprised by the peculiar word.

She was aware that the Schiva was acquainted with the Allfather, familiar even to some degree of comfortability, but not to the extent to which they addressed one another as *friends*.

There was a definite playfulness, a delight in his tone—an obvious indication of closeness.

"Do not bow your head in my presence." He chuckled, a frightening sound in a formidable throat. "Such false modesty is not becoming of you, Schiva."

The Schiva raised his head and looked upon the glistening visor that covered the face of the ruler of Skana, the man who called him "friend."

The Schiva said nothing, thus coaxing another snicker to reverberate through the helmet once more.

The Allfather raised his armored hands, encased in gauntlets that curved into points akin to talons. He grasped at the bottom of the helmet, removing it slowly to reveal a man who completely embodied every characteristic of a Valeriaan royal. His silver hair, though tousled from the helmet, fell elegantly about his forehead and around his face. His dark brows arched over the most alluring pair of violet eyes, a preternatural sharpness in his gaze, honed by his experiences and indicative of his cunning mind. A strong jaw complimented equally prominent, but elegant, cheekbones and the openness of his expression, well-trained to maintain the demeanor expected of an Allfather—of the ruler of all of Skana, of all of Njörden. Ordinarily flaunting no sentiment, his face broke into a soft smile upon the sight of familiar amber eyes meeting his gaze.

"I would recognize those eyes and robes anywhere." His voice was as refined and regal as his appearance, the product of the finest upbringing and instruction.

"Allfather," the Schiva responded, almost bowing his head in respect out of habit before he caught himself. "I hardly thought to see you here."

The Allfather scoffed with a click of his tongue, a sharp turn of his head to the sky.

"Sitting about the High Seat does not compare to the thrill of battle, to the exhilaration war begets. Moreover," the Allfather turned his head back to the Schiva, and his expression sharpened. "I could not resist such a temptation. To see for myself, or perhaps now," the soft smile altered into a sneer, his violet eyes narrowed to dagger points, and he spoke akin to a snake in all its seduction, "to hear it for myself."

He paused, and had there not been such familiarity between the two of them, the Schiva would have submitted before such a presence.

"Is it done?" the Allfather inquired.

The Schiva did not respond, and it was all the answer the Allfather needed. His expression, one which exuded such confidence, soon grew solemn as he contemplated the unspoken news. "So…" the Allfather turned his head forward, gazing upon the emptiness of the fields, and beyond them a city laid to ruin by his own forces.

"I may lose our wager after all..."

"Is such an outcome not enough to persuade you otherwise?"

It was the Allfather's turn not to answer. Instead, he kept his brilliant gaze fixed on the fields for some time before he was ready to face the Schiva once more.

"No," he answered curtly, his chin lifting. "Take me to him."

The Schiva was taken aback, his eyes betraying him with a rather dramatic flinch. "Allfather—"

"I may consider you a friend, a confidant," the Allfather was quick to interrupt. "But do not think it spares you from following my direct orders."

The Schiva was equally as quick to silence himself, and the Allfather was satisfied that his request was understood without further resistance. And so, the Allfather's attention shifted, his eyes wandering down to the Schiva who had yet to unbend her head in his presence. He found it both amusing and peculiar.

"Raise your head, Schiva," he commanded with a smirk, a note of scorn in his voice.

Ygrayne was hesitant at first, confused as to whether the Allfather was addressing her. It didn't help that her nervousness was making her doubt herself, and had it not been for a gentle touch of the Schiva's hand to her shoulder, she would have remained motionless. Ygrayne raised her head, her back straightening. For the first time, she gazed upon the man at the center of her hatred. She found herself staggered. He was by no means an ordinary-looking man—far from it—but he wasn't as frightening as she had imagined him to be. As ashamed as she was about it, Ygrayne couldn't help but feel enraptured by his gaze. It seized her attention effortlessly, fixing her gaze on him with astounding ease. He held power over her with a mere glance. By just his presence alone.

"This one's green," he spoke, glancing from the corner of his eye to Ygrayne's companion for but a moment.

"Indeed," the Schiva responded. "Falkhearth was quite the educational opportunity."

"Pleasure to be of service to the Brotherhood once more." The Allfather smirked again, looking to Ygrayne. Deep blue met mesmerizing violet. There was an intensity about his eyes which left her unnerved. She was not merely being regarded, but studied. The entirety of her being was the subject of thought in his mind. What he was trying to decipher in the silence, she didn't know. She feared it so, what she was unknowingly giving him.

"Any companion of my friend here—is a friend of mine." The Allfather spoke to her with a softness she would have thought unbecoming of him, but the way the words left his lips, it felt as though such words belonged perfectly.

"Allfather," she responded, mimicking the Schiva in the hope that it would appease the reigning lord of Skana.

The Allfather was hardly flattered by her response, and he dismissed it so as he turned his attention back to the Schiva.

"I had the pleasure of being in the company of your—more acquainted brethren, shall we say. The tall one," he tittered at the sparse description. "And the woman with the green eyes. They tended to my child in my absence."

"I hope all is well." The Schiva narrowed his eyes slightly.

"It is now." He sighed, his head still held high despite the slightly melancholic look about his face. "Took a rather nasty spill from the saddle while out on a ride. Your brother and sister were most tender and accommodating, as I would expect. My many thanks to your Brotherhood."

"There is no—"

"No need to thank me." The Allfather threw up his hand to dismiss the deflection he already anticipated, and the Schiva couldn't help but let out a snort of his own. That is, until he felt Ygrayne's steely gaze as she side-eyed him. He cleared his throat and said, "Allfather."

The Allfather looked to him.

"Is this truly what you want?"

The reintroduction of the previous and more imperative subject dissipated the playful banter, and the Allfather grew solemn once more.

"Yes." There was no hesitation in his response despite the mounting tension. "I just…I want to see—" the Allfather paused a moment, shooting a quick glance to Ygrayne.

She was privy to neither the exchanges nor secrets shared only in the utmost confidence between himself and the Schiva, and he was determined to keep it so.

"Nothing more." The Allfather looked to the Schiva, and the Schiva knew there was no persuading him otherwise.

It was indeed an intangible exchange, one that instilled much uncertainty in Ygrayne. But if there was one thing the Schiva was certain of, the Allfather meant no ill will by the favor he was asking. The Allfather knew his limitations, what was to be and what wasn't to be, his awareness of what has been tested sharp.

"Very well." The Schiva sighed. "We were just on our way to Trivaden."

This caught Ygrayne's attention, a gasp nearly escaping her lips.

"Please do resume your journey, Schiva. It would delight me to follow your course." The Allfather pulled on his reins to turn his mighty steed around.

Before his soldiers, those of the utmost skill and greatest trust—the Drengr—could follow suit, he held up his hand to halt them and instructed them firmly, "Proceed on to Falkhearth. The Schivas will be my escorts from this point."

Though weary, the Drengr dared not protest nor voice their concerns. They had their orders and they were to abide by them lest they face the Allfather's wrath, and none were keen to provoke it. Without a word, the Drengr continued their route, and when all the dust settled and it was but the three of them left, the Allfather grinned at the Schiva and said, "Shall we?" He then looked to Ygrayne and said, "You will be joining us, yes?"

"Do I have a choice in the matter?" The words slipped out before Ygrayne could stop herself, and her eyes widened at the indiscretion. Even the Schiva, though he said nothing, visibly tensed and looked from Ygrayne to the Allfather. But the Allfather only let out an amused laugh and replied, "I fancy this one. Where did you find her?"

"As I found all the others." The Schiva relaxed a bit. "Her grasp of tact leaves much to be desired yet."

"Nay," the Allfather protested. "It is a most amusing trait. Allow her to retain it so."

"You misunderstand." The Schiva smiled a bit, a glint in his eyes. "It is for my sake."

As the Allfather laughed again, the Schiva felt Ygrayne's cold stare still trained on him, and he quickly shifted back into his poised and stoic demeanor, clearing his throat yet again.

The Allfather looked to Ygrayne once more, a smile spreading wide across his face. His bemused expression hardened into a cunning sneer, the sharpness returning to his eyes. He was rather surprised by how well she continued to maintain her composure despite the fear in her eyes, holding her own in strained circumstances.

The Allfather found himself impressed, but he saw a challenge in her steely demeanor. He very much wanted to test such strength.

"Your eyes." The Allfather spoke. "The blue of them—you're a descendant of the Heríksson clan?"

"Oh…" Ygrayne was taken aback by the inquiry, distinctly remembering how the Schiva had remarked on her likeliness during his own questioning of her.

"I hardly know, Allfather." Her breath trembled ever so slightly. "My sincerest apologies…"

"Hm," was all the response Ygrayne received before the Allfather drew closer. The horses made their discomfort at the encroaching closeness known, their ears flattening back, their hooves pawing the ground where they stood. Then the Allfather reached forward and grasped at the mask over her face. His fingers curled around the edges that covered her chin, using the leverage to draw her forward, forcing her to bend at the waist.

The Schiva grew tense, just as Onír let out a snort in protest of what was transpiring. Both were ready to interfere if needed, but any hasty reactions would only escalate a rather tame interaction, though what was happening was a wonder.

The Allfather gazed into her eyes once more, a curiosity about his expression as those violet irises scrutinized every bit of her blue ones. All Ygrayne could think to do was remain calm, composed, allowing him to conduct whatever perusal he felt necessary in the midst of her mounting fear and apprehension.

"It has been a long time since I've happened upon such eyes," the Allfather whispered, a breath akin to a soft breeze. "Blue as the deep sea. Hair as dark as the raven. Traits that belong to the adversary of my own clan. The bane of our existence."

Ygrayne swallowed hard.

"Allfather," the Schiva called carefully. He knew that the man, despite all his power, was not one to act on impulse. Even so, he could do little to mitigate the threat the Allfather posed.

The Allfather ignored him. Instead, his lips parted in a most amused, soft smile. The sharpness of his gaze diminished.

"Do well to remember this, Heríksson. 'Tis these robes you bear about you which dissuade me from imparting to you a most unkind fate. The hatred between us has festered since the founding of our clans."

"Allfather," the Schiva called once again, and when the words still fell upon deaf ears, he approached just close enough to place a hand upon the Allfather's shoulder.

"Hans-Nelson," the Schiva said quietly, and only upon the utterance of a personal name, not the customary formal title, did the Allfather turn in his head slightly in acknowledgement.

The Allfather looked to Ygrayne once more, finding it rather peculiar for a Schiva to know nothing of her lineage, given how well versed the Brethren were in the history of Skana, their access to extensive knowledge only afforded to them by his family's generosity. The Allfather was intrigued by the novelty. He enjoyed a little mischief, a little excitement.

"Pity." His brows arched up as he spoke with a most mocking tone, but at last, he released Ygrayne.

Straightening his posture, the Allfather took in a deep breath as Ygrayne swallowed all her nervousness, relief washing over her.

"We have other matters to concern ourselves with at present," the Schiva noted.

"Ah well," the Allfather chuckled once more, relaxing his suspicious demeanor. "Perhaps another time. Shall we, then?"

He gave them no opportunity to respond before he kicked at his horse's sides. The beast took off at a brisk trot down the path from which the caravan came.

The Schiva and Ygrayne looked to one another.

"I did say you bore the traits of the bloodline." He gave her a sympathetic glance.

Ygrayne was not the least bit amused by his words and he quickly veered away from the subject. Whether he was right was of the least bit of concern to Ygrayne. The Allfather was heading toward Trivaden—toward her son. If the village hadn't already experienced devastation at the hands of the Valeriaans, it was certain to fall in the presence of such a man.

"Schiva!" Ygrayne breathed. "He's going to Trivaden!"

"I know," he nodded to her. "But do not fret."

"How can I not?" Ygrayne was exasperated. "Schiva, we need to *do* something!"

"There's nothing we can do—"

"Must I repeat myself, or have I made myself apparent?" The Allfather's voice called to them, and both knew they hadn't the time to converse. Sensing Ygrayne's growing distress, the Schiva placed his hand upon her shoulder, and the two of them looked to one another in search of some reassurance in the brief moment they had. They were at the beck and call of the Allfather, and he wasn't keen on waiting. Without another word, Ygrayne and the Schiva followed him.

The Schiva truly did feel for Ygrayne. The Allfather, even after their years of acquaintance, was still quite the enigma, impishly fickle. Their little wager was not yet settled, and there was hardly any indication of the victor yet. The Schiva *knew* Artur to be alive, and consequently he could not expect Ygrayne to do nothing. She would drop her ruse, cast aside the mask which had done well to hide her identity thus far. He would not blame her, but it was the response of the Allfather that he truly feared.

CHAPTER 34

Artur awoke the next morning in a most groggy state, nearly forgetting where he was upon first opening his eyes to the darkness of unfamiliar surroundings. It didn't take long for his memories to flood back to him, however, the peculiar space he was confined in soon shifting to the den which had done well to hide him through the night, remaining undisturbed despite the proximity of the Valeriaans.

Artur sat up to stretch the aching limbs which had grown stiff and sore from the discomfort of his slumber. The ground certainly did not compare to a well-stuffed cot.

It was then, as his once-still body came to life, that Artur realized he wasn't as alone as he'd initially assumed. Just as they had entwined themselves amongst the branches, hidden in the shadows of Urda's garden, the faelora had made of his warm body a bed of their own. Their translucent and squelchy figures clung to his limbs and the fabric of his garments, their bodies leaving behind wet prints.

With gentle coos, the faelora took to the air and drifted about. The movement brought the orange glow to their limbs and the pale blue to their exteriors, illuminating the darkness of the den itself as they scattered to the brush which formed Artur's nest. And he watched in silent awe as the creatures floated about him until they found rest once more, settling amongst branches to prepare for the coming day. The coos quieted. The glow dissipated until darkness again claimed the den.

In the faeloras' dormancy, Artur wiped at his face to rid it of the wet and gummy substance left in their wake with his already stained sleeve. Even in the dark, he became acutely aware of just how haggard he must look and how putrid he smelled, thanks to the spew which permeated the fabric of his clothing.

As Artur shifted uncomfortably in his own filth, he realized his stomach no longer hurt. The queasiness which at one time plagued him, no longer tortured his body. Pulling up his shirt, Artur could discern the remnants of a bruise where the soldier had struck him, nothing more. Even a slight touch with his fingers generated no pain—only a dull ache. It was a small relief in his dire situation.

The sunlight began to peek through the brush in gentle streaks of light, just as it penetrated the breaks in the clouds above. The deep greens now glistened with a lightened yellow glow. But the momentary lift of the gloom that had hung heavy the past weeks was not to last. The sunlight disappeared as quickly as it came, and the den grew darker and colder than it had been when Artur first awakened. The brown sky became a shroud once more.

Artur crawled to the entrance, his face mere inches from the wall of brush and bent branches. As he tried to piece together the world beyond through the thicket gaps, he listened. The wind he could hear again, could even feel as a gentle brush against his face. The birds in the trees overhead still called out, but their harmonious hymns had become cries of distress. It was still a welcome change compared to the events of the night prior, when all he had heard was the twisted orchestra of the screams of his neighbors, and the cackling of the fire as it ravenously laid waste to everything it touched.

The sounds of nature offered some respite, but Artur longed to hear footsteps again, approaching as opposed to leaving him. To hear Vána's excited breathing while her tongue hung out the side of her mouth, giving her the appearance of a kindly smile. And to hear Urda's voice calling for him once more, uttering words of reassurance as she always did. Yet, there was nothing.

The time passed by without any relief to his ever-growing despair. As much as he thought to brave the outside and to roam about in search of something, anything, he did not attempt it so. The soldiers could still be searching for the boy who had brought about the untimely death of their brothers, seeking retribution in their stead, to bring about a death much befitting the crime at hand. His curiosity wasn't worth the expense of his life. He lay on the hard ground, clutching the book within his hand, knowing well there was nothing to do but wait for Urda. She had made an oath to return to him, and he trusted her word.

With a sigh, Artur held the book before him in the dim light to see what damage it had sustained in the ordeal, and indeed it had not remained unscathed. The cover was dented at the corners and the pages were torn in several places. Dirt stained the vibrant blue cover he so admired, tarnishing its beauty. Only the golden script of the title was left unaffected. Touching them carefully, Artur felt the engravings etched in leather, the gold shine reminding him of how Lovisa's silver hair shimmered at the slightest touch of sunlight.

The unchanging sky and the darkness enveloping the forest made it difficult to measure the amount of time that had passed. But there soon came a disturbance amongst the sounds Artur had grown accustomed to: hoofbeats, growing louder, light and measured. And then, the unmistakable snort of a horse. Artur perked up promptly, his head lifting from the ground, looking through the brush that obscured the figure of a horse approaching through the gloom. It couldn't be anyone else but Urda, the only one aware of his hiding place. Artur crawled to the entrance once more and waited in eager anticipation, overjoyed that Urda's oath would be so promptly fulfilled.

The horse came to a stop just before the den, the white of its coat now visible, albeit stained with grit and soot. Boots appeared as the rider swung down from the saddle with a thud. Someone was standing right before the den, but making no move toward it, and the delay in movement made Artur so restless that he nearly called forth to the folk he believed to be Urda. But he held his tongue. The chance that his judgment would prove incorrect gave him pause.

Fortuitously for him, Artur needed not make a motion. The silhouette of the figure standing just beyond the den went about parting the brush in his stead, slowly separating branch from branch. The faelora, whose sleep was once again disturbed, detached themselves and sought shelter elsewhere, far from the intrusion. The figure slowly being revealed before him bore no resemblance to Urda. On the contrary, he could hardly recognize it as man—the face pale and smooth, a gaping hood cascading around it. Artur let out a gasp and quickly scurried to the back of the den, finding nowhere else to go once his back hit the thicket behind him. He had no choice but to watch the unfamiliar intruder continue to breach the den.

When the brush was finally cleared away, and the opening provided an unobstructed view of the intruder, Artur turned away his gaze, fearing it was but a matter of time before his inevitable demise. Yet nothing happened. Artur expected to be removed from his hiding place with unyielding force. But he was left undisturbed, and the moment stretched long and silent.

Artur opened his eyes with great apprehension to look upon the face staring back at him. Yet the being who knelt before him was indeed akin to none he had ever seen before. A white mask completely concealed the folk's face, and cream-colored robes cascaded around the figure adorned in a similarly colored tunic. Gloved hands held back the parted brush. Artur couldn't help but gape at the figure, his eyes searching for some hint of familiarity and Húgar beyond the attire. Even the eyes, which often gave some hint to the nature of the person they belonged to, were hidden by a thin sheet of fabric.

Confusion and curiosity overcame Artur, drawn as he was to the stranger in front of him who possessed some kind of unspeakable allure. There was nothing threatening about such a presence, and the being appeared to be equally curious about him.

Still, when a gloved hand came forward as a request for his own hand, Artur shrank even deeper into the den until he could feel the scratching of branches and the prodding of thorns, teasing tears in his clothing and cuts in his skin. Considering his response, the robed figure withdrew the offered hand ever so slightly, so as not to cause further distress.

The fear in his expression was not due only to the uncovering of his hiding place by a stranger, but also to the fact that the one folk he had been expecting had not appeared. He was waiting for Urda, and Urda this was not.

"Your friend is not coming," spoke she, in a voice akin to the delicate chime in the wind.

Artur's lips parted slightly upon hearing her speak, and fell open completely at the revelation the words brought—she knew of his circumstances, for whom he was waiting for.

"I am here in her stead."

Her hand went forward once more, her delicate gloved fingers uncurling as a flower bud to the sunlight, and it waited there with the utmost patience, unwavering and obliging. Artur hardly noticed the tear that fell down his reddened cheek, his sorrow and sense of loss manifesting involuntarily. Even if he didn't completely comprehend it in the moment, Artur was mourning. The world at once seemed so much darker, so much emptier to know the one person he hoped would appear at the entrance of the den wasn't coming after all. And this robed silhouette in her place? Artur had never seen such a figure, and yet there was a sense, a pull, drawing him toward her. A blind kind of trust that she asked him for—and he answered.

Artur reached for her hand, as if he were no longer in control of his own body, his own movement. The way his hand fell into hers seemed so natural. There was a tenderness apparent in the way her hand closed around his own, a gesture so reassuring she might as well have spoken the words of comfort.

She led him from the den with the most calculated and deliberate of movements. Artur was entranced, a moth to flame. He went with her without protest, tears intermittently slipping down his cheeks, until they were standing before one another as two would be upon first acquaintance. The white horse beside them watched on as they familiarized themselves with each other's presence, waiting patiently.

Artur observed the robes cascading around her figure and the hood that framed the wrapping around her neck and the pearlescent mask. The mask's curves, the delicacy of the lips, and gentle shape of the eye lent her a look of elegance and femininity. Even gazing into the darkness of the eyeholes, Artur felt no repugnance, only peace.

He had no name for her, but to the world, she was known as a Schiva, and she possessed all the grace and aptitude characteristic of the Brotherhood. And suiting her character, the Schiva knelt before Artur to give a sense of equal footing, an air of security in this encounter with an unexpected stranger. To leave no doubt in his mind that she was a friend, the Schiva removed her robe and placed it about Artur, pulling it tightly around him. Once it was secure, Artur held it in place as he basked in its weight and warmth, the feeling comparable to that of the blankets on his bed. She gently wiped his dampened cheeks dry, the redness fading and the dirt diminishing at her touch.

Artur wanted to ask her a thousand questions—who was she? What happened since the burning of Trivaden? What of his mother and father? Of Urda? Vána? And yet, no words came to him. Perhaps there were no words to be had in the moment.

The Schiva squeezed his arms ever so gently. Artur found it comforting. He followed as she led him to the horse. The Schiva lifted him up into the saddle with a swift movement of her arms, as if he weighed nothing to her. A moment later, she swung herself up behind him.

A gentle nudge to the horse's sides and the two of them set off down the hill at a steady walk, along the route Artur had taken just the night before. Already the prints had been swept away by the winds and natural shifting of the land.

Artur turned back and looked for the last time at the den as it slowly disappeared behind the summit of the hill. He wondered where Urda was, wondered why she hadn't come for him despite her oath.

He felt almost hesitant to leave the area, panic arising as he pondered if she was indeed still coming for him. What was she to do if she found the den empty and him gone? Artur surmised that she would stop at nothing until she found him.

Or perhaps…Artur dropped his gaze as the thought occurred to him. Perhaps Urda had perished sometime in the night. Perhaps the soldiers found her. Whether or not they were aware of her crimes, they would have no doubt killed her. The only reason she wouldn't keep her oath was that she was no longer alive to do so. She would take her words of reassurance and responsibility to the grave.

CHAPTER 35

There were no words suitable to describe the dread Ygrayne felt when the black smoke of what remained of Trivaden appeared in her sight. No amount of imagining had prepared her adequately—not even the destruction of Falkhearth could measure against the loss of the place she called her heart and home. And as they breached the tree line, the cool touch of shadow provided no comfort, overtaken as it was by the heat and the suffocating ash in the air. It helped none that she found herself riding alongside the man who was the bane of Skana's prosperity and contentment.

Why he had insisted on joining them, she could hardly fathom, and the conversation the Allfather had shared with the Schiva had done nothing to satisfy her curiosity.

What are you both up to? she thought to herself.

Fortune had done her one small favor: had she not experienced the horrors of the city, she would've crumbled at the very sight of her home when they rounded the corner—for it was the remains of her quaint cottage that first to came into view.

The village was reduced to ash and embers, as expected, but it was the sight of her home she could hardly bear. The façade which she had maintained so well throughout the entire journey was already on the brink of collapse, and not even the presence of the Allfather could stop her from reclaiming who she truly was underneath—a mother in mourning, the widow of a husband taken too soon. The chances that Artur had survived were already minimal, and if he too had perished, she hardly cared if she engendered her own death at the hands of the Allfather. She cared not if he saw her for who she was. Death would be a reprieve. Death would reunite her with her son and husband.

And so it was Ygrayne who was the first to pull hard on the reins, her horse coming to a sudden halt with a loud snort of protest at the harshness of the command. She nearly tripped in her haste to dismount. Catching her balance in the most ungraceful of manners, Ygrayne scrambled for the remains of the place she once called home, helped none by her still very-sprained foot. With a quivering voice, she instinctively called out for her son. "Arturias!"

Surveying the charred foundation did nothing to ease her distress. The beams which once stood strong, now lay across the living quarters, splintered and fractured by the impact of their fall. The stones of the fireplace barely remained standing, the integrity compromised by the intensity of heat and flame. The loft was nonexistent, reduced to the pitiful remnants of the base. She could hardly tell the pieces of the structure apart. If there was any hint of her son amidst the debris, Ygrayne wouldn't have been able to tell. In her desperation, she pushed past what was left of the door, a swirl of hot embers flying about her. The robes did well to shield her from their merciless touch, allowing her the protection she needed to search the wreckage for some kind of sign, to be granted a bit of resolution, regardless of the outcome—to find some peace in closure.

The Schiva and the Allfather, still mounted, watched the frantic mother, her ruse fading away before their very eyes. And though the Schiva wanted nothing more than to go to Ygrayne, to aid her in her search, he couldn't help but look to the Allfather beside him. In this moment he could observe a man completely out of his element, to gauge his reaction to the sight unfolding before him.

The Schiva found himself rather taken aback. The Allfather, in all his cunning and unpredictability, seemed rather curious in the way he scrutinized Ygrayne, watching as a mother put her love for her child on display for the world to see with neither thought nor hesitation. His scrutiny resembled that of a child looking about the world with all the curiosity afforded to youth, and none of the knowledge to understand it. The intrigue of transpiring events captured his complete attention. But lacking in relatable familiarity—even to an emotional expression as basic and intuitive as a mother's love—he therefore lacked the most simplistic understanding of Ygrayne's distress.

The Allfather was deadened. The demonstrations of her pain could pierce neither the metal of his chest plate nor the frigidness around his heart, hardened and beating only to supply resources needed for survival and bodily functions. And though it was clear to him that this was no Schiva, and the threat he had imparted in their previous conversation still stood, his sole intent in such a moment was to witness her pain from an intimate standpoint, as he had never done before.

The Schiva felt satisfied that there would be no immediate repercussions, even though Ygrayne had clearly revealed herself. He dismounted, and went to her as the Allfather watched on, unmoving. The Schiva was only another specimen to observe rather than an interruption to the study.

Ygrayne, who was frantically checking under anything and everything still standing for some sign of her son, did little to acknowledge the Schiva's presence. Her search would produce no sign of Artur, for he knew the boy to be alive. But to maintain the pretense of ignorance, the Schiva had no choice but to play the part. He did so effortlessly, arguably, even pitilessly, in a sense, given Ygrayne's torment.

In his objectivity and more studied examination, the Schiva looked about the ruins with but the movements of his eyes. He knew what to look for without shifting any part of the wreckage. Bone did not burn as wood did, was not as brittle or frail in the way it gave to flame. There would be some sign of where the body lay, of the remains left behind no matter the charred state. There was nothing, as he knew, though this was hardly a relief. With the rest of Trivaden lying in ruins, they would find plenty of bodies.

The Schiva looked to Ygrayne once again. How he wanted so dearly to bring an end to her despair. To inform her of his knowledge.

"He's not here," the Schiva said to Ygrayne, placing his hand upon her shoulder.

"What?" Her head turned sharply to him, her eyes red and filled with tears.

"He's not here."

"How do you know?"

"Man's remains are distinctly different than wooden ones. Come."

He remained composed for them both, a stable fixture for the poor mother and widow. He led her out of the wreckage of her home, but Ygrayne hardly made it past what was left of her porch before she could bear it no longer and collapsed to the floor. The Schiva was quick to aid her, kneeling before her as she deteriorated at the prospect of her son's death. Tears and phlegm gathered in the contours of her mask as they poured down her face. It was hardly comfortable, and knowing so, the Schiva carefully unbound the mask from the hood. The hollow veneer fell to the floor with the gentle guidance of his hand, revealing the mourning woman beneath.

It was then that the Allfather dismounted from the saddle, the pieces of his heavy armor clanking when his boots touched the ground. Not once did his gaze leave the two of them, his expression completely unchanged as the woman beneath the mask came into view: the pale face with reddened cheeks, the thicket of raven-colored hair he earlier suspected falling about her shoulders.

The Schiva turned to the Allfather, a frown evident in his gaze. He wanted nothing more than to comfort Ygrayne in her moment of weakness, but the approach of the Allfather seemed to him an immediate concern. Tearing himself from her side was painful, though his deportment showed it not.

The Schiva approached the Allfather with a haste that halted his advance, far enough away from Ygrayne to be out of her earshot.

"Enough of this," the Schiva said in a hushed tone, his voice nevertheless harsh.

"You were so certain the *boy* was alive," the Allfather sneered, intimidated not by the Schiva's fierceness. "I think you mistaken."

"Nelson—"

"Gravely indeed, when we are met with such a glorious sight. I am certain of it."

"You are too clever to arrive at such a conclusion with haste," the Schiva said. "Do not attempt to prove the gods you spite wrong. Fate has decided."

"If this proves anything, it is that the Valeriaans are not subjected to this concept of fate we chose to cast aside long ago. Such concepts are meant for the olden ages. The folly of man is superstition."

"Then why are we still here?" The words were a menacing growl deep in his throat as the Schiva took a step closer to the Allfather.

"To see it for myself and to prove you wrong. To establish that I—this Dark Lord—have prevailed against all odds. Against all the hearsay. Against all that was so wrongly determined." The Allfather followed suit, taking but a single step which placed them mere inches from one another.

"Was your proclaiming his survival to spare that woman despair for a moment? You care for her well-being? Perhaps desire her affections? How quaint—a Thórdarson and a Heríksson together."

"It was to dissuade you from continuing this endeavor. You have lost, Nelson."

"I have lost nothing," the Allfather grasped at the Schiva's tunic, drawing him closer with a forceful tug. Through gritted teeth, and with a piercing scowl about his face did he continue, "Nothing is decided until I see that boy—whether he be living and breathing, or the unrecognizable remnants of a fire."

The Schiva did not respond, no matter how the Allfather searched the amber eyes for an answer.

The Allfather took a breath and composed himself, though his hand remained firmly upon the Schiva's robes. He could feel the heat of anger igniting every fiber of his own being, a ferocious passion for the Empire he was endeavoring to maintain, a legacy he needed not only to pass, but to preserve. There was no other option but to be right, to be the victor in this wager. Defeat was much more than a gamble made and lost. The implications were much more dire, much more severe, if they were to be believed. The Valeriaans prided themselves on their freedom from the gods, from the old customs and cultures which had influenced folk in olden times. But was it truly liberation, or was it fear? Was the obstinate renunciation in fact a roundabout acknowledgement that no one could escape the tethers of powers unseen? The Allfather was to find out for himself presently.

"Shall we proceed?" It came out as a request though it was no suggestion, and with a shove did he release the Schiva's garments from his quivering grasp.

The Allfather proceeded forward, stopping only a close distance from Ygrayne as she continued to weep.

The Schiva was quick to come to her side once again, his body shielding her from the ire that could have been directed to her then. His gloved hands went to her face, tenderly wiping away those unending tears in a gesture the Allfather had never witnessed between a commoner and a Schiva. Though passed to him in rumors and speculations, it was the first time such an interaction had ever taken place before his eyes. Peculiar as it was, he slowly drew his hands behind his back, his refined posture such that even the highest of nobles would blush in his presence.

He was a silent spectator, a statue atop a platform overlooking the masses. Neither the Schiva nor Ygrayne acknowledged his presence, their conversation carrying on as the Schiva attempted to reassure and reanimate her.

"I won't stop searching until I find him," said she.

"I know you won't." There was a smile in the Schiva's tone. "We'll find your son. Gather yourself, and when you're ready, we press forward."

The Allfather proceeded on without them nonchalantly, looking about what was left in his army's wake, still so certain of his conquest. Such devastation could only mean such an outcome. If anyone understood the way his warriors operated, it was him. Such knowledge guided him first to the tavern. The largest building, the Allfather knew, would be the ideal location to house a considerable number of folk in the process of exterminating them. The opportune site for a mass grave, a cemetery made of wood and stone. Turning to gaze through what was left of the tavern, he found everything he was looking for. Amongst the twisted charred beams and burning red embers lay the remains of the village folk. The mass of contorted skeleton limbs hinted at their last moments of pain before their bodies stiffened, letting the flames devour their fleshy husks. The bones now lay about the tavern as morbid markers of the terror wrought.

There was a certain satisfaction at such a sight, though the Allfather hardly reacted in any capacity, even as it strengthened his resolve in believing he was indeed the victor. A smug smile across his lips was brought on by the ease which overcame him, a relief that only such an outcome could grant.

Wanting to boast in his triumph, the Allfather turned his head to his two reluctant traveling companions. The smile on his face now hidden by discipline and practice, he called out to them. “Schiva.”

Both the Schiva and Ygrayne looked to him simultaneously, and the Allfather only gestured to the tavern with a nod of his head before he turned his back to them and unconcernedly continued deeper into Trivaden.

The Schiva let out a sigh, displeased with the Allfather’s lack of grace, his obvious attempt to rouse the woman once more to despair. When the Schiva felt Ygrayne shift beside him, did he attempt to hold her at bay. “It’s best we don’t, Ygrayne.”

“I must see for myself!” Ygrayne protested.

Ygrayne tore away from him with a strength born of desperation before he could persuade her otherwise. To the tavern she limped to see what the Allfather had beckoned them to witness before the Schiva could reach her. There, Ygrayne saw the bones of everyone she had known, contorted and transformed by the fire—folk on top of folk—as if they had become one in the event of their death. Arms and hands protruded as if they were reaching for some divine intervention as they screamed their prayers, stretching toward the heavens above for a savior’s hand in response to their pleas. Even their faces, the expressions frozen in the moment of death before the flames wiped away the physical traits that identified them and reduced them to charred flesh stretched over skulls, appeared desperately beseeching.

When there were no cries, no elegies, the Allfather glanced over his shoulder to the two companions still in his wake. It was only a matter of pondering the sight before her, he was certain, anticipating the chorus of bereavement that would soon happen upon his ears when it dawned upon Ygrayne that this son of hers—the one for whom she so desperately searched—wasn’t found amidst the wreckage of their cottage because he was safe, but rather because his remains were mingled with the others, lost in the grotesque mass before her.

He wanted to see her suffer. Suffering, he was familiar with. He knew the keening wail in response to losing someone, the writhing of the living as if the stiffness of death beset them too, immobilizing them in the most grotesque and painful of postures. Pain was his pleasure, the spoils of victory in battle. He cared not for gold or possessions, for he had it all. It was power over the commonfolk that he craved, the knowledge that his deeds possessed such influence, and could call forth such responses.

“Ygrayne—”

“My boy…” At last, her voice quavered, a preview of the sheer unraveling to come. “My boy!”

The realization of her son's fate was stronger than her will to keep herself composed. No amount of preparation could have rendered her detached.

The Allfather turned his head away before Ygrayne's screams filled his ears. Had he still been watching, he would have borne witness to the Schiva pulling her away from the tavern as she fell into hysterics, attempting to get her as far from the petrifying sight as he could. Though he kept his own composure, he could not impart a sense of calm great enough.

Even across the distance the Allfather had put between them, he could hear her lamenting—the cries of a mother's unmatched grief and sorrow.

"My boy!" She cried out to the heavens as if she were cursing whatever gods that had allowed this happen. "My boy!" She was a banshee shrieking in the night. No consolation could ease the grief and pain she was feeling.

"Ygrayne, please." The Schiva fell to the ground with her, enveloping her within the confines of his arms as she wept. "You must listen."

But his pleas fell upon deaf ears. She would hear none of his carefully enunciated words, none of his condolences. Still, he tried.

"Artur is alive. You must trust me."

She believed it only to be a pitiable attempt to console her—empty words and equally empty oaths.

"I only ask that you be patient."

Still, she wept and she wailed, to the Schiva's dismay. The failure of his attempts left him exasperated at the circumstances she was forced into. It was hardly ideal, nor was it to be painless, but he had only one other tack with which to bring Ygrayne peace.

The Allfather came upon the execution site, where the bodies of the Oathbound lay strewn about the ground. The gaping mouths of their severed heads, and the tongues hanging limp from their lips, were befitting the mourning off in the distance, as if the woman's cries were an echo of their own. But just as he was unfeeling to the woman's loss, he cared little for the lumps of flesh and blood at his feet. Those he stepped over as he passed, as though they were nothing more than the cobblestones of a paved street.

He was ever more confident in his conviction, his mind now contemplating the subsequent measures to take. He thought about executing the woman, for several reasons. Impersonating a Schiva, certainly. Her supposed Heríksson lineage, an adversarial clan that had given his family much grief throughout their many ages of conflict, was another demerit against her. But also, it would do her a favor—to put her out of her misery. To grant her a peace that she would achieve nowhere else. Yet, the more he pondered, the more he considered that death was indeed too generous. Would it be better if she were to suffer in life, as was expected of the commonfolk? Should he grant her such a gift as death? Given the lightness of his mood, he felt that he had enough generosity to spare. It was only a matter of desire.

The Allfather had no more time to contemplate before he stopped in his tracks, for his gaze fell upon something rather unexpected.

Through the heat, ash, and smoke which shrouded the path ahead, the Allfather could make out a silhouette. A flash of white. A rider upon a saddle…no—two riders. His lips parted as his eyes narrowed to scrutinize the sight manifesting in front of him, incredulity overtaking his confidence.

CHAPTER 36

The Schiva let Ygrayne cry, let her grieve to her heart's content, until there were no more tears left to be spent. Schiva were meant to be objective, to keep their wits about them, for their judgments and engagements could mean the difference between life and death. But they could not remain indifferent to a mother who felt the loss of her child and her husband all at once, in the face of her cries of grief for the ones she loved the most. The Schiva had heard enough anguish to last multiple lifetimes, but such a sight weighed heavily on his own heart. For in the woman he had found companionship, and a closeness he hadn't felt in many a year. His stoic demeanor was put to the test, and had circumstances been as dire as Ygrayne believed, he would have wept beside her.

Words had failed him, but at last came reprieve. There was shift about them. A presence which prodded at a sense beyond the known, which made the air tremble and the trees whisper with the rattling of branches, the land quaking with excitement. And the Schiva looked in the direction that called to him in unspoken words and unearthly gestures. The remedy he needed to ease the mother's pain was fast approaching. And it would have arrived sooner, had their progress not been impeded by the formidable figure in their way.

As they parted the mirage of smoke, the Schiva and Artur were greeted by none other than the Allfather, who gazed back at them. This was unanticipated indeed, but even more frightening, as the Schiva knew of the man standing before them and the consequences that would follow if he should discover the book tucked within Artur's arms—the forbidden object the Schiva had chosen to ignore when she first saw it against his breast. Given the drastic change in circumstances, she could no longer continue to do so.

"Hand me the book," she whispered to him, and Artur recoiled at the request.

The thought of parting with his prized possession was unthinkable. He shook his head in opposition.

"Artur," she breathed. "This man is a Valeriaan. If he sees you with it, you'll be killed." She purposefully neglected to specify which Valeriaan this man was, as she didn't want to make him panic.

"I'll relinquish it to you when it's safe to do so. You have my oath."

Oaths were something Artur had little faith in at the time, but he couldn't deny she was right. If any of Urda's words did hold integrity, it was those of warning. He had no choice but to relent, moving the book to the very edge of the robe while keeping it covered. The Schiva cascaded the thickness of her sleeves in front of him as she took the book into her hand, pulling it within them without flashing so much as a corner. Artur swallowed. The very mention of the name *Valeriaan* made him nervous after everything that had transpired with Lovisa. It helped none that the Allfather, though Artur did not know him to be such, had his gaze fixed upon him so, only adding to the tension as they approached.

When the Schiva brought the horse to a stop just before the Allfather, the word which came from her lips was suffused with respect and modesty. "Allfather." A bow of her head followed.

All Artur could do was stare at the man looking directly at him.

The Allfather did indeed stare back at him, with a veiled fear. Though he did well to mask it, there was uncertainty in the otherwise vibrant eyes of violet, a rare change from his naturally confident temperament and poise. His fixation upon Artur was so unwavering, he hadn't even acknowledged the Schiva paying respects to him. She was quick to notice. Watching on in acute silence, she was baffled by the Allfather's display of vulnerability. What could cause the otherwise indomitable demeanor of a man who possessed all the power in Skana to falter, she was trying to fathom.

The Allfather, in turn, was hardly aware of how he presented himself. He was still grasping the sight before him, coming to terms with *this boy* right before his very eyes. Sentiments he had never experienced overtook him, overwhelming his otherwise imperturbable and unyielding composure. He had believed himself to understand everything he needed to know about life. The path laid out before him was always clear, the knowledge of his duties instilled in him per the established course of the life of an Allfather, the High Seat otherwise unthreatened by any number of adversaries. Yet, it was this mere *boy* who stood to tear down the walls of an empire with no effort, nor awareness.

The Allfather's first instinct was to act, to defend his empire, to assert his power as the almighty, and still, he didn't—couldn't.

Flustered by fear, and the power which the uncertainty possessed, he was reduced to nothing, his authority torn from him. Above all, he feared the repercussions. Even holding all the power in the world did not render him impervious to the superstitions he claimed to have cast aside. He knew better than to overstep unseen bounds laid out by powers much greater than his own, should they exist. He did not want to run the risk, however slight. The Valeriaans' deep hatred of the gods was matched only by their fear of the taboo they believed to exist, but dared not admit. Given that they had already tempted the wrath and scorn of said gods, he knew this *boy* right before him was a measure of such might. The Allfather feared any impulsive attempt to dispatch him would only bring premature misfortune. With a deep inhale, and a strike to his pride as he stepped away in imperceptible trepidation, the Allfather gestured to the ruined Trivaden and said, "Your mother awaits, child."

Mama? Her likeness instantly sprang into his mind.

"Take your leave, Schiva." The Allfather dropped his gaze, ignoring once more the bow of her head in acknowledgement, and the utterance of his title before she continued into the village.

Their time apart, and the tragic events which had destroyed the rhythms of life as they knew it, had Artur truly believing he was never to see any of his loved ones again. A hopeful optimism buoyed him, even as a realistic outlook kept him grounded and subdued as they proceeded through the remnants of all he once knew.

The Schiva was the first to meet his gaze, his arms encircling his mother's back as she wept, her face pressed against her palms, the lengths of her hair pooling around her as a dark veil. Her likeness was unmistakable and there was no doubt in his mind now that it was indeed his mother in the flesh. His mouth fell open with awe, and though there was hesitation in his voice, he could not stop himself from calling to her.

"Mama?"

The unexpected voice made Ygrayne lift her head sharply, her blue eyes swimming in tears yet unshed. Ygrayne could hardly believe it. She would rather be convinced her mind was merely playing cruel jests on her in a twisted attempt to subdue the grief which plagued her—her reality distorted by the wishful thinking of seeing even just a glimpse of her son once more. Had it not been for the Schiva reacting to the sight as well, with a deep sigh of relief of his own, she would have dismissed the manifestation before her.

"Mama?" The voice sounded too real to be an illusion. It was him—her son. Sitting there in the saddle in a robe much too big for him, a Schiva seated right behind him.

"Arturias," Ygrayne whispered, and a smile spread across her lips as the revelation dawned upon her. Artur couldn't help but smile in turn.

"Arturias!" Her voice rang in his ears, the chime of a bell in the wind, and no longer could he sit as he did.

He had to go to her, needed to embrace her as she would embrace him. To hold her at last after a time apart that felt akin to an eternity.

"Mama! Mama!" Desperation rang clear in his voice, prompting the instincts within her, forcing her to scamper to her feet as Artur tumbled from the saddle.

He would have collapsed, had it not been for the assistance of the Schiva.

Running to her as she did him, he felt the robes fall away from his shoulders. They fluttered to the ground, coming to a rest in a heap. And for Ygrayne, though the pain in her ankle flared, threatening to hinder her approach, it did little in the face of her conviction.

"Arturias!" she cried once more, just as he came crashing into her arms with all the force of longing and need, only strengthened by circumstances which had done well in their attempt to separate them.

They held each other as if it were the first time and the last, as if they were the only ones to exist where nothing else mattered to them. In the face of death, whose mere gaze struck fear and hopelessness into all those caught within its sight, their resolve grew stronger.

"Oh, my boy! My baby boy!" Ygrayne couldn't wrap her arms around him tightly enough, overwhelmed with sputtering tears and elated laughter.

Before their separation, hearing her call him "my boy" would have sent Artur into a fury in which he would insist himself too grown to be called such. But in this instance, it was a melody in his ears. How he yearned to hear her say it again. It was true: in this moment, he was a boy who only wanted the affections of his mother.

He couldn't help but cry as he buried his face within the crook of her neck.

All the time apart, the worry and the pain they both shared, was felt in their embrace, in the tears they shed, in the smiles gracing their faces. Amidst the darkness, it was a sweet glimpse of the light that still shone beyond.

The Schiva watched on in composed contentment. His mask's fixed expression hid the smile spread across his face. But he could not keep the exhilaration from dancing in his eyes, which radiated the fondness unique to a spectator of such a display of adoration, one in which he knew he could not partake. Still, he needed no personal familiarity to recognize the bond between mother and child, to know the boundless strength it possessed—the equal of the steel and might of an empire.

His eyes did not dim either, when his sister dismounted beside him. And for a time, she too watched, admiring what was also forbidden to her.

"He's the only one to have survived." She turned her head slightly to him.

"I know," the Schiva responded solemnly, recalling the villager folk found within the tavern, the decapitated Oathbound.

"Eight villages destroyed—only him."

"And her." The Schiva added. "Her husband perished in the Falkhearth siege."

The pause hung in the air.

"I understand."

The conversation waned when the Schiva's attention was torn away. His eyes drifted from the touching sight before him, to the figure who stood off in the distance—whose violet eyes glimmered as he too observed the reunion of mother and son. He raised his gaze to meet the Schiva's gaze once he sensed such amber eyes upon him. The Schiva could decipher the apprehension in the stare of the man whose grip on the whole of Skana had been shaken in a moment. The words exchanged were clear without so much as an utterance from either of their lips. The thoughts that passed between them left no room for uncertainty. Both recalled previous conversations, whose conclusions all led to this moment.

The sister noticed this silent exchange, glancing between both brother and Allfather even as she could not interpret what was being discussed between them. But there was one thing she knew for certain now—the Allfather was not in Trivaden by coincidence, and it was no accident that he was accompanying her brother.

"Why is he here, Brother?" she asked him, quietly.

The Schiva still did not answer. Regardless, it was all the answer she needed.

"Brother," she called to him again, and it was only then he looked to her. "You hide too much from me."

"On the contrary—I don't hide enough from you."

The Allfather made his way around the scene. Both Artur and Ygrayne hardly paid him any mind, engrossed as they were in one another. He said nothing to either Schiva, though their gazes followed him with the utmost scrutiny, as he made his way to his horse and swung into the saddle.

Still, he was acknowledged by no one until he rode beside Artur and Ygrayne. It was only then, in the presence of such an imposing beast, that they could not keep their attention away from the Allfather towering over them. The sister made a motion to go to them, but the Schiva held her back with a grasp of her shoulder, and a confident gaze, a nod of his head.

Apprehensive, she stopped herself and watched on tensely.

Neither were as nervous as Ygrayne, who knew well the capability of the man before her—his status, his power, his entire existence. He was the man who could end their lives in an instant should he simply choose so, and she wrapped her arms even tighter around her son. What Artur saw was nothing more than another Valeriaan.

"I bid you farewell," the Allfather spoke, his voice cold and unfeeling. "You're leaving here with your son because I choose it so—never forget this. But be warned, woman. Should we ever cross paths again, neither of you will be so fortunate. I will do what I should have done, the gods be damned. Until then." His words were as sharp and threatening as the tip of a blade, but that blade had been fractured and dulled, no longer possessing the same capacity to wound. But they would never know of his failed integrity, his crippled might. He only needed them to believe it to remain intact.

Without another word, the Allfather gathered his reins and made his way back to the Schiva. It was the sister who bowed her head in respect. Her counterpart hardly flinched when he felt the heat of the beast penetrating the thickness of his robes. His gaze rose up to the Allfather, who returned it in kind. There was silence, one last glance between the two of them, before the Allfather shifted his eyes forward to the barren road ahead.

"This changes nothing," said he, curtly.

He gave the Schiva no chance to respond before he kicked at his steed's sides. The beast took off into the forest, ash and debris kicking up in their wake. It was rather disheartening for such words to be the final ones spoken between them, and even more so to know that in some part of all this, the Schiva had failed. There was indeed no victor.

"The Schiva called that man the Allfather." Artur looked to his mother. "Who is that?"

The two of them watched the prominent figure disappear amongst the trees before their conversation continued.

"Just another Valer—" Ygrayne caught herself.

She looked at Artur, the evidence of his ordeal discernible on every part of him. All that he had seen—she could only imagine. The naïveté and innocence she once tried to preserve for his own sake with lies and falsehoods, had been shattered in her absence. If she had learned anything from her own involvement in the war, hiding the truth had not protected him, and instead had only served to hurt him in the end. She could not indulge her own fears any longer, at the expense of her son's perceived safety. No amount of justification would convince her now. Still, this was not the moment to reveal all to him. Times were dire and the matter of his father remained. She believed there would be an opportunity for the rest.

Ygrayne pursed her lips as she swallowed her nervousness, pushing aside her own trepidation, then parting them again to say, "That man…Artur…is the ruler of the Valeriaan Empire…and he's the man responsible for all of this."

"Ruler of…" Artur spoke in a whisper, his voice trailing off. Such a title he had heard cross Urda's lips when she had explained the history of Skana, the war, in the simplest way for him to understand.

She touched at his cheek and stared deeply into the eyes of the boy she knew she had failed.

"How?" she breathed. "How did you survive?"

Had he possessed the courage to tell her of how he had left the rest of the village to their damnation, about what had transpired on the riverbank, she might have been forced to think of him differently. How he had cavorted with the enemy, an enchanting and forbidden enemy, and possibly provoked Valeriaan ire once they understood what had happened to her, one of their own.

The event would be forever concealed. The two other folk who knew the truth had taken it with them to the grave, a permanent silence. It was to be Artur's secret, and his alone to harbor for the rest of his days.

"Urda saved me," he said, hoping she would pry no further. "She found me and hid me. But I haven't seen her or Vána since. She promised she would come back, but…"

Ygrayne knew she had made the right choice entrusting Artur's care to Urda. Her closest friend had kept her word until the very end. Ygrayne expected no less.

"Where's Papa?" Artur asked, realizing his father had yet to return to him as his mother had. He longed to embrace him, to speak of how much they missed each other. The anticipation in his eyes pained Ygrayne greatly, knowing she had no choice but to shatter such expectancy with the grim revelation of a promise unfulfilled.

Ygrayne looked at him, struggling to keep her face composed, flattening her lips into a hard line and blinking quickly to fight the tears.

No mother should ever have to tell her child that their father was never coming home, was gone forever. It was the hardest truth she would ever have to speak. Ygrayne took in a deep breath, a tear she could no longer hold back falling down her cheek. The strength she wanted to emanate, to be a bastion for both herself and Artur, was slipping from her grasp with each passing moment. She pushed a shuddering breath through her lips, and the words finally came forth.

"Papa…" She nearly choked. "Papa isn't coming home, my boy."

She placed her hand on his cheek once more. Artur awaited the moment he would be overcome with the rush of bereavement upon hearing those words, and yet, he felt nothing. The impassiveness engulfed him, left him completely unfeeling. Whether it was pure disbelief at such an admission, or a subconscious part of him trying to protect him from any more heartache, Artur couldn't know. He wanted to cry. Wanted to scream. Wanted to collapse under the weight of grief. Instead, he remained unmoving.

"Just know," Ygrayne's voice kept him from falling into the void of his thoughts, to be lost to a world which he could not effectively navigate, "that he loved you more than anything in this world. He thought of you every day he was gone, even until the end. Your father sacrificed everything, because he loved you so much…"

Hearing her own voice speaking the words aloud was a way to convince herself of what had only been revealed to herself upon Thelric's death. There could be no questions, no conversations, only speculation. The only justification of his involvement with the Oathbound was the belief in a better world for his family, a conviction was so true that he had been willing to sacrifice his life for it.

"Right now, we need to be strong for him. All right?" The tears continued down her face, liberated showers of her pain and the acknowledgement of the love her husband had for his wife and his son. "Be strong for your papa…for us."

Ygrayne clasped her hands around Artur's and held them between their bodies. "Be strong with me."

Artur looked at her, tears streaming down his own face, though he did not realize it until one fell atop Ygrayne's fingers. He had believed himself done crying, thought there was nothing left.

But there was no impeding the weeping of a boy who had just learned of the loss of a most beloved father—the fixture of his family, the man he idolized, adored, and looked to for wisdom and guidance—all taken away from him in a moment, never to be replaced.

Artur withdrew his hands from under Ygrayne's and wrapped his arms around her, burying his face into the nape of her neck. She wrapped her arms tightly around him once again. There was nothing more to say. Silence and time to weep was all they needed now.

The face of the man he called Papa was but an image in his memories—unchanging, unageing, a fixture in his past. Those days spent by the river were ended. The way his father would tousle his hair when they were playing, when he was proud, when he caught more fish. Gone. The way his eyes had narrowed at Artur when giving a scolding. The way his father would look at his mother. The way he held her. The way they smiled at each other. Artur would react in disgust. The display of any affection was something he found repulsive, and he'd vowed to never behave in such a way with anyone.

The more he dwelt on thoughts of his father, the more Artur was able to feel...something. His subconscious couldn't protect him forever, though he wished it would. Perhaps it was better to feel something, to allow himself to experience grief and all that came with it. It was akin to a gaping hole in his chest, and the ache that spread through him was a greater pain than anything he had ever felt before. Greater than the destruction of Trivaden, and the death of everyone he knew. The impassiveness relinquished its hold, and it was then he felt with all his being. Suddenly overwhelmed, he clung to Ygrayne as if she were his very lifeline. And he wept, the depths of sorrow darker than any night he'd ever known. Had his mother not been there, there might have been nothing left of him.

CHAPTER 37

The Allfather's thoughts were dark and burdensome, consuming him so completely that the world no longer existed around him. Had it not been for his steed's keen sense of direction, they both would have been led astray. But it knew well its master's destination, and the remains of Falkhearth awaited them at the end of the road.

Never in his life had the Allfather found himself taken aback, without the upper hand. He prided himself on his superiority and foresight, on the control and influence he held over the entirety of Skana.

He could have a city burned for no stated purpose with a single command. He thrived on the way the masses trembled in his presence, the napes of their necks exposed to him as if they were sacrificing themselves to the fangs of a beast come to devour them.

There was no force that could oppose him.

To say he was humiliated in the presence of a mere boy would have been an understatement of grand proportions. He had been forced to his knees in defeat with only a gaze. The fires into which he'd cast the land burned with a vengeance inside of him, for he had been bested. He had stared into the eyes of Fate and the supposed power of olden gods and had been shown who truly still had the power. The might of man was nothing compared to the omnipotent. Was it revenge? The Valeriaans had boldly gone against the powers that be, spat in their faces as they defiled their altars and statues and purged their very existence from culture and cognizance. All this to show that they were the ones who held the authority and influence over all of Skana. And yet, he'd felt but a touch of the gods' capability, and he trembled. His forefathers would be disgusted with the feebleness of his resolve, the implications it could have for the Empire. He would be a disgrace of a descendent, unworthy of the almighty title of Allfather.

"Allfather." He heard the voice of a Drengr call to him, and it was only then he realized he had arrived at the gates of Falkhearth. His personal regiment and foot soldiers alike bowed in his presence, dropping to one knee in a show of respect and obedience.

"What are your orders, my lord?" the Drengr inquired.

But the Allfather could see a suggestion of disquiet about his Drengr's face, sensing the distress within from the mere expression about his face.

The impassive, confident air his men expected him to carry was absent. The Allfather knew so. His Drengrs knew so. To let anyone see any indication of weakness was not only unbecoming of an Allfather, but it was also entirely unheard of. Valeriaans looked to strength, to confidence, and should any of their leaders display anything but, it would mean the immediate forfeit of respect and the likelihood of being deposed, executed even.

"My lord?" the Drengr called to him again when there came no response.

A small gasp escaped his lips when his mind returned to the world he claimed as his own. Violet met violet, and though it was a relief to the Drengr to be acknowledged by his Allfather, the situation remained dire.

The thought of having his own men doubt his stature, having them look upon him with uncertainty, only heaped more humiliation upon the Allfather. This enraged him beyond measure, for it was one thing to acknowledge hesitation within himself. It was another matter altogether for it to be felt by his subordinates.

The muscles about his face began to twitch with rage, burning even hotter than the fires that had purged Skana and made the name Valeriaan one to be spoken with trepidation. His brows furrowed as his eyes sharpened with the focus of anger and his breath became harsh and deep, his shoulders and chest heaving.

This was not to be. The Allfather was not going to bested, particularly by a boy of common birth. Fate be damned. The gods be damned. The wager be damned. The Valeriaans had dared to meet the gaze of the Almighty once before, and they could do it again with the boldness they always possessed—to curse, to spite, to tempt the wrath of the divine and laugh when they emerged victorious in the battle of great powers. The Allfather would show them, as his forefathers once had, that the name Valeriaan was to be spoken with that same trepidation even on the tongues of gods.

"Burn it all to the ground," the Allfather said to his awaiting Drengr, for fire was their element, their greatest weapon to wreak great destruction upon the whole of Skana.

"My lord?" The Drengr was rather intrigued by the demand, but as to what was to be burned down, he needed clarity.

"Falkhearth," the Allfather said, his voice a disdainful hiss. "Burn it to the ground. Let there be nothing left."

The Allfather pulled on his reins with force, turning his steed sharply to the men around him as he addressed them in a commanding voice, one they knew well and respected.

"And to the forests—leave not a tree standing! Not a village to be mourned! Burn the entirety of the region to the ground! For in the ashes we dwell and in the flames we thrive, and we will remind all of Skana of the might of the Valeriaan clan!"

From his soldiers came a loud war cry, propagating the veneration for their Allfather and the eagerness to carry out the tasks given. The Allfather needed not utter more commands for them to go about realizing his objectives. Torches replaced the blades in their grasp, and they took to their saddles to traverse the land once again.

Before the Drengr could take to the orders themselves, the Allfather halted them. He had a rather more personal request in mind.

"You are to come with me," the Allfather said, a grin spreading across his face. "To Trivaden we go."

"What in Trivaden beckons your presence, my lord?" one of the Drengr asked, for he knew his Allfather well—he would not make such specific request without a specific reason.

"There are survivors of the village—Heríkssons—who eluded our initial efforts with some finesse. But not this time."

"Fucking Heríkssons." The Drengr sneered with disgust. "We should have done away with the lot of them ages ago."

"Then shall this be the beginning of the end of their bloodline." The Allfather returned the sneer. "I want their heads on pikes. Let it be a testament—that old grudges have not been forgotten and our thirst for reckoning has not yet waned."

The Allfather then looked to the Drengr about him, and into the air he raised a closed fist, and to the heavens he spoke as if addressing the divine directly, personally.

"And to the gods, who dare believe they stand against our might. I say fuck the lot of them!"

His Drengr let out a howling cheer, lifting their own fists in the air.

"Let our hearts be hardened! Let Skana herself and these gods know who possesses the almighty power. For us Valeriaans, we are gods. We are the omnipotent. We, and we alone, decide the fate of Skana. Let us remind her folk of it. Let us show them the true might of the Valeriaan Empire."

Amidst the cheers and high spirits, the Allfather took to the road once more, his destination Trivaden, and Trivaden alone. And as his steed's hooves beat thunderously against the ground, and the Allfather's silver hair glinted in even the modest light of the sun in a sky long tainted, he smirked.

"Leave the Thórdarson to me. He comes alive—as my prisoner."

The Allfather had spoken. While the rest of the region suffered still from fatigue and wounds left open, a flood they could not hope to stop was unleashed from the gates of Falkhearth. What was for a moment believed to be the end of bloodshed and devastation was only the beginning of a long campaign for the eradication of the commonfolk. Once again, the screams of the despairing called out to the skies above as a veil of black shrouded the clouds. The air was filled with suffocating heat as the darkening horizon was set alight with a flush of red and auburn seen from afar. Felt from afar. Smelled from afar. The cascade of ash spreading across the land was a plague coming forth, an unspoken oath fulfilled.

In remembrance of the pain of past tragedies now repeating, even Skana began to tremble with the onset of tears. The wind brushed through the grasses of the valley and the trees of the forest, bringing a chill in the air with the threat of a storm. From the clouds came a great roar, and a spark of light burst through the darkened mass. In its unpredictable nature, the wind strengthened and made even the boldest of soldiers shudder at what was to come.

They did not have to wait long before it was felt. A single droplet fell upon his cheek and the Allfather brought his steed to a halt, his Drengr following suit. To the sky his face turned in disbelief at the sudden appearance of the most unexpected of guests.

Another droplet landed on his forehead, and he involuntarily blinked his violet eyes, his mouth falling open.

The mortification he felt inside was revealed only briefly on his face. With each droplet falling about him did the realization become clearer. The rain was swiftly pelting the Valeriaans' armor now, the cold of its touch creeping between the gaps of the protective plates. Their breaths appeared before them as plumes of white mist, heat meeting cold—fire meeting water in a never-ending battle for superiority.

The Allfather turned back toward Falkhearth, now far off in the distance, and he could see the once-thriving flames about its walls withdrawing from the withering touch of their adversary with hisses of smoke. The ease with which the rain fought the flames put their show of power to shame. And not once did those flames flare back to life with the vigor they had previously possessed. The dampness of the surroundings halted the advancement of the fire altogether.

The Allfather looked on with a despondency that only compounded his own fiery wrath. He had spared no thought to opposition, hardly expected his prowess to be tested any more than it had already been. He knew exactly what this was—so-called *Fate* intervening in her attempt to thwart a path divinely set forth, the gods spitting upon him and the name Valeriaan. Just as he challenged their supremacy, they were now returning the favor, and with a chuckle heard through the thunder roaring about the skies, and a contempt seen in the relentless downpour that doused the Valeriaan flames.

The Allfather scowled, his deep and utter hatred as much his birthright as his title. What was meant to dissuade him only angered him further. He was not to be intimidated. He was not to allow the gods to best him. He gave his steed's sides an aggressive kick, provoking a powerful neigh and sending the beast down the path as fast as the lightning above. His most loyal Drengr, the personal guard of all Allfathers, followed. Valeriaan victory was at the end of the path, close at hand. It would leave no room for doubt in the true power *he* possessed over Skana.

CHAPTER 38

Ygrayne held Artur until he absolutely exhausted himself, finally drifting off into a deep sleep within her arms. She cradled him as she used to when he was but a baby, rocking him as she held his head ever so tenderly.

The day was already fading quickly behind an encroaching storm. The clouds deepened in hue to shroud the sky in a blanket of deep grey, obscuring entirely the sun's piercing rays and the smoke that had recently dominated its domain. Ygrayne was wholly unaware of the threat hurriedly coming their way, an unbridled wrath not to be stopped.

However, her blessing was the presence of the two Schivas. In all their heightened awareness, they felt the sudden frigidity in the wind, smelled the increase of moisture within the air—never mind the confirmation in the sky above their heads. The signs picked up by their finely tuned senses had both turning toward the entrance of Trivaden, toward the road leading to the condemned city of Falkhearth. They could feel the thundering hooves beneath the soles of their feet, the heat of the vast flames approaching them, the ash bound for their lungs. It was not over—not even close—and they would soon be swept up in the turmoil once more.

Just as they turned their gazes to one another, did they hear the thunder in the distance, a flash across the darkened sky. The rain would follow shortly, and if they attempted to flee, a rainstorm would make it all the more difficult to do so. They needed to leave—immediately. Grieving mother and son or not, there was nothing left for them in Trivaden, and staying would only ensure their own demise. They had already bided their time for over an hour for such a moment.

The Schivas nodded to each other in an implicit agreement that it was indeed time to press forward. The two parted ways temporarily—brother to Ygrayne and Artur, and sister to tend to the horses and prepare them for travel.

He hardly wanted to disturb the tender moment, but the Schiva had granted them as much time to mourn as he could. He navigated the intrusion delicately, with the utmost respect for the fragility of their well-being, but also with the haste such a dire situation required. He knelt beside Ygrayne, setting a gentle hand on her shoulder. He nearly sighed at her state—her eyes were swollen and weary, red from the tears which had yet to stop. Her cheeks were flushed, her breathing heavy and choked.

She spluttered and wiped at her face to be more presentable to him, though it did little to ease her state.

"Ygrayne." He whispered so as not to disturb Artur or prompt any panic. "We must leave at once."

"What?" Ygrayne was taken aback. She'd known they would need to leave Trivaden, but she had not imagined it would be with such haste, the urgency evident even in the Schiva's voice.

"There's nothing left for either of you here—only death."

She contemplated their situation. They could not rebuild their life here even if she wanted to. The land would be barren. Folk would avoid it out of sheer superstition, as if the land herself was now cursed—forever to be haunted by great tragedy. There was no other choice but to move on.

Ygrayne did not ponder these conditions under the same duress as the Schiva, unaware of the terror fast approaching, only bothered by the sudden onset of rain now falling upon them with growing ferocity.

"Is there somewhere you can go?" The question prompted Ygrayne to look to the Schiva once more.

"Yes." She nodded her head. "A village called Sarek. In the region of Varäm."

"The village of Mount Valjäk, the Seer. Northeast from here," said he. "About a week's travel."

"That's right," Ygrayne breathed, though she could hardly be surprised that he knew the exact village of which she spoke, given the nomadic ways of the Schiva. "It's the only family we have left—my mother and father are there."

"Well." The Schiva nodded. "We must cover as much distance as we are able before the rain makes travel too difficult."

"Shouldn't we settle somewhere and wait for the storm to pass instead?"

"We can't, Ygrayne," the Schiva was quick to respond. "We need to leave."

Alarmed, Ygrayne looked to the sister hastily tending to the horses—ensuring the saddles were secure, their bags fastened for a speedy retreat. It was only then Ygrayne knew something was gravely wrong.

Looking to the Schiva once more, she asked, "What is happening?"

He hesitated a moment, and his silence prompted her to ask again with greater insistence.

"Schiva. What is going on?"

"The Valeriaans are coming." He forced himself to speak the words aloud, though the sudden fear in her expression was exactly what he had wished to avoid.

"How do you know this?"

"I just do." He shrugged lightly. "I beg you, trust me, Ygrayne."

The Schiva removed his robes and placed it about Artur to shield him from the sudden shower of rain, and the motion made him stir vaguely.

"I do trust you."

"Then let us go to Sarek." The Schiva stood and held his hand to her.

"You'll come with us?" Ygrayne was genuinely surprised.

She would have expected the two of them to part ways, seeing as the Schiva would be needed elsewhere. And given the distance between the two villages, it was too much to ask after everything he had already done for her.

"We will," he answered. "I made an oath—for you to return home safe. If your home is now in Sarek, then to Sarek we will go. "

Ygrayne would have responded had the Schiva not quickly interrupted, "And there is no need to thank me."

With no further questions, but full trust in the man who had, on more than one occasion, saved her life, Ygrayne accepted his hand. Artur sleepily followed her. They made their way to the sister and awaiting horses and mounted with great haste.

"They'll track us," the sister said in warning.

"To the river," the Schiva responded. "We'll follow it for some time before returning to the roads."

Ygrayne still did not know how the Schiva knew they were in imminent danger, or that the Valeriaans were approaching, or of the endeavored devastation of the land. But she followed them willingly through the remnants of her own village, casting silent farewells to the folk she once called friends and neighbors before the party disappeared into the forest.

Cold, wet, and shivering, they made their way as the Schiva had proclaimed: taking to the river so that they would leave no tracks, traversing it until the waters became too deep, and then returning to the adjacent road once again.

They pressed forward as the torrent of rain poured down upon them, soaking through even the thick robes of the Schiva. It did nothing to deter their escape—being miserable was preferable to death.

To the Fjallands they went, following the back road that cut through the craggy landscape, passing the fields Artur and Lovisa had only just frequented, in the hope of hastening their travels and creating safety in distance. Though it provided them the protection they sought, it was not without its perils.

The trail along the edge of the mountain provided a sweeping view of Falkhearth and her once-proud region. Only then could Ygrayne see how close to their demise they truly had been. The land she once called home was blackened and barren, and had it not been for the sudden rainstorm, the entire region would have been reduced to an inferno promised. In the wake of attempted destruction was the white smoke of flames extinguished, the smoldering remains of bested Valeriaan ire.

A tear fell down Ygrayne's cheek. She could hardly recognize the land she loved and venerated, so cruelly desecrated as it had been. Had she not been breathless, she would have bid her former home farewell. But there were no words to be had, nor were they needed. Her pain and despair were felt and understood without the agony of speaking them. With one last glance, the traveling party turned into the mountain range, and Falkhearth and the surrounding land disappeared behind a veil of trees.

CHAPTER 39

A week it was but a week it did not feel. The roads were longer, the days often colder than usual for the approaching spring, and the ash and smoke which overtook the skies seemed intent on following them. The party wished their presence would remain in the past, but in the past they were not satisfied to dwell. They resisted being forgotten, as the events in Falkhearth soon would be. The fear they struck into the minds of the folk who witnessed them was fated to be but a tale told in passing, the conversers removed and apathetic to the tragedy long behind them.

It was a few days before they could see the blue of the sky and smell the freshness about the air which wafted through the deep green fields and their flamboyant flora as they passed through. There had never been a more beautiful blue, nor whiter, fleecier clouds, and come night, the stars had never shone so brightly and the moon had never been more welcoming in its radiant touch. Everything seemed so tranquil and picturesque again.

Ygrayne was also given a rather pleasant surprise when she realized that the white mare the sister had ridden into Trivaden upon, was in fact Mara returned to her. She hadn't known how much she had missed the beautiful mare until she could pet her coat once more, brush the mane which hung beautifully about her neck. And it wasn't just Ygrayne who was grateful for the reunion. Onír too had missed the lovely Mara, and in their moments of rest did he do well to parade himself in front of her, to woo her with his own wit and charms. As amusing as it was, to everyone but the Schiva who found his steed's behavior rather humiliating, the elegant Mara showed little interest and ignored him for the duration of their time together. This did little to discourage his attempts. The horse was stubborn, and his efforts only became bolder to win her affections.

But the restored beauty of the world and the lighthearted moments much missed failed to ease the mind of the travelers, for they were a mere bandage over a gaping wound very far from healing. A solemnity hung over the group, their hearts heavy as their minds recalled the calamity which had changed their lives forever. Even the Schiva, with his familiarity and good intentions, received little reward for his attempts to lighten the mood amongst them. What had once won him a smile or a titter from Ygrayne now only brought about a look of sympathy. He quickly learned it was best to leave her to come to terms with everything that had happened, in the company of silence—a company she now welcomed much more readily than his own.

Artur was not in the spirit to entertain either of the Schivas, or his mother, to her despair. He didn't even grant them a glance when they addressed or approached him, his eyes always fixated on the nowhere before him, his expression blank. He might as well have been a husk of a boy, he seemed so empty and departed from the world. No one blamed him for the almost catatonic state. The pain they knew he felt was immeasurable, and no amount of forced exchange would do him any service.

"He won't even look at me," Ygrayne once told the Schiva when the travelers stopped one night in the middle of an open field, beneath the blanket of stars above. At this moment was she still wearing a splint about her ankle, and a makeshift crutch under her arm to assist in her wanderings. The saddle was cruel enough on her still aching limb.

"He's in mourning," he told her. "'Tis his way of managing."

"I feel it would help him if he just talked to me about it."

"No, Ygrayne," he calmly interjected. "It would only serve for your betterment. You must consider Artur's feelings, not your own."

She could hardly argue his point. Her son's silence did well to agitate her nerves and add to her overall dismay.

"He'll speak when he's ready." He placed a hand about her shoulder. "Allow him such time."

In truth, Artur did not know when that time would be. There was no one in his presence who could bring him the solace that seemed impossibly far from his reach. Neither the Schiva's attempts to comfort him, nor the times Ygrayne took him into her arms, mattered to him. There was only one person in whom he would consider confiding, and she was gone. The woman who did not hesitate to indulge his curiosity, who was honest with him in all the questions he presented to her. The woman who saved his life. The disputes and spats he and his mother had shared in her unyielding need to conceal the truth from him, had left Artur pained and scared, his trust in her shattered. He could not confide in her even now. For the time being, he would keep the truth to himself, and perhaps it would always be so.

One night, Artur turned on his makeshift cot about the ground where they had made camp for the night, to see his mother and the Schiva standing several paces away past the fire, talking as they always seemed to do after her break in silent mourning. But it was only this time Artur truly paid attention to them after doing well to avoid anyone for so many days. The way they stood in each other's presence, the openness of their postures, the light touches they exchanged from time to time—it was clear to Artur that his mother and the Schiva were close, that they shared a bond forged in their time away. His mother had a confidant when he no longer had anyone, and what a bitterness it evoked inside of him. As unfounded as the feeling was, he felt as though the Schiva was already replacing his father in his mother's life.

It should have been his father beside his mother in such moments, not the Schiva.

The Schiva touched at Ygrayne's shoulder, the two of them engaged in a conversation Artur could not hear, and his lips twitched into a quivering frown, his face wrinkling with the anger brimming inside of him. He couldn't stop a few tears from falling down his reddened cheeks. The Schiva turned his gaze to him, and flickering flames danced within those amber eyes, glowing in the darkness that encompassed him. That would have been the moment for Artur to turn on his side and avert his own gaze. Not this time, however. He let the Schiva see the displeasure about his face, the hate and anger the Schiva evoked in him. Artur expected a reaction, some sort of disbelief for the loathing on display, and yet, there was nothing of the sort. Only sympathy for one who had lost everything. Even as the Schiva withdrew his hand from Ygrayne's shoulder, the eyes did not falter in their expression of commiseration. Artur hated him even more for that—for the lack the of reaction he had hoped to inspire.

Only then did Artur turn his back to the Schiva, as those amber eyes were still upon him. Artur didn't care. He shut his eyes and did well to hold back any further tears, cursing at both his mother and the Schiva within the darkness of his thoughts.

"Schiva," Ygrayne said, drawing his gaze. As she gazed upon the moonlit fields before her, she continued. "I've been meaning to ask...well, for a while now."

The Schiva held his hands before him, listening.

"How did you know my son was alive?"

"Hm." It was a thoughtful hum.

"When you were first trying to tell me, it was as if I couldn't hear you. As though I couldn't understand words any longer. After days of traveling, I now understand what you were trying to tell me. How foolish I was to not have known."

"Hardly foolish," said he in response. "You were grieving. Not of the soundest mind. I never blamed you then as I don't blame you now.'"

Ygrayne glanced at him with a grateful expression.

"As for how I knew—I received a message only the night before from my sister there. She had been informed by your friend Urda of his location, as well as the demise of Trivaden."

"Urda." The name was a gasp upon her lips as they fell open, her brows furrowing. "Did she…did she survive?"

There was an ache in her chest. How dearly she missed the friend she thought to have perished with the rest of Trivaden. To hear that her fate might have been different was disheartening even as it was hopeful. They never should have left without her. They should have brought her along as they escaped to Sarek.

"What happened to her? Is she alive?" Ygrayne's words were more forceful than she intended, but she was desperate.

"For all we know, she perished that night as well. Once she passed the information to my sister, she wasn't seen again."

Ygrayne went silent. The wind blew through her hair, brushing against her dress, chilling her skin. She believed herself foolish for hoping for but a moment. A howl whispered across the field as the fire cackled behind them.

She and her son were most certainly the only survivors of Trivaden.

"I see," was all she could muster before she looked out to the fields once more.

"I'm sorry, Ygrayne," said he in response.

"Don't be sorry," said Ygrayne as she shook her head with a sigh. "I'm tired of you having to be sorry for everything."

That would have been the moment he would have placed a hand upon her shoulder, but he refrained this time. Instead, his gaze went to the boy whose back was turned to him still. Who had only just made his attitude of disdain known. The Schiva refrained. Whether observant eyes were still upon him or not, he did not wish to inflict any more pain that night.

The Schiva did not blame Artur for what he was feeling. The poor boy had experienced a horror no child should ever have to, and his grief left him fragile and volatile. He knew well to leave the boy be, even in the face of such openly flaunted contempt, a purposeful exhibition meant for his eyes and his alone. Given the timing of the silent exchange, the Schiva contemplated whether the platonic and unassuming contact with Ygrayne was what had elicited such a severe response. As amicable as their relationship was, it was a close one, solidified by the events that brought about such great bereavement. He knew that in the eyes of his brethren, it was cause for suspicion and scrutiny, as so clearly demonstrated by the accompaniment of the sister. The boundaries already set naturally seemed insufficient in proving the innocuous nature of their relationship. Ygrayne, however, needed him still. She found comfort in his company, their familiarity providing some form of stability where she had lost all others. He would've been all the happier to provide the same for Artur if the boy would allow him to do so. But Artur continued to rebuff the advances of both him and his sister.

"Pray tell, who gave you this book?" she once asked him.

Artur was keener on taking it back for himself than answering her question, and his attempts to do so were only met with a greater opposition, a test of his physical reach.

"It would be wise for me to keep this until we reach Sarek," she said to him, to his dismay. "In the event we happen upon any more Valeriaans. 'Tis safer with me."

As irritating as it was to not have his most cherished possession, Artur couldn't argue with her. Upon further questioning, Artur would only begin to weep and find solitude elsewhere. He wanted nothing to do with her questions, even if he fancied her company over that of her brother. He had to admit, he admired the softness of her voice and the way she spoke to him, seeking conversation rather than talking down to him as adults often did to children. In some ways, it reminded him of Urda and how she had conversed with him, how easily she had won his trust by simply being candid with him when no one else would be. But she still wasn't Urda.

Such a reminder only saddened him more, pushed him further from everyone else and deeper into the pit of darkness he found himself in. From that day all attempts to reach him ceased. How thankful he was that they finally did. He only wanted a reprieve from everything.

On the verge of nightfall, they finally arrived in the sleepy village of Sarek, a small settlement within the Staghart Forest, situated at the base of a mountain known around Skana as Mount Valjäk—the Seer. The mountain range was the largest in Skana, splitting the entire continent. From the summit one could see north and south, east and west—the tip of the mainland to its southernmost border. The prominent location held a power bestowed upon it by the folk of Skana, and it was rumored to have been the site of one of the most sacred temples devoted to a goddess long ago worshiped and long ago forgotten. *Rumored*, it is said, because all documentation of the temple's existence was destroyed in the war, the pathway up the mountain desecrated in the Valeriaans' rage. No one had since made the trek up the mountain, and the tales had largely passed from memory. But the mountain was not without its own magnificence. The waters which fell from its snowy peaks were cold and fresh, providing a flowing river behind Sarek and giving life to a forest whose trees grew tall and sturdy, their foliage lush and green, and whose wildlife came to rely upon it as did the folk of the forest.

The unsuspecting village folk had already returned to their homes for the night to enjoy their supper. The towering mountains shaded the town long before the night did, the orange of the setting sun beaming between their silhouettes. Torches lit the roadway for the unfamiliar traveler passing through, and lanterns hung in a cascade above on interweaving ropes strung between buildings. If not for the crackling of fires in hearths, the sounds of chatter and laughter muffled by wooden walls, the only sounds would have been the evening melodies of crickets and the stirrings of nocturnal life. Even the river skirting the village seemed tamed, slumbering.

Ygrayne felt so foreign in the village she had once called home, and yet all the roads, the cottages, the smells, and the sensations seemed the same to her, completely unchanged from when she'd left to begin a new life in Falkhearth. All her senses recognized her long-forgotten surroundings as if they called to her with a familiar voice. Overwhelmed was she by the pure reminiscence of it all, as old memories flooded back to her and she recalled her desire to leave such a modest village in favor of the bustling life of a city now gone. Now here she was, back in that modest village once again. And despite her eagerness to be rid of it, Sarek was only too content to welcome her back, guiding her down a torch-lit path straight to the to the cottage she once knew as home.

She felt a momentary guilt, given how easily she had discarded Sarek and how readily forgiven she felt, but there had been no offense committed. Still, in a moment of uneasiness, Ygrayne pulled her sleeping boy closer to her as he sat within her arms in the saddle. His slack body swayed with Mara's gentle walk, the motion akin to that of a cradle rocking, enticing him to sleep long ago. Ygrayne felt she would be separated from him all over again, and in the blink of an eye Sarek would be cast to flames—a flood of silver and violet taking to the homes as if they were consumed by an unholy storm. The screaming would commence, and the streets would be stained forever crimson. All over again. But this wasn't Trivaden, and the Valeriaans were nowhere nearby. Reminding herself of that, Ygrayne took in a few breaths before she regained her sanity, dispelling such ghastly thoughts.

It was not to happen here.

Ygrayne's parents owned the inn, so appropriately named "Staghorn Inn," and the wood mill in the village, and are the largest producer of cut wood and carpentry in the region, the family having cemented their roots in Sarek upon the village's founding, hundreds of years ago in the current age—the tenth. The mill stood beside the river, which served as a natural source of energy for the woodworking and woodcutting that was done there. Their cottage lay adjacent to the property, a place of escape from the daily bustle of the inn and the toil of the mill work. In her younger years, Ygrayne had found the unchanging nature of routine dull and unsettling, believing it best to advocate for them to leave such a secluded village, for there was no future in Sarek.

How foolish she felt now for failing to see its beauty and purpose.

After all those years away, she could see a future for herself here. Perhaps it was always going to be. There was pain in such a thought, but also relief.

In the time she had been away, Ygrayne had hardly visited or made any effort to send news of her life in Trivaden. After Artur was born, it was only more of a justifiable excuse not to make such an endeavor. She was living her own life, busy with the trials of motherhood and the maintenance of her home in her husband's absence. There was no time to make the week-long trek to visit. Only now did she think of how her parents might have been affected, to lose a daughter because of perceived inconvenience. Not once did they express sentiments of disappointment, nor complain to her about it, treating the circumstance with the utmost understanding. Ygrayne never thought she would have to face a reckoning with her failures as a daughter.

How would she be able to explain herself? What excuses were enough to warrant her negligence? She did not know.

The light inside the cottage glowed through the open windows, welcoming her as it always did, even after her prolonged absence. Ygrayne lightly pulled the reins and brought Mara to a halt. The Schiva stopped beside her.

"Their residence, I presume?" the Schiva asked. Ygrayne nodded, her eyes fixed upon the place she once called home.

"Yes," Ygrayne answered quietly.

The Schiva noted her apprehension with curiosity.

He tilted his head slightly and said, "Do you want me to—"

"No," Ygrayne was quick to say, knowing well what he was about to ask. "No." She let out a long sigh and followed with, "I can do it, it's just…I haven't seen them in almost twelve years. I don't know what to expect."

"There be only one way to know." His brow arched teasingly, and he nodded toward the cottage.

"We shall remain with your son," the sister said to ease Ygrayne some, and she nodded in acknowledgement of the offer.

Ygrayne dismounted softly while the sister held onto Artur. The boy hardly stirred, exhausted from the interminable travel of the past week. As Ygrayne approached, her hands began perspiring as her nervousness mounted, her body running hot despite the chill in the air. Her footfalls sounded gently on the steps of the porch, and she hoped the slight creak did not alert her parents to her presence before she was ready to face them. She flinched, stopping just before the door as she waited a moment to gather herself. She hesitated again, the weight of the unknown on her shoulders. She could hear her parents chatting quietly as they always did during supper, and just the sound of their voices brought her to silent tears she couldn't hold back anymore. All at once she missed them acutely, the sum total of all the years she had been away a deep and heavy ache.

And so, her hand went forward and gently tapped on the door, which brought a silence from inside. Then came the sound of benches scraping across the floor as her parents left the table, the subsequent shuffling of feet coming closer to the door until it opened before her.

There they stood, aged in the intervening years by wrinkles and experiences, but still so recognizable in her eyes, still much as she remembered them.

No one could have been more shocked than her parents themselves. The years apart had convinced them they would never see their daughter again, let alone unannounced. They were stunned, their words caught in their throats as they gaped at Ygrayne with soundless joy.

Ygrayne pondered what to say, tried to reach for any excuse at her disposal to explain away the lost time. Even a simple "hello" evaded her grasp. It was her mother who was the first to reach out and bring Ygrayne into her arms with a choking sound in her throat, and soon after did her father follow suit, wrapping his arms around the two of them. He was hardly one to show outward emotion, but the sight of his daughter was something he could not overcome.

"Mama. Papa," Ygrayne whispered as she cradled them both in her arms. The words felt strange upon her tongue, so long it had been since she had uttered them.

"Oh, my dear sweet Ygrayne," her mother, Sigrida, couldn't help but sob to her. "I'm so happy to see you."

To Sigrida, it didn't matter why Ygrayne was there, nor how. All she knew was her daughter was right there before her once again. Rikulf, her father, in his own way of showing that he had missed Ygrayne, went straight to inquiries.

"Ygrayne, are you well? What are you doing here?"

Ygrayne pulled away from their embrace a moment, and it was then the two of them realized how haggard their daughter looked, how worn and exhausted her suffering and traveling had rendered her.

"What's the matter?" Rikulf placed a hand upon her forearm, sensing something was amiss.

He surveyed their surroundings, quickly noticing Thelric's absence and the presence of the two Schivas—indications which revealed to him the most tragic of events.

"What has happened?" he asked, looking to Ygrayne once more. Despite her pain, Ygrayne took in a deep breath and placed her hands on their shoulders.

"I will explain everything." She nearly choked. "But for now, Artur and I have spent a week getting here and my boy needs his rest. Once he is settled, I will tell you."

"What about Thelric?" Rikulf asked, worried for his son-in-law. "Why is he not with you?"

Ygrayne didn't answer right away, for the very mention of her late husband's name twisted a knife deep within her chest. She had known she wouldn't be able to avoid the question for long.

"He's not of this world anymore, Papa…"

Both Sigrida and Rikulf needed no more explanation, taking her meaning immediately and wishing to impart no more pain upon their daughter.

"You and Artur rest for tonight." He nodded his head to her. "No need to explain until you're ready."

"Is it really all right if we stay?" Ygrayne nearly gasped.

It would have been an insult that she assumed otherwise if the circumstances were different. They did not hold her disbelief against her, for she was weary and exhausted from her travel. It was Sigrida who told Ygrayne with utmost confidence, "My dear, this is your home. You are always welcome here, should you choose it."

Artur did not stir when they lifted him from the saddle, and the Schiva carried him inside while Ygrayne followed them up the stairs and to the spare bedroom her parents always kept at the ready should she ever visit.

The Schiva gently laid him on the bed, and Ygrayne went about removing his socks and leather shoes before tucking him in under the quilt, a welcome alternative to the ground and rough woolen blankets. The Schiva excused himself to the doorway, waiting patiently as Ygrayne gently whispered good-nights to Artur, finishing with a loving kiss upon his forehead.

When Ygrayne joined the Schiva, they shared a gentle glance and smiled at one another, for Ygrayne was as grateful for his help as he was content to give it.

They descended to the main room where Rikulf and Sigrida were waiting alongside the sister, and when both were in sight of the other, their eyes met in understanding that their duty had been concluded, their oath fulfilled.

It was time for them to depart, and Ygrayne could sense so when the Schivas moved to stand together. She was not ready to see either of them go—not yet—but she had no say in the matter. What she did have some control of was the nature of their farewell. The Schivas said not a word as they exited the cottage suddenly, and Ygrayne would have called to them if it weren't for the presence of her parents. Instead, she composed herself and said, "I'll be just a moment."

They had no objection when she followed the Schivas.

The sister was already going about relieving Mara of her saddle and packs, for the horse was weary, and the modestly sized garden behind the cottage would suffice as a resting place. 'Twas rather warm and welcoming, sufficient to serve the horse's immediate needs.

It was the brother, the one Ygrayne would have regarded as a friend had the oath allowed her to, who remained close to the porch and looked to her as she closed the door gently behind her and approached.

How she wished she could beg him to stay, to house him at the inn for even a single night as a gesture of gratitude for all that he had done for her. But he wouldn't accept, not because he wouldn't be appreciative of it, but because he was needed elsewhere. It would be selfish to keep him around for one more night, regardless of how worn he looked and felt. Ygrayne approached gingerly, pondering her next words carefully, rubbing her forearms to stave off the slight chill in the wind as it brushed her hair about her.

"Will the both of you be all right?" The Schiva broke the silence, and Ygrayne felt ashamed for being so hesitant.

The nodding of her head was the final acceptance of their departure.

"We will." She spoke up at last. "Thanks to you and your sister. Without you neither of us would be alive."

The Schiva resigned himself to silence, recognizing the impending accolades for everything he had been more than willing to do.

"Regardless of whether you accept it, I will say it—thank you." She said the words with a faint, fatigued smile. "Thank you for everything."

Ygrayne could hear a quiet snort under his mask, and was pleasantly astonished when she heard him utter, "You're welcome."

It only strengthened her smile.

"What will you do now?" she asked.

The Schiva took a deep breath, and upon his exhale he replied, "Go where I am needed, as always."

She had expected this response, though it still pained her when the words graced her ears. She would miss him, dearly. Would miss his awkward jests, the snort of a laugh on an otherwise dignified figure, the kindness of his words, the calming presence he had bestowed upon her. That she might never see him again was a difficult prospect to accept, and she felt foolish for desiring the presence of someone who devoted his life to the service of others, roaming the world wherever it called him.

"Will I ever see you again?" Ygrayne let the words slip from her lips.

She could hardly believe what she asked, wishing too late to recant such words, and she stood there a moment rather discomfited at herself.

The Schiva did not consider it so ridiculous. He was flattered, honored, though he did well to hide it from his eyes and the response he gave to her.

"I would say so." He nodded. "My travels will eventually bring me back to Sarek."

"Well," Ygrayne couldn't help but smile. "I hope you will stop by for some catching up when you do come here again."

His eyes narrowed. He was smiling.

"I look forward to it so, Ygrayne. But." The Schiva stepped toward her. He lowered his voice, for the words he was about to utter were for her ears alone.

"Before I depart, there is something I must give you."

"And what is that?"

"Walk with me." He nodded his head at the road leading out of Sarek and deep into the forest. Although confused, Ygrayne complied.

CHAPTER 40

The forest felt unfamiliar. Unakin to Sarek, the trees she used to call her playground were now wary of her presence, not at all remembering the girl who used to run about them as she screamed with joy. But the silence and the solace the forest provided was exactly what the Schiva needed for the conversation ahead of them. The forest was often nosy, but it spoke not a word of anything it heard or observed, and any idle gossip would be kept between the leaves and the wind, neither of which spoke the native tongue.

They came to a cobblestone bridge that spanned the same river that ran behind Sarek. This too was a place where she had spent many enjoyable hours, sitting and playacting about the water. Ygrayne let out a breath, the longstanding bridge a wonder to see again, and leaned over the stone parapet to glance down at the rushing waters below. Her reflection danced about, and the moon beamed proudly. However sentimental it all was, Ygrayne alleged that the Schiva had not brought her there to reminisce.

"Why come here, Schiva?" She looked to him.

"I must turn something over to you in utmost secrecy."

The Schiva produced from the inner pocket of his robes the blue book Artur cherished so dearly, and atop it, a folded piece of parchment that had seen better days. Ygrayne couldn't believe her eyes as they took in the unexpected objects, and she couldn't help but ask breathlessly, "Where did you get this?"

Ygrayne was as cognizant of the forbidden nature of such a commodity as every other folk, and the Schiva's possession of it made her blood run cold with an understandable fear. Even as she reached to hold it, it felt so wrong.

"The book belongs to your son," said he. "It was in his possession when my sister found him."

"And how did Artur get this?"

"That," the Schiva intoned solemnly, "is only for him to tell. He has refused to entertain inquiries into the matter."

Ygrayne looked at the book with an almost morbid curiosity, never having seen, let alone held, one before. Her understanding of the object was a product of her imagination based on the descriptions she had received throughout her life.

It was no doubt beautiful, beneath the dirt staining the cover, and Ygrayne felt the power of the unassuming object—one whose mere possession had decided the fates of so many in the past.

"I should burn this," she stated simply, forcing down her nervousness.

"I wouldn't be so hasty." The Schiva placed his hands atop the book to shield her eyes a moment, and to protect it from a deed provoked by impulse. "No one will know of its existence, should you keep it hidden. Tell no one. Not even your parents."

"He should never have had this to begin with," Ygrayne was quick to argue.

"I understand, Ygrayne." The Schiva was loath to add to her mounting distress. "But, you have hardly any idea of how important this is to your son. He has yet to speak in its favor and its value to him is very apparent regardless. Destroying this will only hurt him beyond measure, and if he won't speak to you now, imagine the silence you will prolong if you go through with this."

"But…Schiva—"

"The Valeriaans have no reason to presume the commonfolk have anything akin to this, and therefore will not be actively looking. Hide it well, and you'll be spared suspicion."

The Schiva hadn't led her astray before and would not do so now. It was frightening to possess such an item, but she knew he was right. So, she nodded in acceptance even as tears began to prod at her eyes, the worst outcomes marauding through her head.

"And the parchment?" She was scared to even ask. Never had she written on one, due to her own illiteracy.

"It was in your husband's possession." The Schiva eyed her carefully. "We found it when we prepared his body for cremation. We always examine the bodies beforehand, should they possess items of inherent value—such as this. My guess, a letter for you and your son."

"But…" Ygrayne let out a breath. "My husband doesn't…didn't…know how to write."

"On the contrary, Oathbound are taught to be literate. For communication purposes within the Rebellion."

Ygrayne looked at him in disbelief, although she felt she shouldn't be surprised.

"I-I can't read…"

The thought of not being able to indulge in her husband's last words pained her greatly.

"Do you mind?" He gestured to the letter, and Ygrayne nodded her head.

As he carefully unfolded the parchment, she murmured, "I'm thankful the Valeriaans didn't forbid it to you as they did to us commonfolk."

"They may have raided our temples, but they did 'allow' us to retain our practices and libraries—under the hardly subtle threat of what would befall us should our knowledge be shared with the commonfolk, or used to undermine the Empire."

"I'm surprised your temples weren't burned down anyway, given that a Valeriaan oath is no oath at all."

"They do not see oath-bound pacifists as threats."

"So, the Schivas are just as beholden to the Empire as us commonfolk."

"We have no choice in the matter. No more than you—one of the commonfolk. The reverence they may have for the Brotherhood, and the privileges it grants us, haven't spared us entirely from our own suffering. We do what we must to preserve what we can."

"Hm." Ygrayne eyed him carefully. "Seems the Allfather has a little bit more respect for you than you confess."

She scrutinized his reaction. The Schiva did well, as always, to maintain his calm demeanor, the steadiness in his voice.

"It's…rather complicated," he answered. "But I gather it bothers you nonetheless."

"I'm just curious…" She dropped her gaze to the stone bridge, ducking her head slightly.

The Schiva let out a snort, knowing well that her annoyance of the perceived bond between himself and the Allfather had only grown.

"I did say you can ask me anything, and in the same regard, I can answer almost anything." He lightly touched at her chin, raising her head and lifting her gaze once more to him. "This, however, is neither something I can, nor will, speak about."

There was clear disappointment about her expression, and it pained him to deny her curiosity.

"Let us continue with the matters at hand."

Ygrayne watched in silence as the Schiva unfolded the parchment until the handwritten words upon the page were finally revealed to her. She couldn't help but gawk at such fine penmanship, a hidden talent of her husband's—one amongst many, she suspected. Only now she wished she could read the letter herself.

"What does it say?" she asked with a desperate eagerness, and when he did not respond, she believed the darkness to be an impediment.

"Shall I fetch a torch?"

"No." He was quick to respond. "I can read it as is."

"Then what does it say?"

My love,

There were so many things I wanted to tell you.

But the secret I bore on my shoulders was something I never wanted to burden you with. I made my decision long before I met you—when my parents were killed only years prior.

To have their lives taken by the drunken escapades of Valeriaan soldiers was something I could not abide, and the pain I felt that day I never wanted anyone else to feel.

When we had our son, I knew I wanted better for him.

I wanted him to grow up in a world in which he didn't have to worry about his well-being. To thrive, and be without fear.

I was willing to fight this war so he would never have to, in the hope of leaving him a better world than the one left for us.

I know you wanted nothing to do with the Rebellion, and I never wanted you to ever have anything to do with it either. I'm sorry for deceiving you all these years…

I don't know if you'll ever receive this letter—I very much doubt it. But perhaps, I also write this in the hope that you will happen upon it by some chance, and understand that the sacrifice I chose to make was for the both of you. For I know I will not survive this siege, and that Falkhearth will be my final resting place.

This letter is the companion I can confide in one last time.

But, in the event that you do get this letter. Just know that I love you with all my being. Never doubt that. I fight and I will die for you and our son.

I will wait for you in the great paradise beyond.

We will see each other again.

When the last word of the letter was spoken, the Schiva grew silent, giving Ygrayne time to process the contents. Looking to her, he saw that she was gazing to the parchment with a tortured expression, fighting back tears again. How she wanted so much to cry. She hadn't done so in the past week on their way to Sarek, and thus the tears that had at one time run dry, had refilled their reservoirs and now threatened to overflow. It was as if Thelric was talking directly to her, the words sounding so much akin to him. How she desired to hear those very words coming from Thelric himself, spoken in his own voice. The words now only etched upon parchment would have graced her ears upon his return. Even if he would omit the truth of his endeavors in Falkhearth, she would have done anything to hear his voice once last time. As comforting as the Schiva's own voice was, it still was not Thelric's.

Ygrayne rubbed at her eyes and turned to the river flowing behind her, her hand coming to rest atop the parapet. She wanted to be alone with her tears and thoughts for a moment—to not burden the Schiva once more with her mourning. And in turn the Schiva left her be. He did not need to hear her desires spoken to know what she needed. He simply folded the parchment once more and waited for her in all his patience, though her moment did not last long. She was not to let herself be swept up into her sorrow once more. Ygrayne turned back to him, the testimony of her internal battle evident upon her face. She held her hand out to him and the Schiva handed the letter and the book to her. It felt as though a small piece of Thelric had finally returned to her. Her husband lived on in those words.

"Thank you," Ygrayne whispered.

"You're welcome," he said, placing his hand upon her shoulder. "I hope this only proves to you how much he loved you. Rid yourself of any doubt."

"It does," Ygrayne nodded. "Though I'll have to wait until I'm dead to beat his arse for keeping such a secret from me."

A small titter accompanied the sentiment as she wiped away a single tear, and the Schiva's eyes glimmered gently in response.

"You brought him back to me." She looked to him as the breeze slightly picked up around them, and the locks of hair around her face appeared to dance. "This…means more than you will ever know."

"My parting gift to you," the Schiva replied. "And I will have your late husband's ashes forged into something befitting you, and your son—so that he may always be with you both."

"That would be wonderful." Ygrayne smiled at him.

They looked at each other. It took everything inside of her not to express her thankfulness to him the way she wished she could. Had he been a commoner, she would have embraced him, would have even kissed his cheek as one did to show platonic affection amongst friends and kin. She wondered how it would feel if her lips graced a mask such as his. She imagined it would be odd. The masks, as she knew from personal experience, weren't the most comfortable to wear, let alone interact with. Even something as modest as holding his hand she thought to be too much, though it was already evident that he didn't insist on stringent adherence to the olden oaths. Where the contemporary Schivas stood as far as ancient tradition, she did not know. But there was no doubt a sort of ambiguity which she was curious to explore further. Such contemplation brought an idea to mind—one simple, and innocent in all its pretenses. Only but a mere foundation of one's acquaintance. Ygrayne took a breath as she prepared herself to speak.

"I think it's selfish of me to ask this of you, after everything you've done." At last the words found their way to her lips.

His head tilted ever so slightly as he listened, intrigued.

"But..." She paused a moment, biting her lip in one last attempt to silence herself. The restriction proved ineffective.

"Could...could you at least tell me your name?"

It was obvious that a brow lifted about his eye. He wasn't at all taken aback by her request, more so titillated by it.

"My name?"

His response made her nervous.

"I know it is against your oath. To avoid—um—fortune and favor... whatever the reasoning. But I ask not to praise you. I ask because I wish to thank someone whom I regard as a friend. To be better acquainted with him."

He said nothing.

"It feels wrong to me that I can't at least grant you the most common of pleasantries...especially given everything we've been through."

The Schiva still remained silent, contemplating. It was indeed against the founding oath of the Brethren. But he could hardly argue opposition after all that had already been broken. He would have to trust her with it. To give a name would be to create a secret shared only between the two of them, never to be uttered to another no matter the relationship.

His prolonged silence worried Ygrayne further, and she began to regret her impulsive request.

"I'm sorry—"

"Varden." The Schiva spoke before she could finish her monologue of apology, and it completely took Ygrayne by surprise. She was asking much, and she hadn't believed he'd actually agree to grant her request.

"My name is Varden."

It took her breath away. To be trusted with the name of a Schiva—such a thing was unheard of. When the astonishment finally wore off, Ygrayne smiled softly and said, "Thank you. For everything, Varden."

And of course, he replied, "You're welcome, Ygrayne."

"Is he still sleeping?" the Schiva sister asked Sigrida and Rikulf, the two of them sitting by the fire to patiently await their daughter, a melancholy about them. A downtrodden air had filled their warm and welcoming cottage. Even as the Schiva made her way into the main quarters from outside, they were visibly disappointed to see an unfamiliar façade of a face meeting theirs.

"He hasn't stirred at all," Sigrida answered.

It was just as the Schiva expected, and she acknowledged the confirmation with a nod. In her hands was a common plant—the Ilyndór known for easing one's mind and assisting the body in repose, its sweet scent recognizable.

"Do you perchance have a vase for this?" The Schiva presented the plant to the couple. "I wish to put it beside the boy's bed."

Sigrida fetched her one, having no objections to the kind gesture, particularly from a Schiva. The Schiva went to the bedroom in which Artur slumbered soundly, his back at the edge of the bed. She looked to him, relieved he was at last slumbering after their punishing travel. It was a great trial for a young boy to have his entire life uprooted and moved to an entirely different part of the world without any preparation to speak of. Her steps were silent as she proceeded into the room and gently placed the vase at the nightstand. She rearranged the bundle of Ilyndór to look aesthetically appealing. And when she was satisfied, the Schiva looked once more to Artur. She couldn't help herself. To see a child suffering as he had burdened her heart greatly. She reached out and tenderly brushed his hair with her gloved hand, the strands gently falling through her fingers and coming to rest about his face.

"I'm sorry, child," she whispered, and with one last parting gift of benevolence, she adjusted the blankets about him. She then withdrew her hands to her sleeves as she clasped them at her chest and bid him a temporary farewell.

"Be well, Arturias."

By the time she took her leave, Ygrayne and Varden were returning to the village, their silhouettes deep shadows within the forest, only touched intermittently by the light of the moon piercing the foliage of the trees above.

She observed them from the porch, cognizant of the conversation they had shared. The two Schivas' eyes met and they exchanged another unspoken conversation, the understanding that their respective roles were at last coming to an end and their time to depart was upon them. The Schiva nodded, retreating to the brown horse that Ygrayne had ridden while she posed as a Schiva sister herself, to wait for the two to bid their farewells in kind. To allow them the privacy a vacant room had provided her.

Varden walked with Ygrayne as far as the door, and the two looked to one another in the moment of their inevitable separation. Ygrayne was going to mourn his company, the stability he had provided to her in the hardest of moments. It was going to be a weighty absence.

"I bid you healing and peace in the future, Ygrayne," he said to her.

"And I wish you good luck on your travels," She flashed a tight smile. "I will miss you."

There was a risk in saying this, but given the bounds already breached, it was fairly easy to say and she felt little guilt in doing so.

Varden paused a moment, and then said to her in a whisper, "I will miss you too, Ygrayne. But I will see you again. You have my oath."

"You know where to find me." Ygrayne chuckled awkwardly and brushed her hair behind her ear in a nervous gesture, her eyes drifting to the floor. When she finally did gaze up once more, she directed her attention to the sister waiting patiently in silence.

"And thank you," Ygrayne said to her. "For bringing my boy back to me."

It would have been a disservice to not acknowledge her part in all of it, and even still, the gratitude was not enough to address the magnitude of the Schiva's actions.

The Schiva tilted her head for a moment, as if grasping that the kind words spoken were directed toward her, and then she nodded in acceptance and said, "No need to thank me."

A likely response, and one Ygrayne expected.

"I wish happiness on you and your child."

Ygrayne smiled and nodded to acknowledge the sentiment.

"Goodbye," she said to Varden, and it pained her more than expected when he responded, "Goodbye, Ygrayne."

It was so final. This truly was the end.

Ygrayne strained with every fiber of her being to keep from embracing him then. She would have wrapped her arms tightly about his abdomen in an impulsive gesture prompted by deepest regard. He would have been understandably stunned, though he would have accepted it all the same, even without reciprocating himself. He would have held his arms about him to prevent contact while looking to his sister in both awe and bewilderment. She would have nonchalantly shrugged her shoulders, declining to indicate any particular opinion on the matter. It would have been what it would have been.

No such show of affection transpired in that moment. Varden merely gave the customary bow of the head as was expected of a Schiva before departing from the porch, to both his and Ygrayne's dismay.

She felt she was losing yet another person she cared for, and in case their reunion was prolonged by the circumstances of the world, she wished to have at least made their leave-taking one to remember for that long time coming.

But she didn't give herself the opportunity to act on the desire, retreating quickly into the cottage.

When the door closed behind her, Varden felt a twinge of guilt. He knew of her desires, of how she wanted their parting to transpire. The Brotherhood's position on outward affection and reciprocation was clear, and yet it felt so wrong withholding it from Ygrayne. Even as he retreated to a rather cross-looking Onír, he could not stop thinking about it. The horse let out a snort as if he were laughing at the awkward situation, pawing the ground with a hoof.

"Well now," the Schiva sister sighed. "'Twas quite uncomfortable."

He was not the least bit pleased to hear her jest. Without another word, Varden swung up into the saddle and kicked gently at Onír's sides, sending him into a trot and leaving the Schiva sister to snicker to herself quietly before following in his tracks.

Ygrayne listened until the sound of hooves was swallowed by distance, and their shadows vanished into the night. Loneliness overtook her promptly, their company something she had grown accustomed to. Even as her parents came to her, she could feel the emptiness left in the Schivas' wake. Sigrida and Rikulf embraced her once more, wishing her a good sleep before she retreated to the spare room. Ygrayne stealthily crawled into bed next to Artur, the exhaustion already clamoring for her to submit to slumber. Before she wrapped her arms around Artur, she placed the book and letter under the pillow. She was so thankful she could hold her son, feel his warmth, know he was alive.

CHAPTER 41

The Schivas stopped to rest at a cliffside beyond the valleys and the forest from whence they'd come, overlooking the sleepy village and all that surrounded it. A gentle glow of orange crept up through the trees from where the torches and lantern lights gleamed, outlining the bristles and branches. The mountain acted as a great protector, overlooking the lands that surrounded it, its magnificence still not on full display at the distance the Schivas observed it from. They could, however, witness a singular phenomenon not visible from Sarek. As the moon rose high above, glistening white and silver—a welcome sight after its prolonged absence—it brought forth a certain beauty only the night afforded. The White Maiden, a species of flora found only on Mount Valjäk's cliff faces. The flower was so named for the way it bloomed during the night, white petals awakening to the touch of the moonlight and emanating a blue radiance. Come morning, their petals folded back into a condensed pod as if they shunned the sunlight, awaiting the rise of their mother moon in the evening once more.

All had been quiet since the Schivas arrived atop the cliff. Both were exhausted from their travels, the horrors they'd seen, and taking the burden upon themselves to bring reprieve to a distraught and displaced mother and son.

It had been a long time since the conflict between the Oathbound and the Empire had heightened. The dissention was considered a cold war by many—handled in secret with only the occasional scuffle for Skana to see. However, it was now apparent from the siege of Falkhearth that the Empire was growing weary of those they once would have only considered pests. Regardless of whether the Oathbound were a mere thorn in the side, they were still a thorn in the side—a nuisance lulled into a false sense of safety by the Empire's seeming dismissal of them as a disorganized, inconsequential band of disgruntled commonfolk.

This was more than just a single battle in a long-standing war. The fall and complete annihilation of Falkhearth and her villages was meant to be a warning to the Oathbound that the Empire retained a power which should not be tested. And if indeed it was tested, the warning would then turn into reprisal. The number of Oathbound had dwindled through the years, in part from casualties but also the failing support from the long-defeated commonfolk, exhausted by the unending conflict. The time of the Oathbound waned in a world much divided and unable to withstand the tension that plagued it. The defeat in Falkhearth stood testament to the truth that the greatest efforts of the Rebellion would always be met with the brutal veracity of defeat in the end.

This knowledge weighed heavily on both Schivas' minds. How many more folk were to suffer and die before one of the opposing sides admitted defeat? They could not say. The only certainty was this: the pain and suffering were far from over.

The Schiva sister looked to Varden, and she could sense how distracted by his thoughts he was. The way he and Onír simultaneously sighed with great heaviness as if they shared one breath, one body. She could only speculate, but given the revelation of the alleged rapport between her brother and the Allfather, she was certain he was privy to details she, and the rest of the Brotherhood, were not. She would leave such questioning for another time. They were both spent, and such a conversation she feared would only evoke contempt. His bearing spoke volumes—the way he hung his head slightly, where ordinarily he held it high regardless of his circumstances. His disposition was subdued, and he was distraught over his departure from Ygrayne—a development she found rather intriguing. Perhaps their relationship was just as fascinating as the one he held with the Allfather, though she hadn't had the opportunity to observe his interactions with the Valeriaan firsthand. The woman, she felt, would be a matter touchy enough for a stimulating conversation.

"She lost her husband only recently," the sister said, eyeing him with cautious scrutiny.

Just as she expected, Varden shifted his gaze to her with a sharp turn of his head, and she prided herself on the provocation.

"Do tell me what you're alluding to," Varden said in a tone that indicated he wasn't about to suffer teasing on the matter—not that night.

The Schiva looked to him with a gaze so piercing, Varden could sense it through the fabric of the eyeholes.

"Don't give me that look." Varden sighed, his shoulders sagging.

"I was making a modest statement." She feigned innocence.

"I know of your supposed modesty." Varden was not to be fooled by her pretense. "Ygrayne is merely a companion, and confidant…and as you so eloquently stated, she just lost her husband. I would never make such inappropriate advances given the circumstances. Moreover…" Varden paused a moment, his sister waiting expectantly for him to continue. "I hardly think she will fancy another man anytime soon. Particularly one without a face." There was a certain pain in his tone that he could not hide from her.

"And such a relationship is forbidden," she noted playfully. "You failed to mention its impermissible nature."

"I didn't think it necessary to do so."

"Hm…if you say so." She chortled at him and looked once more to the village. It was so peaceful. A welcome departure from the destruction they had witnessed. She thought of Ygrayne. Even the sister had noticed the mannerisms, the similarities. She wouldn't blame Varden for harboring some attraction to the woman, though she would vehemently advise against any such dalliance.

"She bears a strong resemblance to her," she said in all manner of softness, the teasing absent from her voice. "I would hardly blame you…"

They looked at each other, and when Varden offered no response, she spoke once more.

"If you did indeed have affections for her."

"'Twas a long time ago." Varden said quietly, the alarm in his voice all but dissipated. "We've talked about this many a time."

"That was also a long time ago."

"There is no comparing the two."

There was silence between them, filled by the soft whisper of the wind and the dancing of the grasses below them, murmuring quietly at the exchange. Regardless of the nonchalant tone of their conversation, the sister could not promote such affairs, no matter how improbable. She would make her sentiments known.

"All jests aside, I give you warning, Brother. Do not court possibility."

"I won't."

"I don't believe you."

He looked to her once more, as she did to him.

"I must staunchly disavow it, as unpremeditated as it may be. Please, Brother, I beseech you. Do not…"

Varden said nothing in response.

"I know my pleas may fall upon deaf ears. I have no say in what you determine for yourself. But you must understand how I feel…"

"I do—"

"Do you truly? Or are these unbecoming false placations?"

"Sister—"

"I must forewarn you, if I bear witness to such undertakings, I will take matters into my own hands. Shall I make you uncomfortable as you would make me uncomfortable?"

Varden parted his lips to speak but found their discussion ceased by his awareness of a third presence hurriedly approaching, recognized by them both long before the sound of hoofbeats filled their ears. Neither of them flinched, nor felt pressed to see who was approaching, for they already knew it was someone they had long been expecting.

If the moon had been less luminous, he would have been indistinguishable from the plains, his silhouette a manifestation of shadow itself. In the presence of the moonlight, a Schiva clad in black, from robes to boots, came forth, silver tracing the edges of his figure.

The horse he rode was a night-coated beast who would make even the ravens caw with a burning jealously, who put to shame even Onír's impressive frame. In tow was a white mare of the Valeriaan breed, her pristine elegance a stark contrast to the stallion's brooding strength.

"You're late," Varden said as the Schiva came to a halt beside his sister and handed the reins off to the unridden mare's rightful master.

"Greetings to you as well, Brother," the Schiva scoffed, his voice deep and rich with a haunting appeal, as if it resonated from the depths of his chest.

"Ah. There you are, my sweet Ériu," the Schiva sister cooed to the mare, and in turn the mare let loose a delighted whinny, tapping her nose against the Schiva's white mask.

"I've missed you too," the Schiva chortled as she went about brushing her fingers through the thickness of Ériu's mane, patting her soft neck.

"Did I miss anything?" the brother asked.

"Matters have proceeded according to standard," Varden replied, looking to his brother.

"The standard-standard," the sister emphasized ever so cheekily, and her brother at once gathered what she was referring to.

"I don't remember that being part of your duties this time," the brother couldn't help but chime in teasingly, unaware of the banter already exchanged.

"All right, all right! Enough, the both of you!" Varden groaned. "What was required has been done. That's what matters."

"And fuck, that was a storm of shit." The brother let out a boisterous laugh, as if the events in Falkhearth were as humorous as a minstrel show. "The Valeriaans aren't taking kindly to the Rebellion any longer. The Oathbound are but foxes biting at the ankles of a bear. Eventually, the bear is going to bite back. And what a most frightening and deadly bite it will be."

"I shan't lie—'twas a beautiful analogy," the Schiva sister said.

"How did you find it?" Varden directed the conversation back to more important matters.

"Perfectly. All things considered." The Schiva was quick to respond.

"And the girl?" their sister asked.

"On the mend," he answered her in kind. "I find it all rather...peculiar. Quite interested to see how everything will unfold."

"What are you planning?" The sister was alarmed by the guile in his tone, suspecting the presence of a rather cunning smirk beneath his mask.

"I can't reveal everything I have up my sleeve." He scoffed. "What fun would that be?"

The Schiva sister let out a sigh and groaned begrudgingly, "Not you too."

"Whatever do you mean?"

"Oh, so he hasn't told you either." She turned her head sharply to Varden, drawing the gaze of their brother as well.

Varden did well to not look at either of them.

"Hasn't told me what, exactly?" the brother asked coaxingly.

"It's nothing of importance at present," Varden growled at them both.

"Oho!" The brother jeered once more, and his deep voice lowered into a menacing purr as he added, "I can't wait to pry the truth out of you."

"Have there been any signs?" Varden redirected the conversation once again, giving his brother a rather stern and critical look. He, however, was hardly castigated. On the contrary, the brother preferred a little excitement in their conversations.

"Very few," he answered, and withdrew for the time being.

"This one has yet to become aware," said Varden, gesturing to Sarek down below. "In due time, no doubt. Yet, I dare say, not anytime soon."

"Some simply take a little longer than others," his sister commented. "We'll observe in the meantime."

"Until then." Varden took the reins into his grasp and Onír needed no order to know their time there was coming to an end. "We shall let them be. They've been through enough as it is."

After the sister moved her saddle to Ériu's back, the three of them made their way into the valley. The conversation was done, for now. It was only a matter of time before the future would begin to unfold before them, and their sense of foreboding for all that lay ahead told them that close and continual observation would be necessary, just as it had been in years past. It was exciting, it was terrifying, but for the moment they were left to wait with much anticipation.

www.ingramcontent.com/pod-product-compliance
Lightning Source LLC
LaVergne TN
LVHW090549110826
845146LV00001B/82

* 9 7 9 8 9 9 4 3 7 6 8 0 5 *